Published by
Hybrid Global Publishing
333 E 14th Street
#3C
New York, NY 10003

Manufactured in the United States of America, or in the United Kingdom when distributed elsewhere.

Christopher Loric
Minurva
    ISBN: 978-1-967598-04-5
    eBook: 978-1-967598-05-2

Cover design by: Julia Kuris
Copyediting by: Wendie Percharsky
Interior design by: Suba
Author photo by: Byron Wiggins

WEBSITE

www.christopherloric.com

Thank you, Dad, for waking my imagination.

My Wife, you are my Northern Star with your constant devotion

CHAPTER 1

Space. Dark and cold. Only lights from distant suns blazing and galactic materials broke the darkness. Silence prevailed except for those who knew how to listen.

The hyperspace well opened and a single ship came through.

It was a small transport with limited range. The transport could only make the jump between Earth and Alpha Centauri. The craft was built for relative comfort and lacked any form of combat capabilities.

ADM Ralph Nabum, Chief of Space Operations, stood up out of his chair, went to the porthole and peered through it.

"So, that is hyperspace."

ADM Kevin Brannigan, Commander of the Space Fleet, lifted his gaze from his hand pad and grinned. "Yes, that is hyperspace." He closed his hand device, went to a view screen, and brought up the Alpha Centauri station. The station, at this point, was a glorified International Space Station but was under construction to house several labs and engineering facilities for the production of the fleet. Kevin then keyed the comms for the pilots.

"Let's head over to the shipyards."

"Yes Sir," came the response.

Kevin then brought up the shipyards on the viewer.

The superstructure of an enormous ship came into full view on the monitor.

"There is the new battle carrier. Its design should carry one hundred fighters. In addition, reconnaissance ships, drop ships and transports. She will have the latest in weaponry to include planet killing rods, but she will also have nuclear weapons."

"Indeed. So much firepower and she is huge! Why do you want such a large ship, Kevin?"

"We will need nine of these as the center ships for three fleets."

Ralph stared in astonishment at Kevin. "What? We are programmed for only three with the escort ships. You want nine of these and I assume all escort ships."

"Yes, I do. You saw the report and video. Karen and her awesome crew destroyed the *Intrepid* with four nukes onboard. She vaporized her ship and did not destroy the Kammorrigan. Yes, she blasted such a hole in it that it vented its atmosphere. But if they had sealed off parts of the ship, we would have been killed. I need warships to exceed and destroy their capital ships."

Ralph just shook his head. "The materials and costs not to mention the manpower to man those."

"I know. That is the main reason I want all manufacturing for ships moved to this system. We bring the raw materials here; we manufacture what we need. Then we construct the ships here without undue waste of shipping. The process to manufacture those parts, if you have not noticed, creates a lot of pollution. Better to protect our system than pollute it. Meanwhile, with a better station here, we can improve the process and eliminate as much pollution as possible. We don't need any of the planets in our system to be a dumping ground. Let's recycle here or dump here. One of my orders for this station is to scan these planets for life forms or the possibility of life forms. I don't want to harm anything that might be alive."

"Wow. Kevin, I didn't realize you were such an advocate or such a grand schemer. I see the value in what you are saying, but…well, the politics of it."

"Fortunately, that one is your problem. The resources and time factor required to provide a space fleet is what I am sending you. Ralph, time, manufacturing, construction; it is best done here for not only the two reasons I gave but also other ones. Those reasons are in the capability request I will transmit to you."

Ralph went to the port as the transport was approaching the battlewagon. He stared at the immensity of the superstructure. It was five times the size of the largest aircraft carrier in the US Navy's inventory. A pure warship, just like the other escort ships would be.

"Speaking of politics, Ralph, is that why we have the Chinese Colonel onboard?"

"Yes, part of the negotiations among the nations was to give important positions to them. Colonel Chang will be this station's commander and he will be responsible for the construction of the fleet. He will report directly to me."

"I've noticed the academy structure. Will we require all the other contributing countries to send their forces through the academy?"

"Yes, everyone must go through the academies. We only made a few exceptions, such as in Col Chang's case. That is why the Deputy Director will be Mr. Ray Osborne and the Deputy Commander will be Col Mark Adams. They will ensure Col Chang is properly supported." Ralph smiled. "All others will go through the academies."

Kevin asked, "Academies?"

"Yes, we are setting up different sites. All enlisted will attend the academy in Venezuela and the officers will go to Argentina. Pending their graduation scores, there will be other areas of study. Pilots will go to Mars for their pilot training. Ships will come out here to Alpha Centauri, which Colonel Adams will be in charge of. We are still working on the training sites for other disciplines to include planetary assaults, etc. Mars seems to be a good candidate, along with the various moons and the asteroid belt. Safety will be a concern, but I'm sure we will get that worked out."

Kevin just nodded.

The transport continued to fly by the various ships in the yard under construction, ensuring the Admirals could see them.

"Oh, I almost forgot; what do you want to do with CAPT Lindsey? She isn't enjoying her time on my staff. As you may recall, she was supposed to command a carrier before we made her your operations officer."

Kevin nodded. "Let her finish out her time on your staff. I want her to learn more about Space Force." Kevin made a motion to the ships. "I want her to command one of the battlewagons if not a fleet. So, we need to move her in about nine months or so and give her a Space Action Group to command. Give her a commodore position. I'm sure we will need to send out a SAG in the near future. What I don't like is the quality of our current ships, but speed made us build lower quality ones. I'm determined these ships will be of greater quality. Especially sending our people into deep space, we need quality ships. That is why I asked you to build three ships for a SAG. I want Josephine to command them."

Ralph nodded. "I see why you want her on my staff till then. Ok, I'll have her start reviewing those ships and the crew manifest now."

"Thank you."

The shuttle had toured the shipyard and indicated they would be heading for the station. Kevin keyed an affirmative and the two Admirals returned to their seats, discussing other aspects of the new fleet and the way ahead for their next encounter with the Kammorrigans.

* * *

The moment *Excalibur* pulled into the docking ring; Mike O'Shea received orders to depart the ship. The orders told him not to speak to anyone but to depart at once and go on administrative leave. Now, after two weeks, he found himself at the State Department building in Washington DC, in front of three men. This definitely was an inquisition.

"Mr. O'Shea," started one of them, "You were to negotiate a trade deal with these Kammorrigans, not unleash nuclear weapons on them."

Mike started to respond when another man interrupted him. "Quiet. This is a board of inquiry to see if you are fit to stay in the State Department. If I had my way, you and that homicidal idiot of an admiral would be in jail."

At which point the other man stirred nervously and cleared his throat.

The first inquisitor continued. "Yes, we hold you accountable for everything that happened out there. From the incident at the station to the issues on the Kammorrigan home world. You should have ensured that maniac didn't ruin the negotiations and drop a holocaust on those poor people!"

This time Mike did speak, and when they tried to interrupt, he raised his voice.

"Gentlemen, you were not there nor do you seem to understand I was not in charge. For Admiral Brannigan, he is a good and just man. He did what was necessary to save our lives, including yours. The Kammorrigans were never interested in a diplomatic solution. They are conquerors and slavers. We were about to be captured and tortured so they could send a fleet here and conquer us. You must have read the reports. Turns out dropping the nuclear weapons was the best option. It bought us time to build a true defense for the planet. Our best option is to garner allies out there. But we have learned since the collapse of three major civilizations that space is now an extremely dangerous place, and we must figure out how to engage with the other life forms."

As the first two started to speak, the third gentleman raised his voice to silence them.

"Enough. This is a waste of everyone's time." With a heavy sigh, he continued. "Mr. O'Shea, no one at State approves of your handling of the whole affair. If we knew what the mission was, we would have sent someone else, but we didn't. You may not know but the President, while not happy, does approve of you and your role at Kammorriga. He is the one who, despite our objections, has decided you will assist his Special Envoy to a summit about space and the way ahead. The Special Envoy is a retired Marine, General Malcolm, former Commandant of the Marine Corps. You will depart immediately upon a new shuttle to go to Switzerland to assist him. The President believes your experience will aid the US greatly in this summit." He glanced at the other two. "Admiral Brannigan's fate is not up to us but the President, DoD and Congress. We have given our opinion but we don't decide in this matter. So, off you go, and we will hope you perform better."

Mike stood up and left the room. A person was waiting for him and led him to a car.

Three hours later, he was at Langley, where he boarded the shuttle, and an hour later, he was in Zurich. He was picked up from the airport in a State Department vehicle and driven to meet his new boss, Special Envoy Ambassador Malcolm.

* * *

Ms. Linda Powell was ecstatic. Her company, Eleanda Designs, just won its first defense contract. She was on her way to inform her team when she received a call. It was from the new Space Force Academies Deputy Commander, CAPT Paul Ramirez recently returned from the space voyage she had read about.

It was a sobering conversation, and she was now wondering how they would meet this requirement. She turned into the company garage and parked. She quickly proceeded to the design room, where her team was already assembled. She entered the room, took a deep breath and drank some water.

"Ok, we got a contract." They all applauded and were about to celebrate.

"Wait, we already have a change to the requirement. What we said we were going to do is no longer applicable." They all stopped their celebration and started sitting down, watching Linda closely.

"I just got off the phone with CAPT Ramirez, you know one of the EXPLORER's officers that just returned from deep space." She ran her eyes over her team who were listening.

"He now is Deputy Commander of the new Space Force Academies. He wants us to design and produce space suits. Not the big clumsy suits we have seen on the net. These are to be combat suits for the, let's see, how did he put it? Oh yes, the hard vacuum of space. He is sending specifications over now, but they are to be able to operate in a planet's atmosphere, which may be totally hostile to humans and in space. They are supposed to be sealable and unsealable and take a direct hit from grenades and high-powered energy weapons. Different style suits are to be made for regular combat troops, special operations forces and maintenance crews among others. This is going to take all of our resources, I fear. We most likely will have to subcontract out to some of our other partners." She stopped in thought and scratched her head while the team started to speak among themselves.

"Ok, you know, we wanted this, and now we have it. Lots of money to be made here, but we need to produce high quality suits. People's lives will be in our hands." That sobered everyone up and started to scare some of them.

"I know, this isn't what we thought we would be doing. But, well, you know, here we are. So, let's see what the specs are that the Captain is sending over to us. Oh yes, he and others will be working with us, so we should be able to get our questions answered. Oh, he wants the first designs delivered in a month to ensure we are on track. So, let's get started."

* * *

The last ten months had been a whirlwind. Mike still felt overwhelmed by it all. Soon after arriving at the summit, he was in the middle of the whole mess. The other nations were complaining about how the US violated agreements and laws, and another two weeks for blaming them for putting the world in danger before they could discuss the real issues. He was surprised how John Malcolm handled the whole affair with calm and sympathy. Finally, they got down to discussing the details of global defense and an Earth Space Fleet. So many times, the summit almost ended in disaster. The US had to make concessions on some key items. Such as the Chinese wanted a commander in a key position, so it was decided they would command the space station at Alpha Centauri and oversee the construction of a new fleet of warships. They turned to the discussions of academies for training. The US could stay in control of training, but other nations desired the basic academies to be in their own countries, so Venezuela and Argentina secured them. Soon, they hoped that several member nations could contribute their people to the academies and new science areas. Parts of Europe and Asia would be able to support important laboratories and engineering facilities. The climate was key; the US insisted that actual manufacturing be done off world. This was reluctantly agreed upon. The crystal technology was another major issue. A new energy source safer than nuclear and less polluting than oil was discussed. Finally, all parties agreed to replace manufacturing and power plants with the technology. However, oil still had to be drilled for its value in composites. There were still several topics for discussion. After ten months, though, AMB Malcolm said it was time for them to start the next phase, so they left after turning the summit over to new special envoys.

Now, Mike found himself looking out a port window at the planet as he and Malcolm headed for the Operations Space Command in orbit about the planet. He was given two weeks of leave before the trip with orders to pack for a long voyage. He sighed as he thought about this, *another space voyage, damn.*

"We should be arriving at the station within the hour," Malcolm said as he approached him.

"So, what is this about?"

"We will be meeting with the Space Fleet Commander and find out what is up."

Mike rubbed his chin in thought.

"You know we never had time to discuss what happened at Kammorriga. I couldn't stop ADM Brannigan from dropping the nukes, and while I won't openly contradict him, I still disagree with the decision."

Malcolm thought for a moment. "You believe he acted out of anger and without thinking about the consequences?"

"Yes, sir, I do."

"I have known Kevin for a long time. I can assure you he thought about it and even put aside his anger. Yes, he was very angry when you lifted off the planet, but I can assure you he gave it a rational thought. After all, there is enough evidence to tell us what the Kammorrigans are. He bought us a lot of time. As we learned, their home world was their manufacturing plant with several research labs. By nuking it, he stopped their ability to produce more ships and weapons. Now, they have to find a new place to make into a manufacturing world. That takes a lot of time. Plus, the other life forms they have enslaved; we have given them a morale boost."

Mike turned to him with a confused look.

"Oh yes, the news of the planet's destruction will have traveled by now to many civilizations. Those who were harmed, destroyed and enslaved will see that they are not invulnerable and there is a new race willing to fight them. The survivors of those worlds and others that may be threatened will now have hope and perhaps be willing to work with us to utterly defeat the Kammorrigans."

Mike thought about that while gazing out the window.

The shuttle slid into a docking ring inside the space station and was maneuvered automatically into the pressured side of the hangar deck. The hatch opened, and the two stepped out of the shuttle onto the hangar deck. A young crewman was standing there waiting for them.

"Good morning, Gentlemen, she said. "Your luggage will be transported to your office. If you follow me, I will take you there now." She moved off smartly as they followed. They moved quickly to a set of elevators. The crewman punched in the Diplomat section and the lift began moving. She then moved to a monitor and brought up schematics of the station to show their progress so both the Ambassador and Mike could follow their progress. When the elevator came to a stop, the doors opened and she led them to their offices. "Good day, Gentlemen. The Director is being notified of your arrival, and I am sure you will meet him soon." She closed the door and departed. The two watched her leave with blank expressions then moved further into the Diplomatic section. No one was present, but John saw a door with his name on it and motioned for Mike to follow him.

The office had a desk with chairs and a small table off to the side. Book shelves lined part of the bulkheads and view screens took up the rest. John moved behind the desk and found a keypad. He keyed a couple of buttons when a voice responded.

"May we have coffee sent up for two, please?"

"Yes, Ambassador, it will be there shortly."

"Thank you."

Mike peered at the empty shelves and blank view screens then moved over and took a seat.

"I guess this is home now. I wonder what my office will be? A broom closet?"

John smiled at him as he took a seat and opened and shut the drawers on the desk.

"Well, this won't be too bad. I'll have a look around the spaces after we meet with the Director."

There was a knock at the door, and John said, "Enter." A steward entered with a cart with a coffee thermos, milk, creamer, sugar, cups and spoons on it. He set them to one side and quietly left the office. Mike got up, poured the coffee, fixed it how they liked them, and handed John a cup.

"Now what?"

John shrugged his shoulders and said, "We wait."

It wasn't long till another knock came at the door. John said, "enter," and a nice, professionally dressed lady stepped into the office.

"Good morning, Gentlemen, the Director is able to see you now if you wish."

John stated, "That would be nice," and both men followed her to the elevator. She keyed in the command deck when the doors shut. The elevator rose two levels in the station, and the doors opened. They followed her to the double set of glass doors. Over the doors, it read Director of Space Fleet. She opened the doors for them and gestured to the closed doors at the far end.

"He is expecting you; please go on in."

She took a seat behind one of two desks and pulled up a screen.

Mike looked at John, who just shrugged and headed for the doors with Mike in tow.

After shutting the doors, they looked around the office they had just entered.

It was long, similar to a tube. A window at the far end had Earth in its view, with the two bulkheads going the length of the room slightly curved inward. A massive view screen filled up one of the curved walls and a smaller one on the other. Between the door and the desk was a table with four chairs and a computer. It was full of various items. Next to it was a cart from the galley with coffee and food items.

Between the desk and the window stood a man looking out the window at the planet.

As they approached him, he turned with a smile and came around the desk with his hand out. Mike was astonished to see Admiral Kevin Brannigan.

Kevin chuckled as he saw Mike's expression.

"John, Mike, it is good to see both of you." He first shook hands with the Ambassador and then with Mike. Then led them to the table and started pouring coffee for them.

"So, you are the Director." Mike started. "I was wondering what happened to you and, of course, what is happening." Kevin nodded and took a seat after handing them their cups.

"Yes, they appointed me as a director. But I am planning on having name changes made. This position will become Chief of Space Operations. Ralph Nabum, who is the Chief, ought to be Chief of Staff of Space Force. That should align better. But that isn't why you are here."

He took a drink, put the cup down, and waited.

Mike noticed they were staring at him which started to make him feel a bit apprehensive.

"Ok, what? Why are you staring at me like that?"

"Good show, excellent, thank you for volunteering," John said with a devilish smile. Mike went a bit pale and both started to laugh at him.

"Now what? What have you two cooked up?"

John leaned over and put a hand on his shoulder.

"It was decided a bit ago to send you out as Earth's diplomatic representative."

Mike started to get really apprehensive then.

"No, State will have my head."

"No, they won't" John replied. "In a real sense, you no longer work for them. Besides, the President has nominated you, and the Senate has confirmed you. You are Earth's first ambassador to the stars. Congratulations. We are here for two reasons. First, for me as the new head of Earth's Diplomatic Corps, led by the United States, to establish our positions here at the station. And second, for you to be briefed and sent on your way."

Mike gaped at them with shock.

Kevin spoke. "The President was impressed with your work and advice. The members of the summit you were at also were impressed. The member states also voted for you to head out to represent us. So, part of my job has been preparing a ship and crew for you. Now, we will explain your mission to you."

"I get a say in this, yes?" Mike asked both defiantly and timidly.

"Well, yes," John replied. "I suppose you do. Do you really have any objections? After all, you know what we are facing better than most people. Everyone who was on EXPLORER has important jobs here to prepare us for the next encounter. You are trained and experienced in diplomacy. Also, you have practical experience."

"Besides," Kevin added, "you have credibility. You were there at Kammorriga when we destroyed it and saw what we could do against them. That will be of great value."

Mike sat back and thought for a bit. Then started shaking his head. "Ok, I see the points." He sat quietly for a moment. "Ok, I guess I am going back out."

Both men smiled and said ok. Kevin turned to the computer and started keying in items he desired to come up on the larger viewer. As the Milky Way galaxy spun into view, Kevin started, "First and foremost, and always, Earth's location is never to be revealed. This is the first and most significant law. Never reveal our location." Mike nodded.

The viewer then showed a spiral with a green dot for Earth and a red dot for Kammorriga.

"This demonstrates the relative positions of our two worlds," Kevin continued. "Now, we have some rough figures of the three great civilizations," Kevin keyed up areas of space as he said, "This region appeared to belong to the Zumeera Empire, this one to the Odaessumada Federation, and this one to the Daemoulaoumari Republic. This information is what we have been able to glean so far from all the databases we have acquired. We still don't know much about them."

Mike studied it, then said, "It appears Kammorriga is on the outer edge of the Daemoulaoumari Republic, yes?"

"That is what we believe. It appears as though they were insignificant during the great civilizations. You may need this information as background, and it is already being uploaded to your ship. Now, you are to seek out a species called the Alia."

Kevin keyed in another set of instructions, and a few planetary systems were highlighted.

"One of our recon teams on Kammorriga came across an Alian. They are a short, furry, yet highly intelligent species. They may be our best introduction to the other civilizations out there." Kevin pointed to the highlighted systems. "We believe they may be found here. Go out there and find out. If you find them, see if we can start a coalition of races to take on the Kammorrigans." Kevin paused. Mike just turned his head toward him and back at the screen.

"Mike, we have sent Paul Connington with a Strike Group to take out the unknown threat from the first space station we encountered. Soon, we will launch an anti-piracy group to eliminate the pirates threatening Plymouth, the mining planet we discovered. We hope to launch a Space Action Group shortly. Both the SAG and the anti-piracy will seek out a world for refugees." Mike focused in on him.

"Part of your negotiations will see if there are any refugees willing to join us in a coalition, and we would offer this system for them to hide, train, and share technologies and techniques for us to destroy the Kammorrigans. Perhaps, they would have a system they can offer, closer to their own worlds, that would be better. But even if they don't want to; you must pull together a coalition with as many civilizations as possible. We are building a fleet to lead such a coalition. You will see it as you go to your ship."

Kevin continued, "Also, we are supplying you with a new communications system. It is a hyperspace drone that carries messages, data, star maps, etc. Your ship will have a few onboard. Now, with this information, we have some preprogrammed locations for your ship to meet up with the *Sabachi*. She is an intelligence ship already underway. She is in deep cover, spying on the Kammorrigans. You will link up with her, download all of her information, and send it to us via one of these drones. This is a top priority. Her mission is to discover key strategic points of the Kammorrigans so we can plan our campaign. Also, she will give you critical information for creating a coalition. Don't share everything, but you should have valuable information that, in your judgement, you can share to get a coalition formed.

Mike sat there, taking it all in.

"Now, you will be the Mission Commander and the Ambassador. Your ship is designated," Kevin smiled and shook his head, "the *USS Diplomat*."

Mike turned to him, and Kevin again shook his head.

"Don't worry, it will have the latest weapons and shields. Her hyperdrive will take you possibly farther than you may know. But its primary mission is diplomacy. Use her weapons if needed. Colonel

Jennifer Nelson is her commanding officer. You command her, and she commands the ship. You and she have orders. Enforce your authority as the Mission Commander but leave the running of the ship to her. Got it?"

Mike affirmed the positions.

"Chief Petty Officer Seymour will be a part of your personal staff. He was the team leader who came across the Alian on Kammorriga. He is to take your orders. Now, he is a SEAL, so listen to him. He has practical experience you will find useful. You will have a couple of reconnaissance teams onboard for your command. Chief Seymour will know how to use them. You will have two aides and a linguist to assist you."

Kevin paused and looked at them.

"Any questions?"

Mike thought for a moment, then shook his head. He was still assimilating what he'd been told.

"Ok, no worries. All this information is in your packet, waiting for you on your shuttle." Mike lifted his head and gazed at Kevin.

"Your luggage is already on the shuttle."

Both Kevin and John stood up as Kevin keyed for an escort to come in. Mike slowly got up. Looked around the room. This was fast, and he was glad he had the leave to handle his affairs.

Kevin extended his hand, and Mike took it.

"Ok, well, success and all the best to you."

Mike said, "Thank you," as the escort knocked and entered. With a nod from Kevin, he took Mike by the arm briefly to start him moving. The door closed quietly behind them.

John watched as they left, then started to leave.

"Just a moment, please." John stopped and turned toward Kevin.

"On a different note, why am I policing the system, and why is that other station in orbit if it is their job to police the system?"

John sighed. He knew this would be a thorn in Kevin's side and hoped he wouldn't have to deal with it so soon.

"Simply put. They are the police in the system to stop piracy from Earth, but they lack the resources. You have the ships, crews, and the sensors to do the job. So, for the meantime, you have to provide those resources."

Kevin started when John interjected. "No, no use saying anything at this time, Kevin. You have to cooperate with them. You don't have to like it, but you do have to share the resources. And I already understand your arguments. But this is the area in which you must bend, especially if you want your fleet."

Kevin stood there staring at his old friend while that sunk in. He turned away with a growl in his throat and headed to the window. John joined him and they both stared out the window. Then he left Kevin to his thoughts.

* * *

Two months after Mike O'Shea left on his mission, Lieutenant Colonel Clark stepped out of the elevators and looked about the hallway. His eyes rested on the glass doors to his right and the title above them: Director of Space Fleet. He turned, walked to the doors, and entered. He approached one of the two secretaries, identified himself, and was informed that the Director would see him shortly and to take a seat. As he sat down, she told the Director that he was here.

As he sat there, he pondered this part of his career. His first space mission was the FAST Platoon leader protecting VADM Brannigan. Those final hours on Kammorriga, seeing the Admiral's Aide killed and his own sergeant carrying the dead woman, still haunted him. That was not how he saw things going. He had been transferred to the Space Force as one of the first Marines in the new Space Force

Galactic Marine Corps. Still, he held the same Marine Corps thinking of always faithful. And now he was heading back into space. He looked around the office and watched briefly the quiet efficiency of the two secretaries while waiting. Why would the Director want to see him?

He scanned the room again and noticed one of the ladies staring at him. When she saw he was returning her gaze, she said, "You may go in now." He got up and gave his thanks, went to the door, and knocked, and, after a brief moment, entered the office.

He was surprised to see Admiral Brannigan, now a four-star, come out from around the desk and head toward him with a gentle smile.

"It is good to see you again, my friend. Congratulations on the promotion." As they shook hands the Admiral led him to the table with chairs and poured him a cup of coffee.

"I am glad to see you were promoted and selected for this mission," the Admiral said as he sat down.

"Thank you, Sir."

"I will be brief since you have an actual mission briefing to get to. After all you did for me and my staff on our last mission, I just wanted to see you again."

LtCol Clark nodded.

"So, you will be the Commander of a Landing Force on a Space Action Group or SAG. The Commander of the Action Task Force, formally Amphibious Task Force, is Colonel Doug Kirby, he is the Commodore. SAG LIBERATOR's mission is anti-piracy. Primarily, that is. Secondarily, you will be seeking a system to house refugees. But you are to destroy the pirates that threaten Plymouth on system 237 Prime, the mining planet we found. You won't have the MEU numbers that we did, but you will have the capabilities to get the job done."

Kevin looked around the room, then continued, "man, it is good to see you again."

They chatted a bit longer about the people who were part of EXPLORER and where they were now. After fifteen minutes, a chime sounded, and Kevin stood up with Clark following. They shook hands, and the Marine left while Kevin watched him go.

Then, he turned back toward his desk and thought how Earth was fortunate to have men and women like Clark. It was a dangerous mission, but he needed those pirates gone, and between Kirby, Clark, and the three-ship SAG, they should get the job done.

CHAPTER 2

Colonel Jones was in his command center when the hyper-space well opened and the alert klaxons sounded. He ordered them silenced while his defense force readied itself. Out of the well came five ships that were already transmitting their IFF, Identify friend or foe, signal. He sighed in relief when it showed SESG RETRIBUTION from Earth was entering their system.

He ordered a hail to the command ship.

"Mining Station Plymouth, this is SESG RETRIBUTION, requesting permission to orbit"

With a nod of his head, his communication officer sent the affirmative.

"Comms, send to the Commander of the Strike Group an invitation for him, his commanders and staff to join us for dinner here at the station. Also, inform the galley of our guests."

"Yes Sir."

SESG EXPLORER discovered 237 Prime during its mission to Kammorriga. The planet was inhabited by pirates which the EXPLORER Marines destroyed. When Earth received the planet's location with the valuable energy crystal deposits, they sent another expedition to the planet. The pirates had returned and after a short battle, Earth claimed the planet and established Plymouth Station. However, the colony has remained under a constant threat from pirates.

When the Earth forces arrived at 237 Prime, they found an inhospitable planet with pockets of surface water and vegetation. They soon discovered the majority of the water was underground. The main value of the planet was and remains the various energy crystals and rare earth minerals, among others, included platinum and gold.

Plymouth Station was established as a mining, research and processing center for the energy crystals. A Central Command Dome was constructed with tunnels spreading out connecting other domes; including crew quarters, a large galley, multiple research domes, hydroponics and planetary hangars for a variety of equipment and workshops. West of the settlement, the designers placed three hangars for the space and planetary fighters with crews housed nearby. They connected the hangars to the central complex with a series of tunnels.

The mine was connected to the central complex by a tunnel and airlock system enabling the miners, engineers and scientist to transit between the two facilities without environmental suits. The main cavern at the entrance of the mines was enlarged and outfitted with several machine shops and laboratories for the mining and researching of the crystals. The heavy mining equipment used in the extraction of the crystals were maintained in a nearby cavern. From the main cavern, the settlement dug a tunnel to a different cave for the processing of the crystals. The processed crystals were then conveyed to Earth for its power requirements and space fleet.

Colonel John Jones, originally an officer with the US Air Force who later transferred to the US Space Force was the first and current commander of Plymouth Station. He interned at an energy company, learning several aspects of mining and processing materials. He has a deep understanding of these areas affording him the ability to lead the various technicians, miners and scientists making up the business end of the station.

He also commands Defense Force Zeta, the planetary defense force. The US Army provided a Striker group as the ground component of the defense force. Part of their mission is to escort scientists to other parts of the planet for research but primarily to repel any ground attacks. Zeta also has atmospheric ships for transport and close air support. A squadron of space fighters make up the orbital defense force. Finally, he has five combat ships in orbit around 237 Prime. ADM Brannigan has promised him newer and better ships, but they haven't arrived yet. Col Jones understands the Admiral has to update all the Earth Defense forces around Earth and Alpha Centauri, so he doesn't expect the new combat ships anytime soon.

Plymouth Station is the point of entry and departure to Earth. Col Jones has four missions: mine, research and develop a processing station for the energy crystal, defend the planet and station and finally, be the border control point for Earth.

LtGen Connington's shuttle slid into its berthing spot within a hangar. They waited as the hangar closed and sealed, equalizing the pressure. After a short period, the shuttle doors opened and the General with two staff officers and his five commanding officers stepped out onto the hangar deck. Col Jones greeted and led them to the main galley for dinner. Dinner was made up primarily of fruits and vegetables with small amounts of chicken. The beverages included wine and water.

"Thank you for the dinner, Col." Paul Connington stated.

"Glad to host you, Sir. The hydroponics domes can produce sufficient amounts of good-quality vegetables and fruits. We plan to deploy a few other farm domes to house animals with a processing center for meat, but that is probably a year or so out. We still rely on supply ships from Earth for other items. Glad they see fit to include alcoholic beverages for us." Col Jones smiled as he stood up and lifted his glass. "A toast." Everyone made sure they had wine in their glasses.

"From us at Plymouth Station, we wish you a successful mission. May you have victory without losses." They all took a drink and Col Jones sat back down.

General Connington glanced around the table and finally back at Col Jones. "How is the defense force working out? How is the fight against the pirates going? Do you require assistance since we are here?"

The Colonel thought for a moment.

"They are still coming. Our combat ships and fighters are doing a good job of preventing them from landing. Although three attacks ago, they came with sufficient forces to enable a landing. Thankfully, we had the strikers here and adapted to this planet's atmosphere to fight them off. Since then, their attacks haven't been that frequent."

After further moment of thought, he said, "Thank you General for the offer but I think you ought to conserve your combat power for your mission. I know you are going to Station Zeta Prime, as it has been designated now, to reinforce your victory over them during the EXPLORER mission. That might be a fight. Besides, you may need everything you have to complete your primary mission."

"You seem well informed about our mission." The General said, sounding slightly annoyed.

"Yes Sir. While it is classified, Admiral Brannigan wants me informed about the departures from Earth and any known arrivals. Since I am the entry point to Earth, he wants me ready."

General Connington thought for a moment, then sighed, "I see. Well, in the end it makes sense."

Colonel Jones continued, "Besides, soon after you depart, perhaps in a few months, the Space Action Group LIBERATOR will be arriving. Their mission will be anti-piracy. It will consist of three combat ships with transports and a Space Force Marine rifle company. LtCol

Clark, whom I believe you know as Major Clark from EXPLORER, is the Marine in charge. Colonel Doug Kirby is the overall mission commander."

General Connington nodded. He knew both men quite well. He remembered hearing something along this line when he was at Space Force plans reviewing his own mission.

"Very well. We will be making a jump in a couple of days. I want to use 237 Prime for some drills before we depart."

Colonel Jones nodded, "By all means. Just let my Operations Center know your schedule and any needs you may have." He smiled, "Using my combat ships and strikers as a red force wouldn't be a bad idea. I would like them to have additional training here, and they might surprise your group with a few tricks."

Paul looked over at his staff officers and commanders. "Yes, I think that would be a good idea." He turned to his Operations Officer, "Make that happen. Get with the Commander's Operations Center to schedule a few events."

"Yes Sir."

The rest of the evening's discussion turned to other topics. One of them was the *USS Diplomat* carrying Ambassador O'Shea. Colonel Jones was expecting the ship in about four months as she began her mission to build a coalition. General Connington was both surprised and pleased to hear Mike O'Shea was being made an ambassador and heading out to build a coalition. He thought how this could help Earth and wondered how he could be involved with the coalition. What might his Strike Group mean in this regard?

The evening ended pleasantly enough with the station's Commander escorting them back to the hangar. Their shuttle lifted off easily, and they returned to the command ship. From there the other commanders would depart for their own ships. Paul was happy with the station, Col Jones, and the news he received. His thoughts turned back to the days ahead and the drills they would undergo.

After three days of drills between the Strike Group and the station, Colonel Jones sat in his chair in the Command Dome, watching the status boards and screens.

"SESG RETRIBUTION is signaling they are ready for departure and will be opening the well in one minute, Sir." The Communication Officer reported.

"Very Well, the Colonel responded. "Please send them my regards and hopes for success in their mission."

"Yes Sir." The officer said and relayed the message.

The screen displaying the fleet showed the well opening, and SESG RETRIBUTION and LtGen Connington slipped through on their way to complete their tasks.

The Colonel sat back in his chair.

Four months later, Colonel Jones was in the cave that housed the crystal refining laboratory.

"Well, Doctor, how long before we can process these crystals?"

The Dr., the lead researcher, shook his head in thought.

"Colonel, we have discovered not only the crystals that are clear in color, but also other crystals with different colors which seem to have different yet similar properties. We also have found that cutting the primary clear crystals into different sizes and shapes affects their energy outputs. As such, we are not ready to process them through a production plant."

The Colonel drew his lips up tight indicating a level of frustration.

"Ok, I get that, but we ought to be able to produce the clear crystals now. Earth can do that but the commanders and lead politicians want production here."

"Yes, yes," The Doctor responded, showing his own level of annoyance. "But it is more important to understand each type and fraction of the crystals before we start producing. IF we don't do this," the Doctor raising his voice as he saw the Colonel start to answer, "WE will be wasting resources!" He finished with a defiant tone and a hard look in his eyes.

The Colonel stared at him, about to respond, when his communication radio sounded. He picked it up and saw it was the Command Dome.

"Go ahead," he spoke into it.

"Sir, a ship just came through the hyper-well and identifies itself as the *USS Diplomat.*"

"Good, have them make orbit and send an invite to the Ambassador and Captain of the ship. Colonel Jones out." He flipped the switch to off before waiting for an acknowledgment and turned back to the Doctor.

"All right. Meet me in my office tomorrow at 1000. Come with a plan to start production within one month, Doctor." As the Doctor was about to object, the Colonel raised his hand to silence him. "We will begin production with the primary crystals. We cannot wait for more research, though I expect that to continue. This isn't a pet project of yours. We are talking about the defense of all humanity. Now, get to work on that plan, Doctor." He quickly turned toward the exit and left the cave to greet his visitors. *Yes, I will send a message to Command to get a replacement for the Doctor,* he thought. *He is too much trouble, wasting time and resources.*

As Col Jones headed to the hangar, he noticed the stranger with an escort approaching him. He stopped and waited. The young man approached and saluted him, saying, "Col Jones, Sir, may I present Ambassador O'Shea." The Colonel returned the salute and acknowledged Ambassador O'Shea. He then dismissed the escort.

"Welcome to Plymouth Station, Ambassador. Is there anyone else?"

Mike looked the Colonel over. He was a tall, slender man. "Thank you. It is only myself," he said as he shook the man's hand. *Yes, a strong man.*

"If you would follow me, Sir." The Colonel turned, and the two traveled down the tunnel, made several more turns, and came to the Command Dome. The Colonel then led Mike to his personal office. With a touch of the keypad, the doors slid open, and they entered. The office was round with a door to their right. Mike noticed the desk was simple and transparent, with a monitor and computer. He also noticed two other view screens on the walls. One of them displaying a tactical display of the planet's orbit. There was a short cabinet behind the desk and a bookshelf against another wall.

"Please sit, Ambassador. Would you like some lunch or a drink?"

"A drink would be nice, thank you."

The Colonel went over and poured a couple of glasses of brandy and offered one to the Ambassador.

"I'm surprised Colonel Nelson didn't join you, Ambassador."

"Mmm, she is an interesting person. She didn't want to stop here at all. Claimed we needed to make the next jump and be on our way. I know she is new to this and doesn't realize how long each leg will be before we get anywhere. But she seems quite competent other than the impatience."

John thought for a few moments.

"I've known Jennifer for several years now. She was Air Force like I was before joining Space Force. She decided to spend time on a Navy cruiser to get a feel for ships." He took a drink while thinking about what to say next. Mike knew he was debating saying something, so he took a drink and asked, "What is it, Colonel? She seems cold and yet efficient."

John smiled.

"Actually, she is a very passionate woman, Sir. She is very proficient and cares deeply for her ship and crew. Don't worry about that. But to command a diplomatic mission or, rather, a diplomatic ship is not what she was seeking. She desires a combat mission. She will do well but wants this assignment over quickly."

"Oh," Mike said, "then she won't understand that we could be at this for a few years. This type of mission requires a level of patience and can't be rushed. Yes, we are in a time crunch. Who knows when the Kammorrigans will find us? And yes, we believe they will eventually. So, we have to take the fight to them. Mine is one of the key missions and needs to be done right."

John nodded. "You are right, Sir. She will avoid you at first. Give her some time to get comfortable. Then you will need to impress upon her the importance and to follow your lead. In the end, she will."

Mike smiled his appreciation and took another drink.

The Colonel looked hurriedly at one of the viewscreens. It had begun to blink to get his attention. As Mike turned to see what caught the Colonel's eye, he noticed John was keying his communications.

"Command Room, what is happening?"

"Sir, the *Diplomat* is signaling they are ready whenever the Ambassador is."

Mike stood up. "Well, you have your own duties and we should get on our way. Thank you for the drink, Colonel."

"Before you go, Ambassador. I have a disk for you from Admiral Brannigan. I don't know why you didn't receive the briefing on Earth, but here it is." The Colonel handed him the disk. "You should know a stealth ship is already in deep space. They departed almost a year ago. They were heading for Kammorriga space. The XO of the *Nautilus* is commanding her. She is the *USS Sabachi* on deep reconnaissance. She has contact info for your ship and you have several key locations to meet up with her. She may have the information you require for a successful mission."

Mike thought for a moment and pocketed the disk. "Thank you, Colonel, I appreciate it."

The Colonel finished his drink and took Ambassador O'Shea to the hangar.

Approximately two months after the *Diplomat* left his space, Colonel Jones was in his office with the desk monitor displaying various statuses of the station and mining operations. He was expecting the replacement doctor for crystal production any day now. One wall screen displayed the orbital tactical situation with ships' status reports. The other wall monitor was linked to the scanning monitor in the Command Dome displaying the system. His desk monitor had various symbols in the upper right corner, when one began to blink. He keyed his communication button.

"Yes, Command Room, what is it?"

"Sir, a group of ships just came out of hyper space. We are hailing them now."

"Prepare to put the station on alert and bring the ships about."

"Yes Sir......Sir, we just received a communiqué from them. They are SAG LIBERATOR."

"Ah, good. Have them establish an orbit. I want to see both Col Kirby and LtCol Clark before they start their mission." After the Communications Technician acknowledged his order, he switched it off and sat back in his chair, feeling relief flow through his mind. The last year had been intense with all the pirate activity in the region.

His door chime sounded; he pressed a button on his desk to open the door. Two officers stepped through. Colonel Jones adjusted the live feed viewscreen, and the three ships of SAG LIBERATOR came into focus. He gazed at the two men, taking stock of them. Finally, he motioned for them to take a seat. They each took a chair and sat down.

Colonel Jones then punched up information on his desk monitor regarding the two men.

"Colonel Doug Kirby, I see you are a Space Force serviceman your entire career. For a year you were assigned to the Navy with a Surface

Action Group and an Amphibious Readiness Group to prepare for this mission. Mmm, good. Then I expect you will know how to command the three ships in pursuit of these pirates."

He glanced over at LtCol Clark and keyed a few items.

"Ah, now I recognize you. You were in charge of the Fleet Anti-Terrorism and Security Team with Admiral Brannigan's expedition. Now you are the second in command and in charge of the Marines taking down the pirate stations. Good."

Colonel Kirby started to speak when Colonel Jones held up a hand while keying in a few items. He then indicated for them to watch one of his viewers. The image of Admiral Brannigan came up.

"Colonel Jones," the image began, "you will maintain your current complement of defense ships. I cannot replace them, but you can look forward to additional combat ships to defend 237 Prime. Further, I'm sending you a three-ship fleet with Marines onboard. This is a Space Action Group. Colonel Kirby will be the commander of the SAG. He falls under your command. Make no mistake. His mission is to destroy the pirates in the sector under your authority. That is the authority you will gain when you destroy the pirates. The SAG under Colonel Kirby is your Strike Group. Ensure you can recall them if necessary to augment your defense force. I suggest you ensure the system you are in is clear of all pirate activities and listening posts or stations. Secure your system then send the SAG to clean out the pirate strongholds. Oh, by the way, you're being promoted to Brigadier General. You now have general court-martial authority, along with all policing and judicial authority over your sector. The Senate has already approved your promotion, Brigadier Jones. Brannigan out."

Colonel Kirby sat there a bit dumbfounded. He had believed he would be free to command without any oversight. Now, he discovered he had been assigned to Plymouth Station and was not free to do as he pleased.

Brigadier General Jones stared coldly at him. "Colonel, as my strike force, I want to ensure you have total communications and station protocols between your three ships and my operational command. We will run a few drills over the next few days, then, I want you to proceed with clearing this system of all pirates. As intelligence comes in, you may proceed to the pirate strongholds for elimination. Understood?"

"Yes Sir. We will get on it right away."

LtCol Clark sat watching. He noticed how Colonel Kirby had strutted into the station and office but now seemed downcast. BGen Jones turned his gaze toward him.

"How many Marines do you have?"

"Two reinforced rifle companies, including a squad of Recon Marines and a squad of support Marines. They are spread out across all three ships with myself and the command group on the lead ship with Colonel Kirby."

"Good. Ok, I'll let you two get started with linking to my Operations Center. Good day, Gentlemen."

"Good day," they both responded as they stood up and departed the office.

John sat back in his chair, satisfied. Command had told him about Doug Kirby. He was an excellent officer and a good tactician but a bit on the arrogant side. This humbled him but didn't break him. He knew he would have to watch him and ensure he received timely communications from them. But he also knew this team would break up the pirate activities. Earth and Plymouth needed the pirates destroyed and a smooth and constant flow of the crystals back to Earth. He sighed heavily. Damn, now he had to get production going and get the engineers and scientists to figure out those new colored crystals. He rubbed his eyes, then keyed his system to review the reports.

CHAPTER 3

Lt Gen Connington sat in his office reading reports concerning his Strike Group when the door chime sounded. He keyed a few buttons, and on his screen, he could see Brigadier General John Roberts, the MEU Commander from SESG EXPLORER, now his Deputy Commander, outside his door. He keyed for the door to open.

"Come in, John."

John entered the room. He still had to duck to enter rooms, since the designers hadn't enlarged them. Paul got up and fixed them both some coffee as John sat down at the desk. Paul took his seat, keyed in few items on the computer, and the information was displayed on a monitor.

"Well, Sir, I've looked over the fleet reports and have spoken with the ships' commanders and the different functional leads."

Paul nodded.

"Our flagship is in full readiness. The *Hood* can do all her mission sets without any problems. CAPT Murphy has her in tip-top shape. His job on the *Excalibur* paid off. I'm glad he is here with us like he was at Kammorriga." LtGen Connington nodded. He thought how good it was to have CAPT Murphy, who had commanded the ship *Excalibur*, and Col Williams, who commanded the second command ship and Marine transport, the *Chesty*, from the EXPLORER mission. Experience counts out here.

"What about the *Levant* and Colonel Johnathon Williams?"

John stared at his palm device for a while, sighed heavily. "Well, I'm concerned about Colonel Williams. This is our main ground force, but he behaves as if he is only a transport commander. When we were out with EXPLORER, he was solemn during the entire mission." Paul watched him.

John shrugged with a downcast look.

He then continued, "Paul, he never liked transporting the Marines onboard the *Chesty*, and he sees his role much in the same way, not even a second fiddle but just a pure transporter. His ship isn't ready and the Marines are allowed limited sustainment training. It will hurt us when we need them the most."

"I see," Paul said, sitting for a moment in thought. This isn't what he wanted to hear. Their first real test was coming up and he didn't need a ship's captain not performing at his peak level, especially one that had to deliver Marines on a target and protect them while protecting his own ship. He performed well enough during the mission to Kammorriga as Paul's flagship commander, but Paul was in command and John his deputy when they had to leave the Admiral behind. Paul sighed, "well let's come back to him. What about the others?"

John keyed a few items on his pad, first came the *Chesapeake*.

"Ok, our lead cruiser, the *Chesapeake*, commanded by Colonel Joe Meyers. Her readiness level is a bit lacking. She is C2 overall. Her response times are not at their peak. Her equipment, weapons, drive and other machinery are good. It is her training and response times that are pulling her readiness down. As you know, Colonel Meyers was in charge of the Mars Defense Force. He commands the *Chesapeake* in much the same manner. Good enough is good enough is his philosophy. He thinks he is ready, but I don't."

John keyed a few more times and the *Vengeance* came up.

"Our other cruiser, the *Vengeance*, commanded by CAPT Ned Holmes. She is C1, fully operational, and ready like the *Hood* is. No issues here."

As John started to key his pad, Paul said, "Ok, wait. Let me get this straight. The two Navy guys have their ships ready and operational, and the two Space Force guys are lacking."

John looked up from his pad and drank his coffee while watching his boss.

"Ok, got it. We need to lean on Meyers. You will do that. I'll have a chat with Johnathon. Now, what about the *Cyane*? How is Colonel Jeanine Smith, our last Space Force commander?"

John finished keying up the *Cyane*.

"Well, Colonel Smith has our one and only destroyer and is ready. She is C1, fully operational. Colonel Smith is great at commanding this ship. I've seen her with her crew. I think her time at Mars Defense Force as both a shuttle and, later, a fighter pilot has paid off. Jeanine Smith has a relaxed manner around her crew but is commanding their attention and respect at the same time. The *Cyane* is ready and able."

"Good, glad to hear that. So, I have three out of five ships locked and loaded for bear and two lacking. One that is particularly vital since they carry the Marine attack force I need."

Paul looked at his own computer, keying various statistics while thinking. John just waited.

"All right," Paul started, "when we come out of the well, you get over to the *Chesapeake* and get her in shape. I want her at peak readiness. I'll summon Colonel Williams and see if I can't motivate him. I want the fleet at full operational level when we jump to Zeta Prime. I'm expecting a fight when we get there. I want to go in ready to recapture the station and fight off a fleet or two of pirates while doing it. All commanders must be ready."

John nodded and made some entries into his palm device.

"I want a good battle plan for the Marines, which means I want you onboard the *Levant* when we make that jump. You have the authority to relieve Colonel Williams if he isn't performing correctly but ensure the Marines go where we need them to go. Got it?"

"Yes Sir. I'll have her ready, both ship and the Marines. This means we may need to stay in normal space a little longer, though. I'll want to run more drills with *Levant* and the Marines before we make that jump."

"Yes, I agree. We have made several jumps since Plymouth, and I agree with you, we need drills to achieve our efficiency."

John finished his coffee while Paul was sending command instructions to his flag bridge for the fleet.

"Alright, John, you best get going."

"Ok, see you in a bit, Sir."

John left the office.

Paul watched his viewscreen. He thought how Admiral Brannigan would look at the well out of the port hole at a time like this. He admired the way Kevin handled these things. Well, he now was the one to handle these things. He thought, *I need Johnathon onboard the Levant. He knows what we are facing and I can't afford him to slack off.*

He keyed for his communications officer and told him to have Colonel Williams report to his office upon entering normal space.

* * *

Colonel Williams stood at the Fleet Commander's door. He had rung and now waited. The General's Aide assured him that he was in the office. While traveling from his ship to the *Hood* he wondered why he was being summoned to the General's office. What happened to cause this? He wondered if the other ships' commanders were being summoned or just him.

The door opened and he heard the General say, "Come in, Colonel."

Colonel Williams entered the office and stood at attention in front of the desk while the General ignored him, reviewing his computer monitor. Several moments passed. Finally, LtGen Connington turned toward him and Colonel Williams saluted him. The General returned it and motioned for him to take a seat. The General watched him for some moments.

"Colonel Williams, good to see you. How are you? How are you doing?"

Colonel Williams was confused and showed it.

"I'm good, Sir."

The General nodded. "You are good, no issues? You're not ill or anything then?"

The Colonel was confused by this line, "I am fine, Sir. Nothing wrong. Why do you ask?"

"Just wondering." Paul turned back to his computer and keyed in for some information on the *Levant,* including crew readiness, equipment and overall ship's status.

The Colonel waited, wondering what this was really about.

"I'm a bit confused, Colonel. I'm trying to ascertain why the *Levant's* readiness is C2 and declining. In fact, you are about to hit C3 status. Not good, especially for the ship carrying my Marines who must be ready to assault stations and planets. I could only think your health is failing you. Care to explain?"

Colonel Williams thought. *Oh, that is why I am here. What to say now? How do I respond? Those Marines are troublesome; what am I to do?*

The General sat waiting for a response.

After a few more moments of silence, the General stood up and stepped to his port hole and looked out at the stars. With his back turned to the Colonel, he sighed and said, "Johnathon, you are putting me in a difficult position. I was glad that Admiral Brannigan picked you for this mission. He has the final say on ship commanders and chose each of my commanders with a purpose. You, for instance, were with me from the start with the EXPLORER project and you did a damn good job on that mission. I need good ship commanders, and having you and Captain Murphy out here is a good thing. But your performance is making me wonder what is wrong. Why are *Levant* and the combat forces declining in readiness? What needs to be done to get them to peak performance?"

He turned and looked at the Colonel with both sadness and determination.

"Are you still up to the job or do you need to be relieved? If I need a new commander, now is the time. I do need an operations officer."

Colonel Johnathon Williams was shocked. That statement struck him to his core. He had been with Space Force since the start of his military career. He'd commanded the International Space Station and served briefly with the Navy onboard an Amphibious Readiness Group, to learn about ship functions and Marine landing support. He was honored to be part of EXPLORER but quickly felt totally irrelevant. His ex-girlfriend, Captain Lindsey, was the Fleet Operations Officer, now Brigadier General Roberts, who was the Marine commander on EXPLORER, was the Deputy Fleet Commander and once again, he was the ferry guy. He was not even third in command, and now the General was telling him he was about to be relieved. Why did he get stuck with the Marines and this terrible situation? But what to do now? How to respond? Isn't command better than everything else?

He started to say something and then closed his mouth and looked down with furrowed brows. The General pursed his lips, then relaxed and chose to wait. Colonel Williams started thinking. This mission is a hunt-and-kill mission. The Space Command sent them out to destroy enemies. Battles will be fought, and men and women will die; perhaps his and other ships could be lost. He had failed to prepare his own ship for battle. How many crewmembers and Marines could die because he failed to prepare them?

The Colonel looked up at the General with determination in his eyes. The General felt some gladness at this.

"No Sir. You don't need to relieve me. I'll get the ship ready."

"Good. Then you can tell me what is wrong; why did the readiness drop?"

Johnathon breathed heavily.

"Me, Sir. I was happy to be a part of EXPLORER, but during the mission, I felt like I was nothing but a transport commander and not a combat commander. I started feeling left out. I was surprised to get this shot, but those feelings are still there. Yet, I now fully recognize this is a different mission. I thought we were just a transport ship."

Paul shook his head and sat back down.

"I see. Admiral Brannigan and I had discussed this once or twice when we were on our way to Kammorriga. He expressed how ARG ship commanders, at times, would feel that way. They could start feeling resentment toward the Marines and vice versa. Perhaps when I came aboard the *Chesty*, you and I should have discussed this matter. But that is in the past. You need to snap out of this. The *Levant* is just as important, if not more so with this mission. Yours is the ship that will go into the thickest part of the battle to deliver my combat force to stations, planets, asteroids, and even other ships. You have to provide fire suppression, fire support, and protect those Marines to and from the objective. I have to have you sharp at all times onboard the *Levant*. I can't have a resentful, envious, or bitter commander. I need you fully alert and prepared with good judgment at all times. Understand?"

"Fully Sir. I will get the ship and Marines ready Sir. No more issues, I can assure you."

Paul looked him square in the eyes. "Ok. I intend to spend time here before we make our final jump to Zeta Prime. See that you get with General Roberts and get drills done to improve readiness. You will command the *Levant* to the upper portion of the station and deliver an assault force on the station. I'm going into this as a combat operation since Space Command has assumed we will be attacked the moment we arrive. Got it?"

"Yes Sir. We will be ready."

"Good. Now, get back to your ship. I look forward to the next report."

Colonel Williams stood, saluted, and left the office.

Paul felt better and was glad that Johnathon had recognized his situation and snapped back from it. Now they will be ready.

* * *

General Roberts entered the airlock of the *Chesapeake* and, after being welcomed aboard with the proper protocols, turned to Colonel Meyers and softly said, "We need to talk, Colonel."

Colonel Meyers responded, "Yes Sir, this way to the briefing room. My officers are ready for you."

"Ok, but I want to talk to you alone first."

"Ah, yes Sir. Then should we go to my office?"

"Sounds good."

General Roberts observed the crew while they went to the Colonel's office. Upon entering, the General took a seat in front of the desk while Colonel Meyers moved behind it.

With a serious and matter-of-fact tone, the General started, "Colonel, your readiness is at C2. That is not good. When we make this last jump, you must be at C1 and ready for combat. When we come out of the well, we expect to be in a firefight. Understand?"

"No Sir. C2 is fully ready; besides, the station is allied with us."

General Roberts scowled while staring at the ship commander.

"Really? C2 is below standard with this fleet. Both the Fleet Commander and I are unhappy and we want this ship at combat readiness. You will get this ship to peak performance before we jump.

And besides, who are you to tell the General that Zeta Prime is no problem? Have you been there? Do you have intelligence that we don't have?"

Colonel Meyers realized he had angered BGen Roberts.

"Colonel, I am here to get you back on track. Is that clear?"

"Yes Sir. We will be ready before we jump. I can guarantee it."

"Good, I am not leaving till you show me one hundred percent ready. Got i?."

"Yes Sir."

General Roberts studied the Colonel and saw his point was made, "Ok, now let's go see your officers and get this ship ready."

They both stood up and headed to the briefing room.

* * *

Five days and multiple drills later, LtGen Connington was pleased with the improvements in the fleet's operational and combat readiness. Now, he knew they were ready to make the jump to Station Zeta Prime; as Space Command had dubbed it.

All his ships' commanders, Marine landing commander, and CAG were in his briefing room.

BGen Roberts began.

"All right. Sir, we have achieved C1 status across the fleet. All ships and functional combat systems are fully combat ready. We can now accomplish our first objective."

"Thank you, General Roberts," Paul said.

He shifted his gaze upon each officer who was gathered around the table.

"Ok, listen up. Those of you who were with EXPLORER know this is a dangerous situation we are jumping into. The last time we were here, we had to take the station and nearly lost a ship due to, well, let's call them ship traps. Thankfully, we had the firepower to defeat the station plus a fleet that appeared out of hyper space."

The General looked about the room, and seeing he had their attention, continued.

"When we departed the station, Admiral Brannigan was positive any future travels to the station would find a hostile administration prepared to attack us. Space Command still believes this, as do I. We have ensured each ship has the signature of these traps. We suspect there will be more than one and expect that the station will call for another fleet to come to their defense. This station is a trading out-post. The last time, the battle didn't involve any of the visitors. We do not assess they will partake in any battle this time, but we must watch them in case they do."

Again, the General measured the status of the room.

"Space Command wants us to go in ready for battle. Admiral Brannigan wants us to reestablish our authority over this station. Once we do, we are leaving behind our own governor. Colonel Burnhart of the US Army, now part of Space Force, will be the governor."

He turned to the Colonel, who nodded.

"You will be alone here with your own security force. A bad situation but this fleet needs the station to be neutralized if it can't be a friendly spot for us."

The Colonel acknowledged him.

"So, when we come out of the jump, I want to appear next to the station. The *Levant* will appear at the Administration level. Colonel Williams, I want you to launch the Marines ASAP when you come out of the well. Have them ready. The Marines are to lock onto all the docking ports and enter those airlocks at once. Take control of the Command Center and Administration levels and capture the Administrator."

They acknowledge the orders.

"The *Hood* will be midline to take out any attack ships or sta-tion defense. I want the *Cyane* to cover us. The two cruisers will take up two different positions. *Vengeance* will take the lower section, while *Chesapeake* will be across the *Hood* and a bit lower to cover those sections. All ships will launch their fighters to provide cover and be ready to combat any fighters from the station or any other ships.

Upon our jump, I want the station to be jammed so they can't call for anyone, plus scan for those traps. When a trap is discovered, I want the fighters to destroy them."

Captain Murphy raised his hand. When the General acknowledged him, he said, "Sir, I recommend that instead of destroying the traps, we mark their locations. This way, Colonel Burnhart will be able to use them once he is in control."

The two Generals sat back and looked at each other in thought.

"General Roberts, Colonel Burnhart; thoughts?" Paul asked.

General Roberts responded. "We planned to destroy them, but that is a good option. We can always take them out if we can't use them."

Paul turned his gaze upon the Colonel.

Colonel Burnhart thought for a bit, then nodded. "I like the option to be able to use them in case I need to trap any inbound ships and use the station weapons to destroy or capture them as necessary."

Paul thought for a few moments. "Ok, I agree. Scan and mark. Avoid them if we have to maneuver for battle. We will need to find their controls and, if able to use them turn them over to Colonel Burnhart."

The General looked around the room for questions or comments.

"All right, if nothing else, get to your ships and get your coordinates from Fleet Operations. Prepare to jump in two hours."

All Commanders and Staff departed for their ships and stations.

Paul turned to BGen Roberts who had remained behind.

"Ok, how are things onboard the *Levant*? Is Colonel Williams ready?"

John simply smiled. "He has come around. The ship and Marines are ready."

"What does Colonel Darcy think? Does she think the Marines will get the required support? Paul asked.

"Yes, she is actually quite happy with Johnathon now. She told me she has seen marked improvements in his behavior and command. She has no issues with him."

Paul sighed. "Good." He thought for a few moments. "You think I should have you onboard the *Levant*?"

John shook his head no. "If I went over there now, with these improvements, we would be signaling that we don't trust him. I'd rather have a confident commander than one who doubts everything he does."

Paul nodded. "Ok, then let's keep you here. Besides, I like the idea of having you onboard here to aid in the command and control when we make that jump."

Both men stood up and departed the conference room.

* * *

The five ships were lined up, ready for their jump. Each had its destination coordinates. The wells opened and the ships jumped into hyperspace. They were one day away from their end points. Paul Connington left the flag bridge and went to his office. He sat down at his desk, looking over the reports as each ship was preparing their fighters and loadouts. The *Levant* was prepping their Marine drop ships. They will have one night or sleep period before they come out of the jump. Each unit would be rested and fed. Their timing would have the assault begin mid-morning period.

Paul was satisfied with the reports and dictated a letter to his wife and ensured the logs would be up to date. The fleet had the new hyperspace communication drones. After the assault, Paul planned to launch the first one to Space Command. A nonevent was the desired outcome, then, he could leave Col Burnhart in command with only his Soldiers to man the station garrison. An actual assault would be a different story.

After a while, he read for a bit then got up to go to dinner. His table was set for four. Besides himself, it would be BGen Roberts, Colonel Burnhart and CAPT Murphy. He only desired a small group before the assault. Breakfast would be the same. He was feeling melancholy tonight.

The night went and came, and again, he found himself at breakfast with the same feeling. They ate in silence as they hurtled through hyperspace. Paul did find it difficult to fall asleep the previous night, but as he looked at his fellow diners, he felt energized. Today would be a good day.

After they ate, they each went to their stations. Paul and his Deputy were on the flag bridge while CAPT Murphy went to the ship's bridge. CAPT Murphy would ensure the *Hood* would be in position to provide covering fire while the flag bridge would oversee the entire operation.

They were in the final hour of approach. Finally, the reports came in from the other ships through the well. They had made communication improvements for hyperspace travel but it still wasn't where Space Command wanted it. Nevertheless, Paul had what he needed. The green light for the assault was sent.

"Damn fine astrogating." BGen Roberts stated. "All ships are on station as planned. *Levant* has already started her assault on the Administration and Command levels."

Paul nodded his affirmation to the report as he watched both the main viewer and the tactical display.

"Ensure each ship is scanning for those traps."

"Yes Sir." His Operations Officer responded.

The assault crafts from *Levant* were making their way to each of the station's airlocks.

"We have them by surprise. No shielding is up and just now some weapon systems are coming online." BGen Roberts said.

"Good. Communications, hail their Operations Center and tell them to stand down. Inform them we are a Strike Group from Earth and are here to enforce our rights."

"Roger, Sir."

The Marines began entering the station through force entry protocols. There wasn't a response from the station except for laser fire from the mid and lower sections. Each ship of the Strike Group quickly silenced those guns with their own laser fire.

"Sir, we have located six ship traps."

"Mark them on tactical and ensure all ships and fighters have them."

"Yes Sir," Responded the Operations Officer as he keyed in the instructions.

"Ok, launch the cover fighters now," Paul ordered.

The ships promptly launched their fighters which circled the station and the visiting ships.

"Reports are coming in from the Marines, Sir." Operations stated.

"Go ahead."

"They are meeting resistance from station personnel; however, it is light at this point. The reports indicate they are internal security at this time. They didn't have any time to prepare for an assault."

"Ok," Paul said, "tell them to ensure they capture the Administrator. It will be the one who directs a robust counterattack if it gets away."

"Yes Sir." Operations began sending the orders.

Paul watched the screens. The ships had jammed the station's outgoing communications the moment they had jumped into normal space and so far, the station was not able to get any communications out, though they had made the attempt. The signal they had attempted was aimed in the direction of Paul's actual destination. This confirmed to him the orders Admiral Brannigan had given him. The station was controlled by an unknown entity that was definitely hostile and had to be eliminated by any means necessary.

"General, the Marines have the Command Center and Administration levels under their control." Operations reported.

Paul got out of his chair and moved over to BGen Roberts.

"John, time from assault."

"Thirty minutes Sir."

"Seems too easy, don't you think?"

BGen Roberts thought for a few moments while reading through the report channel.

"They met with light resistance since we took the station by total surprise. They have the Administrator in custody." He read some more, "I think we got a good jump on them, so, no Sir, thirty minutes may seem fast since we planned for a longer fight. Now, as they move down the station into the mall area and the other areas, that may present more of a fight. I would say the station is not yet secured."

Paul stood straight up.

"I agree. Begin phase two of the assault. Have the *Levant*'s Master-at-Arms force take control of the upper levels and have the Marines begin securing the rest of the station. Ensure they have enough reinforcements. No surprises by not taking the entire station with our forces."

Paul moved back to his station as the Operations Officer keyed in the instructions.

The Marines were finding the situation easier than anticipated. They were methodical in the way they moved from level to level. Only internal station security was facing them vice an organized militia as they planned. The top section was secured. They posted guards at each level to watch over the mall and posted fire squads at the openings to the ships' berthing ramps to counter any offensive from berthed ships. The internal security forces were either quickly dispatched, ran away or surrendered as the Marines moved into the second disk.

Paul watched quietly the tactical display of the station's internal monitoring as the Marines moved down. Finally, he stirred in his chair and turned his attention to the few ships in their berthing housings.

"Have we scanned those ships?"

Operations looked about the bridge and after getting a thumbs up from the scanning stations responded, "Yes Sir. So far, the ships have kept their weapons and drives off line. A couple have activated shields, but that is all."

"All right, Communications send a general message to all the ships that as long as they stay in their current posture, they will be safe. Tell them this is an internal manner."

"Yes Sir," responded the Communications section.

Six hours later, the Marines reported they had the station secured. The *Hood* flag bridge acknowledged the update.

"Have CAPT Murphy prepare a shuttle for us. I want to keep the ships in an orbit about the station. Ensure the Control Center has those traps turned off and mark all of them. I want Colonel Burnhart and his security with me on the shuttle. I'm heading over." Paul said.

"Yes Sir." Operations affirmed as they sent the instruction.

"John, you have the fleet." Paul left the bridge and headed to the *Hood*'s landing bay.

As the shuttle was departing the bay, Operations radioed that the berthed ships were requesting permission to depart the station. Paul told them to deny departure and inform them that if they attempted to depart, they would be fired upon. He didn't want them to leave until he had a chance to discover who they were and where their flight plans stated they would be going.

The shuttle traversed the space to the Administration level easily. One of the Marine landers moved off to the *Levant* providing them the direct access to the Administrator's office. Four fighters had accompanied the shuttle to the station airlock. They made a hard seal easily and the airlock opened to receive the General, Col Burnhart, and the security team. They moved through the airlock and were escorted to the office.

As they entered, they noticed four of the *Levant*'s security team watching a tall, three eye, furry being. It stood at seven feet with hair that could be described as medium length and coarse. It had two legs and four arms.

"Have you been able to communicate with this creature? Is it the Administrator?" Asked Colonel Burnhart.

"Yes Sir, it is the Administrator. We have tried to communicate but it has remained silent," answered the Sergeant.

"I see." Colonel Burnhart was handed the translator and he spoke to the creature.

"What race are you?"

The creature opened a mouth with all flat teeth and answered, "I am a Cdeaybaayuuraa."

The Colonel studied it for a bit, then asked, "Where are you from?"

"From Cdeaybaayuuraa."

The General gave a closed mouth smile and chuckled under his breath.

"Where did you send the signal, and is that your planet?"

"Not my planet, no. My planet was destroyed by another species. A very deadly species. One you don't ever want to meet."

The Colonel glanced at the General who gave a very slight hand signal to be quiet.

"What race is that?"

The Cdeaybaayuuraa smiled and said "Kammorrigans."

"Ok, are they at the other end of that signal?"

"No and you best be glad though they will come and either take this station back or destroy it."

"So, you work for this other race?"

"Yes, but I will be killed for losing this station just like the last Administrator was."

"I see. So, who is the race you sent the signal to? How many ships and what level of technology?"

The Cdeaybaayuuraa just smiled at them.

The General nodded while Colonel Burnhart just stared at the creature with its broad mouthed smile.

"All right, take it to a holding cell. Ensure it can't escape and post a twenty-four-hour guard on it."

The Sergeant acknowledged the order and, the four guards took it away.

"It appears it or he, I suppose, doesn't know its signal didn't get through," the Colonel said.

The General glanced around the room. It was a circular room with a desk, adjustable, and a high back chair. The desk had a type of monitor within it and a monitor on one of the curved walls. He walked behind the desk.

"Thankfully, it didn't go through, so we will have the element of surprise. I'll be leaving soon but." The General went quiet while thinking. The Colonel stood there waiting. The General then keyed his pad on his right forearm.

"*Hood*, this is Ombre."

"Ombre, this is *Hood*."

"We will stay in orbit for a few more days. No more than three. Get inspectors over to those other ships. Look for a species called Cdeaybaayuuraa. Arrest them if you find any. Beware, they are big and potentially dangerous. Have the Marines recheck this station no less than three times. Scour it for listening and communication devices. Have a team check for traps and explosives. I want a team to secure the Command Deck of this station for Colonel Burnhart and have the shuttle ready to take me back to the *Hood*. Ombre out." The General closed the link as the acknowledgment came through.

"All right Colonel, your station. I'll be onboard the *Hood* while you take command. I suggest you make your quarters at the Command Deck along with your team. Ensure you have the supplies you need to hold off any forces. We will talk before I depart."

"Yes Sir." The men left the office and the security detail broke into two teams to escort them to their respective destinations.

Upon his arrival at the *Hood,* the General wanted the hyperspace communication drone prepared for immediate launch. After he ensured his message was prepared for Admiral Brannigan, he wanted it to launch immediately at the highest speed possible. Meanwhile, load it up with other messages, he instructed.

* * *

Space Command Headquarters defense systems unexpectedly came online and klaxons across the station sounded blaring their warnings of an intruding ship.

Admiral Brannigan woke up to the blaring klaxons and the voice calling for battle stations. He immediately keyed his comm system.

"What is it?"

"A single ship on the monitor just came out of hyperspace, Sir. We are trying to identify it now."

"A warship?"

"No Sir. Too small and scans aren't showing any weapons or shields."

"Then shut off those damn klaxons and go to yellow alert. Stand down from battle stations."

"Could be a missile, Admiral."

He thought for a moment, "Well is it headed for us at a high rate of speed?"

"No Sir. It is decelerating at a notable rate."

"Then follow my orders and check it against the databases."

"Yes Sir."

An hour later, CAPT Jorgensen was in the Admiral's office reviewing the message from LtGen Connington. The Admiral entered his office.

"Good morning, Admiral. The General desires a fleet of cruisers to support Zeta Prime."

"When did the General launch the drone?"

The CAPT checked his pad, "One month ago."

"Umph, a three-month trip reduced to one month with this drone. Good. What ships are in the pipeline that we could send him?"

"Only the SAG we were setting up for CAPT Lindsey."

"Damn." He rubbed his chin while moving behind his desk thinking.

"Crews ready?"

"Yes Sir."

"What ships are behind them in the pipe."

CAPT Jorgensen checked his pad, then answered, "A cruiser and two destroyers. They could be ready for CAPT Lindsey."

The Admiral grimaced, then nodded.

"Ok, get the SAG into launch sequence and prep a transport full of either Marines or Soldiers to accompany them. Let's see if we can get it there prior to three months."

"Yes Sir." CAPT Jorgensen left the office while the Admiral was thinking about the mission. So, Zeta Prime was taken but there was trouble out there. Paul wouldn't have asked for more ships if not required. He could only hope Colonel Burnhart would still be holding the station by the time those ships arrived, and Paul was achieving his objectives.

CHAPTER 4

Colonel Doug Kirby entered the ladder well returning to his cabin. The Commodore of SAG LIBERATOR was not happy with his Chief Engineer or CHENG as they were called. He had woken up in the middle of the sleep period and believed he felt something wrong with his ship. He woke up the CHENG and ordered him to meet him in the Engineering section. He wanted to ensure there wasn't anything wrong with the ship. The CHENG assured him there wasn't but would run diagnostics on the engines and reactors. The Colonel, while not quite satisfied demanded he report to him at the earliest possible moment. Now he was returning to his cabin. Revelry had yet to sound on the ship.

As he climbed the ladder, he was steaming on the inside. He hated being assigned to Brigadier General Jones. After all, he was promised his own command. He had expected only to answer to Space Force Operations but that damn Admiral Brannigan was able to place him under the Plymouth Station Commander. When those thoughts entered his mind, he grew red with anger. *Brannigan, that bastard* he thought. He had tried to keep Kirby from this assignment. He had argued Kirby was a fighter pilot and should stay commanding squadrons, possibly a wing. But Kirby had greater ambitions. He wanted to command one of the new battle carriers. The powers that be agreed Kirby should command one of them. Which meant he needed this assignment as Commodore of SAG LIBERATOR. Those powers had forced Admiral Brannigan to accept him in this role. But the

Admiral won a battle. He forced Kirby to spend a year as an executive officer onboard a US Navy cruiser, which was part of a Navy Surface Action Group or SAG, which the Space Action Groups were based on.

He spent his year with them learning how a three-ship action group operated. He had tolerated that well enough but they made matters worse. His last two months saw him reassigned to an Amphibious Readiness Group (ARG) which transported Marines.

He had nearly reached the deck where his quarters were and started to fume even more as he thought back to the ARG. *Damn Marines, they goofed off and lounged around. Turned out*, he thought, *Marines are lazy*. The Sailors did all the work while the Marines played. There were a few that did what they called "sustainment training" but most just lounged. Then he discovered why he had to spend time on those ships, Marines were being assigned to SAG LIBERATOR. He reached his deck and stepped out of the ladder well noticing a Marine. The young man instantly came to attention against the bulkhead. Cleaning supplies were on the deck where he had been scrubbing.

"Good morning, Colonel." The Marine said.

Colonel Kirby scowled at him, "It is Commodore." He turned and stormed off to his cabin. The Marine stood there for a moment then returned to his duties.

That is right, thought the Colonel. *Better not say anything and get back to work*. He was determined the Marines onboard his ships would not lounge around.

To make matters worse, he discovered that Admiral Brannigan had assigned his personal pet, LtCol Clark to the SAG as Deputy Commander and Commander of the Marines. He nearly went into a rage over this. His face twisted in anger as he remembered that LtCol Clark, the famed Marine who supposedly saved the Admiral back on Kammorriga, was here to steal his glory.

Of course, the Marine was here to spy on him for the Admiral. He wished the Admiral had died on Kammorriga, after all, the Admiral had started a war placing everyone on Earth in grave danger.

Hellfire, that Marine even requested, which sounded more like a demand, that his Marines perform "sustainment training." Well, he knew what that meant, the Marines would lounge around the ships while the Guardians did all the work. That wasn't going to happen. He smiled to himself at his disciplining the Marines.

Colonel Kirby approached his door and held his hand against the hand sensor, the door slid open and he entered. A few seconds later the door closed. He took a deep breath and let it out slowly. Sanctuary at last. He would have an hour after revelry then that pet Marine would arrive to discuss the mission. After clearing a pirate outpost in the Plymouth Station system, they had gathered some intelligence of a pirate base out here. They would hunt them down and the Colonel said softly, "I will make those Marines behave and do their job."

LtCol Clark stopped outside Col Kirby's office and read the tag; Commodore Kirby, and was annoyed at the method he used the title to show his authority.

As he pressed the call button, he closed his eyes and slowly let out the deep breath he'd been holding. The door slid open and he entered.

"Sir, the ship is still heading on the same course and we are following. No changes at this point in time." He reported to Colonel Kirby.

The man turned his chair from the screen behind his desk so he could see Clark standing there at attention. His office had two chairs in front of the desk, but he didn't offer any to Clark.

"Ok," he replied.

"Since we cleared that base back at 237 Prime, this ship has led us on a chase. I'm starting to think about overtaking it versus following it."

Clark just stood there. He knew the Colonel didn't like any input to his thoughts. When they found the pirate station in the system with Plymouth Station, he had offered different courses of action or COAs for the taking of the base. The Colonel attacked him or his staff on a personal level with each COA. So, in true fashion, he waited.

The Colonel finally shook his head. "Continue following the ship for another day then I'll decide."

"Yes Sir." Instead of leaving, Clark just stood there. Finally, Colonel Kirby looked up and said, "Dismissed."

Clark turned and left the room.

An hour later, the SAG dropped out of hyperspace. The pirate they were following had made the transition and was heading toward an asteroid field. They continued to follow the ship. Commodore Kirby stepped onto the bridge of *Liberator* and took his seat. LtCol Clark finished his communication with the Marines in the landing bay and turned toward Kirby.

"Commodore, the Marines will be ready for boarding within thirty minutes."

The Scanner Officer turned and reported, "Commodore, the pirate is moving into the asteroid field with a course for one of the larger asteroids."

The Commodore acknowledged both then asked his Helmsman, "How long before both the pirate ship and we reach that asteroid?"

A moment later, "It appears they will reach the base in an hour and we can be there in an hour and a half."

The Commodore sat back in his chair in thought.

"Increase speed. I want to reach the base no more than five minutes after they do. Let's not let them get any defenses set. Clark, get those Marines moving. I want you ready to board the moment we get there."

"Yes Sir," Both men responded. After keying in instructions, LtCol Clark got up to leave the bridge. The Colonel swiveled his chair in his direction.

"Clark, where are you going? Get back to your station."

"Commodore, I need to join my men."

"I said get back to your station. The Major can lead them. I want you here."

"Sir, I need to join my men."

"Get back to your station," Kirby said with menace in his tone, "or else you are relieved."

LtCol Clark returned to his station, picked up his headpiece and informed his Deputy Commander to take control and lead the assault.

With a satisfied look, Commodore Kirby ordered the attack to begin.

The frigate-sized ship, the *USS Jackson*, rolled onto a plane taking it to a Z positive position to the station. The destroyer class, the *USS Revolution* tacked onto a course taking it to a position in front of an opening that appeared to be a hangar bay. The *USS Liberator* continued onto a straight path setting it to the starboard of the *Revolution*. As the three ships took positions around the identified pirate base, they launched the Marine assault crafts. As the transports headed to the base, laser fire erupted from it. Two assault vehicles were destroyed almost instantly. LtCol Clark's face ashened, and he turned to the Commodore, who was glaring at the view screens.

"Fire upon those base guns now." Commodore Kirby ordered.

The three ships targeted the base lasers with their own. The assault crafts turned out of the way in the nick of time for the *Liberator*'s own lasers nearly struck them. They began returning to their ships.

"What the hell are those cowards doing?" Yelled Commodore Kirby, turning to LtCol Clark.

"Get them back into the fight!" He ordered.

LtCol Clark turned back to his station to give the orders to proceed with caution regarding the guns to the base. Five pirate ships came out of the hangar bay heading straight for the *Revolution,* which was busy targeting the base guns. Before she could redirect fire onto the ships, they made the jump to hyperspace. Kirby looked angrily about.

"Have the *Jackson* swing about to support *Revolution* and GET ME IVERSON NOW!" He screamed at his Communications Officer. About a minute later the voice com came online.

"LtCol Iverson here Commodore."

"Damn you, idiot. Target all ships that come out of the hangar bay. The *Jackson* will take out those base guns. Got it?"

"Yes Sir." The commlink closed.

The *Jackson* received new maneuvering orders after taking out four of the six base guns. LCDR Fox thought for a few seconds and then signaled to comply with the order.

"Weapons Officer, fire upon the remaining two guns as we make our move. Ensure you can at least damage them. As we come upon the port side of *Revolution,* target and destroy all base guns around that hangar. I'm guessing that is how the Marines will enter this base."

"Aye Aye Sir," Came the reply.

Meanwhile onboard the *Liberator.* "Scanning officer, besides the hangar bay, are there any docking areas for my transports?" Asked LtCol Clark.

Kirby shot him an annoyed look but kept quiet.

"Sir, there appears to be two, maybe, though I can't be sure."

"Thank you," LtCol Clark responded. He then turned to his board and instructed his Marines onto the new assault path. Four assault craft peeled off, heading to the two ports. The other ten assault craft began heading for the hangar bay, slowing their approach waiting for the all-clear sign from the two warships.

The *Revolution's* shields were struck with five laser beams. Within a minute they started to show the rainbow of colors as they dissipated the energy from the beams. All five were coming from ships within the hangar bay as they were making their way out.

"Scanning officer, how many ships are hitting us? Which ship has the most powerful beam?" asked LtCol Iverson.

"Sir, there are three ships, one of them has three beams on us."

"Ok. Weapons Officer lock our beams onto that big one and fire. Fire missiles at the other two ships."

The Weapons Officer fired the laser beams onto the larger ship and its shields began to glow as it displaced the energy. "Sir, if we fire the missiles and destroy any of the ships in the hangar bay, the Marines won't be able to land."

"Damn, you're right. Ok, don't fire the missiles, but keep your beams on that ship. Helm, start backing us away, and let's see if we can't draw them out. Communications, advise the *Jackson* what we are doing and for them to engage the other two ships as they come out. After that, best advise the Commodore."

All the crew acknowledged the orders.

The *Revolution* began backing away from the hangar bay and the *Jackson* began repositioning herself in order to fire upon the other two pirate ships as they emerge. Commodore Kirby was seeing these actions on his screens and began to give counter orders when his Communications Officer informed him of LtCol Iverson's communication. He sat back in his command chair mulling this information over. Meanwhile, the remaining ten assault craft lined up near the hangar bay as the other four approached the docking ports.

"Sir," the *Liberator* Weapons Officer began, "we have destroyed all the targeted guns. We can assist the other ships."

"Thank you Weps. Helm, begin moving us around to destroy those ships as they emerge."

"Yes Sir."

As he thought, the three pirate ships began to emerge. LtCol Iverson ordered his fire to intensify on the lead pirate ship and he noticed how the *Jackson* had repositioned herself. Soon, she should begin her fire upon the other two ships. At this moment, the *Liberator* swung around and placed two of her laser beams onto the lead pirate ship and two onto one of the other ships. LCDR Fox, skipper of the *Jackson*, noticed this and redirected his weapons to fire upon the remaining ship only.

With all enemy ships firing upon them, the pirates realized they couldn't make a jump and began another maneuver to try and break the laser beams upon their shields. All three turned to their starboard and began a Z minus maneuver attempting to place the asteroids between themselves and the ships attacking them.

LtCol Iverson saw what they were doing and sent orders to the other two ships to follow and match the maneuvers.

"Weapons, fire missiles at those ships once they are clear of the hangar bay," He ordered. "Let's see if we can't destroy them or if we can't, then disable them." His Weapons Officer acknowledged the order and readied missiles. As the pirate ships swung into their maneuver, the Weapons Officer launched two missiles each at the ships. Meanwhile, their shields were weakened by the constant energy being deployed on them by the SAG's laser beams. When the missiles struck the shields, they obliterated what remained of them allowing the laser beams to strike the pirates' hulls and, in a matter of moments, penetrate them. The two smaller ships exploded while the larger one began showing damage and fires from the beams. The *Liberator* sent out a cease fire order for the ships and authorized the Marine Assault Crafts to enter the hangar bay to continue their assault.

While the space battle was occurring, the four Marine Assault Crafts had engaged the docking ports, and the Marines had successfully opened them. The forty-eight Marines deployed into the ports. At first, there wasn't any resistance. They continued down the tunnels, and when they entered what appeared to be internal corridors, they were fired upon. They were able to quickly dispatch this light resistance. Half turned one way along the corridor, and the other half proceeded along the opposite direction. They continued to meet very light resistance and were able to dispatch each Pirate team they contacted.

The other assault craft entered the hangar bay and emptied their Marines who quickly took control of the hangar. There wasn't any resistance. After they secured the bay, they found the airlocks leading into the rest of the base. They quickly breached these locks and entered the station. At first, they met light resistance, and after a short exchange of fire, they overtook the Pirates. Every Pirate they encountered fought till killed or took their own life. After approximately thirty minutes, the Marines had the base and zero prisoners. Commodore Kirby was disappointed they weren't able to capture anyone but at least they had the base.

Commodore Kirby and LtCol Clark entered the control room of the base. Four Marines were standing at attention, looking stiff in their combat space suits. The five Marines were comfortable in their suits, but Commodore Kirby felt restricted. Eleanda Designs made the suits for space combat, and the Marines had trained in them till they felt like a second skin. But the Commodore never had one on before. LtCol Clark had insisted he wear one in case they found hostiles. Now, they needed them since the station's atmosphere was hostile to humans. A couple of technicians from the *Liberator* were attempting to make the atmosphere suitable for them.

Kirby looked about the control room. The systems were intact.

"I don't see anyone looking at these controls Clark," He stated flatly.

"No sir, the priority was the atmosphere, but we can redirect if you desire."

The Commodore was stuck. He was the one who had ordered the atmosphere to be corrected immediately. Now, he was faced with staying with that order or redirecting them to get information for the pirate hunt. He didn't want any more personnel on the station and wanted to get on with his hunt. He sighed heavily.

"Stay on task, Clark. Once they have the atmospherics adjusted then get on the databases."

"Yes Sir."

Kirby turned and left the room, heading back to the hangar bay. LtCol Clark stayed behind to discuss the operation with his Marines. As the Commodore entered the hangar bay, he noticed the Marine had not accompanied him. This irritated him. He started to call for him but decided against it. Maybe the light colonel had something to attend to. *Oh well*, he thought. He headed for his shuttle. Once inside, with the seals engaged and pressurized, he removed his helmet.

"Head over to the *Revolution*," He ordered.

LtCol Iverson was at the hangar bay doors, waiting for the Commodores' shuttle. He wasn't happy about this upcoming visit. He'd known the Commodore for a long time. Both had joined Space Force from the start. Iverson had several space assignments during his career. While SESG EXPLORER was out, Iverson had played an important role in securing 237 Prime and knew how these ships worked. Unfortunately, the Commodore didn't seem to know despite being assigned to the Navy to be part of a Navy SAG in the Pacific Ocean. Iverson knew this wasn't going to be a pleasant meeting, but he braced himself. At least the Commodore wasn't the highest authority in this sector.

As the Commodore's shuttle departed, LtCol Iverson let out a heavy breath. Yep, a chewing out for the loss of five pirate ships and the destruction of two assault craft. His own crew was berated for their actions despite Iverson attempting to stop the Commodore from doing it. At least he was able to draw the Commodore's ire onto himself, which stopped the Commodore from taking any more actions against his crew.

As he entered his bridge, he noticed the Marine Assault crafts were heading back to their respective ships. He nodded at the screens. Soon, he knew they would get directions to another target. He just wondered if the Commodore would do some reconnaissance this time vice just charging in. The Pirates now knew they were being hunted and would be more dangerous. He shook his head; twenty-four Marines and two pilots were lost in this assault. LtCol Iverson knew that LtCol Clark would be angry over this and he felt the loss also. These lost personnel were from his own ship. He was thinking about the morale of the crew and Marines when the new coordinates began coming in. Soon, they would be making the jump to hyperspace.

CHAPTER 5

The *USS Diplomat* was a sleek ship, cylinder in appearance with smooth skin. She had one hangar bay to launch and recover transports. Her weapons were standard lasers and missiles, upgraded with crystal technology. Her shields were exceptionally strong. Her jump drive was among the most advanced Earth had devised up to this moment. Both her sensors and communication arrays were state-of-the-art. Colonel Nelson was very proud of her ship and crew. However, this was not the mission she desired. She had been a Space Force officer from the start of her career. Her previous assignments included a tour on the space station and an exploration of the moon for a possible base. She had hoped for a combat command but the outgoing Space Force General and the two new Admirals thought her skills were best utilized commanding a diplomat's ship. She was in command of the ship and crew; it was the Ambassador who was in charge of the mission.

For two days, they have been in normal space. After weeks of making jumps, the ship commander wanted to perform maintenance and give her crew some rest. They had taken the jump drives offline for routine maintenance ensuring they would function normally. During this time, half the crew spent one day doing nothing but recreational activities, while the other half performed maintenance duties. The next day, they switched. Engineering was reporting their activities were done, and the drives would be online by the end of the day. Colonel Nelson acknowledged.

"Mr. Ambassador," she keyed up Mike O'Shea, "we can make our next jump when you are ready." The Ambassador sat in his office with Chief Petty Officer Seymour, who had been part of the special forces that landed on Kammorriga.

"Acknowledge Colonel, at your discretion please." Mike closed the communication system.

"Well, Chief, nothing so far. We have been trying to find the Alia and yet no sign of them. How in this galaxy are we to find them if the databases we have acquired don't reveal them?"

"Sir, the one we discovered on Kammorriga showed a lot of technical insight and was quite clever, self-sacrificing even. We may need to change our objectives if we are to actually locate them. The survivors are most likely hiding, and we won't find them without help."

Mike thought about this for a moment or two.

"Ok, Chief. I see your point. Please look through the databases for any other species or civilizations that may be able to help us. Once you find them, let me know and we will seek out their planets."

The Chief acknowledged the Ambassador as he stood up and left the office.

Three days later, they made normal space. They were near a solar system with five planets. The Chief was still pouring through the databases, seeking another civilization to find. Colonel Nelson agreed with the Ambassador to search for another race since they had not been able to locate the Alia.

Moments after entering normal space, the Colonel had her ship scan the system ahead. Long range scanners showed no other ships in the area. After about an hour, Col Nelson noticed her communications officer looking intently at his board and adjusting his systems.

"What is it, Comms?" She asked.

"Well, Colonel, I am not sure," he turned toward her and then back to his board. "I seem to be picking up something on an obscure frequency. Not sure, though. It may be a signal but the way it comes across it could be just some background noise."

The Colonel leaned forward in her chair, staring at the viewscreen which showed the system ahead.

"Are you able to identify a source location?"

The Communication Officer shook his head slowly while making some adjustments. Then he looked up at the view screen and back to his board. The Col waited, knowing he was trying to decide. Then he said, "I think I have something Colonel. The second planet from the sun may be a signal source."

"Thank you. Keep trying to lock that signal down. Sensors, tell me about the second planet."

The Lt at the scanning station tuned her beams toward the second planet.

"Colonel, from here, it appears to be similar to Earth. It may have a breathable atmosphere."

"That is all you can tell me?"

"Gravity is approximately Earth-like. But I'd like to get closer to refine all readings."

"All right. Helm, make for the second planet. Communications coordinate your readings with Helm. Sensors scan the daylights out of that planet. I want to know all we can about it."

As they acknowledged her orders and began their tasks, Col Nelson keyed the Ambassador.

"Ambassador, we are in normal space and may have picked up a signal. We are moving to investigate. Might be nothing but we don't want to ignore a possibility." Mike agreed.

"Definitely a breathable atmosphere, within tolerable limits. No industrial sites anywhere. Not picking up any advanced life signs, like humans, but there are life signs. A couple of oceans and forested areas, but most of it is arid. Some deserts and rocky areas."

"And the surrounding areas showed nothing of a civilization either, Ambassador," Col Nelson reported to Mike as he stood beside her command chair. He rubbed his cheek.

"Thank you, Lt, keep up your scans for more information."

"Helm, are we over the signal?"

"Yes, Col."

"All right make it a synchronized orbit."

The Colonel swiveled her chair to face Mike directly.

"Well, Sir. We definitely have a signal originating from down there. The way it looks, it may be a distress signal."

"Interesting," Mike responded, "something I think we should check out. Hate to miss our only opportunity."

"I agree, though it could be Kammorrigan, we can't identify it."

"Then, Col, I think it isn't them."

The Col thought for a moment. "Yes, I agree. Nevertheless, I don't want you going down. No need to put you in danger unnecessarily, especially when you are needed for the real meetings. Let Chief Seymour lead this with a couple of specialists and two-armed security."

Mike slowly nodded his head, "I agree."

The shuttle approached its landing area. The flight down was uneventful. The journey through the atmosphere lacked turbulence. The shuttle pilot made a soft landing and smiled to himself, easy. One of the Technicians checked the atmosphere and confirmed it was within acceptable limits. Chief Seymour stood up and checked his weapon as did the two security personnel. The Technicians were checking their equipment one last time. The pilot checked his boards. He would respond to any of them to evacuate quickly, till then he would wait at this location for their return. The pilot shook his head. *This was an unarmed shuttle craft, how to respond other than run away?* He smiled.

The hatch unsealed and the Chief stepped out onto the planet's surface. First man to step onto this unknown planet. He looked around as the first security guard stepped up next to him. The Chief indicated for the guard to take a position to his left, which would place him in front of the shuttle. He motioned for the second guard to go to his right. The two techs exited the ship and began scanning.

"Chief, I am picking up the signal. It is coming at four o'clock from the shuttle's nose."

The Chief nodded and motioned them forward. He indicated for the guard on his right to move parallel to them and for the other to stay where he was. The ground was primarily dirt, with rocks either protruding from it or strewn about. As they were moving forward, they noticed a rock, about ten feet high, in front of them, so they moved toward their right side to get around it. They continued to pick their way between the rocks heading for the signal.

As they were making their way, the Chief and both Techs came to a standstill. A creature appeared directly in front of them. They had not seen it till it had jumped in front of them. It was small, maybe eighty-five or ninety pounds. It had four legs, ending in paws, white socks to a fawn color over the majority of its body, two eyes, two ears that stood up, a black face, and a tail with a white tip that curled over its back. The creature had its front legs out with its high quarters in the air and was wagging its tail.

The Chief started to back away while scanning around for signs of anything else.

"Why are we backing off Chief? It is a dog."

"A dog? Out here. Don't think so. Try the translator."

"Really, Chief?" As the Tech pulled out the translator and began to adjust it. "All we will get is barking. Look at it, he wants to play."

The creature was bouncing back and forth or scooting around. But it kept watching them all the time. Sometimes, it would have its hind quarters up while its face was on its front paws. Other times, it was standing straight up on all fours. Always wagging its tail and watching them intently. The Chief noticed it was really fixated on the Tech with the translator. The Chief's eyes widened, and he started to move toward the Tech when the creature flashed forward and, with its mouth, grabbed the translator and took off at a run around a rock. The Tech was shocked as he fell down and the Chief pulled his weapon.

He looked around, and seeing nothing, holstered his sidearm. He then keyed the communication device on his right wrist.

"Security, acknowledge." Both guards answered him.

"We have encountered a creature that looks like a dog. Keep your eyes open. We don't know if it is hostile or not but it took our translator."

The guard who was paralleling them came around a rock toward them. He was scanning the surroundings but kept his carbine weapon relaxed. The Chief nodded at him.

"Well, that was exciting. Do we have another translator?"

The second Tech indicated he still had his.

"Ok, guess we will continue to the signal source but this time let's keep our eyes wide open. And when I say be careful; be CAREFUL." The Chief growled.

As they started to move off, the Guard noticed movement to his right and slightly behind him.

As he turned, he said, "Chief, movement behind and to the right." He started to bring his weapon up.

The other three turned and joined him.

The second creature was four legged also and appeared much like the first, except bigger, possibly a hundred pounds or more. A tail with a white tip curled over its fawn, yet slightly darker fur, and four legs with white socks ending in paws. It was more bear like in its head and face, which was black with a white ring around its nose and whiter under its mouth than the first one. It had some black markings along its four legs also.

The four men stopped and stared at it. The creature had the translator around its neck dangling under its head. They gazed at each other. The Chief motioned for the Guard to stand behind them and scan for the other creature.

"What are you?" The creature asked. While the noise sounded unintelligible, the translator picked it up and made it sound English.

The two Techs looked astonished but the Chief took it in stride. After all, he had spoken with an Alia and seen the Kammorrigans up close. Why shouldn't a species develop which resembled dogs?

"We are humans from a planet we call Earth," The Chief responded. "What are you?"

The creature thought for a moment. The Guard touched the Chief's shoulder who turned slightly to him. He indicated to look up. The Chief turned back and looked up at the top of the rock in front of them and noticed the first creature was lying on it with its black face, staring intently at them.

"I may have heard of you." The second doglike creature said. "What else will you tell me about yourself? Where have you appeared before?"

Now it was the Chief who was thinking. *How many of these creatures are there? What are their allegiances? Should he evade or answer the question?* He slightly crossed his arms in front of him while keying his comm system to the shuttle. It was now an open link.

"Well, let's see. Obviously, we are not from this planet. We do have a ship in orbit. Can't seem to reach them right now." He was hoping the Pilot would link to the *Diplomat* so both the Ambassador and Col would be aware of this meeting.

The creature seemed to smile. "Well, obviously, especially since this planet's inhabitants are low intelligent beings. Humans have no dwellings here nor do we."

"Then you have a ship here?"

"But, of course, Human. So, where might I have heard about you?" The creature returned to its question.

After a moment, the Chief decided, "We destroyed the home world of the Kammorrigans."

The creature on the rock quickly lifted its head. The one in front of them backed off a couple of paces and scanned the area. It then clicked off the translator with its left paw and began speaking to the other one. After a few moments of speaking back and forth in singing style tones, they stopped. The creature in front of them clicked the translator back on.

"How do we know you are the ones to have destroyed that planet? Why would you?"

"So, the word has spread that the planet was attacked." The Chief said. "I was on the planet doing reconnaissance to discover what the Kammorrigans really were. We dropped nuclear missiles onto the planet since we discovered they only desired to conquer all other civilizations. I met a slave on the planet that identified itself as an Alia. Unfortunately, to save me and my team it took off so we wouldn't be captured."

"Well, that is something of a why but not a confirmation." The second creature clicked off the translator and spoke again to the first. After a few moments of conversing, the second creature turned back to the Chief, activating the translator.

"We are Wooxuna. I am Magos and that up there is Thunder. We crash landed here several days ago. Sadly, our third died in the crash. Why did you land here?"

"We picked up a signal from this area. I'm assuming that is a distress signal from your ship?"

"Aarrgh, yes. We have a signal going out but on a very specific frequency. And you picked it up. Rooo aa rooorra." Magos spoke to Thunder, who stood up and bounded off the rock in the other direction.

"I'm sending Thunder to deactivate it. We don't want any other uninvited guests showing up."

The Chief nodded. "We can offer you a ride. We need help in finding Alia."

Magos narrowed his eyes, "why do you want to find them?"

"We are seeking an agreement with them. The Kammorrigans are still out there and are a threat to this galaxy. We are seeking friends to help us destroy what is left of them."

Magos sat down on his haunches, staring hard at the humans.

"You make war on Kammorriga."

The Chief said, "yes."

"You are seeking friends to help you in this." These were statements vice questions.

"Yes."

"You want the Alia."

"Yes."

"You desire others to fight with you."

Magos was sitting there in thought when Thunder showed back up on the rock.

"Why does Thunder go up there?" The Chief asked.

"Aarrgh," Magos stirred and looked up, then back at the Chief. "Oh, well, Thunder is a scout. They like to take positions so they can see everything clearly. He can see part of your ship and the other guard. I am of the warrior class. I am the leader of our trio. Unfortunately, our specialist is now dead."

"I see. May I confer with my ship?" The Chief asked. Magos nodded his head.

The Chief keyed his system.

"*Diplomat*, this is landing party. Come in."

"Landing party, this is *Diplomat*."

"Please inform Ambassador O'Shea, we have made contact with two Wooxuna. They have crash landed here. I believe they may be able to help us, but they need a ride."

"A moment landing party."

The link went silent. The two parties watched each other. One of the Techs started pulling another device out when they heard a deep growl from Thunder. The Tech stopped and moved his hand away.

"You seem to listen," Magos was saying, "yes, please tell us what you are about to do before you do it.

"Landing party this is *Diplomat*"

"I read you, *Diplomat*."

"Please inform the Wooxuna that we are happy to have them as our guests. No return favors required, though we do ask they help us find the Alia."

The Chief turned his gaze onto Magos. After another short discussion with Thunder who immediately took off at a run, Magos turned back to the Chief.

"We will be happy to help you find them. Please wait here while we gather our belongings. We will join you shortly." Magos took off at a run.

"*Diplomat*," Chief Seymour was reporting, "the two Wooxuna are gathering their gear and we will join you shortly. Landing party out."

"Acknowledged Landing party, *Diplomat* out."

It only took a few minutes and the two Wooxuna had rejoined the team. Both of them had back packs on with belts strapped around their torsos. They trotted up to the four Humans and all six of them headed to the shuttle. As they approached the shuttle, an explosion occurred. The Humans jumped onto their stomachs with their hands clasped over their heads. The two Wooxuna just looked at each other and then at the Humans.

"That was our ship. We set the charges to go off and destroy it completely. No need for our enemies to find it," Thunder said.

They boarded the shuttle and it lifted off with the six Humans and the two Wooxuna.

Magos and Thunder sat on their haunches in Mike's office. Chief Seymour sat there along with them.

"How do you find the quarters?" Mike inquired.

"They are good, thank you," Thunder responded. "Does our food requirements make sense to your…, oh yes, cooks?"

Mike turned his head to see the Chief, who nodded yes back at him.

"Yes, it appears they do. Please, though, let them know if something isn't right. We may have to adjust to ensure they do meet your requirements."

Thunder nodded.

"From our scans, this system seems to be uninhabited," Mike said.

"Yes, it is. I mean, there are some low-level creatures on the second and third planets, but yes, it is uninhabited. Possibly a good base location." Magos responded.

"Is that what you were doing? Scouting the area for a base?" the Chief asked.

"No, not really. We were returning from a mission when we had an incident with our ship, resulting in our crashing. We just observed this might be a good location for a hidden base." Thunder said.

"So, do you know how close we are to the Kammorrigans?" Mike continued.

"You might say you are too close for comfort," Magos said.

Mike and the Chief looked at each other.

"This could possibly meet one of our needs," Mike mused.

"Maybe. If we could get word back to the Admiral, he could send a scout out here," the Chief said.

Mike thought for a bit while the Wooxuna watched them both.

The communication system beeped at them.

"This is Ambassador O'Shea."

"Ambassador, we are ready for jump."

"Hold off, please. Let me speak with the Colonel in say…an hour."

"Yes Sir. I'll let her know. Helm out."

The link closed.

"Magos, what would be the best coordinates for us to find the Alia? Do you need to contact your command? How soon do we have to return you?"

Magos stood up on his hind legs to the surprise of both Mike and the Chief and walked over to a view screen. "Are you able to show this area of space and the relative systems?" He asked, then he sat down again.

"Ah yes, I think so." Mike turned to the Chief, who reached over to the keyboard and punched in some instructions. The viewscreen lit up displaying several systems. Magos then turned to Thunder and they spoke in their own language for a bit.

"Thunder can plug in the coordinates to your bridge for the most likely area in this part of the region." Magos said, "We would like to send a tight beam message to our regional headquarters advising them where we are and what we are doing."

"I think we can arrange that." Mike was nodding.

"Chief, please show Magos and Thunder to their quarters while I discuss this with Col Nelson."

The Chief nodded and motioned for the other two to follow him. They left Mike in his office, thinking. *Finally, we might actually get somewhere.*

Mike was sitting in Col Nelson's office which joined her cabin.

"Damn, Sir. How can we trust them?"

"I don't think we have a choice if we want to actually set up a coalition," Mike responded.

Col Nelson leaned forward with her arms crossed in front of her on her desk. She knew the Ambassador was right, of course. But what a risk to the ship and the mission if they were wrong. She was shaking her head when the viewscreen on her desk flashed a few times. She sat straight up and keyed a few strokes. The image appeared on her screen. She shook her head and turned the screen toward Mike. It showed an akita, fawn colored, with a white belly.

"This is what our two guests would look like on Earth," she stated. "What a mystery this is."

Mike smiled, "indeed. But I think that is for the scientists and philosophers back home to figure out. But it is an interesting point. How do our Akitas resemble the Wooxuna? Were we visited by them or by one of those ancient races that are now dead? What are the relationships?"

"You may be right, Ambassador. It is in the back of my mind, though. Something I think we should be aware of and keep in the forefront of our minds. Especially as we work through this mission. Besides, don't they say that dogs are man's best friend?"

"Yes, but I don't think we should confuse these two with a species from our own planet."

"You may be right, Ambassador, but perhaps we can trust them. If we show trust, then they will trust us."

Mike smiled, "now who is the diplomat?"

They both laughed.

"Colonel, when will you address me as Mike?"

She focused intently on him. "I guess in private it is ok. Hello, Mike, I am Jennifer."

"Glad to meet you," they said as they shook hands.

"Now, what do you think about sending one of those extremely valuable hyperspace comm drones to the Admiral, Jennifer?"

"Well, if I were the Admiral, I probably would start having a hundred questions about the lack of information versus the 'Hey, we found a candidate for a base statement. And oh, by the way, we came across two wayward souls looking for a ride."

Mike thought for a moment.

"Yes, I see your point. Ok, let's hold off till we have enough to actually send a coherent message to them."

The following day, the *USS* Diplomat was heading out of the system. Col Nelson sat in her command chair on the bridge with Ambassador O'Shea standing next to her. She watched as Thunder took the Astrogation chair. She was surprised how easily he could sit in it and manipulate the board. It seemed the Wooxuna didn't have dog paws but paws with individual digits to include a thumb that would appear when needed.

She turned toward the Communications station to see Magos sitting in the Comm chair. He was busy with his message, plugging in the coordinates for the ship's system to send a very tight beam to. He was making adjustments that were surprising the Communications Officer. The beam was being narrowed to a level that he didn't realize could be done.

"I'll need more power for this beam to reach its destination," Magos stated.

"Engineering, this is the Bridge. Provide whatever power output Communications requires." Col Nelson said into her comm system.

Magos watched the dials as the power was being increased to the system.

"That is it," He said and depressed the send button. The beam shot from an array and was gone. Nothing else remained.

"Thank you," Magos said as he dialed out the frequency and location then departed the chair.

Meanwhile, Thunder was busy making the coordinate inputs to the Astrogation system. Magos walked over and stood up on his hind legs to watch him. Thunder kept making even more adjustments, honing the coordinates to a fine level of detail.

"You sure there will be an Alian ship there, Thunder?" Inquired Magos.

"Odds are favorable. That is one of their routes through this region. Yes, I know, they change them but this is among their latest adjustments."

"All right. Any idea with this ship how long it will take to get there?"

Thunder pressed a few buttons and looked at the various displays. The Humans could see he frowned a bit. Then, in their way seemed to smile.

"Two and a half days by the way Humans measure time. Not bad considering." Thunder turned his gaze to Magos. Magos looked over at Col Nelson.

"Commander, you may jump at your ready. Thunder has the coordinates in the system."

"Thank you, Thunder. Helm, bring us about and make the jump. Engineering, bring the jump drive online and see if we can't shave some time off." Col Nelson ordered.

The *Diplomat* swung about for the clear area of space to make the jump. The hyperspace well opened, and she moved smoothly into it.

The two days in hyperspace were uneventful. Both parties took the opportunity to learn more about each other.

Chief Petty Officer Seymour was escorting both Magos and Thunder to a conference room. As they entered the room, they noticed Ambassador O'Shea was pouring drinks into four cups, coffee for the Humans and a strange drink for the Wooxuna which they had described before.

As the Humans were taking their seats and Magos was taking his, Thunder inquired, "I noticed you are wearing different clothing from the others. You Chief have dark green coveralls with black boots. While the ship's crew wear black coveralls with black boots. Each one you have insignia on your collars, chest and arms. While the Ambassador is dressed completely different."

"Yes," responded the Chief, "the crew of the *Diplomat* belongs to the regulars in the US Space Force. I am a Navy SEAL." He paused when he noticed the confused faces of the Wooxuna. He smiled, "I am a Navy Sea, Air, and Land member." He thought for a moment then said, "I think I would be the closest person who performs the same task as your team does. My job is normally performing covert reconnaissance. As I told you before, I was on Kammorriga and was the person who spoke with the Alia. I was chosen to assist the Ambassador here." He moved his open right hand toward Mike. "The Ambassador is what we call a civilian. Everyone onboard the ship is military except for the diplomats. They are civilians and wear clothing appropriate for their functions. Though, we will dress them in different clothing if the situation requires."

The two Wooxuna nodded. Everyone took a drink from their cups.

Mike said, "Please tell us about yourselves and your home world. Has it been spared from Kammorrigan occupation?"

The Chief added, "Yes, and how have you avoided capture? Nothing in the databases ever mentions you as slaves."

Both Wooxuna sat in thought for a few moments. Thunder then reached out and pulled the keyboard toward him and keyed in the region of space they were in. He then keyed in an area and after studying the keyboard and symbols which appeared on the screen made some adjustments and an area of space was outlined.

"This is what was Wooxuna space approximately three hundred years ago." He started. "The Kammorrigans arrived requesting trade relations and before we suspected them, destroyed our home world. Most of us escaped them." He fell silent.

Magos followed up. "From the beginning, we understood they wouldn't want us as slaves. Rather, we learned of their savagery in torture and studying other species. We knew they would dissect us after determining our tolerances. They did capture some of our people early on but not since those early days. We have been at war with them for over two hundred of your years now. We avoid capture at all costs. Our orders are to ensure we won't be captured."

Thunder continued, "Exactly. We destroyed our ship on the planet you found us. We also ensured our third's remains were destroyed. We won't even let them find our dead. We will incinerate ourselves before capture."

Magos lowered his head at the mention of their friend. "We have a fleet but it avoids enemy contact unless we are sure of a victory and no Kammorrigan craft can record the ships. Instead, we send out a three Wooxuna manned ship. A warrior." He raised a paw for himself, "a scout." He motioned toward Thunder. "And a technical specialist. They are much smaller than us but quite intelligent." He thought for a moment, "From what I have overheard from the crew, you might say a different breed." He thought a few more moments. "The mission of these ships is primarily intelligence gathering and very specific actions against a target. Rarely, but sometimes we will enter a Kammorrigan center for specific knowledge which we suspect may be of significant importance to us. But we mainly just monitor what they are doing."

Mike and the Chief sat in silence while Magos finished. The Chief especially understood about losing a comrade in battle or in this case an accident. He sympathized with the Wooxuna. He stirred.

"You mentioned before about three great civilizations. Anything you can tell us about them? We found some information but nothing specific."

Mike turned from the Wooxuna to the Chief and when he noticed Thunder began to operate the keyboard, turned back toward the viewscreen. The area of space expanded and a new border encapsulated more of the space.

Thunder began, "As you can see the Wooxuna space was either within or very near this larger area of space. The vast majority of our records were destroyed when the Kammorrigans took our home world and destroyed our civilization. But we know this region of space and perhaps more was controlled by the Odaessumada Federation. They were a warlike civilization. They used our earliest people as rangers or scouts, your words for them confuse me but I think they might be different. Anyway, we were used by them to scout out many worlds. Again, those records are lost and we can only pass this knowledge now by the Elders to the younger."

Mike inquired, "Could your people have settled other worlds, I mean the Wooxuna?"

Magos and Thunder glanced at each other and both shrugged. Magos said, "Possible but we really don't know our origins as a species. We only knew of Wooxuna. But the Elders may know more."

The Humans nodded.

Mike focused on both the Wooxuna, "Would your people be persuaded to join us in a coalition against the Kammorrigans? Your knowledge of this space and of them would be of great benefit. You said you have a fleet. Earth is building a fleet even now to take on the Kammorrigans. We could join forces."

Magos clicked off the translator and the Chief adjusted a pad next to him ensuring the room's translating capability was off. Both Magos and Thunder had a discussion in their own language for some time. Magos turned back to the Humans.

"I understood that is the reason why you are out here. That is the only reason?"

Mike answered, "That is my mission. I am to meet with as many species that we can find to form a coalition. We can use your aid in locating potential members. We have only met pirates and some wayward species during our time in space. Of course, we will gather any information we may find."

Magos nodded, "then that is the true reason to find the Alia. Because you met one on Kammorriga, you believe they will desire to join you." He sat in the chair with his face indicating he was deep in thought.

"I cannot say whether Wooxuna would join you or not. I cannot say whether we can assist you in locating others who might be willing to join you. But, when we come out of hyperspace, I can dispatch another message to our leaders that you are requesting we join this coalition. Only the Elders can decide."

They agreed to send another message to the Wooxuna leadership with the proposal when they returned to normal space.

The *Diplomat* came out of the well into normal space. Magos started moving over to the Communications station to send another message when the Sensor Officer announced there were ships in the area. Everyone stopped and looked around.

"Bring them up on tactical and main view screen," Col Nelson ordered.

The tactical display showed two ships, one apparently pursuing the other.

"That is a Kammorrigan warship," the Weapons Officer said.

"Magnify the ship it is pursuing," Col Nelson ordered. The viewscreen adjusted till the other ship came into view.

"That ship is Alian," said Magos.

Everyone sat back watching both the tactical and viewscreen. Mike thought, *great now what do we do?*

The Kammorrigan warship was a smaller craft but larger than the Alian.

"Col, I want you to engage the Kammorrigan," Mike said before realizing it. Everyone turned to look at him. The two Wooxuna were watching him with a fierce intensity in their eyes.

"We need to allow the Alia to escape or turn to help us. Either way, we need to help them."

"Mr. Ambassador, this isn't a warship but a diplomatic ship," Col Nelson replied. She was astonished at the notion of attacking an enemy warship when the mission was anything but an offensive one.

"I realize that, Colonel. But we need to render aid."

"We could be destroyed or worse yet, captured."

"Yes, I know. Regarding the capture, make sure we are destroyed, even if we do it ourselves. Trust me, we don't want to be captured. The Kammorrigans have no rules regarding prisoners."

Colonel Nelson sat back in her chair. Damn, Mike had given her an order. One that was legal, which compelled her to follow it. But that risked her crew, the ship, and now the mission itself. She let out a heavy breath.

"Weapons, tactical analysis on the Kammorrigan."

"Col, we are evenly matched. Though our shields may be stronger," He responded after reviewing his board. "So far, they don't know we are here."

She nodded to herself.

"Ok, thanks. Prepare lasers and missiles for firing. Helm, keep us behind the Kammorrigan. In fact, maneuver us directly behind her and bring us up fast," The Col ordered. She pressed her com link for the ship. "Red alert, all hands to battle stations. We are attacking a Kammorrigan warship to aid a potential ally. Again, battle stations, this is no drill." She closed the link and watched the boards as each stations showing battle status turn to green.

"Raise shields," she said as she leaned forward contemplating how to destroy the ship.

"No shields?" The Col asked.

"No Col. Their aft shields are still down. I don't think they are aware of us. They do have their forward shields up but nothing else," the Weapons Officer replied.

The Col sat back in her chair and rested her chin on her right fist with her left hand on her armchair. *Strange*, she thought. *Is this a weakness in the Kammorrigan ship design? She may have a chance after all.*

"Helm, keep us behind her and increase speed to full. Weapons, prepare the missiles, best yield." Both acknowledged as they performed their instructions.

The *Diplomat* maneuvered behind the Kammorrigan ship remaining in her exhaust path. Now, she increased her speed coming into missile and soon laser-effective range. The two Wooxuna were watching the screens and the crew's performance. Ambassador O'Shea still stood beside the Col's command chair.

"We are now in laser range," Weapons reported.

"Fire four missiles into her aft side now," the Colonel ordered.

The missiles went true to the target with massive explosions occurring. The Kammorrigan ship began listing to her starboard side with a negative Z axis.

"Fire the lasers and maintain fire," ordered the Col.

The *Diplomat's* forward two lasers locked onto the Kammorrigan ship and fired their constant beams into the hull of the drifting ship. This caused major explosions and decompression across the entire ship, ripping through compartments. The *Diplomat* maintained her lock while the Kammorrigan ship continued to explode.

"You may cease fire now," the Col ordered.

"Any life signs onboard what is left of the ship?"

"No, Col," came the response.

"Ok. Good job. Helm, bring us about so we can see the Alia."

The ship made the maneuver on a positive Z axis and to the port of the shattered Kammorrigan hulk.

The Alia had not made a jump yet and was still moving away from the ships but at a reduced speed.

"Thank you, Col," Mike said, "it appears the Alia are interested in who attacked the Kammorrigans."

"I think you are right, Mr. Ambassador. Should we hail them?"

"Please do." Mike was both excited and nervous.

The Colonel was proud of her crew and their performance while attempting to remain focused on the next task. She flipped her internal communication switch.

"Job well done. We have destroyed the Kammorrigan warship. Go to yellow alert but maintain general quarters. Sensors, scan the area for any other ships to include Kammorrigans. Communications, please hail the Alia." She said as she closed her internal link.

"Col, they are responding." Communications stated.

"On visual and audio," Col Nelson responded.

The viewscreen displayed the bridge of the Alia ship with their captain. Everyone, except for Chief Seymour and the two Wooxuna, were a bit surprised by the Alia. They were short, four legged and furry. The Col turned toward Mike, who stepped forward.

"I am Ambassador O'Shea of the Earth's Space Force. We have sought you out to offer a coalition against our common enemy, the Kammorrigans. First, is your ship and crew all right?"

The Alian Captain looked around its bridge then back at the viewscreen. The translator indicated it had translated Mike's words correctly.

The Alian responded, "We are good, thank you for assisting us against the Kammorrigan. How did you acquire our language?"

"We encountered one of your kind on the planet Kammorriga and it equipped our translator with your language."

"Kammorriga no longer exists. If you were there, how can you be here now?" the Alian asked.

"Chief Seymour," Mike motioned to him, "and I were at Kammorriga. The Chief here met your member who helped him and his team. We were part of the mission to Kammorriga. After seeing what they were doing, we decided it was our best interest to destroy the planet. Now, we are seeking a coalition of civilizations to actually defeat the rest of Kammorriga," Mike responded.

"We have met two representatives of the Wooxuna and are asking them to join us as well," he continued.

The Alia clicked off the audio portion of the communication and began speaking to its crew about what they had just heard. The chatter went on for roughly five minutes. Magos indicated this was a normal thing with the Alia. After all, since their planet was captured and they became enslaved to the Kammorrigans, the Alia had become suspicious and more deliberate when dealing with other species. Finally, it keyed the audio portion of the communication link.

"I understand," the Alian Captain responded while checking one of its monitors. "It isn't safe to remain here. I am sending you coordinates to another location. I will meet you there to discuss what you are saying. After we meet, I will decide if I should let our leadership know. Then, we shall see. Coordinates on their way." The link was cut after the coordinates were received.

"Well, that seems to have gone well," The Colonel said. "Astrogation, plot the course. Helm, as soon as you have it, get us out of here. Engineering, prepare for another jump. We need to move soon." All stations reported they were ready. Colonel Nelson turned her head toward Mike and smiled as the hyperspace well opened and the *Diplomat* made its jump.

The Alia ship stayed motionless for a few more moments as they sent a communiqué. Then they made their jump.

CHAPTER 6

Admiral Brannigan looked up from the report he was reading as his call box chimed. He depressed a button and said, "Yes."

His secretary responded, "Sir, Dr. Vance's shuttle is arriving in the hangar at this time. The galley will be sending up coffee and pastries soon."

"Thank you," he responded and was about to close the comm link when he thought of something. "Is he alone or with an entourage?"

"Just a moment Sir, and I will find out." After a brief moment she came back online, "He is alone, Sir. He is currently making his way to the elevator and the galley is sending the refreshments up now."

"I see, he is bringing me bad news," the Admiral responded.

"How do you know Sir?"

"If it were good news or a successful development, he would bring all the people involved so they could get the credit. If there is failure or bad news, then he comes alone. It is his style."

"Oh, I see." She sounded a bit solemn by the assessment. "Should I send in the refreshments?"

"Yes, please. When the Dr. gets here, just have him come on in."

"Yes Sir." She closed the link and proceeded to escort the Steward with the cart into the office toward the small table. After placing the items on the table, she motioned for the Steward to leave and noticed the Admiral was reading something on his desk viewer. She moved to the door, and as she was leaving, she looked over her shoulder to see that the Admiral had swiveled his chair around to view the Earth through the window.

Dr. Vance entered the office and stopped. The room was nearly dark. The dimming sunlight streamed in from the window at the far end of the office. The only lights on were over the small circular table with four chairs and a computer. The Admiral used this area for informal meetings. He found the Admiral at the small table pouring coffee into two cups.

"Ah, Jack. Great to see you again." The Admiral greeted him with a smile as he put the coffee down and held out his hand. They shook. As the Dr. was about to take his seat he said, "You may not be happy to see me, Sir."

"Nonsense Jack. It is always good to see you. Even when you bring me bad news." The Admiral took a seat and drank from his cup. Dr. Vance just shook his head as he picked up his cup.

"Please have some of these pastries. The Chef takes great pride in her baking." The Admiral took a cheese Danish and shifted the cart for the Dr. who took a croissant with chocolate in it.

"My apologies, Admiral, but we can't get the weapon you desired to work. No matter what we do it burns out all the components including the other weapon systems in the forward batteries. We even extended the firing tube into the secondary battery and that just caused more systems to burn out."

"I see," Kevin said, eyeing the Dr. over his cup. "Absolutely no way to make it work? The different regulating chips and crystals can't channel the power back into the firing tube?"

"We have tried that and other rather ingenious methods but the power generation is too great. Unfortunately, rather than sending the energy through the tube in a controlled manner, it just burns out all the components and threatens to destroy the front of the ship if not the entire ship. It even affects the drive systems."

"Damn," Kevin breathed. "Well, forget it then. No sense in continuing when we need a working fleet vice ships waiting for a system that we can't control."

"We can keep working it," Dr. Vance said when Kevin started shaking his head.

"No, Jack. It is a waste of resources. Keep the plans and idea in a safe place. Maybe new technology will come along that will enable such a weapon in the future but let's go with something else for now."

"Yes Sir," Dr. Vance responded. "The good news relates to the Cobalt Project. We have success and the new systems are functional. We were able to coat the fusion elements with cobalt 60, increasing the radiation fallout. We can outfit the new hydrogen bombs and missile systems with cobalt. Also, the blue crystals from 237 Prime are proving quite useful as added material in the fusion process. We have greatly increased the yield with the crystals and even reduced the bulk of the munitions."

"Well, that is excellent news," Kevin responded. "Let's get those into production as an addition to the planned hydrogen ones. I want options whether to nuke a planet and yet have it somewhat habitable or use the cobalt system to make it uninhabitable. I like the huge rails to simulate a nuclear winter. How are the planet drilling rods coming along? Are you able to outfit them with the fusion hydrogen?"

Dr. Vance thought for a few moments then answered, "Since we won't be deploying the massive energy weapon, we have extra space for additional rails and various nuclear devises. The drilling rails are designed to break the planet's mantle…" He trailed off in thought, playing with his black-rimmed glasses.

After a few moments, he said, "Well, we may very well be able to incorporate them with a hydrogen and crystal system. Let me get with the nuclear physicists and engineers to ensure we can do it. I'll get back to you."

Kevin pressed his lips together and slowly nodded. "Yes, do so. It would be a better use of the forward pod than additional laser weapons. I think it would make more sense having a variety of these devices as options for the commanders. I want you to coat the planet drilling rods, the planet rods, and all planetary bombs with the cobalt additive."

Kevin slumped back in his chair, crossing his arms and lowering his head. Jack thought the Admiral seemed smaller within a matter of seconds. Jack watched him intently as he stood up and walked slowly over to his wet bar. Kevin took a crystal glass out, one which his wife had given him from a trip to Europe, and poured two fingers of Scotch into it. He then took a sniff of the whisky and, in a smooth movement, swallowed it. He then poured three fingers worth of Scotch, closed and put away the bottle, picked up the glass with the fingers of his left hand walked over to his window, and gazed out.

Jack took off his glasses and pulled a cleaning cloth from his pocket. While he started cleaning them, he realized for the first time the implications of what the Admiral wanted and how it must be torturing him. They had been discussing the destruction of entire worlds and entire civilizations. This raised several moral and ethical questions. After they had returned from Kammorriga, Jack had uncovered reports about Kevin during his time in the Sudan. The US State Department had labeled him "The Butcher of Sudan." It was unfair of them. Kevin was there on a United Nations humanitarian mission. He was protecting women and children from rape and enslavement by raiders and in doing so, slaughtered a few hundred raiders. He had to do it in order to save lives. But now, here he was preparing to destroy worlds. Jack realized how this issue must be eating away at him.

Jack continued to clean his glasses and cleared his throat. He saw Kevin turn his head to his left. He had not taken a drink from the glass.

"Sir, I understand your intent but it is a waste of cobalt to deploy on the planet drilling rods. The intent is to break the mantle, which the rods being combined with fusion hydrogen and supplemented with blue crystals will do that nicely. The use of cobalt will gain us nothing. Also, coating all the planetary bombs and the conventional rails will negate the ability for us to inhabit the planet after their use. We desire to emulate a nuclear winter not totally destroy the world's ability to recover from it. The intention is to kill Kammorrigans and their allies and not necessarily destroy all the worlds they inhabit. I recommend we only modify part of the munitions as true world kill-ers. Leave fusion hydrogen bombs and conventional rails for destruc-tion of the civilizations."

He watched as Kevin slowly nodded and turned back to gaze out the window. He then lifted the glass and took a sip of the whisky, turned, and started around the desk. He placed the glass on the desk as he passed it on his way back to the table. Jack noticed he appeared to have returned to his normal self.

"All right Jack, don't place any cobalt on the drilling rods, only hydrogen and crystals. Coat only 25 percent of the conventional rods with cobalt and crystals. We'll have that as an option if we need to have a fallout. Also, 25 percent of the hydrogen bombs slated for planet bombardment. Leave it up to the commanders if they need to use fusion hydrogen or cobalt salted bombs. It might be worthwhile having some of the hydrogen missiles with cobalt in them. Might be useful to deny regions of space from casual entry."

Kevin noticed Jack had placed his glasses back on and was taking notes.

"I'll get with the planners on the last part, if you don't mind. Perhaps there is a way to combine them for space deployment," Jack responded. He began to muse about the possibility and probability of using cobalt to deny an enemy from operating in an area of space. Jack refilled his coffee cup and took a couple of bites of his pastry while thinking about the fallout in a spatial area. *Would it be worth the added material?*

"Jack, anything else?" Kevin inquired.

Dr. Vance looked up with his eyes opened wider and realized he had been lost in thought. He scanned the table quickly. picking up his tablet. He thumbed through several notes.

"Ah, yes. We have been able to get the pulse lasers to work, Sir. This provides for smaller guns with limited range for the battle carriers. With the addition of crystals, we worked out the control mechanisms of the guns. Now, we are able to fire short bursts of lasers which will dissipate after a few kilometers. This eliminates projectiles from being fired at very close range. Further, it gives better fire control, so we don't hit our own fighters. And the fighters won't have to pursue enemy fighters so close to the ships. They can be used against incoming missiles or torpedoes as well.

"Excellent." Kevin was quite pleased with this and showed it. "Now, we can outfit the ships with these new batteries. Keep the big guns locked on the larger ships and give a defensive system against the smaller threats. That will give General Cole more options for strike training for the pilots at the academy."

Kevin started keying up some items on the computer. "How is crystal development coming along?"

"Good," Dr. Vance said, "The red crystals are proving quite an enhancement to the lasers and other potential power weapons. They have increased the power output and have enabled better control and power regulation. The clear crystals are really for overall power and drive systems. The blue ones seem to work best with bombs, missiles, and torpedoes for yield and guidance. The yellow crystals are geared more for communications and various sensors. They have discovered green and purple crystals. Still not sure what they optimize but the labs are working on it."

Kevin nodded, "good. Well, that is positive." He thought for a few moments, then said, "What about pulse lasers for the fighters? If that can be solved then we can eliminate bullets for a more efficient firing system."

Jack nodded. "Unfortunately, we can't miniaturize enough to place them on the fighters. We are working on a laser gun for some of the fighters. Making them into a fighter bomber, so to speak. The idea is simple. When a fighter locks onto an enemy cruiser or capital ship, they can activate the laser gun and rip into the ship's hull. We are having difficulty though with the size of the power plant. It's making the ship pretty heavy."

Kevin pressed his lips together. "Ok, well, we won't go to production with either one till the engineering is worked out. Deal?"

"Yes Sir."

"Sounds like that is about it. Anything else?"

Jack was going through his notes when a chime sounded. Kevin's face indicated he was a bit disturbed but depressed the answer button.

"Yes, what is it?" He asked with a bit of displeasure in his voice.

"Apologies for disturbing you, Sir." His secretary responded, "but Admiral Nabum is on a secure link."

"I see," Kevin replied. "Ok, put him through, please."

"Yes Sir." She closed the comm link and ensured the secure link was made before going about other duties.

The big wall viewscreen came up showing Ralph Nabum, Chief of Staff of Space Force.

"Hello, Ralph." Kevin greeted him.

"Hello, Kevin," Ralph said and smiled when he saw Dr. Vance, "hello Dr., good to see you."

Dr. Vance waived.

"What can we do for you?" Kevin asked.

"Updates, Kevin. I'm going before the Senate Armed Service Committee in two days. I want to know where we stand, especially on this grand weapon."

Dr. Vance lowered his head while shaking it, *great* he thought.

"Well, a complete failure," Kevin started, "but that isn't a bad thing really. We are scrapping it and moving on."

"Wait, what?" Ralph asked interrupting Kevin. "This was to be a massive planet and fleet killing weapon and you are scrapping it and saying not a bad thing."

"That is right," Kevin said. "Look, the power grid can't handle the power generation and we lack the technology to control it. We can't get it to shoot. It burns out so many systems it renders the ship inoperative or destroys it. Rather than waste time and resources on it, we scrap it and move onto systems that work. For instance, they have solved the problem with pulse lasers, providing our ships with better defenses and relying less on shields and fighters. This will allow us better tactics in the field. We now have cobalt bombs along with the huge planet drilling rails for planet killing. Our laser cannons and rail guns don't have to be wasted on planets. A lot of improvements giving the commanders in the field different options to kill Kammorrigan ships and worlds." Kevin said.

Ralph thought for a few moments. "Ok, I get it. No problem. Just ensure I have the information by tomorrow afternoon. I must show the tradeoffs and benefits and answer the technical issues why we can't solve the problem now."

Both Kevin and Dr. Vance nodded.

"All right, guess I'll let you two get back to it if there isn't anything else." Ralph started to close the link when Kevin spoke up.

"Actually, there is, Ralph. I have a big gripe, and I need resolution from these guys."

Ralph grimaced. *Great here it comes*, he thought. With a sigh, he said, "all right Kevin what is it?"

Kevin's tone became a bit sharper, "Sir, how much longer must I play nurse maid to these cops? They have an orbital HQ with an internal shipyard and yet I have to keep sending them ships and crews. Every light and medium cruiser we build goes to them. I need those ships for our fleet and our defense force at 237 Prime. Plymouth station is having to defend itself against attacks with substandard ships. Yes, we have sent them LIBERATOR but that is a strike group not a defense group. I know, we have sent them five new ships but five more require replacements. It is a waste of resources to give a law enforcement entity the cruisers. We need them."

Ralph thought for a bit then said, "Kevin, I get it but you need to understand the position which Congress is in. Both the Senate and House have appropriated for the defense of Earth. The new Earth Council is trying to figure out what their role is and how the defense of the planet will go. Everyone got scared when EXPLORER came back. You guys jumped into the system and frightened everyone. Now, they want the system defenses to be stronger than it was when you came back. There is talk we need the battle carriers here vice going out to attack. Also, the anti-piracy effort requires ships. The President, the Chairman, and I are doing what we can to keep it balanced."

Kevin thought about what Ralph said for a moment. "I understand but we are not in the same situation as then. We now have Plymouth Station, plus we are recapturing Zeta Prime. Our warning systems have been improved and are nearly in place. We will have warnings this time. The defense system is sufficient. It is a waste for the Marshals to have cruisers. To solve this problem, we have plans for corvettes, smaller, faster, and better capable ships for them. We can start production on them now. They include sensors for anti-piracy and other law enforcement practices, weapons, shields, boarding capabilities, and brigs for prisoners. We can get them built rather quickly. We can have ten ships built within weeks. They can be produced here in our system, so they don't have to make that jump. Let me get ten produced as a top priority and give me back ten medium to light cruisers and or destroyers at best, or the next ten we get built so I can get them to Plymouth Station. General Jones needs those ships ASAP, Ralph."

Ralph sat back in his chair. "Corvette ships you say. Specifically designed for our sister service." He steepled his hands together in thought. Kevin and Dr. Vance sat quietly, watching the view screen.

"All right, Kevin. I'll see what I can do to get you some of the ships back."

"Thank you, Ralph." Kevin was getting ready to close the link when Ralph thought of another matter.

"Kevin." Kevin stopped and turned back to the screen. "Yes Sir."

"CAPT Lindsey. I think she is ready to transfer to operations and take command. I know it is early but I like to move her onto her next assignment."

Kevin nodded, "All right. Unfortunately, she was meant to have WOLFPACK, but I had to send it to Zeta Prime."

"Don't you have another SAG for her?" Ralph asked.

Kevin keyed up his computer and read through the build report from Alpha Centauri. "Well, not really, at least not the type of ships we need. We have two destroyers coming off the line. At best, I can make three destroyers available. But those won't do her mission any good and if I can't have medium cruisers for Plymouth. Then I need the destroyers for General Jones."

Dr. Vance spoke up, "Were you not thinking about her finding a planet for the coalition to assemble and train?"

Ralph nodded. "Yes, we are waiting for word from Ambassador O'Shea to inform us of a good location, though."

"Ah," Dr. Vance continued, "well, why don't you give her these three ships and send her out to Zeta Prime to appraise the situation there? Give her the ability to swap out ships so the military governor may have a strike group. Then she can continue with her mission with the ships she requires. Let her have that judgment."

Kevin looked at Ralph.

"In theory, a good idea but not practical. The destroyers would take too long to get there. They are smaller ships with smaller jump drives. No, she needs at least medium cruisers to make timely jumps to Zeta Prime. Also, CAPT Blevins as commander of WOLFPACK, wouldn't take kindly to losing his heavies, besides, she isn't supposed to go to Zeta Prime at all." Kevin said.

Ralph responded, "Good points, Kevin." Ralph was seen keying his own computer for the build schedule. "I see we don't have any heavies coming off the line anytime soon." He frowned. Kevin and Dr. Vance watched as he started keying something else. Kevin started to show some concern and began working on his own computer.

"All right, Kevin. I'm going to fight to get the corvettes for the Marshals and convince our political leadership to let you redistribute the planet's defense forces. You do need the freedom to assign appropriate ships to their tasks." He breathed out a heavy sigh. "Kevin, you are not going to like this, but I want Josephine to have three heavy cruisers for her specific missions. I'm pulling them from your fleet. Make it happen. I'm readjusting the build schedule to replace them."

Kevin clenched his teeth. "Ralph, I keep losing ships from the fleet."

"Enough. It is done." Ralph stated. "I said I would fight to have you repurpose the planet's defense forces and have ships returned to you. Just get those corvettes here ASAP."

Kevin said, "Thank you, Sir. That will be a big help. Put Josephine on a month-long leave so we can get her a SAG that is capable and effective. Besides, she will be away for quite some time."

Ralph agreed.

Dr. Vance spoke up. "Gentlemen, we have a colonel as a military governor at Zeta Prime. Is that appropriate? Also, we haven't discussed his role and the role of Zeta Prime. It may be the right location for a trade station and a central place for the civilizations we are encountering. Better to transfer trade goods there than at 237 Prime."

Ralph and Kevin looked at each other.

"Ralph, perhaps we should promote Col Burnhart to General or at least a Brevet Brigadier General. I agree with Jack, we should look at Zeta Prime as a trade, diplomatic, and customs station."

Ralph nodded. "Ok, we will cut some orders for a Brevet level. That way I don't have to go through Senate confirmation. We can do that later. If we go with the trade station concept, we will need a diplomat to support him. Kevin, you work on that one."

"Get me the info I need for the hearing soon. Out here."

"Will do, Sir. Out here."

The links closed and Kevin smiled at Dr. Vance.

"Sir, I can give Admiral Nabum the information he requires in an hour."

Kevin shook his head. "No Jack, give it to him tomorrow. I don't want him starting to expect information sooner than he asks for."

* * *

SAG WOLFPACK came out of jump near Zeta Prime escorting the troop transport. The klaxons sounded across all ships. CAPT Blevins, the commander of WOLFPACK swung his chair around to view the main screen and called for his tactical display to come up. Zeta Prime was under attack.

"Seven ships are attacking the station, Sir. One of them seems to be listing a bit. So far, they have yet to notice us."

"Very well," replied CAPT Blevins. "Keep us heading for the station at this speed. Communications, open a frequency to Zeta Prime. Let's hope we are still in charge."

"Frequency open, Sir."

"Zeta Prime, this is WOLFPACK from Space Force Command. Do you read me, over?" CAPT Blevins said.

Through static cackling came an excited voice over their speakers, "Thank God you have come. Please, please attack them! Get them away from us. Please kill them!"

Everyone around the bridge turned to the CAPT who motioned for them to be calm.

"Zeta Prime, what is your status?" The CAPT responded.

"We are under attack! Can't you see? Get them!" Came the harried and excited voice.

"Is Col Burnhart there?" The CAPT asked.

"We have sent for him."

CAPT Blevins leaned forward in his chair with his hands on its arms. He was viewing both the viewscreen and the tactical display. "Weapons."

"Sir, six of the ships have their lasers locked onto the station, which is returning fire. Shields are up on all targets. The seventh ship is starting to roll now."

'Understood," began the CAPT when a new voice came over the audio.

"WOLFPACK, this is Col Burnhart. Most glad to see you. I have you on the tactical as four ships but can't tell anything else." CAPT Blevins was relieved. The Colonel seemed to be in control though there was stress in his voice.

"Communications, can you clean up the audio? Col Burnhart, what is your status?"

"It's grim, WOLFPACK. We were attacked unawares. Ten ships came out of jump and immediately fired upon us. Section C of the upper disk has hull breaches. We were able to get the shields up but not before they blew the sensors out. Thankfully, the targeting systems are online. I'm pulling power from other sections to keep the shields up. My Ops Center has burned out systems. We are also repelling attacks from the inside. I really hope you brought ground troops." The Col responded.

"Yes, we have a transport with a reinforced battalion. You've done well. There are only seven ships and one is starting to roll out of control. I'm heading in at half speed. Where do you want the battalion to dock? I'll escort the ship then peel off as necessary to engage the remaining attackers."

There was a moment of silence, then Col Burnhart started to respond when an explosion was heard over the speakers.

"Colonel, what was that? You, ok?" Capt Blevins said.

After a moment delay. "Yes, we are still here. That was an airlock giving away in Section C. It finally collapsed from the previous hits. No new hull breaches there. Please send the transport to the second disk. I think most of the docking bays are empty. Seems a lot of ships left the station when we were attacked. I'll flash the lights continually so you will know which dock. If you can offload two companies there that would be great. Keep the third in reserve to either support them or drop them into the primary section."

"If you give us the coordinates, I can plan on *Helldog* and my ship to peel off to engage the others while *Scout* continues the escort."

"Sending now."

When the *Fenrir*, CAPT Blevins' ship received the coordinates, the Helm plotted the course. *Fenrir* sent to the rest of the ships the path to the docking bay and the location where *Fenrir* and *Helldog* would peel off to engage the enemy ships. Meanwhile, CAPT Blevins had the communications patched through to the transport for the Battalion Commander, LtCol Sarah Marvin, to be part of the battle plan.

"The internal enemy is still trying to break through our control points. But my Soldiers are holding firm," Col Burnhart said. "Thankfully, we have help from other species holding this area. There has been fighting in the lower decks between them and the hostile aliens. I'll need those two companies to break through those lines and come up into the primary section to attack the hostiles from behind."

"Yes Sir. We can do that." Responded LtCol Marvin, "is there a way you can vacuum the docking area, so we don't have to breach it?"

"Not really. Not without hurting both allies and civilians," Col Burnhart said. "But we can deactivate the artificial gravity and slowly bleed the air out."

"That would be good, Sir. We can handle zero grav." LtCol Marvin said. "I notice they are only attacking the primary section."

"Yes, this is where Operations and Administration are located. They want the station intact therefore they are not attacking the power systems. They seem to want to overwhelm us." The Col responded.

As the WOLFPACK reached the peel off point, *Fenrir* and *Helldog* peeled off at a Z positive vector while *Scout* continued to escort the transport toward the second section.

CAPT Blevins was watching the tactical display and saw one of the ships disengage from its assault on the upper section and begin transiting in their direction. CAPT Blevins keyed his comm link to *Helldog*.

"*Helldog*, engage that ship that is transiting down the station. I'll cover you."

"Affirmative," Came the response from COL Michaels, the commander of *Helldog*.

The CAPT continued, "Weapons, put two torpedoes into that ship in the roll. I want hull breaches in her, so we don't have to worry about her coming up behind us."

"Yes Sir," The Weapons Officer said and began programming for two torpedoes to hit her. Within a minute two torpedoes launched from *Fenrir* heading toward the hostile ship that was in an uncontrolled roll. CAPT Blevins watched the main screen for the torpedoes to hit the ship while watching the tactical to see *Helldog* engage the enemy ship heading in their direction. Zeta Prime was in the background.

As he watched the two torpedoes slam into the rolling ship resulting in two different hull breaches with gas and fire escaping, he noticed a new hull breach occur on the station's primary section.

"Helm, increase to full," he ordered in a loud voice. The Helm immediately responded.

"Zeta Prime, we just observed a new hull breach. Come in over."

There was silence on the audio. The CAPT repeated his call to Zeta Prime.

Helldog engaged the enemy ship with its two forward batteries and one starboard battery. Its three lasers locked fully onto the enemy ship whose shields immediately turned rainbow colors as it attempted to dissipate the energy. Within a minute though two lasers penetrated the shields and impacted the hull. The enemy ship had returned fire but was ineffective against *Helldog*'s shields. It began to list toward the station itself.

Damn, thought Col Michaels.

"Get us where we can make that ship miss the station," He ordered his Helmsman, who immediately started to make corrections.

The transport ship successfully docked at the station where Col Burnhart desired it to go. LtCol Marvin's forced entry squad started to set breach charges when they noticed the hatch roll open. No one could be seen so they moved in with caution, weapons at the ready. No resistance was presented but they noticed there wasn't any gravity, so they activated their magnetic boots, which were now standard on all combat armor. They proceeded to the inner hatch and found they could open it easily. They continued into the station and began to set up a perimeter, letting the LtCol know they had successfully breached the station. She ordered the rest of the platoon to enter and began to set up her command post within the station.

"Col Burnhart, this is LtCol Marvin. We have successfully entered the station and are building combat power now." She called to Col Burnhart.

"Good," he responded, "Colonel Marvin, you will find mainly civilians in that area but may encounter both hostiles and friendlies."

She thought for a moment, "How can we tell the difference?"

"I've already started spreading a challenge to all of our friendlies. The challenge is Alpha and the response is Omega," Col Burnhart said.

"All right Sir, we will pass the word to the troops. Hope to see you soon."

"Indeed, please get up here fast. We will leave this channel open."

"Yes Sir," she said while watching the status board as her forces entered the station one squadron at a time.

"*Fenrir*, this is *Scout*," CAPT Blevins heard over his audio. "The transport is docked and off-loading the Soldiers. We are moving up the station to engage the enemy ships on the other side. *Scout* out." CAPT Blevins had his ship send a response.

"*Fenrir*, this is Col Burnhart. Sorry about that. That explosion was one of our communication relays. Only the exterior hull breached not the interior. My shields, in that section, may fail any moment."

"Acknowledge, Colonel. Both *Scout* and I are moving to engage the enemy ships. *Helldog* is cutting one ship into sections now. That leaves five we must deal with."

"Roger that." The Colonel said.

Fenrir came around the primary hull first and engaged two enemy ships simultaneously. She had to be careful since the station's lasers were still locked onto the remaining enemy ships. *Fenrir* hit one ship with its two forward lasers while its port guns locked onto a second ship. She poured as much fire onto them as her tubes would take. One of the ships quit firing on the station, and turned its lasers onto *Fenrir,* while the other one took just one laser off the station and turned it onto her.

LtCol Marvin had moved onto the station with her Headquarters and Service or H&S company. They secured the area and set up her command and control. She had informed Col Burnhart she was now in the station. Alpha Company was ascending the station up one section while Bravo Company was moving forward along a different path. Her Executive Officer was leading Bravo Company. So far only Bravo had encountered some armed aliens. The lead fire team had challenged with Alpha and the aliens had replied with Omega. They joined forces. Since then, Bravo was moving forward faster than Alpha since the aliens knew the station and were leading them upward.

"Col, I would like to bring Charlie Company over to secure this section and send a squad to check the lower levels. Bravo is moving rapidly upward while Alpha is moving along another axis of attack," she reported.

Colonel Burnhart looked around his smoke-filled Operations Center. Several monitors were dark with control panels burned out. His staff was calmer knowing there was help from Earth. He found the system he was looking for and indicated he wanted the internal station schematics brought up. He walked over to it. After reviewing it, he flipped open the comm link to LtCol Marvin.

"LtCol, take a platoon to do your recon of the area. We are showing zero activity but you can check it out. Send the rest of Charlie up the axis that Bravo is traveling and have them secure the joining section. When Alpha reaches the joining section on their axis have them hold. The intensity of combat inside the station seems to be lessening. Not sure why, but I want Bravo up here fast."

She acknowledged the orders and sent her own mirror orders. Alpha began moving forward at a quicker pace. The first two platoons of Charlie she sent immediately along the axis Bravo went while maintaining the third platoon as a recon and reserve force.

Scout had emerged around the upper section to find *Fenrir* engaging two ships. Col Devin ordered his Weapons Officer to fire upon the closest two ships with a similar fire pattern as *Fenrir*. He further ordered two torpedoes to be fired upon each of the targeted ships.

Helldog, meanwhile, had maneuvered herself between the enemy ship and the station thus pushing the enemy away from the station with her fire. *Helldog* had fully smashed the shields of the enemy and was cutting the hull into two halves. The Commander was ensuring the hulls would fall away from the station. When the ship finally broke in half and was falling away from the station and showing no weapons activity, he ordered her to move at full speed to the rest of the fight.

"Col, shift your station's fire onto the one ship we have yet to engage. *Scout* and I are able to handle these four ships." CAPT Blevins informed the station. His lasers had now fully turned the two enemy ships' shields into full rainbow colors along the entire craft. It would only be a matter of moments before he smashed through them.

Meanwhile, he was happy to see how easily his ship was handling the laser fire from the enemy. They obviously lacked the power to sustain a fight against them. He did wonder why they could wreak havoc with the station, perhaps because of the surprise attack?

Helldog emerged and finding the only ship that wasn't under WOLF-PACK attack zeroed in on it. They came upon the ship at full speed, locked the forward batteries onto it, and poured tremendous amounts of energy onto it. Meanwhile, one of *Scout's* opponents lost their shields and the Col slammed three more torpedoes into it along with laser fire. The ship went dead. Col Devin then turned his attention onto the remaining ship. *Fenrir* was able to smash the shields of both its targets at the same time and fired torpedoes into both ships, crippling them.

"Major, are you in position?" LtCol Marvin asked.

"Yes Ma'am, we are ready. I don't see Alpha yet, but this company is ready to attack. I see the enemy. They appear to be bringing larger guns into position to fire upon the Col's forces. Also, I see other aliens under cover seeming ready to attack them."

"Roger Major, hold your position." LtCol Marvin said, then flipped a switch on the comm panel, "Alpha, where are you?" She asked with a fierceness in her voice.

"We are coming up to the mall area now, Col. That firefight surprised us at the joining area. But we came through. I left a platoon there to secure the area while we moved forward. I've also picked up several other alien fighters along the way. Whew, we are here Col." The Cpt reported.

"Good." She then flipped three switches. "Major, a platoon from Charlie Company will be approaching you soon. Col Burnhart, Alpha and Bravo are in position. Both Alpha and Charlie are holding the two joining sections. Bravo reports enemy activity seems to have brought in larger weapons. We are ready when you are." She waited.

Colonel Burnhart was watching the monitors with internal views. His Soldiers and allies were in blocking positions. He could see the hostiles with their weapons getting into position. Their attention was fully on their weapons. They did not seem aware of the forces behind them. Good. Finally, the fight seems to be going their way.

"Attack," was the only word he said. The two companies moved forward firing at the enemy with the largest weapons and the ones closest to them. As they moved forward, attacking, the aliens that were under cover also attacked the hostiles. The enemy forces were facing a full one hundred eighty-degree arc of fire. They were falling away quickly without a real opportunity to return fire. Once they were fully engaged, the Colonel gave a second order and his forces in the barricades opened up fire upon the hostiles. Now, they truly fell from fire above and below their positions. The fight was over within minutes.

Meanwhile, the five remaining attack ships were dead hulks in space. All of them had breached hulls with fires burning inside. They were falling away from the station into the near space. WOLFPACK had silenced their guns watching their enemy die in the coldness of space. They continued scanning the entire area for any other hostiles.

Both Colonel Burnhart and CAPT Blevins were wondering what had happened to General Connington and his Strike Group.

CHAPTER 7

LtCol Clark approached the door and stopped. He took a deep breath and exhaled it as he forced himself to relax. *This isn't Going to be pretty,* he thought, *but best to get it over with.* He pressed the ring button. Over the voice box, he heard enter as the door opened. He stepped into Commodore Kirby's office.

"What is it, Clark?"

The Commodore asked briefly, looking up.

"That is LtCol Clark, Sir." He responded.

The Commodore jerked his head up with his face turning red from anger as he glared at the Marine.

"Watch it boy," he growled.

LtCol Clark shook his head with his own eyes on fire, "No Sir. You cost us surprise and Marines from that last action. After reviewing the regulations, I see my own ignorance allowed it but no more, Commodore!" He stated.

"Oh, what makes you think that, Clark?"

"Space Force Order 3441 states the landing force commander has the ability to plan and direct the assault."

The Commodore interrupted him, "That is only for task forces with an amphibious force."

"No Sir, it isn't. The reg states it applies even in our situation. I am the one that decides how and even when we attack. It further states that I have the option to relieve the task force commander if I see either negligence or willful disregard for life or mission achievement."

"It doesn't say that," The Commodore responded.

"Look it up yourself, Sir. It does and I will exercise all the authority it gives me from now on."

Both men locked eyes and glared at each other.

After a few moments, it was the Commodore who broke the silence.

"Very well. You want it that way, you have it, boy. Let's see if you are smart enough to know when to follow instructions. You're dismissed," he said with malice in his voice.

LtCol Clark slightly inclined his head, acknowledging the statement and left the room.

The Commodore sat there in silent rage for a few moments, then threw his pen across the room and breathed out heavily.

Dammit, he thought. *This job really sucks. First, I find out I'm not to operate independently. Instead, I'm placed under that fool, Jones, only to have him be promoted in front of me. Next, I had to play patty cake with his staff. Now, this upstart Marine is telling me what I can and can't do. And to boot he thinks he can actually relieve me.*

He turned to his system, keyed up SFO 3441, and scanned through it. Now he really got angry, there it was, right there. The Marine can relieve him as he had quoted.

Well, he thought, *we will see who is relieved. I will play along and give the Marine just enough rope to hang himself. In the end, Space Command will see their error and promote me like they ought to have done!*

The ships came out of hyperspace and began breaking prior to reaching the asteroid belt. They began scanning almost immediately. The Helmsman called for Commodore Kirby who simply asked if LtCol Clark was on the bridge. After receiving a positive answer, the Commodore thanked the Helmsman and referred the operation to Clark. LtCol Clark just shook his head and moved to the command chair.

He had them launch three scouts and four probes to the belt in search of the pirate base.

After nearly four hours the three scout ships returned. Each one reported negative findings of a base or any sign of a base. The probes returned six hours later with similar results. LtCol Clark was at his station comparing the probe results with the three scout Marines next to him. He then checked the data they had taken from the pirate base they had raided. He nodded his head. Yes, they had indeed chosen the wrong asteroid belt. He keyed the communication switch for the Commodore.

The Commodore answered.

"Sir, confirmed, no base here. Recommend we head to the other asteroid belt. It appears from the data we have collated the base will be there." LtCol Clark reported.

"How long before we can get there?" He asked.

LtCol Clark looked at Astrogation who keyed his system, "Two days, Sir."

"All right, jump the ships to the other system. Make your preparations LtCol." He then closed his system before awaiting the confirmation.

SAG LIBERATOR began moving away from the asteroid belt to have a clear jump path. The astrogators programmed their next destination into their systems. When the SAG ships had travelled ten thousand kilometers, they opened the hyperspace well and made the jump.

For the next two days, LtCol Clark and his staff made their plans. The Marines rehearsed their take down procedures of the anticipated pirate base. The ships' crew members ran simulations on blockading methods while destroying pirate ships and support of the Marines' assault. The Commodore would check on the Marines and his crews to see how they were doing. He found himself pleased with their performance. He advised LtCol Clark that he should ensure all hands had plenty of rest before entering normal space, which the LtCol thanked him for and ordered his Marines and crews to be rested.

The SAG entered normal space. *Liberator* was flanked on her port side by *Revolution* and on her starboard by *Jackson*. The asteroid belt was ahead of them. The ships were at yellow alert and the Marines were gearing up. The ships headed toward the asteroid belt at half speed. The astrogators were collating where the pirates may be located from the confiscated data they had acquired from the previous base. The *Liberator* launched two probes in the general direction they believed the pirates would be. Now, it became a waiting game.

The system they had jumped into had a single yellow sun with two planets, with the asteroid belt between them. The ships were on the outer side of the belt with the sun shining through it. The asteroids cast shadows across each other but other asteroids were lit up by the sun very nicely. They could see different colors reflecting off of them. The sensors were picking up readings of different alloys which could be useful.

Three hours later they received telemetry from probe 1 indicating the base's location. Within a few minutes, the second probe sent telemetry from another angle, confirming the location. They waited. The two probes were returning to the ships in a more direct path than how they entered the asteroid belt. They readied a scout ship with Recon Marines onboard and the remainder transports were filled with the other Marines. When the probes reached a point the Astrogator indi-cated they had the path and sent the information to the recon shuttle to follow through the belt. They launched and proceeded to enter the belt.

The shuttle proceeded along the path, dodging asteroids or gliding around them as required. They maintained a comm link with the SAG and sent updated telemetry back to the ships. The pilot found it smoother than anticipated. The belt wasn't tightly compacted allowing for better maneuvering. The three ships would be able to make it through without any issues. After two hours the shuttle was approaching the coordinates of the pirate base. Their link with the ships was still good. They slowed.

The pilot chose a Z minus path around the last asteroid, gliding along it to the other side. When they came around, their sensors picked up the pirate base. The pilot and lead Marine were amazed by what they saw. The radiance of the sun shone through the asteroids with a cascade of light and shadows. It was spectacular. The Base itself was set inside a large asteroid. Most of the rock was in shadows, but the hangar portion was lit by the sun. They could see light sources coming from within the asteroid where the pirates had the hangar and several port holes. The Recon Marines began their scans. The hangar doors were open to receive ships. The asteroid itself was circular on the side they could see. They counted five laser guns on this side of the base. They saw two communication arrays and a few items that looked like shield emitters.

They figured the other side of the base would have a similar figuration. In front of the hangar bay doors were three ships in what appeared to be external docking stations. They sent a message to the SAG with the information and made ready to make their attempt at the station.

"Bring up tactical," Commodore Kirby said. When it came up, he continued, "Now, show the line of approach to the base." A green line from them arced across the screen to the aft end of the base indicating their approach would be from its blind spot. He sat back and motioned for LtCol Clark to join him at his chair.

"When we approach at this vector, I would like to disembark the Marines, then speed forward with *Revolution* to take out those three ships and blockade that entrance. That leaves you with *Jackson* as the escort. Does that match your planning?"

LtCol Clark checked his hand palm, "Yes Sir. That should work provided the Recon team takes out those lasers and shield emitters."

"Good. Send in the Recon team now. Helm, let's get moving. Comms let the other ships know to move out and that *Revolution* will accompany us once we have the Marine transports away."

They both confirmed the orders and set about their tasks. The three ships banked to their starboard and began moving along the green path on the screen through the asteroid belt.

The Recon pilot nudged the thrusters and the shuttle began moving away from the asteroid to the rear of the pirate base. The move caused the shuttle to move along a pace similar to the asteroids around them making it appear they were nothing more than another rock. They glided smoothly as the pilot made minor corrections with the thrusters while keeping the engine at a minimum power output. They made it to the Base rock in approximately thirty minutes. The Recon Marines didn't spot any sensor arrays though they felt certain they existed. As they came up on the Base rock, the pilot used his thrusters to angle onto the rock and make as soft a landing as possible. Once they were down, he killed the power.

The Recon Sergeant told everyone to button up since they would be doing a spacewalk. The six Marines then locked down their suits and picked up their packs. The mission: plant charges along each laser battery and shield emitter. They would blow them when the SAG showed up. Then, they would breach an airlock so the rest of the Marines would have an entry point into the base. The air whooshed out as the pilot depressurized the shuttle and opened the hatch for them.

The Sergeant was the first to step out. He looked around the rock with the sun high over the horizon, lighting up the jagged landscape. He keyed his suit comm link to the others.

"Keep it loose and watch your step. No sense in floating away. Remember, this isn't Earth's gravity. Let's move out."

The other five Marines exited the shuttle, leaving the pilot alone. They moved around the shuttle and began working their way toward the front of the rock. They were moving as fast as they could while ensuring they didn't snag themselves on any of the protruding rock projections. Some of them appeared to be very sharp. They made their way toward the first emitter and reached it in roughly fifteen minutes. The Sergeant motioned for a charge and had the other four Marines move on. The SAG would be here soon, and he needed to ensure the lasers wouldn't be of any use to the pirates. He checked to see how the Marine was doing and once satisfied began moving forward himself, knowing the Marine would do the same.

They had four lasers set with charges and all the shield emitters. The Sergeant ordered two Marines to get the last one and then set up near the hangar bay doors. Meanwhile, he and the other three Marines moved toward the docking hatch they had found on this side of the base. He only hoped he had time to breach it before the ships arrived. They were moving as fast as they dared to avoid injuring themselves. He looked back to see his two Marines placing charges on the last laser gun. He smiled and turned to move on when he stopped. Yes, he saw it correctly. The sun had just glinted off the three ships. They are here and would begin their attack soon. He called for his Marines to hurry to the entry point and begin the breach as he set off. He told them, the SAG had arrived.

The three ships began to pick up speed. Commodore Kirby had them launch the transports and then ordered the ship to go to full speed with shields up. The *Revolution* followed suit, launching her transports, and then went to full speed following *Liberator*. Only *Jackson* was staying behind with the transports as they were launched.

LtCol Clark reached out to his Recon Sergeant.

"We have launched. Give us the signal Sergeant."

"Yes Sir," came the response.

"Time to blow the charges, Sergeant."

There was a moment of silence just before lights flashed from the explosions across the entire rock face as the Marines blew the charges. They had reached the docking hatch and were in the process of breaching it. The Sergeant sent an intermittent beam of light toward the transports to guide them in.

Commodore Kirby leaned forward in his command chair. He was excited, perhaps more than he ought to be. But finally, he had caught these scumbags flat footed. Now, he would show everyone his prowess. He checked himself.

Best keep your mind on the battle, he said to himself.

The Recon Marines did their job well. They had disabled the entire defensive grid on this side. He could glide right past them and deal with the ships while Clark led his Marines into the base. He hated to admit it, but Clark was good at this stuff.

"Bring us alongside the two nearest the hangar bay doors," he ordered. "Weapons Officer, fire when you have a firing solution. Hit each ship with a torpedo and lock lasers onto them. Have *Revolution* take care of the third. I want our port to them Helm and keep our starboard to the hangar bay doors to keep any other ship from leaving."

Both officers acknowledged the orders and the Helm poured on some more speed and angled them into position. As he was doing this, the Weapons Officer locked the forward lasers onto the two Pirate ships and fired while sending a torpedo to each one. The lasers reached out and hit both ships in the broadside while the torpedoes slammed into them. However, one ship had its shields up. The torpedo impacted the shield with minimum effect; while the laser hit it and began sending its energy along it. The other ship didn't have its shields up. The torpedo hit the aft section of the ship, ripping into the hull. The laser locked onto the mid-section and began tearing into it. Both of the SAG's crew could see fires within and outside of the hull where the torpedo has struck the pirate ship. Gases had begun to escape from the mid-section that was impacted by the laser fire.

The Weapons Officer read his scanners. "Sir, the one ship is dead in space. Its drive is out and her weapons are down," he reported.

Commodore Kirby thought for a moment as the Helm brought their broadside to bear.

"All right, keep one laser on the dead ship to ensure she is out. Bring our other guns to bear on the other ship. Let's get through those shields fast. Keep the sensors on those doors. I want to fire on anything that comes out of them," he ordered.

Meanwhile, *Revolution* had come up and fired upon the third ship. She had her shields up so the two ships locked their lasers onto each other. Now, would be a matter of energy dissipation and time to see who could cut through the shields first and hit the hull.

All right, the Recon Sergeant thought. They had the hatch breached and it was opening. He checked and saw the transports approaching fast. He motioned, and he and one other Marine entered the hatch and began to move inward. That was all they knew. The other two Marines saw their bodies fly out of the hatch with gaping holes in their suits and smoke coming from them. They both crouched there in utter amazement as they watched their companions float away. Then, one shook himself and pulled a grenade off his bandolier, pulled the pin, and tossed it down the hatchway. It bounced along making a clinking noise and then fire and gas came out of the hatch as it exploded. They both started firing down the hatchway.

LtCol Clark watched out the pilot windshield, and saw two Marines floating away from the rock. He knew an explosion had occurred while he watched the two remaining Marines firing into the hatchway.

Damn, he breathed, *lost two men already.*

He began to tell his pilot to take him in when he noticed another transport was already angling in. He grimaced. He then sent a signal to have the Marines disembark a short distance from the hatchway and tried to warn off the other transport.

All but one transport began to land and disembark their Marines a short distance away from the docking hatch. But one kept going toward it. When it started to line up to dock, fire came out of the hatchway. Sure enough, there were pirates in there trying to destroy the transport. At first, their fire bounced off the hull. The Corporal in charge of those Marines realized if he opened the hatch, they would be taking direct enemy fire. He had the pilot veer away from the dock and unload them on the other side of the hatch. When the transport landed, he had the shuttle door opened, and his Marines scrambled out and headed toward the dock hatch. The Corporal positioned them along the hatch, and they took up firing positions. He looked up to see the other Marines marshaling.

They tossed five grenades into the hatch opening. The resulting explosion blew gas and flame out. Next, he had the Marines with the larger caliber and faster firing rate weapons shoot into the hatchway. After a minute, he led two fire teams into the hatchway. Sure enough, they had killed several pirates that were holding the inner door. They quickly breached the inner door and with a motion the Corporal had two fire teams file through and set up firing fields in different directions. So far, no other enemy defenders could be seen. He signaled that the inner hatch was theirs.

Commodore Kirby was not happy. He still was dealing with the one ship but now he was under attack. Five pirate ships had emerged from the hangar bay and all of them opened up onto *Liberator*. His shields were still dissipating their laser energy but they were turning colors. Engineering had reported several relays had burned out, and Medical was reporting crewmembers presenting with electrical burns. The lights on the bridge even flickered at times. He had his entire starboard laser guns locked onto each ship. He really needed maneuvering space to counter these ships.

Meanwhile, *Revolution* was starting to make headway against its opponent. LtCol Iverson had been sending torpedoes to aid Commodore Kirby and the *Liberator*. They were impacting the enemy ships' shields with some effect. Each hit was making headway. There was something odd though, at times light was coming from a spot above the hangar bay doors hitting the shields of the various pirate ships. Kirby just shook his head at this.

LtCol Clark was inside the inner hatch. The H&S element was operational. The two remaining platoons of his Alpha Company were spreading out in both directions, securing passageways. They were meeting with resistance. His transports were unloading the other company of Marines from *Jackson*. He had stuffed as many of them into her as he could. This was taking time, though. Alpha Company, Second Platoon, led by the new Company Commander, First Lt Meynard, found himself unexpectedly in a real fight. Stiff resistance was coming from the pirates. Third Platoon had only met minimal resistance and was moving forward. LtCol Clark decided to reinforce Second Platoon with the Third Platoon. He kept what was left of the First Platoon with him to hold the hatch. He shook his head. He wished his second company would get there.

Finally, *Revolution* had dealt with its opponent. The pirate ship's hull just floated on its mooring with gas escaping from it with fires burning inside. *Revolution* turned its laser guns onto the other moored ship and fired three torpedoes into it. This action shattered its shields, and both the *Liberator* and *Revolution*'s lasers made short work of the ship. But *Liberator*'s shields were a rainbow of color from the enemy lasers.

Smoke had begun to fill the Commodore's bridge. One of the sensor panels had blown a few minutes ago, sending sparks everywhere. Some of his screens were beginning to fail. *Finally*, he thought, *the moored ship was done for*. Now, he could maneuver, and *Revolution* was available.

"Helm, bring us to Z positive twelve mark thirteen," He ordered. "Comm, have *Revolution* follow our path in our shadow. When we come to the new position, have them cross above us and fire on the same ship we're firing upon. Weapons, when we get in position, we should have the nearer ship blocking the other pirates. Concentrate fire on the one or two closest to us."

As they confirmed the orders, Helm kicked the ship into full gear, and she lurched forward. As she moved along the path, *Revolution* came alongside, mirroring the maneuver. Two of the pirate ships followed the path with their lasers, only to find themselves firing upon one of their own, since it was between the *Liberator* and themselves. In the process, they shattered the third ship's shields.

Bravo Company, with two of its platoons had offloaded and were making their way into the hatchway. That was all he could fit onto *Jackson*. Now, LtCol Clark knew he had sufficient combat power to take the station. He sent Bravo Company with their Company Commander, Capt Raymond, down the opposite passageway from Alpha. They would be used to capture the power room and proceed to the command center. He kept the remaining Alpha Marines with him. Bravo's reports were positive, while Alpha was stating they were still being held up.

"Col, we found the station's power center." Capt Raymond reported. "Good, how many men do you require to take it?" LtCol Clark asked.

"A platoon only Sir. I think the station's passageways may be arching back on itself. I see a diagram. Where is Alpha at?"

"Copy Capt, send in the platoon, and capture the power center. I'll get a status from Alpha." LtCol Clark switched his comm link.

"Alpha, what is your status?"

"We are pinned down Sir. We can't break through."

"I'm on my way," sighed LtCol Clark.

He glanced at the Marines that were with him.

"Stay here and hold this area. Be ready to patch me through to Bravo." He turned and took off down the passageway before the Marines could acknowledge his orders.

He moved briskly along the passageway, checking to see what was around him. There were a few hatches along the way. They were blown open by his Marines, but only debris was in the rooms. It wasn't long before he found Alpha. The area was dimly lit from a few remaining light sources, there was residual smoke from both units firing at each other.

"Status," He barked.

The First Lieutenant turned to him.

"Sir, they have us pinned down here. We can't move around the curve. They have heavy weapons at an intersection and they bounced a laser against the curve, which has been mirrored. We have been debating what to do." He reported.

The Colonel turned to him with a flash of anger in his eyes.

"Debating what to do. That is nonsense. Get me three Marines with grenade launchers on their weapons and bring up our own heavy lasers. Now!" He barked and moved forward.

The First Lieutenant made a motion and three Marines instantly were up and following their Colonel. The Lieutenant scanned the other Marines but four of them with laser weapons were already following the Colonel.

"Sir, this is how far we dare go." A Corporal said.

LtCol Clark stopped and looked down the darkened passageway.

"Ok, here is what I want. I want you three to launch your grenades down this passageway. Place them on a thirty-second timer, not on impact. I repeat, not on impact. You three see the angle you need? I want them to bounce down the p-way to the intersection. That means you have to angle it to bounce down there. Understand?" He turned to look at the Marines.

The three acknowledged while they were setting the timer for thirty seconds on their launchers. LtCol Clark then turned to the other four Marines.

"Once they launch their grenades, take up position and fire your lasers against that mirrored section just like they have been doing. Angle your fire to hit multiple areas on the other side and keep firing till I tell you to stop. Understand?"

"Yes Sir." The four Marines said and took up positions.

The three Marines with the grenade launchers laid down on the floor, crawled up to a position, and stopped. They began aiming their weapons at different angles until they each had a green light in their scopes for an angle shot. Each Marine made a thumbs up motion and stated, "Ready." The four other Marines came close and began looking for their angle.

"Fire." The Colonel said.

The three Marines fired and their grenades hit the curve p-way and began bouncing down the other side toward the intersection. As they rolled out of the way, the four Marines took up crouching positions behind them and began aiming at the mirrored curve ensuring their lasers would reflect down the passageway.

Thirty seconds passed and the grenades went off and the four Marines fired their lasers. They kept depressing the laser triggers. Soon, the Marines could hear screaming coming from the other end.

"Keep firing." LtCol Clark shouted.

Finally, the screams died down.

"Keep firing! Change your angle."

The four Marines shifted to change the lasers' angles.

More screams came from the passageway ahead, followed by an explosion.

"You may stop firing," LtCol Clark said, "First squad move forward and secure that intersection with First Platoon following. Watch your fire. Don't hit anyone from Bravo Company that may be moving up. Give me a read out once you have the intersection."

The Marines moved forward at a fast pace.

The area was dark, so the Marines turned on their suit and weapon lights. They found a lot of body parts and smoking debris. Their grenades and laser fire had detonated the pirate's ammunition stores. The squad quickly took up position at each of the other three openings of the intersection. They reported, no contacts down the passageways they were covering.

Each passageway heading away from the intersection had flickering lights. They could see hatches along the way. LtCol Clark looked down each p-way and found a map on the bulkhead of one of them. He moved quickly to it and began scanning it. He then keyed his comm system.

"Get me Bravo."

"Capt Raymond here."

"Capt, what is your status?"

"We have secured the power room. The rest of us are heading toward Alpha. Over."

"Copy. Alpha is now free to maneuver. We have taken the intersection. Your objective is now the hangar deck. Take control of it. Alpha and I will be heading to their control room to take it down. Over."

"Copy Sir. Bravo out."

Lt Col Clark found the Lieutenant.

"Keep a squad here to hold the intersection. The rest of your company this way." He motioned down the passage he desired for them to take, and a squad moved out in front of them.

The *Jackson's* Skipper, LCDR Fox, saw the Marines had entered the station. His scanners were clear of any enemy ships. He had comms inform LtCol Clark he was moving off to aid the other ships. He had his tactical up. They indicated the *Liberator* and *Revolution* were maneuvering to place a single ship between them and the other four pirate ships. This enabled them to destroy each ship in turn, but it would take time. He decided enter the fight, so he had his ship maneuver to a position along the upper portion of the station. He would be coming at the fight above the hangar bay doors. This should give him cover and an excellent position of fire on the pirate ships.

As *Jackson* was coming over the station, the bridge crew noticed the Recon Marines above the hangar bay doors, firing their laser weapon at the ships. LCDR Fox smiled at them.

"Ok, Weapons Officer, lock onto the ship without any shields and kill it."

"Yes Sir."

Jackson's lasers locked onto the ship and ripped into the hull. There were explosions throughout the ship. The Weapons Officer moved the lasers aft along its hull toward the engine room. When they hit it, the ship went dead and began rolling toward one of the other pirate ships.

The pirate captain must not have seen this since they didn't attempt to maneuver out of the way and the two ships collided. The shields failed and both hulls began venting gas as they were now on fire with explosions.

This action got the attention of one of the three remaining pirate ships. It turned its lasers onto *Jackson*. Her shields began turning colors as they dissipated the energy. Commodore Kirby noticed on his tactical that *Jackson* had appeared and was engaging. More fires had appeared on his bridge as his shields were now overheating. Engineering was pulling power from all areas except Medical to keep the shields up. He was getting concerned. These pirate ships seemed to have better weapons and shields than what intelligence had informed them. The pirates must have done upgrades since the taking of 237 Prime.

"Engineering, how much more can we take?" Commodore Kirby called down.

"We are losing systems across the ship, Sir. I'm holding the hyper-space reactor back in case we need to jump."

Kirby sat back in his chair and put his head in his hands.

Damn, he thought, *I can't lose this fight. I can't let these guys get away.*

He sat straight up, "Take from the reactor if you have to. We have to win this fight." He told his Chief Engineer.

The pirate ship in front of him exploded unexpectedly. His shields were being impacted by debris but no longer from any laser fire. Several of his screens failed.

"Wow!" Yelled his Sensor Tech.

"What?" The Commodore yelled.

"Sir, the station just fired upon that ship and the whole thing just exploded. It's firing on the other ship now."

"All lasers target that ship. Have *Revolution* do the same thing."

Both Communications and Weapons responded.

The Control room was lightly guarded and Alpha Company was able to overcome them and secure the room rather easily. LtCol Clark stood in the center of the room and surveyed the screens. He took in both the tactical views and the screens showing the battle outside. He looked over at the station internal monitors and could see his Marines were in charge of the majority of the station. The remaining pockets could be dealt with. The hangar bay was still a concern but he knew Bravo Company would have it soon in hand.

"Someone get on the station fire controls," he ordered, "I want this station to fire upon those pirate ships with everything we have. Take out the one closest to *Liberator* first. Get that ship off her."

Three Marines jumped toward the fire controls.

"I got it!" One yelled. "I see how to target and fire this." He worked quickly at the controls. LtCol Clark watched the screens above it and could see the aiming device locking onto the pirate ship. It flashed that it had acquired the target. The Marine looked down at the board and excitedly pressed the firing button. The screens showed three lasers reaching out from the station and blowing through the pirate ship's shielding causing it to explode. All the Marines cheered as the one at the firing controls began to target the other ship.

Revolution moved forward to take the brunt of the fire from the other ship while *Liberator* launched its remaining torpedoes into the pirate. With her shields cooling off, other ship systems started to come online. Commodore Kirby kept the laser fire going, telling his Chief Engineer he wanted more power to his lasers. The pirate ship didn't last long with the concentrated fire from the two ships and the station. After they dispatched it, they turned their attention to the last pirate that was engaged with *Jackson*. It started to turn to make for a hyperspace point and both *Liberator* and *Revolution* opened up on it, ensuring it would be destroyed. With all three ships hitting it with their combined laser fire it didn't last long.

Commodore Kirby sat back in his chair. His bridge crew looked relieved but were haggard.

"All decks, report. Damage control teams to all decks," he ordered, "Engineering, report."

"Sir, we are badly hurt. The Hyperspace Drive is still good, but we need to make repairs here before we can move off."

"How long?" The Commodore asked.

"I need at least three days."

Commodore Kirby turned to his tactical monitor; it was clear except for his three ships. He then reviewed the screens that were linked to his scanners. They all had static across them. He shook his head.

"We may not have three days; get started." He then turned to his Comms Officer.

"Get me LtCol Clark."

"TREX here, send it."

"Colonel, how is your position?" Commodore Kirby asked.

"We have the station. Bravo Company is securing the hangar deck. Meanwhile, we are cleaning out what few pirates there are. There are only pockets of light resistance, but we now command the control room and power centers along with the major intersections."

"I might need that hangar bay. Try not to damage it too much."

"Yes Sir. I'll let Bravo know. How bad are the ships damaged?"

"*Liberator* has taken a lot. May take us three days before we can make the jump to Plymouth."

"All right, Sir. We will get that hangar bay for you. TREX out." LtCol Clark looked at the *Liberator* on the main viewer. She didn't look bad from here but he knew she had taken a beating.

* * *

They were still at the station five days later. It took longer to clean out all the pirate positions. The last group proved extremely difficult. They had gathered a lot of munitions and were held up in a strong location. It took the Marines an entire day to clean them out. But five days later the station was theirs and all the pirates were dead. They had fought to the last man.

First Lieutenant Maynard stood at attention in front of LtCol Clark's desk. The Colonel was reviewing an officer's evaluation report. He could tell the Colonel was not happy.

"Lieutenant, your leadership during this action is questionable. From the start, you have shown poor judgment. You don't debate what you are going to do in combat. You have to be decisive. You have to control the tempo of the combat and never let the enemy take it. You could have gotten several more Marines killed." The Colonel said. "Further, I'm concerned you are not making improvements. After all, we prepared for this assault and you got pinned down."

LtCol Clark looked up from his report.

"Sir, I froze at that first encounter. My fault."

"Well, at least you acknowledge that. I'm considering what to do about you and whether you are fit for the Galactic Marines. We are a new subset under Space Force. But Marines we are in the traditional sense. You have to be a leader of Marines, have good judgment, and be technically proficient. I'm not sure you are and therefore may not be a good fit for our new structure."

He looked away from the Lieutenant and tapped his finger on his desk. The Lieutenant swallowed hard.

"Sir, I'll do a lot better; you can count on it."

At which point the Colonel growled deep in his throat.

"We shall see. In the meantime, Major Orvin will be working with you. I want you to review the tactics you are supposed to be employing. Major Orvin will be evaluating you on your performance during various exercises. When we get back to Plymouth Station, we will decide your fate. Better improve Lieutenant if you want to stay with the Galactic Marines. Now, send in that Gunny and you're dismissed."

The Lieutenant started to turn and stopped.

"Sir, I was in charge; why see the Gunny?"

The Colonel just stared at him. "You are dismissed."

"Yes Sir." The Lieutenant exited the office and motioned for the Gunny to go in. He could hear the LtCol start chewing out the Gunny as the door shut. The next time he saw the man, he was busted to Staff Sergeant and no longer assigned to Alpha Company.

CHAPTER 8

Captain Josephine Lindsey rode the shuttle from Space Force HQ toward Space Operations HQ. The ride was smooth as she sat in quiet thought, alone in the passenger area. A few tears ran down her face. She had only been to space three times since her return from the SESG EXPLORER mission to Kammorriga. Now she would be assuming command of a task force into deep space. She had no idea how long she would be gone this time.

Her last night of leave with her family was an emotional one. Her children had grown by nearly three years by the time she had returned from Kammorriga, how old would they be when she returned from this mission?

After the children were asleep, she spent a very heartfelt night with her husband. Between the holding and tears was passionate lovemaking. They didn't know if they would ever see each other again.

A trio of soft tones sounded, indicating they were approaching the space station. She wiped the tears from her face and turned her mind from her family toward her profession. As part of Space Force operations, she had visited the moon base once and the Mars Academy twice to ensure they were performing the necessary functions and training. This was her fourth trip to space. She was supposed to command SAG WOLFPACK, but ADM Brannigan had to launch them early to support Space Station Zeta. Her mission had now changed. She knew it involved a task force vice a SAG but that was all she knew for now.

The shuttle slid easily into its hangar spot and was secured by hangar control. The hatch opened once they were in a pressurized area. A young Second Lt stood on the hangar deck waiting. As she came down the ramp he saluted and welcomed her onboard. He then motioned for some Guardians to take her luggage over to another shuttle. He indicated for her to follow him.

"Jo, come in, come in. It is great to see you again!" Exclaimed ADM Brannigan as CAPT Lindsey entered his office.

"Hello Admiral, it is good to see you again." She replied.

"Please sit down, have some coffee and pastries. The galley here does a superb job on both." He indicated where she was to sit as he moved over to a serving area and poured two cups of coffee. He placed them on a tray along with a plate of different kinds of pastries and carried them over to the small table where he then sat down. They each took their coffee and placed pastries on their respective plates. After eating for a few moments, along with a small chat about family and their respective stations, the ADM grew serious. Jo knew this meant business was now to occur.

"Sadly Jo, you have to leave right away. We are getting indications of problems out at 237 Prime. SAG LIBERATOR has not been in touch with Plymouth Station for quite some time. The area may be in trouble. You're going to have to get out there quickly with your heavy cruisers. The rest of your task force will have to follow. Aid General Jones any way you can but don't stay long."

She nodded, "Do we have any information?"

He shook his head. "Our last communiqué with them didn't show anything urgent around the station but a lack of communication with Commodore Kirby. As you recall, he is General Jones' strike group and his pirate hunter. They have been out hunting pirates but Kirby has failed to communicate with Jones to date. We don't know what is happening out there. You need to find out, but again, that isn't your key mission."

She frowned and took a sip of coffee while thinking.

"Ok, Sir. How long before I depart from there?"

Kevin frowned.

"That is a problem. You have a long way to go, and we aren't positive what your heading is to be. We haven't heard from either Mike O'Shea or the *Sabachi*. We are in the dark when it comes to their missions. We need to know from them where a suitable planet is for an outpost. But we do know where your task force is to head to. The problem is if you launch to the task force site, then we will have that much more delay in sending you to…" he thought for a moment while rubbing his chin, "Well, let's call it the coalition planet for now."

He got up and refilled their cups and added a few more pastries.

He sat down.

"You see, Jo, we are really short on ships and crews. Almost as fast as we get them, they are either sent to the Space Marshals or launched on an emergent mission. Yet we are at war, even though most of Earth doesn't know or want to know we are. Some of the leaders are in denial; others think we can hide forever."

She nodded. She had been in the different rooms where Earth leaders were discussing isolationism or exploring and possibly exploiting the galaxy. Some recognized they were now a space faring people, while others just wanted to stay hidden in their own system.

Kevin continued, "Your task force is to head to the planet we found that had crystals just like 237 Prime. Very few people in our own military, let alone the Earth leaders, know about this find. Recall how we discovered large deposits on the planet and yet it was untouched. We want to set up a colony there to mine and produce crystals for us. Long-term thinking has it as a ship manufacturing site along with various weapons and potentially a communication development location. The task force you will be commanding is made up of escort ships and a group of colony ships. You will have three heavy cruisers, one light cruiser, and two destroyers. These are the escort ships for four colony ships."

He reached over picked up a packet and handed it to her.

"When you leave here on your shuttle to Alpha Centauri, please review these items. They are your mission parameters. Anyway, once you get to the planet, ensure it is a secure area and hopefully still untouched. The light cruiser and two destroyers will remain on the planet with the colony. You will then proceed with your heavy cruisers to the rendezvous coordinates to learn the location of the coalition planet, which we have no idea where that may be. We did want WOLFPACK to locate one, but their mission is now to defend Space Station Zeta. But, in the meantime, when you get to your ships, immediately head for Plymouth with the heavies to provide defense. We will get the rest of the task force headed out there soonest. Hopefully, by then, we will hear from either *Sabachi* or Mike."

She stared at the package with her brows furrowed and exhaled heavily.

"I knew I would be departing soon but hadn't realized we are in a crisis."

Kevin sat back in his chair.

"It may be nothing. Might just be me worrying about a lot of quiet. These delays in communications put me on edge. We are still about three weeks between a message sent from Plymouth to reach us and another three weeks for them to receive our messages. A lot can happen in that time span. Anyway, everything is probably ok, but I'll feel better having a Fleet Captain out there."

When Kevin said, fleet captain, she looked him straight in the eyes.

"Yes, you are now Fleet Captain Lindsey. You outrank Commodore Kirby. Within operations, you are equal to Brigadier General Jones. He commands his sector, and you command your task force and even his ships that are in space. That will present issues of command and control with his defense force, but I have already explained the supporting and supported command relationship between you two, once you arrive. It is in your packet. Oh, yes, a new insignia is in your packet to recognize your new rank. Congratulations, Jo. Now, it is time for you to get to your ships."

They both stood up and shook hands and Jo left the office. Kevin stood there watching her depart as the doors closed. He sighed heavily, turned and walked over to his viewport, and looked down at his Mother Earth.

Jo followed the young Lieutenant back to the hangar deck as she seemed to have a new step and persona about her.

Finally, her own command, she thought.

She held the packet tight in her left hand as they headed for her command shuttle. She had thoughts of high adventure and, as always, her excitement was tempered with the responsibilities that came along with it, but only slightly.

* * *

Colonel Doug Kirby sat behind his desk, his head resting on his arms in front of him. The four computer screens on his desk and bulkhead glowed in the dimly lit room. Three screens displayed each ship and its readiness and damage status. The fourth one showed an overall readiness, including his Galactic Marines. He was still awake but barely. He was sorely depressed. This last battle had nearly wrecked his ship, the *Liberator*. *Revolution* had several areas requiring repair. The only ship that wasn't damaged was his frigate, the *Jackson*. He was waiting for LtCol Clark's report. Meanwhile, he sat there thinking about how this fight could have ended up.

Why wasn't intel better? He kept thinking, *why?*

His door tone woke him up. He slowly sat up in his chair, rubbing his eyes as he brought the lights up in the room. After he felt comfortable, he said, "Enter." The door slid open and LtCol Clark stepped in. Commodore Kirby indicated for him to take a seat. The Marine looked sharp in his uniform but a bit drawn, Col Kirby noted as he watched him sit down. At this point, he decided to be a bit hospitable and turned and poured both of them a glass of water and placed one in front of him.

"We had a hell of a time on this one, haven't we?" The Commodore asked.

The LtCol nodded as he picked up the glass and took a drink, "Thank you, Sir." He said, placing the glass on the desk.

"The last group of pirates fought us harder than we thought they would. Down to the last creature they fought. We had to kill them all; there were no prisoners." He shook his head as he finished.

The Colonel looked down at his desk.

Damn, all of them fought to the death, he thought.

He looked back at the LtCol, "how many losses?"

The Marine grimaced, "Total killed in action is forty-two. Eighteen wounded. The doctors don't expect to return any of them to duty."

"Damn," the Commodore said, "isn't that an entire platoon."

"Yes, but that includes the twenty-five Marines we lost in the initial attack on the other station."

The Colonel just nodded.

"So, we need replacement Marines also." He said it as a statement and not as a question. LtCol Clark sat there silent.

"Damn intelligence!" He nearly shouted the statement, "They failed us again by not telling us how they have upgraded their ships and fighting abilities." He then turned to his keyboard, stewing.

LtCol Clark sat unfazed. He knew this was one time to be quiet. He had seen other commanders blame intelligence for things they could not have possibly known. This was one such case. All the previous encounters with pirate ships indicated the SAG ships were more than a match for anything the pirates had. No one expected the pirates would have better ships or be able to acquire them. No, this was definitely a superior enemy than anyone had expected.

"All right, we have been here six days with an action group that is no longer able to fight," the Commodore began. "We have to head back to Plymouth Station ASAP. I'm putting together a communiqué for the General. We need a shipyard to repair both *Liberator* and *Revolution*, which he doesn't have. That means we must go to Alpha Centauri. I'm not sure we can even make it back to Plymouth, but we must try. I'll also include your losses and request for more Marines."

LtCol Clark just nodded and took another drink of water.

The Colonel continued while writing up his report.

"I noticed a gunnery sergeant is now a staff sergeant."

"Yes, my officer failed in judgment during this fight, which also means the senior NCO failed. I took corrective action on the NCO, and we are now appraising the officer."

The Colonel didn't say anything as he continued with his report. He recalled how the Marines are with their own. They took leadership and judgment, especially in combat, very seriously, almost to the extreme.

"I'm not sure we can continue, Jack. Our ships are pretty chewed up and we lost a platoon worth of Marines."

LtCol Clark sat up a bit more with a curious look. This was the first time the Colonel used his first name in any conversation they ever had.

"I don't think the General will send us back to Alpha Centauri, Sir." He replied, "The data from this station doesn't indicate any other pirate strongholds or entities nor does it state that there aren't anymore. I don't see how he would let us return to the shipyards. We will have to adapt and try to repair the ships there. At least he has a manufacturing capability."

The Colonel sat back, rubbed his chin stubble, and realized he hadn't shaved in two days.

"Yes, there is manufacturing. We might be able to become combat-ready with that capability. I'll send a ship casualty inventory to him as well then. Good thinking. Well, that is what I needed for the report. We will transmit this within the day and begin making our way back to Plymouth. I want to be out of here before the day is out. Please pass the word to the rest of the ships and crew to make ready for hyperspace."

"Yes Sir." LtCol Clark replied as he got up, came to attention, and departed the office.

LtCol Clark was standing beside Commodore Kirby's chair, watching the hyperspace well through the main viewer. He glanced down at the chronometer. "We should be at Plymouth within one minute, Sir."

Colonel Kirby sat in his chair, glanced at the chronometer, and then looked back at the main viewer.

"Well, it's taken us over three weeks to get here, Jack. Just think, I'm actually looking forward to seeing Plymouth," he said with a shake of his head.

The Astrogator announced, "We will be coming out of the well in 4, 3, 2, 1, mark."

Everyone braced themselves for the sudden change in speed.

SAG LIBERATOR's three ships entered normal space above 237 Prime. The two larger ships jolted hard as they came out of hyperspace. The crews had to brace themselves due to the damage both ships had sustained.

"Multiple contacts," calmly called out the Lead Sensor Technician aboard the *Liberator*. "Their configuration is those of the pirate ships we have already encountered," he continued.

"It appears Commodore they have engaged Defense Force Zeta," reported the Tactical Officer.

Commodore Kirby and LtCol Clark were watching the viewscreen and noticed a large flash-like explosion occur and observed several ships firing lasers at one another.

"Holy shit." Called out Colonel Kirby, "What the hell have we flown into?"

LtCol Clark commanded, "Magnify the viewscreen, especially on those ships that seem headed to the planet."

The viewscreen was adjusted to show four ships headed toward the planet with three ships in a screen pattern.

"That is a landing force heading for the surface." LtCol Clark declared and began to move toward his station.

"Dammit," said the Commodore, "Plymouth Station is under attack! Call General Quarters, all hands to Battle Stations! Tactical view on the screen to the right of the main viewer and give me a view of the battle." The Technicians began adjusting the screens and the Commodore sat back in his chair.

"How many ships?" He called out.

Tactical answered, "Fourteen warships and four landing ships." He made a few adjustments, "only nine of Defense Force Zeta, Sir."

"Ok, thank you. Jack, I want you to get every single Marine on transports. And I mean all of them; leave no one behind. Take the Master-at-Arms with you and whatever wounded can be loaded and get down to the planet before those landing ships get there. Plymouth has a Striker Group to repel ground attacks but they will most likely be overwhelmed. You have to take them out."

"Yes Sir." LtCol Clark turned to his board called up Major Orvin and began issuing orders.

"Also, I'm going to send the *Jackson* along with you as an escort. If you need to keep Marines onboard her so you can make the landing do so. She will stay with you until all Marines are offloaded. Then she will rejoin us." He noted that the LtCol acknowledged the order and began issuing additional orders. The Commodore then started pressing buttons on his personal control panels and the screens lit up with the commanders of the other two ships.

"Gentlemen, as you know Plymouth is under attack. It doesn't appear the pirates have noticed us yet, otherwise, I'm sure ships would be headed our way. *Revolution* will join me in the attack on those ships. *Jackson* will escort the Marines to the surface of the planet and I mean to the surface. Protect them. Only after all Marines and whatever extra forces can be provided to them will you rejoin us in the battle. You will probably have extra Marines onboard. I want them all offloaded to engage those enemy forces that are landing to attack the station. From my tactical, there are at least two large enemy ships and we have to give Zeta Force a fighting chance. Get going on moving everyone around. We have to engage at once." They acknowledged the orders and the link was closed. Commodore Kirby noticed the LtCol had departed the bridge.

Good luck and success, he thought as he began to pick his targets.

Brigadier General Jones was standing in his Command Center with his fists on his hips, watching the screens as he noticed one of his ships explode. Space Operation had replaced some of his older destroyers with newer ships. He now had one light cruiser added to his complement of destroyers for a total of ten defense ships. And now one of the older destroyers just exploded. He shook his head at this loss. He still hadn't sent his squadron of fighters up yet, being unsure what would be next. His Sensor Officer had alerted him that four ships had changed course and were headed for the planet's surface.

Great, he thought, *half of my Strikers are out escorting scientists, and now this.*

"Sir, three more ships just came out of hyperspace."

Oh, isn't that wonderful, he thought.

"All right, call for the Strikers that are out to return in haste. If they have to leave their scientists behind that is all right, just get them back here." He turned to Major Walsh, who commanded the Strikers.

"Get your crews ready. I don't want you going out without full strength, so stay close but be ready to get out there. Keep your close air support near; we are going to need them. We will send out some drones to try and locate where they have landed and their strength."

The Major nodded and left the Command Center.

"Ok, so we are facing seventeen warships at this time. Well, let's make them pay for coming."

"Sir, several transport ships are leaving the three newest ships with one of them following the transports as an escort." The Technician adjusted his screens. "I am not sure they belong to the attacking force. The two other ships appear to be heading at the enemy ships and the escort is smaller than our destroyers."

The Communications Officer yelped and the General turned to him. "Sir, we have IFF. It is SAG LIBERATOR." He listened then added, "Commodore Kirby says he is joining the fight and sending every Marine he has to our defense escorted by *Jackson*."

"Good deal, send confirmation to the Commodore. Ok, launch our squadron of fighters to join the space battle. Everyone, let's stay calm and focus. We are in the fight of our lives and we have to keep control of ourselves and the situation." He then turned, found his chair, and sat down.

If only I had planetary defense systems, he thought.

LCDR Fox was anxious. His ship was once again escorting Marines but this time during a major space battle. The station's existence was in jeopardy. He noted LtCol Clark was in the lead transport. He knew the LtCol wanted on the ground first to establish his command and control in order to attack the enemy. They had chosen to land behind the enemy's landing zone. The plan was to hit the enemy in their rear while the Striker Group hit them in the front. But none of this was coordinated with Plymouth or the Striker Group commander. Fox shook his head. They were finally making landfall. He looked around his bridge. He still had ground forces on his ship that needed offloading before he could join the fight in orbit. His anxiety was growing, he really wanted to get into that fight. He breathed in deeply, held it, and let it out slowly.

"All right, get the hangar bay ready to receive the transports to offload the Marines," he commanded. His crew started making the adjustments as needed.

LCDR Fox turned to his XO. "Are you sure we can't land this thing to offload everyone?"

His XO shook his head, "No landing gear, Skipper."

Damn, he thought. "All right, do what we can to get them offloaded. Tactical, find me those enemy landers."

The twelve remaining transports had offloaded their Marines and were headed for *Jackson*'s hangar deck. Since they were in the atmosphere, the hangar deck crew left the doors open. As two transports landed and filled up with Marines, they took off. Then two other transports came in and performed the same function. It took an hour but finally, all forces were off the ship.

"Button up and let's get going." Said LCDR Fox. "Do we have a fix on those landers?"

"Yes Sir."

"Great, head for them. As we fly over them, destroy them, and keep heading for Plymouth."

"Yes Sir." Both Helm and Weapons said.

It only took a few minutes for the *Jackson* to get to the enemy landers. When they came into range, the Weapons Officer fired all the ship's lasers onto each ship. It only took a matter of seconds for each one to explode rendering them useless. The *Jackson* continued on its flight path toward Plymouth. A few minutes later the enemy forces came into view.

"Kill as many as possible as we fly over on our way to Plymouth," LCDR Fox ordered.

The Weapons Officer adjusted his targeting board, these weapons were not designed to hit ground forces. But he figured out a way.

As *Jackson* approached them, her lasers made a sweeping motion from right to left. They struck several of the enemy, killing them as they made their sweep. Several explosions occurred as ammunition packs were hit and several large pieces of equipment. LCDR Fox smiled and expressed his gratitude to his crew.

A few minutes later they could see Plymouth Station.

"All right, get us back into orbit, and let's engage those bastards." LCDR Fox ordered.

Commodore Kirby watched as the Marines and other crew members were being transported to the *Jackson*. He was anxious for them to get started. The four enemy transports were still a way out but they were on course toward the planet with three screening ships between them and Defense Force Zeta. He wondered why his ships were not being attacked. He checked his monitors, all Marines, wounded and Master-at-Arms were off his ship. But *Revolution* still needed some time before they were off of her. He grimaced; time was not their friend in this situation. It would be a race for *Jackson* and the transports to reach the surface which the enemy seemed to have the advantage. At least he knew LtCol Clark and his Marines would make mincemeat out of them once he was on the ground.

They had lost the initiative, more of the enemy ships had begun to engage Defense Force Zeta. The first destroyer was farthest from the planet and when the enemy had made normal space multiple ships had fired on it. It was destroyed rather quickly. But this alerted the rest of the force. They quickly formed into three groups of three ships. Two of the groups were hanging near the planet while the last three, comprised of a light cruiser and two destroyers, had moved to engage the enemy fleet.

The enemy forces numbered fourteen warships, and three of them were escorting the four landing ships. These escorts deployed in a screen between the Defense Force ships and the pirate landing ships. They didn't seem concerned about SAG LIBERATOR, and Commodore Kirby was determined to make them regret that decision. The disposition of the remainder of enemy ships was in four formations. One group was made of three ships, which were between the three escorts and Defense Force Zeta. Two groups had a large primary warship with two escorts; one of which was heading for the Zeta Force light cruiser and its two destroyers. The other primary warship and escorts were angling toward the remaining Zeta Force destroyers. The remaining two enemy ships were further away from the planet and seemed to be watching the impending fight. The Commodore surmised they were reserve ships.

Commodore Kirby checked the tactical and the chronometer. Plymouth Station had acknowledged his IFF, and should have launched the fighter squadron. *Revolution* was almost complete with transferring the Marines, wounded, and other crewmembers to *Jackson* and some of the transports had begun their descent to the planet. The enemy main ship was about to engage Defense Force Zeta. The two other enemy groups were starting the course change to engage with the other Zeta forces; there was another larger enemy ship with them. Commodore Kirby was growing anxious. He was gripping his arm chairs tightly with both hands, and both feet were tapping the deck almost insanely. The bridge crew couldn't help but notice.

It's taking too damn long, he thought.

"All right, we can't afford to wait any longer. Helm, plot a course for the escort ship furthest from the planet. I want to hit that thing with all of our lasers; prepare torpedoes," Commodore Kirby ordered. "Communications, tell *Revolution* the moment she has the Marines off to back us up, come up on our port side, and fire on the second escort ship. Let's hope the lead escort will turn toward us and we keep them off Zeta Force."

The *Liberator's* thrusters fired, and her engines roared to life. The klaxons sounded bringing everyone to their battle stations and her shields fired up. The Chief Engineer monitored his controls and scanned his engine room. Several reactors were still in a damaged state from their last fight with many of them nonfunctional. But he would give the Commodore everything he had. This is one fight they could not afford to lose.

"What do you mean no shields?" Commodore Kirby demanded from tactical.

"Sir, those three ships have not engaged any shields nor are they turning to meet us," responded the Lt.

Commodore Kirby sat back in his chair and scratched his head while frowning. This didn't make any sense to him, unless...

"Sensors, have you taken any readings of those ships?" He asked.

"No Sir."

"What?" He yelled, then he calmed himself. "Well, do so now; these ships may not be sufficiently equipped to deal with the fight. Helm, full speed ahead, let's hit them hard and get to those larger ships. If they don't have any weapons, then I want to blow past them."

Everyone acknowledged the orders and *Liberator* poured on the speed.

When the first ship came into laser range, the Weapons Officer fired all forward cannons onto the ship. Immediately there were explosions along its hull. She returned laser fire at *Liberator* and the middle escort ship turned about, bringing its shields online, and firing upon *Liberator*. Before they knew it, the third ship had turned. *Liberator* was taking fire from all three ships. Only the first ship they hit didn't have shields. It was quickly being torn apart by *Liberator*'s own laser cannons.

LtCol Iverson was beside himself. *What the hell is he doing?* He thought. *Revolution* had finally offloaded all the Marines and others she was supposed to. The Skipper had ordered his ship to follow *Liberator* at flank speed in order to engage the target ships but it was too late. All three enemy ships had locked their lasers onto *Liberator*. Her shields were taking a beating. But the tactic had worked. One of the main enemy attack forces had turned toward them and away from Zeta Force. It was the second group with a larger warship. They could not engage yet, but it would only be a matter of time before they could angle their fire onto *Liberator*.

Finally, the first ship was a dead hulk in space. She was on fire in several places inside and along her hull, gases were venting from several holes. Parts of it were floating debris alongside it. *Liberator* was firing on the other two ships when *Revolution* finally joined the fight. Already, *Liberator* had lost part of her port shielding and was turning her forward starboard shields toward the two remaining ships. *Revolution* locked her lasers onto both ships. Meanwhile, the other incoming three ships were angling themselves to fire upon *Liberator*.

The captain of the Zeta Force light cruiser with his two escorts had angled away to their port to draw the main enemy warship and its two escorts away from the planet and the remaining Zeta Force destroyers. The main enemy ships were following them. Meanwhile, the two Zeta Force groups had engaged the smallest three ships of the enemy fleet and were making headway.

The *Jackson* appeared out of the atmosphere. LCDR Fox was surprised to see where they were. They came up behind the six destroyers that were headed for three enemy ships. LCDR Fox scanned his tactical display. He was too far away to aid Commodore Kirby and LtCol Iverson. What a choice: Help the six destroyers or aid the light cruiser that was playing cat and mouse with the main enemy ship. He still had munitions, so he decided to begin moving toward the light cruiser of the Defense Force. His ship was the smallest in this fight but maybe if he could get behind that big ship...

A cheer went up throughout the Zeta Force when they noticed the entire squadron of fighters, twenty-four in all, come out of the atmosphere. Six headed for the two groups that were engaging three of the enemy ships, while eighteen headed for the light cruiser to aid them against the main enemy ships.

Major Walsh sat in his command vehicle watching his monitors. The wind was picking up; a storm had come up and was nearly on the station. The sand from the storm would obscure their vision, scanners, and targeting systems. Still, he could tell from the drone footage the enemy forces were approaching the outer perimeter sensors. Despite the damage the *Jackson* had done, there were still over one hundred of the enemy with heavy equipment. He knew he would have to take out those pieces to save the station.

The Major had six vehicles formed into two lines of three vehicles each. He was moving them forward toward the enemy. He was in the lead vehicle with two others following him. The other line was to his port side and slightly behind his line. The lead vehicle of the other formation matched the last vehicle of his formation.

The remaining forces at the Station were guarding the airlocks. The personnel at the Station were trying to get ready to receive the attack should the Strikers and Marines fail to stop this enemy. The scientists and engineers were doing the best they could to support the aircrews and security forces. Medical was getting ready to receive casualties.

Two of the Major's six remaining Striker vehicles that were escorting the scientists had returned and were in the hangar dropping them off. They still had to load ammunition and refuel for the fight. He could only hope the other four would arrive soon. They were on approach at a high rate of speed but would require the same off-load of scientists and equipment to make room for the ammunition and fuel required for the fight. He really wanted them in the hangar before the enemy forces arrived.

The four close air support craft could not launch in this storm; they would only crash. The Command Center informed him that LtCol Clark and his Marines were on their way and the plan was to catch the enemy between them. He could only trust that his crews could hold the enemy long enough for the Marines to arrive.

The *Liberator's* bridge kept filling with smoke from several small fires. The whine of the scrubbers trying to clear the bridge of smoke was low but could be heard. Several crewmembers kept putting the fires out and yet more would appear. On a monitor to the right of the main viewer was BGen Jones. Commodore Kirby knew he was waiting for a report from him.

"What Engineering?" The Commodore said.

"Skipper, we need you to disengage. Relays are tripping everywhere. As soon as we get some back online others trip. I need just a little time to stabilize the generators, breakers, and relays. Please give me just a few minutes," the Chief Engineer screamed over the comm system.

Commodore Kirby glared at the main viewer, tactical viewer, status of weapons and shields monitor, and the damage control monitor.

"All right, will do what we can to give you a breather." He closed the link and swung around to the Astrogation station.

"Astrogator, see what you can do with the electronic warfare apps to give us some advantage over these ships. Plus, try and figure out their shield frequencies." Commodore Kirby ordered. The Astrogator was about to object till he caught the look on the Commodore's face and just complied.

The Commodore switched on his comm link to the General.

"Sir, we are having trouble up here. How are the Marines doing?"

"Commodore, don't worry about the fight down here. Our monitors show those three ships are gaining their angle on you. You must disengage and reposition. We need you against the other ships. See if you can't join up with the destroyers." BGen Jones stated.

"Affirmative; will do," he closed the link and said, "Helm drop us under these ships and bring us up on a course to join with the destroyers." Commodore Kirby then keyed his commlink to *Revolution*.

As the Commander of the *Revolution* came up, he said, "LtCol Iverson, we are going to swing under these two ships and head for the destroyers. I have to disengage from this fight before we are caught in a crossfire." LtCol Iverson agreed and both ships began moving off.

BGen Jones was standing in front of his chair as he read the status reports displayed on the Command Center's monitors. It was clear to him this was a pirate force.

Incredible, he thought, *they have definitely upgraded their ships.*

Before this fight, his Defense Force and even a damaged *Liberator* would have been enough to dispatch them. And now both *Liberator* and *Revolution* were in a bad situation. He had lost one of the older destroyers right off when the pirate force had appeared. His one light cruiser with two escorts were playing a cat-and-mouse game with the pirate's main ship while the fighters were chipping away at their shields. At least his six other destroyers had dispatched three enemy warships and were angling toward a rendezvous point with *Liberator* and *Revolution*.

"General Sir," an overexcited technician yelled. "Three more warships just appeared on the scope"

"Calm yourself," General Jones said, "Now identify them as friend or foe."

He sat down thinking; *God help us if these aren't friendly.*

Fleet Captain Lindsey had her back to the main viewscreen, watching her Astrogation station and its view screens. She was interested in how they tracked themselves in hyperspace and curious about how it would appear when they would emerge into normal space. The readings on one screen changed as they came out of the well. They went from a spinning tube to a set of streaming stars to what appeared to be nonmoving stars. Another screen was taking readings with four lines moving from left to right. When they came out of the well, all four lines jumped up and then fell below where they were in the well.

To her surprise, the klaxons went off. Fleet Captain Lindsey lost all interest in the Astrogation station and wheeled her command chair about to the main viewer.

"Captain, it appears there is a battle above Plymouth Station," said the Sensor Technician.

Calmly, Captain Lindsey keyed up the other two ships of her task force as she said, "Call battle stations and bring the shields online. Send IFF code to Plymouth Station at once."

As the other two Captains appeared on her screen, she said, "Gentlemen, it looks like we have jumped into a fight. I want you to close up on me. Now is the time to test the joining of our shields to amplify them. If Dr. Vance is correct, we should be able to dissipate their laser fire more efficiently. I see three Defense Force ships drawing off what may appear to be the main enemy ship. We will move in that direction." They acknowledged the order as she closed the link.

A brilliant flash of light on her main viewer caught her attention.

"Tactical, that appeared to be a ship being destroyed. Confirm with both Comm and Plymouth Station." She ordered.

"Yes, Captain."

"Helm, how quickly can we close with the enemy ships?"

The Helmsman checked his systems, "Forty minutes at this speed. If we go to full power, we can close in twenty minutes."

She nodded, "Coordinate with the other two ships and go to flank speed."

"Aye, Aye, Ma'am."

BGen Jones slowly sat down. Damn, he'd just lost both *Liberator* and *Revolution*. They were making their maneuver to disengage and join the destroyers. But the move was anticipated by the pirates and they got them as they came around. They had the combined firepower of five ships hit them. The enemy lasers ripped through their shields and blasted their hulls into nothing. All that remained was one large ball of bright fire which burned out, leaving a debris field. Now, the five ships were forming into a five-ship formation and began heading for his destroyers.

The storm had indeed hit the station. The high winds were kicking the dust up into the atmosphere. The drones had been recalled and the close air support was useless. Their targeting systems were scrambled and Major Walsh knew his laser's integrity would be weakened. Only two other Striker vehicles had made it back. Two other vehicles were still on their way. The enemy forces had breached the outer perimeter and were marshaling just inside it. Major Walsh ordered the eight vehicles he had to move forward and when in range open fire. The two vehicles that were in the hangar had caught up to the second line and had joined with them. Each vehicle had a main laser cannon along with a smaller tube for artillery-style shells plus two other smaller projectile guns, one on each side of the vehicle. Each vehicle also carried six men besides the crew and the vehicle commander. Major Walsh was the commander of the lead vehicle, he had extra monitors to affect command and control. The Marines had yet to reach the enemy forces but were moving fast.

All eight vehicles were moving at half speed ensuring they maintained their formation to maximize their firepower. Despite the speed, they were able to move quickly toward their enemy. The dust was scrambling their sensors and made targeting difficult but the crews were attempting adjustments trying to improve their targeting capabilities. Each vehicle's map showed the outer perimeter and their progress. They were closing to the effective firing range on the enemy. Before anyone knew it, Major Walsh's vehicle was vaporized.

BGen Jones was shocked when the Striker XO came over with the report. This ground enemy was disciplined enough to have set up their heavy weapons. He ordered the Striker XO to close rapidly with the enemy and take out those guns. Meanwhile, he demanded his comm station to get him the Marines.

"Yes Sir, we are point five klicks away. We will pick up speed. Clark out." LtCol Clark closed his link and ordered his Marines to pick up their pace. Every Marine was in their EVA/Battle armor suits. They carried either energy or projectile weapons depending on their role in the formation. They were weighed down with all the munitions they could carry. They had filled their water tanks to the maximum level just as they started the march toward the enemy. They were making double time to try and close the distance between them. Now, the LtCol just ordered them to increase their speed. If providence was on their side, they would hit the enemy from their rear and take them by surprise.

"You heard correctly. I want all Defense Force ships to form up behind my three task force ships. My ship will coordinate all maneuvers and fire from here on out. I want the remaining fighters to move off and regroup to my starboard flank." Captain Lindsey informed all the Defense Force Zeta ships. She had a brief discussion with BGen Jones who provided her Communications Officer with all the links for the entire Defense Force. He wished her success as he would concentrate on the ground fight. Admiral Brannigan ensured she was both a Task Force Commander and a Fleet Captain. This gave her authority over every Earth ship she would encounter and gave her immense authority over a coalition fleet. She now exercised it, bringing the Defense Force ships under her authority and redeploying them to a close formation in which her shields would provide better protection, and concentrate their firepower on the pirates. Further, she could coordinate the remaining nineteen fighters into a better strike mechanism against the enemy.

CAPT Lindsey stood behind the Tactical Officer's chair as they both ran quick simulations on his computer. They were five minutes out from possibly engaging the enemy.

"Captain, it makes me wonder why they have the two smaller escort ships slightly in front of the big one. I mean, we haven't picked up anything on the scans," the Tactical Officer said.

"Yes, I know what you mean. What surprise might they have up their sleeve?" She responded and then moved toward her chair.

"Comm, get me the Defense Force light cruiser," She ordered.

When the Skipper appeared on her monitor she said, "Ok, I want you and the other two ships to make straight for me. Pass me on your starboard side then turn about and support my port flank, understand?"

"Yes, Ma'am," He replied.

"Good. Comm, open to all Defense Force ships. *Jackson*, I see you are trying to angle behind the enemy ship. Watch your six. Be ready to get out of there and join my formation. The other six destroyers, I want three on my starboard flank with the other three behind all of us. Fighters break into two groups. When I attack the central ship, I want each group to attack the inside of those two escort ships. Ride through their shields if you can. Watch out for our fire. The three heavy cruisers will be firing on all three ships. But I don't want any surprises from those two. Fleet Captain out." She closed her comm system and sat down. When the Helmsman turned to her, she just nodded and he engaged the engines while the Weapons Officer prepared his targeting.

The light cruiser with the two destroyers executed their orders right away. They straightened out their path and went to flank speed along the course the Fleet Captain told them. The enemy Chief Captain saw this and smiled.

At last, he thought, *they are finally going to fight.*

He knew he was going to have to take on those three new ships, and now he would get his chance.

The *Jackson* picked up speed and began her angling. However, the two floating pirate ships were to the starboard flank of the main enemy ship. One started veering toward her. At the same time, the other Defense Force ships were moving into position with the remaining five pirate ships moving after them and one of them was a primary warship. The fighters broke into two groups, one of nine fighters and one with ten. They began to take positions to make the runs as the Fleet Captain desired.

In a brilliant show of dazzling light, the six ships fired upon each other. The three pirate ships locked their lasers onto Captain Lindsey's ship while her three heavy cruisers locked onto them. Her ship fired its forward lasers directly onto the main ship. The other two cruisers split their fire between the main ship and the smaller ones on their respective sides of the Fleet ship.

Josephine smiled to herself. *Excellent, the upgrades were marvelous.*

Her ships' shields were effectively and efficiently dissipating the enemy fire. But the pirate shields lit up like a Christmas tree. She checked the shield status screen which showed minimum impact. She had the ships slow to a mere halt with thrusters, ready to move in any direction needed.

The two groups of fighters began their run. They maneuvered through the beams hitting the two lighter pirate ships. They shattered their shields and blasted holes in the hulls. Between the two heavy cruisers and their fire, the two ships erupted in internal fires and began to drift off while their lasers sputtered to dead cannons. CAPT Lindsey had the fighters move off and take up escort positions to the destroyers. Meanwhile, all three heavy cruisers locked all lasers onto the main enemy ship.

The pirate ship made a turn toward its starboard to attempt an escape. Its sensors must have been damaged since she collided with its escort on its starboard side. This shattered its shields, and the Earth ships' lasers ripped through its hull, causing major breeches. The enemy ship lurched back onto itself and began to drift. The Earth Task Force kept firing, though, to ensure it would neither be able to maneuver nor fire back. They ripped big gaping streaks and holes along its port side as it continued to fall away from them. Finally, they hit its engine room with major disruptions. At this point, they stopped firing. *Jackson* never got a chance to fire on it. Instead, it veered off to avoid the other pirate ship and make for the six destroyers.

Now that she knew her ships' strength, Fleet CAPT Lindsey was confident this fight would end in their favor. She ordered the heavy cruiser on her starboard side to change course with her and head for the other primary ship with the remaining four pirate ships. She ordered the port side heavy cruiser to take the light cruiser and a destroyer and finish off the remaining two pirate ships near them.

"Don't let anyone escape," she ordered. All other destroyers were to continue to form up on her. The fighters would regroup into three groups and attack the remaining five pirate ships from their engine side. *Jackson* would be joining her main group.

The three ships on her port side peeled off and picked up speed. They wanted to catch those ships before they made a jump. Within five minutes, they were in effective firing range, and they unleashed their lasers on the two ships. They were dispatched rather quickly. Meanwhile, the rest of the ships veered toward the remaining five pirate ships and her fighters changed course and took off. They had chosen a vector that would hide their intention from the remaining five pirate ships.

The enemy ships changed their formation. They placed their primary ship in the middle. The two landing escort ships moved to a port and starboard forward position. This placed their three most powerful ships forward with their laser cannons. The two weaker ships maneuvered to the starboard and port flanking positions as a rear guard.

Josephine slowed her approach. She was watching the destruction of the other two pirate ships and had signaled that, at the moment, they were ineffective and for the three ships to rejoin her. Meanwhile, she had the other ships scanned. When the results came back, she smiled. BGen Jones had told her Commodore Kirby tried to move underneath them. That turned out to be the mistake of his engagement. These three ships had less armament and weapons on their top side vice their underside. Apparently, they could also be used as a planet bombardment platform. Her maneuver would go topside and, she could use her underbelly cannons as she passed by.

She keyed up the heavy cruiser she had sent to dispatch the other Pirate ships.

"How long before you can rejoin us?" She inquired.

"Twenty minutes," The Skipper of the other ship said.

"Ok, how long to position on the enemy's starboard side?"

The other Skipper ran through a couple of items, "thirty minutes."

"Ok, I want you to head your ships to their starboard side. The broadside is fine. Just stay above their midline. Their firepower is midline and below. The rest of us will maneuver to their port and above. Not a crossfire, per se, but one that doesn't allow them to concentrate fire. Those two front ships have greater firepower. Let's ensure they can't use it."

The other Skipper acknowledged. After a few more minutes of coordinating the Defense Force ships, they all moved off to their new positions.

The primary pirate ship Captain saw them maintain their divided force. He thought it was strange since they seemed to fight better in a consolidated formation. He shrugged and decided his force would take on the larger one. The five ships began to angle toward CAPT Lindsey's complement.

Seeing how they adjusted, she ordered all ships to put on more speed. She wanted to get into position before the pirates realized what was about to happen. All nine ships increased their speed to full. Meanwhile, *Jackson* continued to move toward the rest of the main group.

The Earth ships had the better range. When they reached effective firing range, both heavy cruisers locked lasers on both the primary ship and the one to its port forward. Instantly the enemy shields lit up with multi colors. The two landing escort ships had taken damage with their fight against *Liberator* and *Revolution*. Soon, their shields turned to blurring, swirling colors showing it was having a difficult time dissipating the laser impacts. The primary ship shields turned to rainbow colors almost instantly but were more stable.

As the Earth ships began to take their positions, two of their destroyers added their firepower to the heavy cruisers. It wasn't long before the two ships returned fire. The heavy cruisers had joined their shields and were easily dissipating the laser fire, but a destroyer was also locked onto. Soon its shields began to fail. They attempted to break away, but their shields shattered and the lasers ripped into its hull. Fires began breaking out along its forward section. They were able to break from the group, but it was too late. They exploded, leaving a debris field for the other ships to maneuver around.

"It was one of the older destroyers, Captain." The Tactical Officer said in response to her question.

CAPT Lindsey wasn't happy with the loss. "All right, let's kill these two ships quickly."

The other heavy cruiser with the other two ships had taken position on the other side of the enemy ships and all three of them fired broadsides into the primary ship and the other landing escort ship. Their shield reactions were the same but the primary ship's shields were impacted even harder so the rainbow colors began to shift even faster than before.

Soon after the three bigger ships were engaged, two Zeta Force destroyers swung about the two heavy cruisers and locked their lasers onto the smaller port side aft pirate ship. One group of fighters made a pass on the ship that was engaged by the two destroyers, and the other two groups hit the remaining pirate ship yet to be engaged on the starboard aft side. Their runs made strafing fire from the aft toward the nose of the ship. They pulled up, made an arc, and repeated the runs.

After approximately five minutes, the shields of the pirate ship that was port side forward of the primary ship failed. Instantly, CAPT Lindsey had other ships bring their lasers onto it making short work of it. The ship quickly caught on fire within its hull and began to list to its starboard, threatening its mate on the other side of the primary ship.

At this point, two other destroyers swung about to aid their fellow ship against the smaller one. The heavy cruisers shifted their entire fire onto the primary ship while the remaining destroyers ensured the wounded ship would be a kill. Not long after the other destroyers started aiding against the flanking ship it became a dead hulk in space. At which point all the fighters concentrated on the remaining starboard aft ship as the destroyers came about to hit it.

The light cruiser and destroyer were keeping the other escort ship busy while the heavy cruisers were impacting the primary ship.

CAPT Lindsey pronounced the two ships on the port side of the enemy's primary ship as kills, then she had the other Defense Force ships shift their fire onto the two starboard enemy ships. She ordered two fighter groups and her heavy cruisers to concentrate on the enemy's primary ship. The enemies on the starboard flank of the primary warship were dispatched in short order, the forward ship received so much concentrated fire, that its shields collapsed, its hull torn asunder and rendered ineffective. Then, all Defense Force Zeta ships turned their fire onto the primary ship. Within a few minutes, they had shattered its shields and started ripping long streaks of fire and holes in its hull. It was killed within a matter of minutes.

Fleet Captain Lindsey, her Task Force warships, and Defense Force Zeta had won their fight.

While the space battle waged above, the battle on the planet's surface had begun. The storm intensified to the level that no one was sure of their targeting. The pirate forces had arranged themselves into three groups. The majority of their heavy weapons and equipment was on the left, with four units guarding them and one unit advancing. The enemy Headquarters was set up in the center with a heavy weapon unit just to its left, with four units guarding them, they had an additional unit slowly advancing to explore the enemy's strength. There were two additional units linking the center with the left heavy weapons. To the right of the Headquarters were seven units and one heavy weapon unit. Their plan was to use the heavy weapons on the left to target and destroy any attacking forces and breach the station. The units to the right of the headquarters were to advance into the station and kill everyone.

The Striker vehicles had moved forward at full speed to attempt to get under the heavy weapons fire. Two more had been destroyed upon approach. The remaining five vehicles were able to find and range the enemy's heavy weapons and began engaging them. Their lasers were having difficulty locking onto the heavy weapons and they turned to shelling them. But the storm made accuracy difficult. The vehicles deployed their Soldiers to set up two defensive lines of eighteen men each. While the vehicles were deploying their Soldiers, the two vehicles that were in the hangar were joining the fight by focusing on the center of the enemy line. The remaining two stragglers made it to the hangar to begin swapping out the scientists for ammunition and fuel.

The pirate force was surprised by the Striker vehicles arriving. Their shells were not proving to be effective at hitting them. This caused the Pirate Commander grave concerns. He ordered the forces to his right to engage the vehicles that were in front of him. He wanted them destroyed fast before they could hit him. Meantime he had the two linkage units, plus one of his own guard units move to engage the larger group of enemy vehicles. Then came the blow that shook him to his core. He was being attacked from behind.

LtCol Clark and his Marines finally arrived and did surprise the enemy. The storm had covered their rapid approach to the enemy's rear lines. However, his power weapons would generally be ineffective in the storm, and they would have difficulty targeting the enemy. This meant the Marines had to get a lot closer than desired. Their interlocking fires would be jeopardized since they would be too close. He might not even be able to use his mortars out of concern of hitting his own Marines.

He had Major Orvin take Alpha Company with three Recon Marines and six of the Support group to attack the heavy weapons on the left and give aid to the Striker Group located on that side. He then had Capt Raymond take Bravo Company to attack the forces on the right with the remaining six Recon and six Support Marines. At first, LtCol Clark was going to set up his HQ in between the two companies until he realized the storm interference was too much for his communications. So, he moved to Bravo's Weapons Platoon and set up his HQ with them.

Capt Raymond deployed Bravo Company with his First Platoon taking the extreme right, Second Platoon in the middle and he would lead Third Platoon with his Weapons Platoon behind them in a protected area to fire onto identified targets. He split the Recon Marines into two teams of three and sent one off with the First Platoon and one with the Third Platoon.

Major Orvin kept his Weapons Platoon in the middle and to the rear with the remaining First Platoon of Marines to provide security. Meanwhile, he had the Second Platoon take position on his left and the Third Platoon on his right. His three Recon Marines he sent forward from his own position so he may be able to direct the mortar fire once the Marines identified targets.

Once, all the Marines had deployed, LtCol Clark ordered the attack. He had to yell into his communication system to be heard through the storm but the Marines received the word and all fronts attacked simultaneously. The three Recon Marine squads did not fire initially, rather they kept moving forward to find the high-value targets.

The enemy was shocked to be hit along their entire line, but they did not fall apart. Rather the forces maintained their ranks but were a bit disarrayed as to what to do next. The two Human vehicles that came at their Headquarters had stopped and deployed their forces in a defensive position and began firing at them. The Heavy Weapons unit was able to target one of the vehicles and destroyed it just as the enemy from behind hit them. The orders from the pirate HQ became confusing. The units on the right were to somehow attack the forces in front of them and turn and attack the forces from behind. The Marines added to the confusion with their shock tactics. The units guarding the Heavy Weapons on the left turned to attack the enemy that just attacked them from behind.

Major Orvin received communications from the Alpha Third Platoon. There were several huge creatures. Each stood approximately ten feet tall. They had two or four arms and two legs, some had one head while others had two heads. These creatures operated the heavy weapons. After Third Platoon engaged them and started destroying equipment the huge creatures waded into them attacking. They were having trouble killing them, especially with the powered weapons due to the storm.

Capt Raymond's company wasn't faring much better. First Platoon initially was making headway against two of the three enemy units until the third one turned around and attacked them. The one Heavy Weapons' unit creatures charged into them killing several Marines. One Marine used his energy weapon to cut a huge four-armed one-headed creature in half at the midline. However, this didn't kill the creature. The upper body continued to hit Marines scattering them while the hindquarters fell over. The creature only died when another Marine jumped onto its back and put three rounds into its head. With the discovery of how to kill the huge creatures, the Marines informed the rest of the Battalion to hit them in the head or cut off the head in order to kill them.

Bravo Company's Third Platoon was taking a beating from the huge creatures to the point that the Marines started firing their grenades into them at extremely close range. This had the effect of blowing the creatures apart but also injuring the Marines. Capt Raymond's Second Platoon fared better, chasing down their assigned units and decimating them before they realized where the enemy fire came from.

Major Orvin's Alpha Company, Third Platoon was losing several Marines. Major Orvin ordered First Platoon to engage and support Third Platoon before they could be killed. In the engagement, several Marines died and the Major was wounded.

At this time, the remaining two Striker vehicles had arrived on the far right and disembarked their Soldiers. LtCol Clark received word these vehicles had arrived and was relieved. He looked up from his board in time to see an explosion on his right flank in front of the enemy's line. He soon received news that one of the new vehicles had been hit and destroyed by enemy fire. He quickly checked his board and was about to issue new orders when he was informed that another vehicle was destroyed on the left flank. He was frantically trying to get ahold of the Striker Group but the reports from his Marines made him turn his attention back to their fight. He could only hope the rest of the Striker Group could hold on.

The battle was extremely difficult. The storm made the Marine's targeting system nearly unusable. The power weapons could only be used at very close range to be effective due to the dust particles. Mortars were nearly useless since they would hit the Marines along with the enemy forces. After an hour of intense fighting, the Marines and Soldiers of Plymouth Station won the fight. Their discipline and training along with their indomitable willpower won the day. They called for the landers and whatever assistance could be provided by the station to collect the wounded and dead. Plymouth Station's Medical department would shortly be overwhelmed.

* * *

Brigadier General Jones sat in his office with Fleet Captain Josephine Lindsey, LtCol Clark, and LCDR Fox. The General had a glass of Scotch between his hands and rolled it back and forth with his fingers. LtCol Clark just stared into his cup of black coffee. Captain Lindsey slowly sipped from her glass of Scotch while LCDR Fox was fidgeting with a bottle of water but not drinking from it. The General was gazing at each of them but especially at the two lower-ranking officers. They were not taking the battle too well.

"Well, we had a hard day." The General said, "LtCol Clark, what are your total losses from the battle?"

LtCol Clark stirred and took a sip of his coffee, "We had fifty-seven killed in action and sixty-nine wounded and not all of those will make it."

"I see," said the General, "Overall, what are your losses from all the different missions?"

Again, the LtCol stirred, "The total loss of my Marines is one hundred sixty-eight for a combat loss of forty-nine-point seven percent, Sir. I still have one hundred seventy Marines in good enough shape to give us a reasonable sense of combat power."

The General nodded and took a sip of Scotch, "We lost fifty percent of the Soldiers in this engagement. We also lost six of our twelve Striker vehicles. Ok, I want you to keep the Marines here. You are now the ground combat power to defend the station."

LtCol Clark nodded, "Yes Sir. I'll deploy them after I review the layout of all the structures. We used up all the ammunition we took into battle. At the end, it was hand-to-hand combat. Our suits proved to be a vulnerability, the helmet in particular. That needs to be fixed along with ammo resupply."

"Ok, we will include that in the report, see the Quartermaster for the ammo. LCDR Fox." The General continued after LCDR Fox looked up at him.

"The *Jackson* isn't strong enough for planetary defense. I want you to reconfigure the ship to transport all the wounded back to Earth. If there is room, take the dead also. Otherwise, we will have to bury them here and I think their families would prefer them back home. Reduce your crew to only what you need to care for the wounded and operate the ship back to Earth. I will be reassigning the remainder of your crew to the ships that lost their Guardians."

"Yes Sir," responded LCDR Fox.

The General turned his gaze upon Josephine. "Captain, how long can you stay? I may need your ships and your ability to command my defense forces in case any more pirates show up."

Josephine finished her Scotch, "Not long Sir. When the rest of my Task Force arrives, we have to depart immediately for our designated site. Once there, I drop off the majority of the Task Force and head for a rendezvous location where I should receive follow-on coordinates from either HQ or the *Diplomat*. While I am here, I will do what I can but my mission is to take priority over other concerns."

The General nodded and sat in quiet thought for a few moments. He then took his Scotch in one drink. "Ok, we know what needs to be done, let's hop to it."

Everyone stood up and headed out of his office.

CHAPTER 9

D r. Jack Vance sat at the small round table in ADM Brannigan's office. The Admiral was across from him, reading
the treatise on his device. He watched the Admiral as he
furrowed his brows while reading it. He waited, knowing the Admiral would understand.

"Ok Jack, what are you trying to say here? With this material, we
can increase the reactor output and reduce both the storage of plutonium and the waste it produces? If that is the case, why haven't I ever
heard about it?"

Jack shrugged. "Most likely because it didn't have the explosive
properties of uranium."

Kevin looked up at him and waited. Jack knew not to push it.

"Sir, back in the 1930s and going into the 1940s, the Manhattan
Project was in full swing. Various materials were being tested. The
National Laboratory at Oak Ridge, Tennessee, was one of them. They
developed a reactor fueled by thorium. It produced more energy
with less material and less waste than uranium; however, it couldn't
produce the same amount of explosive energy, so it was shelved. But
one of our colleagues at the Research Center remembered a doctoral
thesis he did on thorium. We pulled it and visited Oak Ridge, finding
the research and all updates in their archives. At once, we recognized
something special for our battle carriers, if it would work. So, we
took the materials along with some thorium back to the Research
base. We performed several tests, and yes, the thorium energy output

exceeded the battle carrier's requirements. We then tested plutonium and uranium against the thorium with the energy crystals. The results were incredible. thorium works best with the crystals in producing a stable and less radioactive source of energy than either plutonium or uranium. Therefore, we recommend, we quickly redesign the reactors on the battle carriers for thorium."

Kevin had continued to study the treatise as the Doctor was explaining the bottom line. He reached over to the computer that was on the table and punched up the construction timeline of the battle carriers onto his wall screen. He then studied where they were at on the construction schedule and noticed the reactor rooms wouldn't begin construction for another three months. Dr. Vance said, "Now is the time to make the change, Sir. If we can do this in the next couple of weeks, we can reduce the storage and even the reactor room itself allowing us more space for either living quarters, ammunition, other equipment, or just more storage."

Kevin reached over to his communication buttons and keyed for Space Force HQ, in particular the Chief of Staff of Space Force. Soon, Admiral Ralph Nabum appeared on the wall screen next to the construction schedule.

"Kevin, what is it?" The Chief asked.

"Hello Ralph, how are things?" Kevin replied.

"Busy. I have a Senate Armed Services Meeting in four hours and I'm trying to prepare for it. After that, I'll be meeting with the World Organization regarding space operations. So, I don't have a lot of time."

Kevin nodded. "All right, to the point, I need approval to make a major change to the battle carriers."

Ralph grimaced and looked instantly unhappy, but before he could say anything Kevin continued. "We are three months away from starting the reactor room construction. Dr. Vance here," Kevin motioned toward the Doctor, "has brought a new, or rather an old, type of material that can increase the reactors' outputs and with less material than planned for. Also, it will have a mass reduction in waste being produced and is a safer and more stable material, meaning, less radiation exposure to the entire crew. Plus, if one of the reactor rooms should be hit, there's less chance of an explosion occurring since this is an energy source vice an explosive source. I recommend Sir, we move on it at once. We have up to two weeks to make the changes without affecting the overall schedule."

Ralph sat back in his chair somewhat puzzled. "What is this source?"

"Thorium," answered Kevin. "Yes, I never heard about it till today myself. But according to Jack here, it was discovered in the 1930s during The Manhattan Project and while it proved to be a good energy resource it lacked the explosive punch of uranium; thus, it was shelved. Also, it performs better with the crystals than the other materials. It can increase energy output for the ion drives, hyperdrives, various weapon systems, and the other multitude of systems onboard the ships."

Ralph shook his head. "I don't like these changes appearing, but is this really what you are saying it is?"

Dr. Vance answered, "Yes Sir. We have run a multitude of tests at our Research base. It has proven itself over all the other materials. We can make it happen and it ought to reduce the costs also. Thorium is actually safer and less expensive than the other materials. We don't require all the safety protocols as uranium and plutonium. A savings could be realized."

Ralph did a closed mouth smile. "Fine. Two weeks. All right. I approve. I'll get approval from the SASC. Dr. Vance, I want you and your team on a shuttle to Alpha Centauri tomorrow to affect these changes. I'll have my Ops Department get you your orders and the production change orders to you before you depart. But get this done within a week, not the whole two weeks. Understand?"

A klaxon sounded on the station before Dr. Vance could answer. Kevin's wall screen's border started flashing yellow as a voice over the intercom announced yellow alert. Before Kevin could reach his communication device another window opened up on his wall screen showing his Senior Watch Officer.

"Admiral Sir, I apologize for the interruption. We have received a communiqué from Plymouth Station. They are under attack by a pirate fleet that includes a landing force. I have set the Earth Defense forces on yellow alert. We are monitoring communications for any other reports from the station. Meanwhile, we have increased all sensor ranges in case a ship appears."

Ralph could see both Kevin and the Senior Watch Officer on his monitor and waited. Kevin nodded.

"Acknowledged. Good Work Colonel. Maintain yellow alert and ensure the Defense Forces are out of their berthing when they are fueled and armed. But no action is required. This communiqué is one week old. Whatever happened at Plymouth Station is over. Let's wait for at least three hours to see what other reports may come in. Admiral Nabum, Sir, I need ten heavy cruisers now. In twenty-four hours, I want to be able to launch them to Plymouth Station to either recapture it or defend it."

"Capture?" Ralph asked. "That will be a hard sale. Those cruisers are still being used by the Space Marshals and until those corvettes arrive, you won't get them. And now with this news, everyone won't want to weaken Earth's defenses. Besides they may abandon the station if we have lost it."

Ralph could see Kevin getting angry as he punched up another screen. "Colonel, thank you. Continue to monitor the situation and advise immediately when another report comes in." He clicked his Senior Watch Officer's screen off and turned back to Admiral Nabum. "Sir, the ten corvettes are already loaded onto the transport and are due to make the jump to Earth tomorrow morning. They will be here in less than a day and delivered to the Space Marshals. There is no viable reason to keep those heavy cruisers from us any longer." He then took a deep breath and let it out. "Regarding Plymouth Station, it is a strategic necessity to keep it or recapture it. It is the only source of crystals we have. It is also the gateway to and from Earth. If we lose it, then we lose a vital energy source for the planet. And if the politicians think we can become isolationist at this point in time they are dead wrong. Besides the Kammorrigans who are looking for us, we will have every pirate in this quadrant looking for us. We MUST maintain Plymouth Station and even build it up militarily to provide both a proper defense and strike capability out there."

Ralph stared at him. "All right, Kevin. I'll get the President to order the ten cruisers back to Space Marshal HQ, offload the Marshals and return them to you. Meanwhile, I'll have to include this in my SASC briefing. I agree with you on its importance." He shook his head and then smiled at them. "Thanks a lot for changing my entire briefing. Ralph out." He really smiled and then keyed his monitor off.

Kevin got up and paced quickly back and forth in his office, thinking while Dr. Vance sat watching him. When he noticed the Doctor, Kevin said, "Well, Jack, best get moving. You and your team have to get to Alpha Centauri by tomorrow. Best get back to your top-secret base now and make your preparations. Safe journeys." Dr. Vance got up and they shook hands and he left the office. As he headed to the elevator, he thought, *there is always something that Kevin has to handle, poor man.*

An hour after the initial report, Kevin made his way down to his Operations Center. When he entered the room, a Yeoman started to announce his presence, but Kevin simply waved him to be quiet and continue his work. He walked about the room looking over everyone's shoulder and made small talk with them. He finally made his way to his command chair and sat down, noticing a fresh cup of coffee was in his Admiral's mug. He smiled to himself, greatly appreciating this crew.

Two hours later, an excited Guardian yelled out, "A ship. Alert! A ship has just jumped into our space." He then reached over and hit a button and a klaxon went off. The Senior Watch Officer immediately canceled the klaxon from his desk and told everyone to calm down and check their systems. He then checked his own system.

"Admiral, the ship that just jumped into our system is in the correct lane for a friendly approach. Communications, request an IFF on the ship. Let's find out who it is." The Colonel said.

A few tense moments later the Communication Technician announced, "It is the *Jackson* coming in from Plymouth Station. We have both IFF and voice confirmation. Admiral Sir, LCDR Fox requests medical assistance for the wounded onboard the ship and permission to report to you."

* * *

The room was circular. A semi-circular table was at one end with a door off-center to it. In the middle of the room was a chair and a second door behind it. There were nine chairs at the table. Over each of the chairs was a light. LCDR Fox sat in the middle of the room facing the semi-circular table. Each of the Service Chiefs, along with the Chairman of the Joint Chiefs of Staff and Vice Chairman sat behind the table. Admiral Brannigan sat beside Admiral Nabum.

The Air Force Chief of Staff laid into LCDR Fox. "Why did you lose this fight? Why all the losses to the Marines, the Defense Force, and SAG LIBERATOR?" He demanded.

At this point, Kevin couldn't take it any longer.

"General, stop it! Asking one of my officers such questions is bullshit and you know it. The man to ask those questions isn't here. Colonel Kirby isn't with us and to expect this officer to know his thinking isn't right. LCDR Fox's job was to provide an escort to the Marines, and he did it with the most professional conduct possible. Hellfire, he even laid waste to the pirate force on the planet's surface. thus giving the station's Strike Group and Marines a fighting chance. He saved LIVES! This is no place for an inquisition!"

At which point Admiral Nabum placed his right hand on Kevin's left forearm. Kevin glared at the Chief of Staff then sat back in his chair.

Admiral Nabum then spoke. "Gentlemen, you all know that Kevin always gives it straight. And definitely I have to agree with him. LCDR Fox did his job exceptionally well and brought his ship back home, intact and with all the wounded from Plymouth Station. He is not the man to answer for the events that took place and quite frankly, I don't believe any one person is at fault. Remember, we have enemies out there, and they get a chance to decide when to attack. We went after them, and, in return, they came after us. Now, were there mistakes made? Yes, in particular, by Colonel Kirby. It was a mistake to give him that command and the persons to blame for is here in this room and it isn't LCDR Fox. We need to own up to our own mistakes."

At which the Chairman nodded.

"Well that all may be fine," started the Commandant of the Marine Corps, "But LtCol Clark is mine and he screwed the pooch. I want him back here now so I can take corrective actions on him for these losses."

Kevin sat forward and glared at the Commandant. "Like hell you will, buster. He is my man, and he did the job he needed to do. He took care of Kirby's mistakes and saved lives. He performed very well out there. Besides, we have created the Galactic Marines. I like that they have their basics in the U.S. Marines Corps, but if you think you can destroy careers for events you know nothing about, think twice. Believe me, we can separate the Galactic Marines from you, though I really hate that thought, but I will do it!"

Both he and the Commandant stared hotly at each other.

Finally, the Chairman spoke up, "No need for that you two. I see Admiral Brannigan's point and agree with him. But, let's keep the relationship between the U.S. Marine Corps and the Galactic Marines alive and well. It benefits us all."

The Commandant glanced at the Chairman, "All right Sir. But I believe Clark needs to return and be taken out of operations, at least for a while."

Everyone looked over at Kevin who sighed.

"Well, we can bring him back. But I want him promoted to full Colonel; his actions rate it. I also want him to aid in redesigning the combat/EVA suits. The main vulnerability was their helmets. That needs to be resolved. With that mission plus command of the Galactic Marine Advanced School, he can greatly contribute. But he needs to command a regiment for us when we go out to meet our main enemy. We need him."

Everyone around the table nodded, including the Commandant of the Marine Corps.

"What about LCDR Fox?" Inquired the Chief of Naval Operations.

Kevin answered, "he is one of our best combat-experienced officers now. I want him promoted to full Commander and given a light cruiser to command. We need him to get to Zeta Station ASAP. He can also transport the Secretary of Space Diplomacy team out there."

Again, everyone nodded. They knew these times were a period of discovery and every officer and crew had to be retained for the valuable experiences they had gained.

The Chairman asked, "And Plymouth Station?"

Admiral Nabum answered, "Sir, we need to militarize it now. Brigadier General Jones has requested heavier ships, a space yard to make repairs and provide maintenance to the ships, and planetary defense systems for both ground and space threats. Dr. Vance and his team have been working on such defensive systems. They have a new ion gun that can target ships in orbit from the ground along with perimeter guns with new targeting systems to counter the planet's dust storms. We need to replace the destroyers with heavy cruisers and provide him with a strike capability of additional heavy cruisers. A side recommendation is to scrap the frigates. They are too weak. Our smallest ships ought to be destroyers."

The Army Chief of Staff let out a deep breath. "Wow, Ralph, that is a lot." He thumbed through the reports. "The cost of it all. Is it really worth it?"

Ralph said, "Yes. It is our only source of crystals at this point in time. It is our strategic outpost. We better do this, or we will lose it and before we know it, alien pirates will be here in our system."

The Chairman knocked on the table. "All right, enough. Ralph, sees to the militarization of Plymouth Station to include the ship maintenance facilities, defense systems, and the replacement of its orbital defense ships with heavy cruisers. Also, let's get CDR Fox promoted and get him to his new ship. Admiral Brannigan, bring LtCol Clark back to the system. He will get his promotion but ensure he goes to the training academy to train the new Galactic Marines and work to improve those suits. I'll help you, Ralph, on getting the funds to do all this."

With the Chairman's summation, everyone stood up to leave.

"Oh yes," the Chairman said, "any word on Strike Group RETRIBUTION?"

Kevin and Ralph glanced at each other.

* * *

Paul Connington sat at the conference room table sipping his coffee while watching the team of astronomers and astrogators at the far end of the table working their problem. The past four days, the Strike Group had stayed in this area of space as the team was attempting to find the system they had been searching for the past several months without any success. He noticed when John Roberts, his Deputy Commander and Commander of the Landing Force stirred. BGen Roberts had difficulty staying still. Men of action often found it difficult to just sit and wait. Paul knew this from the days they were with Strike Group EXPLORER. To fill the time, John had the ships conduct training. He had fighters flying different formations to either defend or attack the fleet. He had the fleet ships performing various battle drills. They had discovered a small planetoid and John had the Marines assaulting it or defending it while the fighters would attack it. All in an effort to maintain combat readiness and, just as importantly, combat boredom.

Paul repositioned himself in his chair to get more comfortable and began dozing off while John would occasionally stir on his own. Paul's eyes were getting heavier when his brain noticed something, and he came wide awake.

"Oi," he said, and the team at the other end of the table turned toward him, "these maps are about two years old, right? We got them when we were with EXPLORER. Has anyone considered the galactic shift?"

The Technicians looked at each other quizzically, when one of them suddenly slapped the palm of his hand to his forehead and began working at the computer furiously. He stopped and lifted his gaze to the screen and made some more adjustments. He stopped again, and turned back to the screen, and made some more adjustments. Both Paul and John watched him and the screen on the far wall, which showed the green line they had followed from Zeta Station. The Technician made some more adjustments and then pressed the enter key. Instantly there was a change to the screen and two systems moved onto the green line's path.

Both Generals leaned forward and furrowed their brows gazing intently at the screen. Two systems now showed on the green line. The Technician made another set of adjustments and a red flashing dot appeared on the green line showing the Strike Group's position. The two systems were behind them, closer to Zeta Station. Paul nodded and John stirred.

"My apologies, General," the Technician said, "we assumed the drift was accounted for all along. I guess no one realized just how old these star maps are."

BGen Roberts slammed his open palm down on the table. "All right, we got them. I know in my bones one of those two systems is our target."

Paul nodded, "Yes, I agree. How far away is the closest system to our position?"

The Technician made a few calculations, "Two weeks in hyperspace, Sir."

"All right John, finish your drills for today. Tomorrow, I want to launch for the closest of the systems?"

"Yes Sir. Should we send a ship to the farther system to scout out?" John asked.

Paul thought for a few minutes. "No. No, I don't want to separate the fleet. I want to maintain maximum firepower. I do not want to risk losing a ship on a scouting mission. The system farther away may be the correct one but we have wasted too much time looking for these guys. Let's do it right this time and maintain our fleet integrity. Prepare your teams, John. Gentlemen, thank you for the hard work. Lay in the course for the first system and let's get underway."

Both the Generals left the room as the Technicians made the adjustments and sent the coordinates to the Strike Group ships.

* * *

Baroque classical music was playing softly in the background while Kevin sat at his dinner across from his wife, MaryAnne. He was home on leave and would be returning to the station the next day. For now, though, he was enjoying a quiet night with his wife. He took a bite of his steak, wiped his mouth with his napkin, picked up his glass of Corte de Rhône red wine, and took a sip. As he was putting it down, he thought about their son, "How is Gary doing?"

She looked up at him a bit surprised and played with her mashed potatoes with her fork, "Oh, he is doing quite well."

"I gather he is enjoying himself with the US Marshal Service?"

MaryAnne glanced at him before looking down at her plate. She took a sip of her wine and a bite. Kevin looked over at her slightly puzzled.

"Well, he has transferred to the Space Marshals." She responded.

Kevin took another drink from his glass.

"I see. Is there a reason he went with them?"

She sighed, seeing there wasn't going to be any way around this. She took a bite of her potatoes and another drink.

"Gary told me they kept finding contraband from the asteroid belt. He always felt behind the criminals and decided he wanted to get in front of them, so he requested the transfer."

Kevin rubbed his chin.

"He wants to go out there to stop the piracy in our system, eh."

He picked up his butter knife and started tapping the end of the handle against the table softly. MaryAnne knew he was in deep thought and about to make some decision. Suddenly, she remembered a question she had, and thought now would be the best time to ask.

"Don't family members get to go to the station to see their families?"

Kevin stopped the tapping and slowly turned his gaze toward her and then his eyes opened up with the realization that MaryAnne had not been to the station.

"Why, yes. They are allowed to come up and spend some time with their members. We just don't have the space to house them all. That is for Lunar Base and the one on Mars."

She then got a look in her eyes while stirring her potatoes and Kevin realized the question was why not her?

"Of course. Let's arrange for you to come up."

"Tomorrow will work for me; what about you?"

He saw this question for what it was, a trap. "Why yes, that's a wonderful idea. I'll get the arrangements made tonight, while we can pack what you need."

"Oh, that. Well, I'm already packed. I went onto the station's website and read what is allowed and therefore am packed. I just need my last-minute items for tomorrow."

Kevin smiled and got up from the table. He went over to the table where his communication device was and called his Aide to make the arrangements.

CAPT Ramirez stood outside of Eleanda Designs with Ms. Linda Powell. They were watching the shuttle make its landing down the hill at the pad. The shuttle door opened and out stepped three people, two men and a woman. They watched as they made their way up the path to the doors. Ms. Powell looked excitedly at her staff. Finally, they get to meet the man that made all this happen. As Admiral Brannigan approached, CAPT Ramirez saluted him and the Admiral returned it.

"Admiral, welcome to Eleanda Designs. This is Ms. Linda Powell, the founder and owner of the company."

The Admiral shook her hand and she turned slightly to her left and with a sweeping wave of her arm to indicate her team. "Admiral, welcome. Please, I would like to introduce my team..."

"Thank you, Ms. Powell, but I don't have time to meet everyone. Please let us see the suits." He then proceeded to the doors as everyone rushed to get them open for him, his Aide, and the woman. Ms. Powell led the way down a winding ramp to a galley where there were a number of people wearing the different space suits.

The Admiral motioned for CAPT Ramirez to accompany him while he approached each person and began inspecting the suits. MaryAnne went with the Aide over to a table and started looking at some interesting items on it. After looking over each suit, the Admiral returned to the first person in a suit.

"This is the one for the Marines?"

"Yes Sir."

Keven then pointed at another person, "And this for the Soldiers?"

"Yes Sir." CAPT Ramirez answered again.

"I see. All right, I want changes made right away."

At this point, Ms. Powell's team pulled out either recording devices or pens and papers and began taking notes.

The Admiral turned toward Ms. Powell and CAPT Ramirez.

"A group of our Marines and Soldiers recently fought a pitched battle. We suffered fifty percent casualties. A key area of vulnerability were the helmets. The large number of polymers made for them to see through also made them extremely vulnerable. I want that shrunk down. Give them a heads-up display inside their helmets. Let's shrink the size of the helmets for a better fit. Also, make the Rangers and Marine armor alike. They both do breaching tactics, and it doesn't make sense to give them separate armor. I want them protected. Standardize all other armor across the Guardians. Only the fighter pilots should have something slightly different for their craft as well as the Special Forces."

Kevin walked over to the person wearing the Special Forces armor/suit. "Yes, this is more like it for them. We don't need all this for the standard Guardian, but we need better helmets, neck connectors for the assault troops, and figure out how to remove the other vulnerabilities."

He turned and looked at CAPT Ramirez directly.

"We have Major Orvin in a hospital, he was seriously injured in the battle. When he is able to leave the hospital, I want him over here to explain these vulnerabilities. Also, Colonel Clark will be returning from Plymouth Station. He will be spending some time here with you to aid in the redesign of the suits."

"Yes Sir. Will do," The Captain acknowledged.

Kevin then turned around and saw another suit he was interested in. It was a space suit with very little armor, and a rather large helmet, for the wearer to see through. Kevin walked over to it and began pointing and said, "Is this the armor for the Space Marshals?"

As Ms. Powell answered, MaryAnne stood up and turned to watch them.

"I want this suit to be discontinued. Start production so the Special Forces suit is provided to the Space Marshals as well." Kevin said.

Both the Captain and Ms. Powell looked at each other puzzled and she said, "But Admiral, the Marshals said this was good for them."

Kevin nodded, "Yes, I understand but things are changing. They will be far more independent with their own spacecraft and won't be with the military any longer. Therefore, I want them with better armor and suits to perform their missions."

"But Admiral," Ms. Powell said, "I haven't received any request for a change from them."

Kevin nodded again, "Well, don't worry about it. Since I am the one paying for their suits, they get what I want them to have, and I want them to have the same suits as our Special Forces. Any questions, Captain?"

"No Sir, we will make the change. How soon do you want the new suits?"

"Send thirty up to the Space Marshal's station immediately. They have their first ten ships now. Of course, they need to fit the first thirty Marshals appropriately, but I want them going out with these suits right away."

The Captain acknowledged the order and the Admiral began walking toward the ramp with MaryAnne and his Aide following. Ms. Powell and CAPT Ramirez followed. They made a quick farewell at the door, and the Admiral, MaryAnne and the Aide began walking toward the shuttle.

"Thank you," MaryAnne whispered to Kevin while slightly squeezing his hand.

"An error in judgment that I should have corrected a long time ago." He replied.

Kevin and MaryAnne entered the outer area of his office and noticed their old friend, Ambassador Malcolm, standing along with two men in suits. MaryAnne went over to him, and they hugged in greeting. Kevin noticed Space Marshal Devlin and a Deputy Marshal were there, along with the recently promoted, CDR Fox.

Kevin turned to his secretary and said softly, "Please have the galley send up some coffee, pastries, and hot water."

She smiled at him and replied, "Already done."

He nodded and turned toward his doors as they opened and motioned for everyone to enter. As he was walking over to the small table, Ambassador John Malcolm said, "I spoke to the Commandant earlier."

"Oh," Kevin replied.

"Yes, he was concerned that you meant what you said about separating the Galactic Marines from the US Marines."

MaryAnne had walked over to the small table, poured two cups of coffee handed them to Kevin and John. She then placed some green tea leaves into a cup and poured boiling water into it.

"What did you tell him?" Kevin asked after taking the cup and thanking his wife.

"That you did and may actually be able to do it. That startled him. Seems everything comes down to LtCol Clark for you."

As the two were speaking, MaryAnne handed the civilians a cup of coffee each and indicated they should fix it the way they desired.

She turned to Marshal Devlin and CDR Fox, handing each a cup of coffee, and asked them to fix it the way they like. Then poured herself a cup of coffee and sat down.

"John," Kevin started as he moved behind his desk, "The Chiefs of Staff have not been to space, or, at least, not from orbit, let alone to deep space, and have seen what we have faced. We need everyone like Clark who has combat experience out there. To sacrifice them out of pride or whatever, organization or personal reasons, only weakens us. I need Clark back here to start training the future Marines plus I need General Roberts back. I want to make him the first commander of the Galactic Marine Expeditionary Force. We need all of our Guardians to protect Earth."

John nodded.

MaryAnne then handed her son his cup of tea while looking up into his blazing blue eyes. He glanced at her and his gaze softened momentarily, then hardened as he turned his gaze back onto the Admiral, his father.

"There are people who don't want us going out there anymore," John continued, "But so far, they are a minority. We need better successes than the one we just had."

Kevin sighed and sat down, "Then they should never have sent us out there. But that is moot. We went, and we won't be able to hide forever. Better we establish ourselves with diplomatic and military power now, so we don't have to fight off an attack in our own solar system."

"Well, I agree. I was able to convince the Commandant to get Clark promoted and right back to you." He smiled as he turned to the two men in suits.

"Kevin," John continued, "I would like you to meet the Trade Negotiator, Johnathon Merce, and Special Legal Affairs, Mike Alsonso."

Kevin walked over shook their hands and asked, "Are the two Space Marshals, three Customs Officers, and the Immigration Officer here?"

John nodded, "Yes, they are gathering their belongings in my office area and will head over to the ship with everyone else."

"Good." Kevin responded, "So, Gentlemen, you fully understand that you will be working directly for General Burnhurt, right?"

"Well, about that, Admiral." Mr. Merce began before Ambassador Malcolm cleared his throat interrupting him.

"Mr. Merce, remember. This has already been sorted out. You shall be working for the General." John stated, then turned to Kevin with a puzzled look, "I thought he was a Colonel."

Kevin walked over to the small table and picked up a folder and handed it to CDR Fox. "This has his promotion to General in it. We figured since he is the governor out there, he best be a general officer."

Mr. Merce continued, "Yes, all right. But why do you need all of us out there?"

"Simple," Kevin said. "Zeta Station is under our military control with a military officer as governor. But it is full of civilians from other worlds. Different species with their own ways of doing things. Our military force on the station lacks the expertise for policing and trade negotiations. That is why you are going. The force isn't equipped to be a police force, and the General will have to recruit other species to assist, but we want our law enforcement methods to be in place. That is why the Marshals, customs and immigration will be there. Mr. Alsonso, we do not have any laws concerning how to govern space or interact with other species. Your primary job is to write space law defining governance and relations with others. Mr. Merce, you will ensure they are agreed upon by all parties."

Kevin then picked up another set of folders and handed them to Mr. Merce. "These outline your level of authority to make trade deals and space law agreements. Some can be made at the local level with the General's approval. While others will have to be transmitted to

Earth for ratification. The information in these folders will guide you in determining which agreements require which level of approval."

Kevin then glanced at CDR Fox and turned back to the table. He refilled his cup, picked up another folder, and handed it to CDR Fox and returned to his desk.

"Commander, you are transferred to Zeta Station with your ship and are to deliver this team there safely. Now, listen, this is important."

The CDR walked over to the desk and took the seat the Admiral motioned to. When he had sat down, the Admiral leaned forward but said in a tone so everyone in the room would be able to hear. "What I am about to iterate to you is in your orders but with more details. We haven't heard from Zeta Station or Strike Group RETRIBUTION. We don't know their status. When you jump into the area be at battle stations and ready to make an immediate jump out of there. We have programmed into your ship the IFF codes for both the station and SAG WOLFPACK. You are to establish the IFF but also establish visual and voice with General Burnhart and the WOLFPACK Commander. We have given you the challenge statements to ensure the General isn't under duress. If you can't establish communications, or find WOLFPACK's ships or the General is under duress, then you are to jump out of there at once. Understand? Jump out of there immediately. We have provided you coordinates for an emergency jump. You are not to engage any ships or attempt a rescue, but get the hell out of there, understand?"

The CDR took a moment and replied, "I understand, but Sir."

"No buts," Kevin replied. "You are to get out of there if there is no confirmed friendly contact with our people. In addition, if the station is under enemy control, jump out immediately. You need to know; they have traps for space ships. We have collected them but haven't broken them yet. They shut down all your power. You can't escape them. It is standing orders that no ship or person is taken captive. That is General Order One. We have figured out how to manually self-destruct our ships. This method we have provided you and it works. If you are caught in one of those traps, then self-destruct immediately. DO NOT let your ship or crew get taken. Self-destruct is the only option open for you, understand?"

"Yes Sir. It is that serious?"

"Indeed, it is."

The CDR looked around the room. Ambassador Malcolm nodded in the affirmative and everyone else tensed and showed concern.

The Admiral followed his gaze to each person in turn.

"Well, let's count we are still in control and LtGen Connington has taken care of the problem. Now, another point. We have provided you several hyperspace communication drones. If the station is under our control, two things: One, have the General provide a detailed report and launch it to us. Two, if you have to make an emergency jump, then at the other side, send a drone with the logs and all other information. We have already calculated how long from both positions it will take the drones to get here. If we don't hear from you for the longer timeframe, then we shall assume you are destroyed and the station has fallen. All this information and more are in your orders." Kevin motioned to the folder, "And a lot of it is already in your ship's computers." Kevin sighed and sat down, picking up his coffee and taking a sip from it while watching the recently promoted Commander.

CDR Fox slowly started nodding, then stood up. "I understand Sir. We sacrifice ourselves to keep Earth safe."

Kevin nodded, "Yes."

"No problem, Admiral. Let us trust that we are heading to friendly space."

Kevin smiled and stood up, extending his hand to the Commander. "Well, you and the others best get going." The Commander shook his hand then came to attention for a moment and turned, motioning the other two gentlemen to follow him.

John stood up. "I will go with them to say my farewells at the hangar. See you around, Kevin." He then followed the other three out.

MaryAnne brought the coffee and tea pots over, and both Kevin and the Marshal held out their cups for a refill. She asked the younger Marshal if he desired more tea. He indicated no and she took his cup and returned to the small table and sat quietly listening. Kevin motioned for the two Marshals to have a seat while he sat down behind his desk.

"Now, Marshal Devlin, what may we do for you?"

"You just ordered an officer of yours to kill himself and all his men. Really?"

Kevin sat his cup down and breathed heavily out through his nose with a grim look on his face and stared at the Marshal. After a few moments of silence, under the Admiral's stare, the Marshal shifted uncomfortably and said, "Well, I guess that is your business and none of our concern."

Kevin then picked up his coffee, taking a sip, glancing at his son sitting across the desk, staring coldly at him.

Then Marshal Devlin continued, "I would like to introduce one of our newest members to the Space Marshals, this is Deputy Marshal Gary Brooks. He just arrived and is in orientation and training for the new corvettes."

Kevin nodded, "Well, Deputy, what do you think of the ships, so far?"

The Deputy studied his father for a few moments then said, "Interesting design. Seems to handle as a fighter rather than a heavier ship. Plenty of cargo space and jail cells. But only three men." He finished up seeming disappointed.

Kevin took another drink of coffee.

"Yes, we noticed the evidence gathering the Marshal Service has to do. So, you have two types of cargo holds. One for your own supplies and ship care and one just for evidence. Your activities only require a three-man crew: The lead Marshal, plus an astrogator who is also an additional gunner, and finally a ship engineer who doubles as an additional Marshal. Also, you will be receiving thirty new space suits. A team should be arriving at your station to ensure a proper fit. I decided to eliminate the suits you have been using and to provide you with suits similar to the ones that our Special Forces use. They offer better protection in combat, plus you can go EVA and breach a ship with them. Of course, as you use them, we can make the adjustments to ensure they meet your needs as you tell us."

While the Deputy was nodding and was about to say something, Marshal Devlin said, "Indeed what makes you the one to decide our suits and even the ships we use?"

Kevin turned a cold stare onto him, "Simple, I pay for everything." After a short pause, he said, "Marshal Devlin, in the beginning perhaps it made sense for budgetary reasons to place everything into my budget but no more. Your HQ station was designed to manufacture spacecraft and it still has that capability. And you are able to service these new corvettes. Plus, you really need to be separated from the military. We are not a law enforcement agency, but you are. You need your own budget. I would prefer that. You need the freedom to make your own buy decisions and not be tied to a person like me being able to veto what you require or make alterations. Please get your own budget."

Kevin took another drink of his coffee, "anything else Gentlemen?"

Gary spoke up, "Yes Sir, there is."

Both the Admiral and Marshal looked at him.

"Well, Admiral, you are pulling these cruisers from us. I understand, you want to separate the military and the Marshals but what becomes of these ships and how does that impact us?"

He then gulped heavily when Kevin turned that cold stare upon him. He knew how his father didn't like to be questioned. But he held his father's blue eyes in his own without flinching.

Kevin sat there staring at his son's blazing blue eyes for a moment, then reached over and picked up a pen and began tapping it softly on his desk. Gary knew where this was heading but held steady. Finally, Kevin dropped his gaze, nodding and putting the pen down.

"Well, Deputy, let's look at this. The heavy cruisers that we manned for a single Marshal to be onboard to enforce the law is neither effective nor efficient. So, we designed ships to meet those requirements. Your corvettes can outmaneuver a cruiser just like a fighter can. You now have a far more maneuverable ship with range to chase down criminal craft. You can go safely where a cruiser must have full shields on just to go. But more than that. More than that, you just heard me tell a man to destroy his ship and crew to keep Earth safe. If he can't get away, he is to self-destruct. I hated giving that order. I hated signing that order. I despise it. But I have to give that type of order since I don't have control over this space, the space where Plymouth Station is located, nor Zeta Station. I don't have the combat power out there to protect our people. So, the first ten cruisers that I have taken back are heading to Alpha Centauri for upgrades and then out to Plymouth Station to protect them. That way, our planet here can have energy sources that are clean and powerful. But I need more combat ships. Soon, we will be sending approximately a one-hundred-ship fleet out into deep space to combat a mortal enemy to us and the rest of the galaxy. Currently, we have two ships in deep space. One is on an intelligence and reconnaissance mission and another to form a coalition of planets to aid in destroying the Kammorrigans, the enemy of all of us. So, I need those ships and your service needs the ships we are now providing you. Make sense?" His tone had softened while speaking to the Deputy.

"Yes, Sir," Gary started, "and the firepower on the corvettes?

"What? Well, you know you have two forward-firing adjustable lasers, a torpedo tube, and one aft laser. We haven't seen any need for any more firepower. Plus, your shield is a two-fold shield, planetary entry plus a field against criminals firing upon you. What more do you need?"

Gary nodded, "But, Admiral, we are now single law enforcement fighters without all the firepower of a cruiser, and there are only three men per ship. What if we get overwhelmed by multiple criminals, pirates or there are multiple ships, more than one ship can handle?"

Kevin stared at him and thought for a few moments. *He was right. They would be out in the solar system alone attempting to stop piracy and enforce the law. One enemy ship the Marshals could take, all cargo ships they ought to take, they could take most likely two criminal ships down. But what if there were three or more ships?*

Kevin let out a low growl from his throat and punched up his Operations Center from his communication pad. His Senior Watch Officer appeared on the screen to his left.

"Admiral?"

"Is Captain Jenkins available?"

"Yes Sir, I believe he is. I'll send him right up."

"Thank you." Kevin closed the link. He then got up and went over to the small table and refilled his cup. He then took the small tongs and placed a cheese Danish on a small plate. He put down the tongs and picked up a small fork and took the plate and coffee back to his desk.

"Marshals, would you like some pastries and a refill?" MaryAnne asked them. They both declined and she took a cheese Danish and began to eat it.

The door buzzer rang and the doors opened. CAPT Jenkins came in.

"Admiral, you desired to see me?"

"Yes, Ken, please come on in. These are Marshal Devlin and Deputy Brooks. Please coordinate with them for our Operations Centers to work out protocols for assistance."

CAPT Jenkins nodded at the two Marshals and looked back at the Admiral, "Sir, what protocols?"

"Well, they are going to be flying independent about the solar system. We need a shared Common Operating Picture or COP (he said on behalf of the Marshals) of Earth Defense Force stations and fighters and their operating areas. Should, and hopefully a very rare occurrence, they require support, they can reach out to the nearest military ship or station, preferably only the ones assigned to Earth Defense, but any military ship for assistance. They may require a fighter or even a cruiser for support, in case they are met with resistance beyond their capabilities. Can we get this done before the first corvettes head out on duty?

The Captain looked over at the two Marshals and thought for a few moments. "If we are looking at say a month, then yes. I would like to test the protocols before going live to ensure the easiest and simplest methods of communication and call signs to be effective. Would that work for you Gentlemen?"

Both Marshals looked at each other, nodded, and stood up.

Marshal Devlin said, "Captain, we can contact our Operations Center before we head over and get that working if it works for you."

The CAPT nodded and turned to the Admiral, "Anything else, Sir?" The Admiral shook his head as he stood up, "No, let's just get it done and tested before they deploy. Marshals, anything else we can do for you?"

Both men shook their heads, and the Admiral held out his hand and shook theirs in turn. The Captain indicated for them to follow him and led them out of the room.

Kevin watched them go and after the doors closed, he turned and stepped over to his port and looked out. His Mother Earth was in full view. Her brightness always stunned him. MaryAnne stepped up softly beside him and took his left hand in hers. She squeezed it as she said, "Thank you." Kevin simply slipped his hand out of hers and softly placed his arm around her shoulders as she hugged him with both arms.

CHAPTER 10

CDR Fox strode onto his bridge. He instantly noticed both the Trade Negotiator, Johnathon Merce, and Special Legal Affairs, Mike Alsonso, standing by the Astrogation station. They were looking over the Technician's shoulder while speaking with him. CDR Fox continued to his chair, shaking his head. He sighed heavily as he sat down and checked the monitors. They were approaching Zeta Station.

CDR Fox was anxious. He desired to reach the station and finish being a taxi driver. In addition to his crew, he had twenty additional Soldiers, ten Customs officers, and ten Marshals. Before he reached his ship, the Admiral instructed that these additional forces would be added to support the station. That meant his ship, the *Reaper*, would be overcrowded. He had to delay departing Alpha Centauri Station while waiting for their arrival. Now, he was almost to the station with an overcrowded ship. Also, he was transporting extra supplies and the hyperspace communication drones.

He found himself a bit annoyed by the two diplomats on his bridge. He had to grant them free access to all parts of his ship, but they seemed to enjoy themselves most on the bridge. At times, he had to speak with them about bridge operations. They routinely interrupted his crew from their duties. He could bar them from the bridge but that could be costly to him and his career. He tolerated them the best he could.

"Five minutes to normal space, Skipper," Called out the Astrogator. "Thank you," responded the CDR, "Call the ship to General Quarters. Messieurs Merce and Alsonso, please either position near the bridge hatch or depart. I need my bridge crew focused. Prepare both the Identify Friend or Foe signal and the challenge messages, Communication, make sure these are accurate and you monitor them closely. Scans, I want a total scan of the ships and their activities when we enter normal space. Tactical and Weapons, shields up, and weapons fully charged. Engineering station, ensure Engineering is ready to make an immediate jump. Astrogation, I want Helm to have those emergency coordinates now. Execute."

The bridge crew responded quickly; they could find themselves in combat before they knew it. The two civilians departed the bridge. CDR Fox relaxed a bit. He didn't want them interfering with him and his crew. His orders told him not to engage, but rather get out of Zeta Station space fast and on a course to elude any enemy and not lead them back to Earth. But he needed his systems online and the entire crew alert for any situation they may find themselves in.

'One minute to normal space," reported Astrogation.

CDR Fox sat back in his chair closing his eyes.

God, I hope all is well. He thought.

He didn't want a fight or depart. This station was important to Earth. They needed to have trade and knowledge about the people in this part of the galaxy. The hyperspace well changed shape and form just before they popped out of it and came to normal space. They still felt the sudden change in the ship's speed when coming out of hyperspace, from an exceptionally high rate of speed to a relative crawl. The klaxons sounded. The General Quarters screen continued to indicate all stations at green.

Scanners reported a ship was heading in their direction but no hostile movements in the area. The station seemed huge on the main viewer and it indicated ships traversing to and from it. The crew identified the single ship heading in their direction. Tactical reported it to have Earth configuration. Everyone breathed a sigh of relief.

"Send IFF," said CDR Fox and see if you can't get me Station Operations and CAPT Blevins." Communication was doing both soon after the CDR gave the instructions. After a few moments, the incoming ship responded to the IFF and tacked onto a course back to the Station.

"Continue at half speed," CDR Fox instructed his Helm.

"Operations, I say again, this is *USS Reaper*, I am ordered to have both audio and visual communication with Colonel Burnhart. This must happen now. Also, I want to speak with Captain Blevins. Let's make it happen." CDR Fox was saying.

"They are busy; state your business, *Reaper*," the Technician responded.

CDR Fox nodded his head.

"Operations, get me both visual and audio with Colonel Burnhart now. Weapons, prepare to launch all nuclear missiles at the station. Engineering, prepare to make the jump." The Weapons Officer was confused, they didn't have any nukes but he started pressing buttons that the station's sensors might pick up.

"What, wait! What are you doing?" The Tech cried out. "Wait a minute, don't do anything." CDR Fox could see the Technician doing something off screen. His own Communication Officer indicated another link was coming online.

A moment later his main viewer changed. It now showed an office, and a person sitting down in a chair facing him.

"This is Colonel Burnhart, who do you think you are to threaten us with nuclear devices?"

The CDR brought up an image of the Colonel on his command chair viewer and ran the face recognition pattern. Meanwhile, on another chair monitor he brought up the challenge statements.

"Colonel, thank you for responding. Weapons, deactivate the attack for now. Colonel, I have been sent to deliver personnel and supplies to you. Also, to augment your defense. Oh yes, sorry to inform you that your dog ate the canary. I trust all is well."

The Colonel frowned with confusion. CDR Fox waited. After a moment, the Colonel straightened up and clicked something on his desk. He then nodded his head with a slight smile and turned back to the viewer. "Yes, my dog is known to eat canaries. Further, the dogs are keeping all cats away. Some appeared but they took care of them."

CDR Fox visibly sighed his relief, "Thank you, Colonel. As said, we have equipment and personnel. Request permission to dock to transfer them over. Also, I need to speak with both you and Captain Blevins. We need to perform a ceremony before all the staff and alien representatives. This will have to be done before I take up my duties with the Captain."

The Colonel seemed confused. "Ok, I'll have Operations bring you into a docking position and get things started. See you shortly, Commander. Burnhart out."

They closed the links.

As *Reaper* approached the station, the Communications Officer informed the station of the personnel and supplied the equipment list. A berth was made ready near the station commander's office for them. Meanwhile, a message was sent to Captain Blevins that he must report to the station commander's office immediately. Upon receipt of the message, his ship began to head to the station for berthing, so he could meet the Colonel.

Meanwhile, CDR Fox turned his bridge over to his Exec and went to his quarters. He changed into a full-dress uniform and strapped on his Colt .45 1911 pistol. He had an eight-round magazine which was loaded with hydro shock rounds. He ensured one was in the chamber and eight in the magazine. The weapon was meant to be ceremonial but out here all weapons were to be loaded. While he was doing this the two civilians, the lead Deputy Marshal, Immigration Officer, and Customs Officer were notified of a formal setting and to be ready for it. CDR Fox met them at the airlock after his ship had docked. The civilians were in their best business suits and the others were in their dress uniforms.

A Lieutenant met the party at the airlock and motioned them to follow him. He told them the Colonel was in his office and Captain Blevins would be joining them shortly. After a short discussion with him, the Lt called for a sergeant to escort the new personnel to administration for station registration and berthing. He then called the Supply Officer to organize a party to receive the supplies and hyperdrive communication drones from the *Reaper*. The Lt gave a brief rundown on the station layout to the new arrivals as they moved toward the area where the Colonel's office was located. It didn't take long for them to arrive since their ship's berthing was near this area.

The Colonel's office area had an outer room. In this room were several seating items and a desk with a Staff Sergeant behind it. The Lieutenant handed them off and returned to his duties. The SSgt nodded and depressed a key, informing the Colonel of the new arrivals. After the party heard for them to wait till Captain Blevin's arrival, they took the seats suited for humans.

Upon Captain Blevins' arrival, CDR Fox stood up and came to attention. The Captain came over and greeted him. Seeing the CDR in his Dress Blues interested the Captain and made him wonder about the nature of the visit. The Staff Sergeant immediately notified the Colonel and ushered them into the Col's office.

"Good afternoon, Gentlemen, how may we help you?" Inquired the Colonel.

"Good afternoon, Colonel. I am CDR Fox, commander of the light cruiser, *USS Reaper.* May I introduce Mr. Merce and Mr. Alsonso? Also, Deputy Marshal Fredericks, Customs Officer Ray and Immigration Officer Delvin." Started CDR Fox.

The Colonel came around his desk and shook each person's hand as the Commander introduced them. Afterwards, the Colonel returned to his desk and remained standing as CDR Fox continued.

"Sir, my ship and I are assigned to you presumably under Captain Blevins' command. Each of these gentlemen are assigned to Zeta Station. Messiers Merce and Alsonso are from the Space Diplomatic Corps and are assigned to you to assist with trade negotiations and developing space law matters here. The other officers are law enforcement with additional personnel to assist with the various law enforcement matters at the station. I also have your new orders." At this point, the CDR handed a package to the Colonel and continued.

"Sir, you are to be promoted immediately to Major General and made governor over this entire region. This will include political, diplomatic, and military jurisdiction over the area. Presumably, LtGen Connington has yet to arrive but when he does, he will fall under your Governor jurisdiction while he is here. You will find in the packet your new position with all the authorities granted to you by the World Senate, which is a new organization on Earth, plus the US Senate confirmation. The President has provided you with instructions along with Admiral Brannigan. With Captain Blevins here, he is to promote you, Sir. Plus, we have a sash for you along with other implements of your new office. You will find in the instruction this is to be a public ceremony to be conducted at once," CDR Fox briefed.

The Colonel had a stunned look on his face. Captain Blevins chuckled and then burst into laughter.

"Well, well, wouldn't you know it. Come out here and bam, you be the man." He continued to laugh while the whole situation sunk into the Colonel's mind.

"Ok, yeah, it's real funny." The Colonel responded shaking his head and taking his seat. He then pressed his call button and asked for the Staff Sergeant to gather his officers and to notify any of the alien officials that may be on the station to the level below the Administration level. The area he desired to meet them used to be the slave trade area. The Colonel had been busy turning this into quarters for a future and yet undetermined nature.

"Sir," continued the CDR, "Mr. Merce will assist you with inviting diplomats from the other worlds to the station so we can perform trade talks and perhaps even more."

Mr. Merce stepped forward to begin speaking, but the CDR touched his arm lightly indicating he should remain still for now. The Colonel had opened the packet which contained three sets of stars, two for his collar and one for a head cover. It also had a disk that the Colonel took and slid into a disk reader, and turned to his monitor. He indicated everyone should take seats. Captain Blevins excused himself in order to change into his Dress Blues for the ceremony and indicated for the CDR to follow him.

Kulabat of the Boorakus glided along the ramp on his four legs. His body was completely encased in a suit of armor that contained his breathing apparatus. Two of his four arms rested on one of his utility belts as the other two held a device. He was reading an invitation by the Humans to attend a ceremony, though it read like an order for him to be there. He didn't understand why. He couldn't remember how long he had been on the station; it had been so long. He only knew there had been several masters, with the Humans being the latest. All of the holders of the station had internal security but few of them ever had ships in orbit about the station. The Humans now had four with some additional ships out there flying around. As he read, he shook his head, the Humans had defeated the old masters twice since they had taken the station. He wondered how long they would hold it before someone else took it away from them.

The Humans were quick to free all the slaves and had been reconstructing the slave section into quarters for other than human occupancy. He wondered about this but not much. He did find it strange how the Humans seemed to despise slavery. Having them was useful. Kulabat even found it helpful to have his slaves, but the Humans made him free them. Only one stayed with him, but the others fled to their far away homes. Again, he shook his head, now he had to pay the former slave a wage. At least it didn't break him; in fact, he was able to save money since the former slave now had to pay its own way. He chuckled to himself.

As Kulabat rounded the last turn onto the level that was still undergoing refurbishment, he noticed several Human Soldiers standing around. They were in a loose formation but ready to tighten it up. He also noticed a ship captain from Ealianai. He waved at him as he turned to view the center area of the space. The Humans had erected a low stage. On it, were three flags. The middle one was on a stand slightly taller than the other two. It had a flag with a blue field and fifty stars with red and white stripes. The one to the right of it had a blue field with a yellow sun, two plant things along each side, and a red lightning bolt going across the sun. It had some writing on it. The flag to the other side had a darker blue field with the center having a blue globe with lines. An open circle went around the blue globe and there was a silver three-pointed star. To the upper left of the blue globe was a star with smaller stars to the left and right of the globe. It also had writing on it.

Kulabat asked one of the Soldiers what the writing said. He told him on the flag with the yellow sun the words said "Diplomacy through Strength." The other flag had "United States Space Force" with a Roman number for two thousand nineteen, the year that Space Force was founded. Kulabat thanked him and went to stand with the other inhabitants or visitors to the station who were arriving. He was about to speak with them when an official party of Humans came into the room and the Soldiers were called to attention. All went silent.

Six Humans strode into the room and climbed the short steps onto the stage. Kulabat recognized Colonel Burnhart at once. He also identified Captain Blevins, who commanded the Human ships in orbit about the station. One Human he had seen around before, went to the opposite end of the stage holding a book, which he opened when he reached his spot. The three other Humans he didn't recognize. One was dressed like the Captain but instead of four gold stripes on the sleeves of his blue uniform, he only had three. The other two Humans were dressed similar to each other but completely different from the other Humans. The new officer carried something folded up. Colonel Burnhart wore blue pants with a yellow stripe running down each leg. He had a dark blue coat on with various devices on both sides of his chest and epaulettes with the strange device that Kulabat had learned meant his military rank. All the military on the stage and off wore weapons on belts around their waist.

The Human with the book began reading orders which promoted the Colonel and designated him as the Governor of the station and the surrounding space. After the reading of the orders, Captain Blevins approached the Colonel and removed the two devices from the epaulettes, and replaced them with two silver stars, one set of two stars on one epaulette and one set of two stars on the other. Then the new officer approached and the new Major General Burnhart lifted his left arm as the new officer placed a blue sash with gold trim over his head and arm. Once the sash was in place, the new officer straightened it. Then everyone saluted him and he returned it. He cast his gaze around the room and approached the front of the stage.

"Gentlemen and Soldiers, visitors and residents of Zeta Station. My government has promoted me to Governor of this space." He then motioned to the two Humans that were dressed differently. "They have provided me with these two gentlemen as experts in Law and International Trade. It is our fervent hope that we can establish trade relations with each of your nations. We will be setting up appointments with your respective representatives that are currently here and send invitations to your home worlds for ambassadors to come here. As you know, we don't allow slavery on our world. Thus, we are refurbishing this section of the station to house ambassadors. We have destroyed all the cages and started building quarters. The specific design of each one will depend on your home world's requirements for your ambassadors. I look forward to meeting them and engaging in productive talks for trade relations. Thank you for attending this ceremony."

He then scanned the room and departed the stage with the official party following him. Once they had left the room, the Soldiers were dismissed.

Kulabat stood there and thought, *They are serious. They actually think they will hold this station and govern here.* He couldn't believe it. *No one since the great fall has ever been able to do this for long. What makes them different?* He glided out of the space to his quarters. *I guess I need to try and contact my old planet and see if they are interested,* he thought. He wondered if he remembered how to make contact.

CHAPTER 11

The Strike Group came out of hyperspace near the system. They tightened up their formation to provide interlocking fire and readied their fighters for deployment. All the ships had begun scanning the system as they slowly moved toward it.

"I think we ought to send a ship ahead to see what we can see," BGen Roberts said to LtGen Connington as he stood by the command chair. Paul just leaned forward looking at the view screens.

"Scanners, what can you tell us about the system?" Paul called out.

After a few moments, the Technician replied, "It is a yellow star, approximately twice the size of our own. Detecting three planets and an asteroid field between us and the outer planet." She then made some adjustments to the sensors, "Normal background radiation but nothing on the electromagnetics to indicate any stations or alien presence. Will continue scanning for more information."

Paul sat back in his chair. "Thank you. No, John, I want to keep the Strike Group together. Let's not weaken ourselves. Besides, we have probes that we can recover." John nodded in agreement. BGen Roberts stepped over to another technician at another set of controls.

"Ready four probes. Send one to each planet for survey, especially for technologically advanced stations or civilizations. Send the fourth to comb through the asteroid belt looking for stations and, if possible, any readings on the rocks."

The Tech confirmed the orders and started programming four probes. After a few minutes, the probes were launched and streaked off to their respective assignments.

John approached Paul. "Well, now we wait. Do you want to stay here or begin moving into the system?"

Paul was sitting looking at his own monitors along with the ones around the bridge.

"Helm, begin moving us toward the outer planet, but at one-quarter speed." He then turned to John. "I want to survey this system quickly but let's give the probes some time in case we stumble onto an unforeseen situation."

John looked at him. "You don't think they are here, do you?"

Paul slowly shook his head, "No, I don't, but I don't want to overlook anything either. Might as well put us at yellow alert but maintain General Quarters."

"Yes Sir."

A week later the Strike Group was on the other side of the system. Only one planet appeared habitable. The other two could barely support human life. The asteroid belt had a variety of minerals which a colony could utilize. The civilization they were seeking was not here nor any others. They logged the system in their computers so future exploration may occur for a possible Earth colony.

The Strike Group moved into jump position.

BGen Roberts called out for the ships to prepare for jump. The Communications Officer sent the message to the other ships as klaxons sounded on the *USS Hood*. John approached the command chair where Paul sat.

"We will be ready within a minute, General," John said. Paul nodded.

"The Astrogators inform me it will be a month in hyperspace to reach the other system."

Paul simply closed his eyes and thought, A*nother month!*

"I only hope Colonel Burnhart is ok at the space station and we are not too late," he replied.

John nodded his agreement, "I wish we could move faster. The *Cyane* will be pushing her engines hard to get us there in a month. That is the best speed we can make."

Paul grimaced, "Will she be able to maintain speed without any damage? We need to be ready for a fight when we come out of hyperspace."

"Col Smith assures me they will be able to fight when we come out. I consulted with our own engineers and they agree with her."

"All right John, let's get moving. The sooner we get there the sooner we can do our job."

John acknowledged and moved off to give the order for the jump.

The Strike Group emerged from hyperspace one month later. Their sensors picked up a blue star in the distance. They were a day out from the system. It was too far away for detail scanning. LtGen Connington wanted them at a safe distance to ensure all his ships were combat ready. They began their system checks ensuring they would be ready. In a few hours, each ship captain would report their status to the Strike Group Commander. Paul left the bridge to go to his flag office to wait for the reports.

Two hours later BGen Roberts depressed the ring button then opened the hatch and entered. Paul was sitting at his desk with a cup of coffee along with a thermos and another cup. He motioned for John to take a seat and get a cup. John poured himself a cup and sat down.

"Well John, are we ready?"

"Yes Sir. All ships report combat ready and, yes, even the *Cyane*."

Paul fixed a steady gaze upon him.

"I confirmed with Col Smith about her status. She said they can jump if need be and have full maneuverability. Her reactors are undamaged and fully operational. She did admit she needs to make minor repairs to the hyperdrive though. She stated she can move with the fleet and make the repairs at the same time; the issues are minor."

Paul shook his head and then smiled and took a drink of coffee.

"Ok, let's start slow to ensure she gets the time she needs. There are no issues with the other ships?"

"No Sir. We are combat ready for this phase."

"Ok, John. You can move the fleet forward. I want our formation tight. The *Hood* will be the lead ship with *Chesapeake* on our starboard flank. *Levant* will be behind us on a Z positive axis with *Cyane* to her port side as escort. Finally, have *Vengeance* coming up behind. Let's keep the fighters berthed but have a ready fifteen in the tubes. When we find the people, we are seeking, we will change our formation for a planetary assault."

John took notes.

"Since we are so far out and will be starting slowly, should we send in some probes and recon ships? Try to get a handle on what we will be facing?"

Paul brought up some information on his computer screens, thinking about this option. He finally sat back and turned to John.

"I like the element of surprise that we currently have and yet we are going in blind. Doesn't that eliminate our surprise since we have no intelligence on this system?" He asked John.

"Yes Sir, it does. I would like to get intelligence on this area and maybe even find them before we enter the system. Our recon pilots will be able to move smoothly and covertly. The probes would be the issue, but they are small and quick. We could most likely have them make passes at points which would make them undetectable. The other factor is the star. It is a blue star, and the scientists are telling me that may mess with our eyes, plus the sensors will have to be adjusted for it."

Paul frowned, "Really? I guess I didn't realize that would make a difference."

John nodded and took a sip of his coffee, "Apparently, so having the data from the probes would help us with the fine tuning of our sensors, especially the targeting sensors and the fighters. Besides, we may be able to find the planet or station the civilization we are seeking inhabits. We would then have the opportunity to maneuver right to them before detection."

Paul nodded, "Yes, I like that. Ok, let's do it. Any idea how many planets yet?"

"We think there are five planets. One seems to be a gas giant with some moons."

"Ok, have *Hood* and *Levant* launch their recon ships supported by how many probes you think they will need. We will hold the fleet here for now. How soon can you get them launched?"

John smiled, "Within fifteen minutes Sir. I had all the ships prepped already. The probes will take a little longer, but we are programming them now. We will have to add the added parameters before we can launch them. I expect they ought to pass the five ships well ahead of them reaching the system."

Paul smiled, "Good. Thank you."

John smiled, put down his cup, got up, and left the office to ensure all would occur as planned.

Five days later, the recon ships and probes had returned. Paul had decided not to move any closer after he had agreed to the reconnaissance mission. For four days, they had remained at their jump point, which enabled the ships to make any repairs and prepare to enter the system. When the recon teams returned, Paul gave them time to clean up, eat something, and get some rest while the scientists poured over the readings. Six hours later, he sat in the conference room with BGen Roberts, each of the ships' commanders, his Flight Commander, the Deputy Commander of the Landing Force, a couple of his scientists, and the recon pilots.

"Your report Gentlemen," John said.

First Lt Gavin stated, "We found them, Sir. The ships we saw match the configurations and signals of the ships from Zeta Station. They are here."

Paul drummed the table with both hands and smiled at John who winked at him and turned back to the Lt, "Did they detect your ships?"

"I can't say with certainty but we don't believe so. We just don't know enough of their capabilities to know for sure, but we did use every form of covert flying as possible to avoid detection."

LtGen Connington glanced around the table, then at BGen Roberts, "Ok, this is good news. John, let's do this right. Let's start with the system and then close in on our target."

John nodded, "All right, let's bring the system up on the screen. Dr. Montgomery and Lt Gavin, you are the main briefers. Take us through the system and highlight how we can use them. Also, those ship traps at Zeta Station, make sure you mark any of those that you may have found." Both men nodded and stood next to the screen.

The lights in the conference room dimmed as the main screen came to life. It showed the blue star system from the Strike Group's vantage. The image of the system rotated to give an overview for the attendance. Then it began to move into the system. As the viewer zoomed in, the first planet came into view. It was obvious to everyone that it was a giant gas planet.

Dr. Montgomery began, "Gentlemen, this is a blue star system with five planets in orbit about it. Four of the planets are on our side of the sun with the fifth one on the far side. I'll start with the farthest planet from the sun. This first planet is a large gas planet with four moons orbiting it. One moon is like our own Europa, a watery-icy surface with no real atmosphere. It can't hold one. The second moon is similar to our Io, which is full of volcanic activity. The third moon is just a big rock in space. The last moon is similar to Earth in appearance, it has land and water masses but with an atmosphere that is poisonous to humans."

He then made an adjustment and the screen showed another planet. He continued, "This is the second planet and is also a gas planet but smaller in scale to its brother. It has two moons. The first is an icy shell that seems to have a salt ocean covering the planet with no atmosphere. The second moon is also in essence a rock in space. When I say a rock, it is a moon with no atmosphere; heavily pitted but no real magnetic presence to them like a planet has."

Dr. Montgomery made another adjustment, and the screen showed another planet, "This third planet can be compared to our Mars. Very similar light atmosphere, dusty and desert like, no moons."

He then made another adjustment and a fourth planet zoomed into view, "This one is similar to our Venus with one moon. The planet has a thick atmosphere, and our instruments showed higher temperatures than our own Venus. The moon is Earth like, similar to the one orbiting the giant gas planet."

He then made another adjustment, and the screen zoomed past the sun and showed the fifth planet, "this planet is similar to Earth but also has an atmosphere that is non-inhabitable by humans. The system lacks an asteroid belt but there are stray asteroids in the system and evidence of strikes on the rockier like moons and the Mars like planet. It seems the home world of the people we are seeking is the Earth like moon around the giant gas planet. Lt Gavin will continue with the briefing." He then moved to the console to adjust the screen for the Lt. Meanwhile, the Lt took his place by the screen.

Lt Gavin began, "Gentlemen, we found three bases in addition to their home planet. The primary base appears to be on the moon around the Venus style planet with a slightly smaller base on the ice moon of the smaller gas planet. Finally, a third and smaller base is on the Mars like planet. Their civilization appears to be on the Earth like moon orbiting the giant gas planet. What is strange is there isn't a space station of any kind orbiting the moon planet, yet there is traffic between the planet and the bases." He took a drink of water and continued, "In orbit above the primary station at the Venus like planet," Dr. Montgomery adjusted the console and the viewer zoomed to it. "There is a space station that houses fifteen ships which match the ships that attacked us at Zeta Station. The secondary base has a station with five ships. None in orbit around the third base. We did find a huge array between the Venus and smaller gas planet. This appears to be the method they have communicated with Zeta Station. We did not find any ship traps in the system. Also, the Earth like planet does not appear to have a colony on it. Which seems strange to all of us who looked at this planet. The two space stations with the docked ships do not appear to have any defensive weapons on them, though they may have shields. We did detect planetary defense systems on their three bases with some on their home moon. We believe we can over power these defensive systems. I think their strength is in those ships. We have more technical details on the stations and ships, but that is all for this portion of the briefing pending any questions."

LtGen Connington looked around the table at his ships' commanders and his staff. They either were looking at the view screen or down at their pads. Each member of the staff was viewing the area of their expertise. He then turned to BGen Roberts.

"John, we need an attack plan. Our primary target has to be the station with the fifteen ships with the other station as the secondary target. I don't want to damage that array at this time. We need to tap into it to figure out how it works. Plus, we need to know how they can travel so fast. At this distance from Zeta Station, it should take quite some time, yet these ships showed up fast, too fast. Perhaps the array can tell us how. It looks like the leadership is on that moon." He sat back thinking while BGen Roberts was taking notes along with his Operations Officer.

Paul sighed, "Our mission is to neutralize this threat to Earth and Zeta Station. We know they are slavers. My orders say I can use diplomatic means. I am authorized to destroy them without even saying a word. That is how much of a threat this civilization is to us. John, give me three courses of action. You can use the rest of this day. I will see you in the morning. Everyone, get to work."

He stood up and left the room as John ordered everyone to attention, then had them sit back down. He gave them instructions on how to divide up the work on three different courses of action and how to develop them. He then gave deadlines to brief him prior to briefing the Commander. Once he was satisfied the teams understood the instructions, he departed the room and headed for the bridge.

It was afternoon the following day. BGen Roberts sat in front of LtGen Connington's desk. They both had a cup of coffee. Paul had the courses of action on his desk screen while John sipped his coffee. John then said, "As you see, they came up with four. Our scientists are studying the tactical readouts on those ships. All the red teaming and the computer battle simulations show we lose. There is no way we can handle fifteen or all twenty ships. We also don't know how many may be deployed elsewhere that they can call back. The best simulation shows we take out twelve of their ships before we are destroyed."

Paul frowned, "Damn. We have been sent out here with the best ships to destroy this threat and everything points to the fact we don't have the firepower."

John responded after refilling his cup. "We need a totally different approach." He then lit up with an idea. "Hey, instead of talking to them first, what if we neutralize or destroy the ships first? Then we can try diplomacy or just blow them to hell."

Paul slowly nodded. "I am thinking the same way. But if we are wrong, we could start a war with a race that could devastate our planet."

"Only if they find our planet. Every commander knows to blow their ship to pieces to avoid capture in order to protect that information."

"Yes, let's get that reinforced no matter what. That is a priority."

John acknowledged the order. Paul thought some more.

"We have the specific coordinates of the two space stations, right?" Paul asked.

"Yes Sir."

"Hmm, perhaps." Paul reached over and flipped his communication switch to the conference room. "Ops, this is the Commander, come to my office at once." He flipped the switch off when the officer replied in the affirmative.

"You have a thought?" John asked.

"Yes, very similar to yours. I want it red teamed and battle simulated. I want you to oversee the simulations yourself. Let me know how it plays out."

"Yes Sir."

He slumped in his chair with his three eyes nearly closed from sleep. He rested his head against the headrest at his watch station. It was a slow night at the station. All was quiet and no one was around. It was always hard to stay awake, even during the watch at this time of night. His head nodded to his right when the proximity alarm went off. His eyes opened wide, but he was still confused since he just woke up. He quickly rubbed all three eyes to clear them to see what was happening. He touched a switch, and the view screen illuminated to show an alien ship nearby. He saw the trail of multiple missiles heading toward the station. He was blown to smithereens before he could reach the switch to raise the station's shields.

Paul sat in his command chair as they emerged from hyperspace. The *USS Hood* and *USS Chesapeake* had jumped to coordinates near the primary space dock with fifteen ships. When they exited the well, the two ships raised their shields, and the *Hood* launched two nuclear missiles right into the station. Both ships launched four other missiles in addition to the nuclear ones ensuring the enemy ships were destroyed before either shields or alarms could be raised. At the same time, the *Vengeance* jumped near the secondary station and launched a nuclear missile and two hypersonic ones into the station, totally obliterating it along with its five docked ships.

Paul watched as the primary station separated into two pieces, both of which were on fire after the mid-section of the station disappeared into the nuclear cloud. Ten of the ships had just disappeared and the other five had multiple hull breaches with fire and gases escaping from them. The readings showed they were combat ineffective. The station itself was dead in space, with only radiation escaping from it as the two remaining sections floated off in a degrading orbit about the planet.

When the other ships attacked the two space stations, both the *Levant* and *Cyane* jumped to the moon orbiting the giant gas planet which was identified as the center of the civilization. They took up blocking positions to prevent any ships from departing the moon. Once, Colonel Holmes of the *Vengeance* ensured his ship had destroyed the secondary station, he ordered them to move off onto a rendezvous heading with the *Hood* toward the civilization's primary moon. After ensuring the station and its ships were destroyed, the *Hood* and *Chesapeake* moved off toward the primary moon. While they were traveling to the moon, they were joined by the *Vengeance*. Now, they would see if the civilization surrendered or if they would have to destroy it.

The Strike Group had formed a blockade around the moon. They had already destroyed two ships that tried to leave the moon's surface. LtGen Paul Connington, commander of the Strike Group, sat in his command chair. He was wearing an all-black uniform with black boots. His three stars lined both sides of his collar. He was relaxed in his chair with his arms resting on the chair's arms. He stared coldly at the figure on the main viewing screen while keeping an eye on his tactical display. It was the leader of the civilization they came to neutralize. It had three eyes, two on top with a third between and slightly below them. It was covered in blackish brown fur. Below the third eye was a slit for a nose and below it a mouth. The leader of this civilization glared with hatred at Paul.

"Why this unprovoked attack?" The creature mouthed, showing teeth made for an herbivore. The translator picked up the noise and translated it into English. The Leader continued, "You better remove yourselves, surrender or die."

Paul checked the tactical, all was still clear.

"Unprovoked? You need to recall how your ships attacked our exploration fleet a few years ago at a trade station. You trapped a ship and tried to take us as slaves. You recently have attacked our forces on said station. No, you attacked us, and we are now on a punitive mission to ensure no more attacks."

Its right eye along with the lower one blinked followed by the left eye. He looked down at something and then back at Paul.

"Ah, you are the Humans who took our trade station. How dare you!"

Paul shook his head.

The creature continued, "You will regret this. We shall destroy you and take your planet's information. We shall enjoy raiding your planet and enslaving your race. In fact, our new ally will pay us handsomely when we share its location with them."

Paul smiled grimly, "Truly. And who is your new ally?"

Now the creature smiled, fully showing its teeth, "Why the Kammorrigans, of course."

Paul slowly nodded. "I understand. Too bad for you."

A klaxon sounded at that moment. The Tactical Watch Officer checked his screens, turned to Paul, and announced, "Six of their warships have jumped into the area and are heading toward us, General."

Paul nodded while frowning and looked at the creature on his viewscreen who was smiling broadly.

"Now, Human, you die." The creature clicked off its screen.

Paul checked the tactical and saw how they were formed.

"Form up the fleet around us and prepare for attack. Launch the fighters. General Roberts, prepare to launch a ground assault."

Everyone on the bridge went to work to execute the order. Within moments, the Strike Group broke the blockade formation and formed up tightly around the *Hood,* ensuring their weapons would support each other.

The *Vengeance* took up position to the port flank of the *Hood* while the *Chesapeake* took the starboard flank. The *Levant* was aft of the

Hood by several kilometers, while the *Cyane* took positions to the *Levant's* starboard flank. The *Hood* with the two heavy cruisers could interlock their laser fire, establishing a one hundred eighty-degree arc of fire. The fighters when launched would remain in between the ships till they had a target presented to them. Marines began filling the transports onboard the *Levant* for a ground assault.

The enemy ships had formed two three-ship wings. The lead wing was heading directly for the *Hood* followed by the second which was on a slightly Z negative path. All ships were the same size with the same firepower. All of them had shields up. The *Hood's* Tactical Watch Officer was scanning all ships while preparing the lasers and missiles.

"General," he called out, "I estimate their firepower to be equal to *Vengeance* and *Chesapeake*. We should be able to overwhelm their shields."

Paul nodded. "Helm, have the formation move to meet the lead enemy ships. I want some distance between us and the moon in case we need to maneuver."

The Helm Officer acknowledged the order and sent the signal to the other ships' helmsmen to make the move. The two fleets moved to meet each other.

Paul was surprised when *Levant* reported a hit on their aft shields. Everyone on the *Hood's* bridge began checking sensors when they noticed a planetary gun was firing on the *Levant* again.

"General Roberts, send the Marines to take out those planetary guns and provide them fighters for support."

Paul had brought out the two personal screens normally stowed in his command chair. He was staring at the one on the right, which had Col Johnathon Williams, commander of the *Levant*, on it. He kept an eye on the other screen, which had the ships' readiness reports, especially their weapons status.

"What do you mean you can't launch the Marines?" Paul asked.

"General, if we open the hangar doors, we are vulnerable to that planet gun. If we are able to get the Marines launched, that gun can target and kill the transports and drop ships. We can't do it. Either we stay with the group or we have to move to drop the Marines."

Paul sat back in his chair and closed his eyes momentarily. The enemy fleet was closing in on them and the battlewagon and two cruisers were moving to meet them. He opened his eyes to speak with the Col.

"Jonathan, we need the *Levant* in this fight, but we need to take out that gun. I need those Marines on the ground."

Jonathan nodded, "But Sir, I can't do it here."

Paul glanced around the bridge seeking BGen Roberts. He found him standing at his station working through a problem, probably the same one. Finally, the Marine turned toward Paul, who motioned for him to join him at the command chair. As BGen Roberts strode over, Paul breathed, "Damn." Then a bit louder, said, "Jonathan, stay on the line. John is coming over."

As BGen Roberts approached the chair he said, "Sir, we can't launch the Marines at this point. Either or both them and the *Levant* will be destroyed or taken out of commission."

Paul started to get red in the face before he exhaled and calmed himself.

"Suggestions. Do we run? Do we take the enemy fleet on without launching the Marines?" He asked.

Col Williams spoke, "Sir, let us reposition away from the planetary gun and drop the Marines. Then Jeanine and I can join the fight. Send fighters to cover the Marines."

BGen Roberts thought for a few moments. "I agree, Paul. Let the *Levant* move to an angle where that gun is useless. We can't afford to avoid this fight. If we run, they will pursue, and it gives the enemy the operational tempo and a big morale boost. If we move as a group to drop the Marines, then those ships can target our transports. Let the *Hood* and heavy cruisers engage them. Have *Levant* move, drop, then join us. The *Cyane* can take a blocking position between the *Levant* and the enemy to protect them. Then both can join us, or one can provide cover fire for the ground troops."

Paul looked down at his screen. "Well, Jonathan, that is what you desire, yes?"

"Yes Sir. I like the thought of Jeanine and her crew providing cover for us while we disembark the Marines. Then I can join you in the fight."

Paul nodded slowly and then a little faster as he made up his mind. "All right, do it. John, make sure the Marines have enough fighter support. They are primary until on the ground."

"Yes Sir," responded BGen Roberts, "but they will require close air support while on the ground. We have enough to do both."

"Agreed, let's execute," Paul said as the BGen moved off to make the arrangements with the Flight Commander and his Marines. Col Williams acknowledged the order, and they closed the link.

General Connington ordered the entire group to maneuver in a manner which allowed the moon's rotation to take them out of the planetary guns range. The *Levant* increased her speed to get ahead of the rest of the group with the *Cyane* matching her; while ensuring she stayed between the *Hood* and the *Levant*. To everyone's surprise, the enemy fleet was allowing them to make this maneuver, but continued to close on the battlewagon and two cruisers. Paul shook his head and gave a closed mouth grin.

What idiots, he thought.

The best option, for the enemy, was to keep the Strike Group between them and the planet guns. Now, the Strike Group's flanks were no longer at risk.

General Roberts and the Flight Commander worked with the *Levant* to launch their ten fighters, all piloted by Marines. They would provide cover for the assault transports as they made their way to the primary city on the moon, which had the planetary guns. Bravo Squadron; a five-ship formation, would continue to escort the transports to the ground and provide close air support. Alpha Squadron would remain in orbit to either lend support to the ground or join the space fight as required.

During the Strike Group's maneuver to their new position, the *Hood* launched her twenty fighters to provide a screen between the two fleets. This seemed to confuse the enemy and their two formations began to break up. The moment the planetary guns appeared to have rotated out of firing range, Paul ordered the *Hood* and the two cruisers to attack. The fighters broke into four squadrons, five each, two heading to the port side of the group and two heading to the starboard side. They would provide cover against any enemy fighters or close with the enemy ships; firing at their shield and weapon emitters.

The two fleets were closing in on each other. "Tactical, when we get in effective range, I want *Vengeance* and *Chesapeake* to focus their main lasers on the lead ship with their secondary lasers hitting the flanking ships. Hold our guns until we see the effects."

"Yes Sir," the Tactical Watch Officer responded.

A few minutes later, *Vengeance* and *Chesapeake* unleashed their fire upon the three lead ships. Instantly, the enemy ships' shields lit up with the impact of all the lasers hitting them. The lead formation focused their entire firepower on the *Chesapeake*. Her shields took the heat of the lasers effectively and began dissipating the energy around her shields. Colonel Meyers contacted the *Hood*.

"General, our shields are taking a beating here. Those three ships have locked onto us with all of their guns. I need assistance if we are going to hold them."

Paul responded, "I see it, Joe. How long can they hold?"

"We calculate fifteen minutes before we lose the shields," Colonel Meyers responded.

"Ok, prepare for shield merging. Shield control," General Connington called out to the officer in charge of shields. "Have all ships begin merging our shields. I want to have that energy reflected to our combined shielding. Helm, continue to have the fleet close with the enemy fleet. Tactical, prepare to bring *Hood*'s main batteries to bear on the lead ship."

Everyone acknowledged the orders and began sending orders and instructions through their boards to their counterparts on the other ships along with those in the *Hood*.

"Helm," Paul called out, "I want to keep their lead formation between us and their other formation. I don't want them getting an angle on any of our ships. Have the formation maneuver to maintain the block on the other three ships." The Helmsman acknowledged and sent the instructions to the other ships. The Strike Group's three ships, as if one ship, maneuvered to a Z positive to their starboard ensuring the first enemy formation was between them and the enemy's second formation. Both the *Levant* and *Cyane*'s positions kept them from this fight as they maneuvered to land the Marines onto the moon.

The Tactical Watch Officer called out, "Sir, I have the firing solution on the main ship. Waiting for your orders, Sir."

"Fire and maintain till we penetrate their shields then hit them with missiles," the General responded.

The *Hood*'s main three laser turrets turned and locked onto the lead enemy ship. Simultaneously the lasers fired. It was like a shockwave hit the enemy ship. Not only did their shields instantly light up from the energy, but the ship rocked back onto its keel from the impact of the guns. The *Hood* kept the fire up. Within seconds, the enemy shields turned to a rainbow of colors from the energy released by the *Hood*'s guns.

"How long before those shields are gone?" Paul called out.

"Estimate within thirty minutes Sir," the Tactical Watch Officer responded.

"Ok, have *Vengeance* intensify her fire on the lead ship."

Major Montgomery, the Combat Landing Force commander, had prepared the Marines onboard the *Levant* with a very specific landing craft load out. The crews of the ten-landing craft included two pilots, one of which managed the craft's only gun, and a loadmaster. Each craft could carry twenty passengers. Major Montgomery loaded each landing craft with twenty Marines, eight of which had projectile weapons, eight with power weapons, two would handle a sixty-millimeter mortar, and two would carry explosives, torches and a small carbine. He further had a command-and-control ship readied with himself and a group of Marines and Sailors to handle communications and medical support on the ground. The Major realized he required a quick reaction force. He requested the *Levant's* five transports and another command-and-control ship be readied. The QRF would be commanded by his XO, Captain Levine. They would remain in orbit with Alpha Squadron protecting them in case they were needed on the ground.

Captain Luis Chavis, Bravo Squadron commander, had his ships fly to the underside of the *Levant* to pick up the ten-landing craft as they exited the ship. As Bravo Squadron departed the other fighters to perform escort duties, General Roberts ordered the other squadrons to form a screening line between them and the enemy fleet to protect the landing force from enemy fire. Capt Chavis ordered the landing force to proceed to the planet in a single line with a fighter in front of two landing craft each. He ensured the spacing between the escorted landing craft was five kilometers in case they took fire from the moon. His fighter would lead the first group which included the command-and-control ship and two landing craft.

"Bravo One, this is Bravo Five, I don't see any enemy fighters approaching us." the last fighter escort called to Captain Chavis.

"Bravo Five, nothing is coming at us from the moon, except the planetary fire, which is aimed at the fleet. So, just keep your two escorts behind you and maintain the flight path."

"Yes Sir."

As the landing force approached the moon's atmosphere, Capt Chavis keyed his comm system, "All ships prepare to engage your heat shields as we enter the atmosphere. My group will go first. All landing craft energize your guns to repel any enemy ships. Let's hope they don't have any smaller anti-aircraft guns."

As Capt Chavis' ship started to touch the atmosphere; he and his escorted group, energized their heat shields. The shields lit up with a strange orange color but did the job, allowing the ships to enter the atmosphere without burning up. They proceeded to the planetary gun on the western side of the city. As they approached, their sensors identified the generator that was supplying energy to the gun.

Major Montgomery keyed his comm system on the command-and-control ship to the entire group. "Bravo Squadron, please provide top cover for us. Landing craft, I want you to land two craft each at the points of the compass and deploy the Marines. Landing force, form a perimeter around the identified generator structure as briefed. I want the remaining two landing craft to land on opposite sides of the structure, and find the doors. I want you to enter the structure as soon as possible to blow the generator. My ship shall land in between the two generator landers."

Each landing craft acknowledged the orders. Capt Chavis gave his orders to the squadron to provide cover for the Marines.

As they descended, heading for the emplacement on the western side of the city, Capt Chavis thought, *"How strange, no anti-aircraft guns or enemy fighters."*

He keyed his comm system, "Bravo Squadron, this is Bravo One, anything on your scopes to an enemy presence?"

Each member of Bravo Squadron reported their scopes were all clear.

He then switched to the transport channel, "Thunder One, this is Bravo One, we are not encountering any resistance. Your landing should go without any hindrance. Though I can't predict what the ground will be like."

"Roger, Bravo One."

As they made their approach, the landing force and their escorts broke off with ships heading to the compass north, south, east, and west to make their landing. As the landing craft touched down, the escort fighters would lift up and make a formation where they could provide top cover. Once, the landing crafts touched ground, the Load Master opened the hatch, and the Marines deployed. They formed a three hundred sixty-degree circle about the generator building. Their deployment alternated a power weapon and a projectile weapon. The two Marines on mortar duty formed up behind every eighth Marine. While the two with explosives took up positions behind the mortar team. The remaining two landing craft circled the building once, identifying possible entry points and landed next to them, deploying their Marines to assault the doors. The command-and-control ship landed in between the structure and the perimeter.

"Thunder One, this is Bravo One. You have a large force approaching you from the southeast. They appear well armed." Major Montgomery acknowledged the information and passed the word to his Marines. Meanwhile, Capt Chavis sent three fighters toward the group to begin strafing runs to thin them out.

Within minutes the three fighters made their first run, killing several of the creatures. As they began to circle back the creatures split up and started moving in between the buildings, causing the fighters to either break formation or limit their runs. When Major Montogomery received the enemy's disposition, he weakened his northwest perimeter by half and sent them to reinforce the area that would take the brunt of the assault.

Meanwhile, the two teams designated to enter the generator structure had successfully cut their way through the two entrances and began moving in. Each team sent ten Marines with projectile and power weapons into the structure. They were followed by the two Marines with explosives. The remaining Marines held the doors with the two mortar teams setting up to support the perimeter. The Major, ordered four additional Marines with explosives to support them.

"Bravo One, this is Bravo Three. Seeing how we can't make effective strafing runs, why not peel off a couple of fighters to hit the other generators? My sensors are clear of any enemy fighters."

Capt Chavis, at first was annoyed by the Second Lieutenant's communication but started thinking about the recommendation. He keyed his comm system.

"Thunder One, this is Bravo One. Unless you object, I'm going to send two fighters to hit another generator structure to see if we can't speed this up."

"Good idea, Bravo," Major Montgomery responded. He liked the idea since he wondered how they were going to fight their way through this mess to each emplacement. "Please execute that plan."

Meanwhile, he ordered the landing craft to aim their guns at the approaching enemy.

"Bravo Two and Three, peel off and hit the northern gun's generator. See if you can't blow that thing apart." Capt Chavis ordered.

The enemy forces cleared the remaining buildings and began running at the Marine perimeter. They were larger than the humans but bipedal. Each creature was hairy and had three eyes. They had powered weapons and some form of armor. They were attempting to form lines as they headed for the Marines. The three remaining Marine fighters, swooped down upon them with a strafing run to keep them from forming their lines.

Meanwhile, three landing craft began firing their single guns at the enemy to keep them from forming. Major Montgomery watched as the enemy was being pelted by the fighters and landing craft. His mortar Marines were anxiously watching him, waiting for the signal to fire. He smiled at them through his helmet and keyed his system. "Everyone stay calm, breathe, and hold your fire. Let's see how they can hold up against our fighters. We just have to buy time to set the charges and then reload the landing craft and get clear. I want to conserve our mortar rounds till we actually require them."

All the ground Marines began to breathe normally and started to calm down. The Marines on the southeast side of the perimeter were still a bit nervous. Some of them had actually begun to fog up their helmets till they remembered to switch on their defoggers and breathe normally.

The two teams that had entered the structure had met with very little resistance, which they easily dispatched. They met up with each other in what appeared to be a control room.

"Now what?" asked a corporal. The Gunnery Sergeant growled, "Split up and find the actual generators and set the charges." He then keyed his comm system, "Thunder One, this is Boom Boom, we are in what appears to be a control room. We are now seeking the actual generators. Resistance was minimal and eliminated."

"Boom Boom, let's not dither about. We are under assault out here," Major Montogomery responded. The Gunny acknowledged the order and barked to his Marines, "find the generators, now!"

Meanwhile, the two fighters reached the northern gun's generator. It was still firing shots into space as they approached. Bravo Two took the lead and dropped a missile onto the structure blowing a hole through its top and Bravo Three dropped his missile through the hole. As the two fighters climbed there were explosions inside the structure. The gun went dead.

"Bravo One, this is Bravo Two. It worked; the northern gun is silenced. We are moving to the eastern gun emplacement now." Capt Chavis acknowledged the order and relayed the success to Major Montgomery.

"Fire the mortars," Major Montgomery ordered. The enemy forces were forming into smaller groups and began advancing. The landing craft began to target each group as the fighters continued to strafe the forces that were just clearing the buildings. Three mortars fired rounds at different points along the field. As the enemy cleared a hundred-meter spot the Major ordered his Marines to open fire with their projectile weapons but had his powered weapons hold fire till the enemy was within thirty meters.

The enemy fire was erratic while the Marines were disciplined. Nevertheless, several of the Marines were being hit. At first, the Marines' armor was handling the hits, but soon several pieces started to give out and the landing force started taking casualties. Despite this, the Marines held their position and wreaked havoc among the enemy. After several minutes, the enemy gave way and retreated back into the buildings. Major Montgomery started moving his wounded Marines onto a landing craft. At the same time, he started swapping Marines from the southeast side with Marines from the northern side of the perimeter. He wanted to preserve their suits as long as possible.

He was very happy to hear the two explosions in the distance and see the guns go silent. At least he wasn't going to have to assault each emplacement. Meanwhile, the Marines inside the structure had found the actual generators and set their charges. They were on their way back when a missile struck the landing craft with his wounded Marines, totally obliterating it.

"Where the hell did that come from?" Capt Chavis cried out over his comm system.

"Smoke, smoke, everyone take cover," Bravo Four called out over the landing force channel.

Another missile had come in but missed all targets and exploded in a nearby building.

"Bravo Four, where did it come from?" Capt Chavis asked.

"Bravo One, it came from the southwest. My scanners don't seem to be picking up anything though."

"Copy that. Bravo Two and Three, get back here at once. Thunder One, do you have your charges set yet?"

"Bravo One, yes and my teams are heading back out."

"Then load your landing craft and let's get the hell out of here. Bravo Four and Five head southwest and take out those launchers. I'll stay here to provide cover. Bravo Two and Three approach from the southeast and strafe anything that moves. Form up on me soonest."

Everyone acknowledged the orders.

Two fighters moved off fast toward the southwest to find the launchers while the other two fighters formed up from the southern gun and began making for the landing area. Meanwhile, Marines were boarding the landing craft, some taking extra Marines. When the hatches were closed, they lifted off immediately. Better to be a moving target in the air rather than a sitting one on the ground. As each craft lifted into the air, they would move to the northeast side of the gun emplacement to put it between them and the missile launchers.

The Strike Group continued their starboard maneuver ensuring the landing ships were in their shadows and hidden from the enemy fleet lasers. As the landing force increased their distance from the two fleets, the Strike Group increased its rotation attempting to place the enemy ships between themselves and the planetary guns. As they continued the rotation the planetary guns had ceased to be a threat.

Meanwhile, the lead ship of the first wing had traded places with the ship to its starboard flank before their shields failed, successfully transferring the Strike Group's combined fire onto the new ship. Instantly, its shields lit up from the fire intensity. Meanwhile, all six of the enemy ships' lasers were engaging the combined shields. The Strike Group combined shields began to change to rainbow colors with the enemy ships' combined lasers at full power locked onto it.

BGen Roberts approached General Connington's chair.

"Sir, this is taking too long. I believe we need to finish this."

Paul glanced at him and looked back at the main screens, "I agree. We could take them one on one, which may be better than being stuck in a bubble. I like their maneuver of swapping ships on us."

Both Generals took in all the information on the various bridge screens.

BGen Roberts looked at Paul with a furrowed brow, "Aren't shields just energy at a certain frequency?"

Paul turned a steady gaze on him, "Why yes, they are."

Paul sat straight up in his chair and stared at the shield station's monitors taking in both their and the enemy ships' shield statuses.

"Shield station," he called out, "are you able to calculate their shield frequencies? And Tactical, can't you adjust our lasers to those frequencies?"

Both officers began running calculations rather than answering the General's questions. They hadn't thought of those actions and knew they better have a good answer.

Meanwhile, BGen Roberts strode over to the shield station.

Tactical sounded off first, "Sir, we can adjust the laser frequencies but it appears we would drop their intensity until it could build back up. But it appears it would penetrate the shields if we have the correct frequencies. To be sure, though, I need to ask the engineers and scientists we have onboard."

BGen Roberts answered, "We don't have time for that type of analysis son."

The Shield Officer spoke, "Sir, we have not thought about that tactic but I have asked scanning to program in the ability to identify the frequencies. They are working on it and we should get something in a few minutes."

Paul rubbed his chin. "Scanning station, are you able to comply with Shield's request, and how fast?"

The Scanner's main officer spoke, "We are working on it, Sir. We may be able to identify it but it will take us a few minutes. We haven't tried this before."

Paul growled deep in his throat and sat back in his chair. He then keyed up his system and called Colonel Williams.

"Yes Sir," Colonel Williams responded as he came on. The General was using his personal systems again.

"Jonathan, I need you in this fight. How soon before you can get the Marines off?"

The Colonel checked something then turned back to the monitor. "Sir, the landing craft are away. We are now offloading transports with a Marine quick reaction force. When they clear, we will be able to join you."

Paul nodded, "Ok, make it quick, then you and *Cyane* get over here quickly. Make your approach where you can hit that second formation." Colonel Williams acknowledged the order, and they closed the link.

Secondary Scanners yelled out, "Sir, two ships from the second wing have broken off."

BGen Roberts calmly walked over to him and placed a hand on his shoulder and whispered something in his ear as Paul took in both the screen showing all six ships and the tactical monitor. He then frowned while pressing his lips tightly.

"Comms, get the *Chesapeake* and *Levant* after them. And yes, I know they have to leave the bubble. Shields, recalibrate our shields. General Roberts, have two fighter squads go after them. Maybe they can slow them down till the others can catch them."

The screens lit up as one of the enemy ships in the first formation lost their shields and the lasers slammed into its hull. The enemy ship began listing to its starboard as the *Vengeance's* Tactical officer fired three missiles into it, causing the explosion. The remaining three enemy ships formed up into a new three ship formation and swung to their starboard side.

"What are those three ships trying to do?" Inquired the Helmsman.

Main Scanning Officer yelped, "Sir, the *Cyane* is dead in space. She doesn't appear to be damaged just no energy readings."

Paul stood up, saying in a loud voice, "Damn, somehow, they have deployed their EMP net. How did it get through the shields? Never mind, intensify all fire onto those three ships and fire missiles. Get me those damn shield frequencies, NOW!" He ordered.

Both the *Hood's* and *Vengeance's* internal lights started to flicker but their engineering departments caught it in enough time to mitigate the situation and maintain their power systems.

BGen Roberts again approached Gen Connington, who was still standing.

"Well, no question about it now. These are the creatures we were sent out to find."

Paul just nodded and watched the screens.

BGen Roberts noticed his board flashing at his station and moved quickly over to it.

When he got there, he placed his headphones on and flipped the switch.

"Bulldog, this is Bravo One."

The General answered, "Send it, Bravo One."

"Sir, we cannot stay on the planetary surface. We lost a landing craft filled with wounded Marines after we had taken out their planetary guns. The artillery pieces came out of nowhere. We missed them till they had fired. We neutralized those guns; however, I believe they were underground and were brought out after we had beaten back the surface attacks. All Marines are in the air moving to another location, but I believe nowhere on this surface is safe. I think they have an underground network of structures and additional firepower hidden there. My squadron's weapons are spent. We only have close rounds and no missiles. Request we return to the ships."

The General thought for a second, "Request denied, Bravo. We are still in a fight and can't afford to offer you protection from the ships. You will either have to land where you think it is relatively safe or place the moon between you and us. Meanwhile, I'm sending Alpha Squadron to back you up."

"Acknowledged Sir. But Alpha Squadron is protecting the quick reaction force in orbit. I recommend they stay in orbit since we don't need any more targets down here. Over."

"Acknowledge, then I'll send a different squadron to back you up, over."

"Acknowledge, Sir, Bravo out."

The General keyed another set of switches and sent a squadron of five fighters from the *Hood* to back up Bravo Squadron. He then went over to General Connington and reported the situation.

Paul keyed his comms for the Flight Commander, "Colonel Holmes, have your remaining fighters attack the remaining three enemy ships." She acknowledged his orders and after a couple of minutes, ten fighters formed up two V wing formations. One attacked the starboard flank enemy ship and one the port enemy ship.

The *Chesapeake* moved off to pursue the two enemy ships. Colonel Meyers chose a wide path that would take his ship away from the main battle but on a rendezvous path with the *Levant*. He had already started coordinating with Colonel Williams on the track so they could form up and meet the enemy ships together.

BGen Roberts turned to Paul, "I wonder why they haven't fired another EMP net?"

Paul stared hard at him for several moments. "I wonder," he said and moved over to his Helmsman, checked his board, and then looked up at the tactical monitor. He then turned around toward BGen Roberts, "I wonder if they have to be at a certain distance." He then turned back to his Helmsman, "Move us closer to the ship on their port, Comms have *Vengeance* swing around to our starboard flank. Tactical when we get that ship between us and the other two fire all lasers on it along with *Vengeance*. And Helm, keep us at this distance or closer. Shield frequency yet, anyone?"

Everyone acknowledged and began either acting on the orders or coordinating with the *Vengeance*. Meanwhile, both the Scanning and Shield sections were working frantically to discover the enemy shield frequencies.

The two ships caught the enemy ships off guard with the speed of the maneuver. They had swung around and closed the distance on the port flank ship blocking the fire from the other two ships. Between the two ships' firepower, its shields were down within five minutes with missiles slamming into it. The remaining enemy ships had attempted to match the maneuver but were not capable of the same maneuver speed. As the fireball of their fleet mate began to dissipate, missiles began to impact the lead ship's shields. The shield blinked for several moments then gave out. Several more missiles piled into it. Meanwhile, five of the fighters penetrated the starboard ship's shields and were raking fire along its hull. They had taken two lasers out when the second ship listed into it with gases expelling from its gaping holes, propelling it into the remaining ship. The Strike Group fighters kicked their ships into high gear to get out of range of any explosions as the two ships collided.

Both the *Hood* and *Vengeance* came over the lead ship in a Z positive move and raked both hulls with their lasers ensuring they were utterly destroyed. After scanning all hulls, the two ships moved away from them. The *Vengeance* moved toward the *Cyane* to assist her crew and make repairs to her power systems. The *Hood* began to make orbit to pick up the landing force and her escorts after which time she would form up with the *Vengeance* in a blocking formation over the main population center on the moon.

The two enemy ships that had broken formation and moved out were outpacing both the *Chesapeake* and *Levant*. Colonel Joe Meyers was watching as the two ships put more distance between them. He thought, *These ships didn't seem that fast but, in this case, they were not making any maneuvers, they were heading toward some destination and in a hurry. They have yet to make a jump, so,* he thought, *they must be pulling power from their hyper drive and other systems to garner this much speed.* He sat in his chair wondering where they must be off to.

"Helm, they are still putting distance between us?"

"Yes Sir," she responded.

Joe sat back in his chair. *Levant is able to stay with us,* he thought.

"All right Helm, max power to the ion drive and have *Levant* do the same. I'm not concerned about the fighters, have them catch up at their best speed."

The Helmsman acknowledged the order as she called for more speed from the engine room and sent corresponding orders to *Levant*.

"Charlie One, this is Charlie Three. Are they leaving us?" The pilot called over.

"Charlie Squadron, this is Charlie One. The enemy ships are pulling away and our ships are going to full speed to catch them. We are ordered to follow their transponder signal at a speed in which we can still fight. If the enemy ships make a jump, then our ships will return for us. So, just follow them at the speed I set. Charlie One out." He shook his head after he clicked his transmitter off as he listened to the chatter between the four other pilots.

"Hey, Colonel Meyers, this is John Williams. I think I know where They are heading." Col Johnathon Williams, commander of the *Levant* called over to the commander of the *Chesapeake*.

"Yeah, me too John. I bet they are heading for that large antenna. Either to call for backup or do something which will deny us the use of that thing. We best get there before them. Ok, let's redline the reactors to get there." Joe then spoke to his Helmsman, "Captain, push the ship to redline." He then keyed for his Chief Engineer to alert him of his decision.

Forty-four minutes later, both the *Chesapeake* and *Levant* came into view of the antenna. The two enemy ships were already there and were firing all their lasers and what missiles or torpedoes they had into the antenna. There were fires along the entire structure. Both of the commanders had their command communication between them open.

"Wow, look at that will you," Col Meyers said.

"Yep, they are really tearing that thing to pieces and we are still ten minutes out at this speed. They must have pulled power from every system they had to get there this far ahead of us."

"I don't think the boss is going to be happy about this."

"That is an understatement, Joe." Jonathan sighed heavily, "Well, let's get these bastards before they know we are here." He looked up and said in a louder voice, "Helm, shave the time off and get us there now. Tactical, I want a firing solution on the ship closest to us." He then ensured his Helmsman and Colonel Meyers could hear him, "Bring us in on a Z positive arc, and before they can react let's hit them hard."

Both ships pushed their engines well past the redline pulling power from non-essential systems as they came in the arc that Colonel Williams desired. The enemy ships had not scanned their presence yet and still had their shields down.

The *Chesapeake* hit the first ship with all her lasers and tore gaping holes in its hull. She immediately began venting gases and listing to her port, being propelled on a Z negative axis while the *Chesapeake* continued to pour her fire upon her. During the approach, it was decided the *Levant* would travel above both ships and hit the other ship before she could raise her shields. Which *Levant* did while firing four missiles into the second enemy ship which erupted into a ball of fire. Col Williams had targeted two missiles into the presumed engine compartment and the other two along the hull where he thought the bridge and a laser reactor may be. He might have been correct from the way the ship exploded into a ball of gas and fire.

Both *Chesapeake* and *Levant* moved away from the destroyed enemy ships and began scanning the antenna. As both commanders had feared, the antenna seemed completely out of commission. Col Meyers sent two transports to an area that appeared to be the control center of the structure in an attempt to determine if there was any way to salvage the systems. Meanwhile, both ships' Chief Engineers began making repairs on their ion drives. They reported they needed a day to make them operational enough to rejoin the fleet. Meanwhile, Colonel Williams sent a message to General Connington informing him of their condition along with the antenna. He then had a signal sent to the fighters for them to continue traveling toward them.

Paul sat in his command chair staring at the weird three eye creature's face that filled his main viewing screen. He slightly shook his head at this thing which was still being defiant despite the loss of its fleet.

"Your fleet is destroyed; will you not surrender?" Paul asked.

The creature bared its teeth as it closed its lower eye. It then opened it as it closed its two upper eyes.

"Come and take it, Human. We already drove off your assault force. You will never be able to take our planet!"

Paul continued to stare at the creature with both sadness and disappointment. It didn't know it wasn't defeated just like Saddam Hussein didn't know it in the first Gulf War of the nineteen nineties. But it had a point. Paul's assault force was driven off the moon's surface. While the two watched each other, Paul had that queasy feeling growing in his stomach. Is this how ADM Brannigan felt at Kammorriga when he nuked the planet? A very human feeling washed over him as he was deciding this moon's fate along with every form of life on it.

Oh well, he said to himself. *After all these creatures made an alliance with the Kammorrigans which means they have to die.*

LtGen Connington keyed his Communications Officer who after seeing the message on his board, turned off the audio but left the visual of the creature on the view screen. He then motioned to the General it was done. Paul nodded and pressed a button for his personal monitors to swing aside as he stood up from his chair and took two small steps forward. He stood with his legs shoulder width apart and his fist on his hips. He kept watching the creature on the screen.

"Weapons Officer, Shield Officer, and all hands prepare the planet killing rails for launch. Nuclear control, prepare four hydrogen missiles for launch. Targeting, target every major population center and any industrial sites on this moon."

The bridge became a swirl of activities as his orders were being carried out. Signals were sent to the *Vengeance* to ensure they also prepared a battery of weapons.

Tactical confirmed there were no other ships.

The bridge crew could hear the armorers loading the guns with the iron and nickel rods which measured a hundred yards in length into the tubes, readying them for launch.

The Helmsman plotted an orbit, which both the Weapons and Targeting Officers provided him with for targets to strike.

The view screen to the right of the main viewer had been reprogrammed to show the preparations of all systems. Paul maintained eye contact with the creature on the main viewer but was able to see each system turn green in its turn.

When all showed green, the Weapons Officer announced, "Ready to fire, Sir."

Paul nodded.

"Fire the rails and hold on the nuclear. Fire now!"

"Aye, Aye Sir." Weapons Officer said as he pressed the button launching the first rail. The Helmsman then started the *Hood* on its orbital path.

The Creature's eyes went wide and started yelling something. No one on the bridge could hear it; however, the Communications Officer recorded what it was saying for playback later.

Within a minute the rail had hit the center of the government center of the moon and a mushroom cloud formed over the entire region. The main view screen went blank. It then was re programmed to show the moon and the mushroom cloud from the rail hitting the surface. The design of the rail didn't just hit the surface; rather, it bore into the surface in a manner that would eventually reach the core of the moon.

Paul turned to his right and gazed at BGen Roberts for a few seconds then took his seat.

The entire bridge watched as they moved in its orbit coming to each target area in turn and sending a rail to the surface and the responding mushroom cloud appearing. The hydrogen missiles were deactivated and secured back in their storage areas.

After the orbit, scanners were reporting large amounts of debris entering the atmosphere and blotting out any sunlight that could reach the surface. The few scientists that were aboard were analyzing the data and shortly informed the bridge that a nuclear winter had settled on the moon. It would be years before the debris would settle back to the surface. Meanwhile, they saw lava flow from the moon and several volcanoes were erupting. The Chief Scientist informed LtGen Connington that he had effectively killed the moon, and everything on it and several miles below the surface was either dead or would be soon.

Paul just sat in his chair feeling numb.

After two days, the *Hood* had traversed the system to the second of two gas planets having the *Levant* join her after she had recovered all the Marine landing craft, transports, and fighters. This gas planet had two moons, one that was rocky with an ammonia-based atmosphere, the other an ice moon. On the ice moon, the creatures had two colonies. The first was a city like area but the second was an industrial based colony. It had a mining capability drawing the moon's resources to several factory-like facilities and a space yard. Paul launched a rail onto the colony and one on the industrial site. His last rail, he launched against a fault line near the industrial site, shattering the ice planet's surface, and enabling lava flows to erupt along several fissures. The scientists informed him that a nuclear winter had taken hold of this moon rendering it uninhabitable.

The two ships then traveled to the last base which was on a Mars like planet. It was small compared to the other bases. As they were arriving their scanners picked up several ships departing the base. Paul had his fighters launched to destroy them while ordering the *Levant* to launch her rail against the base. Within an hour they were able to destroy all the transports that were leaving and watched as a red mushroom cloud covered an entire region of the planet.

* * *

The two Generals sat in Paul's office. Each had a glass of whiskey. Paul sat in his chair, holding his glass with a blank stare. John took a sip of the whiskey watching his boss and friend.

"Those were the orders, Paul."

Paul stirred.

"Yes, they were. But I never expected to feel such an emptiness knowing I ordered the destruction of an entire species. I have taken human life in combat before. Flying against other pilots, shooting them down. When they were out of weapons though, they would depart and our rules of engagement informed us to let them go. But this…this is different. We were ordered to and I did order a genocide on a species. A hostile species intent on enslaving our planet, yes but still an intelligent and sentient species."

John nodded his appreciation of the situation.

"Sadly, they didn't see they were defeated and I do agree with their leader. They did drive us off their home. Imagine Paul if we tried to force them into a surrender how many casualties we could have suffered."

Paul agreed. "Well, it is done. Do you think we got all of them, John?"

"I don't know but both the *Chesapeake* and *Levant* are visiting all five planets to ensure we did. Though their home planet is nothing but a dust ball. Meanwhile, they are seeing if there are any space stations we have missed. As we are approaching *Cyane*, I'm having *Vengeance* join the survey to ensure we got all of them. Of course, we don't have a clue where they may have any other stations or facilities. Colonel Meyers reports his teams are still at the antennae, but so far, they can't find anything to tell us if there are any more of them and where they could be."

Paul took a sip of the whiskey and said, "The *Cyane*, what is her condition?"

"Bad. The engineers aren't sure if they can get her repaired. Whatever they hit her with has done a job. Hell, not even those traps we encountered during our first trip out destroyed systems, they just neutralized a ship. But this tech really did a number on the ship. Thankfully, the crew wasn't hurt."

Paul took another sip of his whiskey.

"Ok" he sighed, "we will transfer the crew to the *Hood*. We will see if we can't get her repaired, if not then we will destroy her. We can't leave anything behind to give the Kammorrigans or anyone else a hint where Earth is."

John nodded.

"What have they found at the antennae?" Paul asked.

John shook his head, "damn little, I'm afraid. The teams are scouring everything. These creatures destroyed too much of it before our forces got there. They are now focusing on anything that might aid us with transmitting over vast distances. That is perhaps the only thing they have found. The energy source, command and control, were all destroyed. Databanks gone. No usable information."

"All right," Paul responded, "I want you to transfer to *Levant*, pick up those teams and take both *Levant* and *Vengeance* back to the space station. Colonel Burnhart may need your help. Get back there as soon as possible. I'll remain here with the *Chesapeake* and see if we can't get *Cyane* operational. If we can't, we'll destroy her and join you as fast as we can. If all is ok at the station then we get to head home."

John stood up to depart and said, "Yes Sir. I'll get on it right away," he then departed the office.

Paul sat there staring into the glass of whiskey. The remorse was returning and while this bothered him it also reassured him of his humanity.

CHAPTER 12

MaryAnne rolled over onto her right side and reached out with her left hand. All she felt was a cold sheet where Kevin ought to be. She stirred and opened her eyes. The room was still dark with only a little light coming in from the port hole. She blinked her eyes as she shifted her gaze to it and could see Kevin's frame outlined in the port hole.

"Dreams again Love?" She asked.

She could see Kevin turn his head to his left.

"Yes."

"The same dream?"

"Sorta, but now with something new. Now, I see John's cold dead eyes looking at me and asking why?" He dropped his head into his left hand, and she could hear him sigh. He had told her how his Aide had stepped in front of Kammorrigan fire aimed at him and saved his life but at the cost of his own. Kevin had ensured a memorial was set up for all those he had lost during EXPLORER's mission but especially for those who had lost their lives on Kammorriga.

Kevin turned and was walking over to a table when he told the computer to provide a low soft light to the room. The computer turned on the light at a brightness that was enough to see but not full strength. She could see her husband was still unclothed. He touched a call button and ordered up some coffee, fruit and pastries for them both. He then moved toward the shower.

"I have to get ready. Colonel Clark will be here soon and I need to discuss with him his future." He said as he stepped into the bathroom.

MaryAnne sat up and fixed her pillows and leaned into them. *Damn, he is still good* she said to herself and then let out a soft laugh.

Colonel Clark, recently promoted from LtCol, stepped into the office and immediately came to attention when he saw the Admiral was just inside. Kevin smiled at him and held out his hand, "It is good to see you, Jack."

The Colonel took his hand and replied, "Same here, Sir."

The Admiral then took him by the arm and led him to a small table with coffee, pastries and files.

"Have you eaten?" The Admiral asked as he pointed to a chair.

"Yes Sir"

"Well, have some coffee," the Admiral said while he poured two cups and handed one to the Colonel and took the other seat. The Colonel took the cup and then added a little milk to it.

"How bad is it, Sir?" The Colonel said. "The orders were quite curt that I received at Plymouth Station. I was told the Commandant wanted my head on a pike."

Kevin just stared at him. Damn, he was proud of this Marine. Took on the difficult jobs and after hearing this nonsense was facing this straight on in a no-nonsense approach.

"Yes, the Commandant wanted you not only fired but up on charges. But we convinced him to back down. However, there is penance to be done."

Jack nodded his head and took a sip of the coffee. Kevin watched him.

"Right. What options do I have?"

Kevin smiled. "Accept your fate," then chuckled.

Jack stared blankly at him.

"Oh, you have several options but I have it worked out. First, I want you to get to Earth and join CAPT Ramirez at Eleanda Designs, our contractor for our space suits. I have ordered a redesign of the basic suits for all Marines, Soldiers, Sailors, hell everyone who is now really a Guardian. Your experience out there is vital for these redesigns. I want those suit vulnerabilities eliminated. Make them standard. Then CAPT Ramirez will be given the go-ahead for Special Forces suits to be redesigned also. I expect this to be done within two weeks. After that, you can have leave. Next, you will go to Mars and be the Deputy Commander of the advanced training academy. You will review the entire training curriculum and make all necessary changes to the entire training program. Let's ensure we don't have the same casualty rates that you suffered out there. The next Galactic Marines must accomplish the missions without the losses. We can't afford it."

Jack nodded. "Yes Sir. I agree. I shall get this done and improve our odds." He was glad this was the penance and not what he was hearing on the transport back to Earth. But after that what would be his fate?

"Do well in these two areas Jack. I have further plans for you and BGen Roberts when he gets back. You two are now my most experienced Marine officers."

"Have you heard from the General Sir?"

Kevin shook his head. "No. Nothing from the Strike Group at all but I have faith in both Generals Connington and Roberts. They will be back."

They chatted for almost an hour concerning the mission and everything that LIBERATOR had gone through. Kevin was astonished at times over what he heard about the pirates, which the reports could not cover. Yes, he was definitely proud of this Marine.

* * *

Mike O'Shea sat in the conference room with Magos and Thunder. Mike had his coffee and the two Wooxuna had their drinks. It smelled like sweet water to Mike and had a creamy appearance to it. They were enjoying their drinks.

Mike asked, "You two have family?"

Thunder looked at him with a quizzical look. Magos finished his drink.

"We have mates, if that is what you are asking." Thunder responded, "But family is our three Wooxuna unit and then our extended family is the entire unit."

"Yes, and when it is time, we will join our mate and produce a family from our union," Magos continued, "When that occurs, both mates will be taken off the active list to raise them."

"Interesting," Mike said, "so how do you decide what to be when you grow up?"

Both of the Wooxunas made a noise that Mike knew was them chuckling.

"We don't," Magos responded, "We have a clan system. I come from the warrior class and Thunder from the ranger class. We have the technical class along with a government, priest, and great thinkers, among others. It was the great thinkers who came up with the strategy of three Wooxuna units after the Kammorrigans appeared. At times, a great thinker does appear among the various classes. That is why we are taken off the active list to raise them and see if one emerges."

"Your planet, I assume, has different terrain features and ecosystems?" Mike inquired.

"Yes," replied Thunder, "Magos here comes from a mountainous zone and I from rolling hills. Very pleasant in a lot of ways."

Mike took another sip of his coffee while the other two poured more of their drink.

A tone sounded, and Mike keyed the communications system.

"Mr. Ambassador, a ship just came out of hyperspace and is headed this way. We are sending the feed to your viewer."

Mike thanked him and keyed up his viewer. The two Wooxunas turned toward the viewer as the bridge kept magnifying the image till it was clear on the viewer.

"That is one of our ships," Thunder said, "we have been anticipating one to come and pick us up. We will have to report to our leadership before we head on."

Mike nodded and keyed the comm system again, relaying the information to the bridge. The bridge sent a signal to the incoming ship and received one back. They made docking arrangements.

An hour later, the *Diplomat's* commander, Colonel Jennifer Nelson, entered the room with another Wooxuna. This one had cinnamon red hair, unlike the other two, who were fawn in color. His marking followed the top part of his body, giving way to white socks and underbelly. The red coloring covered his ears and went between his brown eyes, giving way to a white face with a black nose. While Magos and Thunder's tails went over their back and were fluffy, this one was thick fur and smooth, but the tail curled upwards. He was much smaller than Magos and Thunder. The new Wooxuna went to the other two, who stood up and greeted him. They spoke in their own language for a few moments.

Magos turned to Mike and Col Nelson, "This is Sol, our new technician. He has arrived in our new ship and, as suspected with orders for us to return to our lead group. There, we are to report on you and what we have learned."

Sol made a gesture to the two Humans which they knew was a greeting.

Thunder continued, "He has a set of coordinates for you to go to. Once our leadership have their discussion, we may provide you an escort to the meeting you have requested. If they decide not to, then they will send word to the Alia who may escort you then."

"I see," Mike said while nodding.

"Colonel, how much longer are we to be in this space?" Mike asked the Commander.

They had been sitting in this area of space for seven days. This was one of the programmed rendezvous locations for them to meet with the *Sabachi* to share any intelligence they had gathered.

She checked her wrist device, "Five days, then we are to get out of here."

The three Wooxuna discussed this briefly among themselves. Sol shook his head and seemed a bit concerned.

"What is it?" asked the Colonel.

"Just that we are at a point that touches Kammorrigan controlled space. You could be discovered."

"I see," she said, "Well that can't be helped since we…" she closed her mouth and tightened her lips. The Wooxunas looked at her and Mike.

Mike responded, "There is an Earth ship out here and this is one of the places we are to rendezvous with it. We just can't tell you anything about the ship or its mission."

Magos let out a chuckling sound.

"You have an intelligence ship out here. No problem. We do that all the time. Ok, we will set your departure date five days from now. We have seen your hyperspace speed and will calculate that into our report for a rendezvous with you at the coordinates that Sol has provided. Well, that is it. Thunder let's gather our belongings. Ambassador, Colonel, till we meet again."

The two Humans shook the three Wooxunas' paws/hands and the three went to the quarters provided, gathered their belongings and within thirty minutes were on their ship. Fifteen minutes later, the Wooxuna craft was moving away from the *Diplomat* and when it reached a safe distance entered hyperspace.

Two days later, the night crew Communications Officer alerted the bridge Watch Officer of a transmission. The Capt looked up at the main viewer and didn't see anything on it.

"Scanners, I don't see a ship"

"No Sir," the Technician responded.

"Comms, are you sure of the transmission?"

"Yes Sir. We have an IFF from them. Decoding it now." She worked her system as the Watch Officer checked tactical and other systems preparing to sound general quarters.

"Got it, Sir. It is the *Sabachi*."

The Watch Officer let out his breath in a sigh of relief.

"Ok, send them docking instructions and alert the Commander and then the Ambassador that they have arrived."

"Yes Sir."

CAPT Ortega entered the conference room where the Ambassador and Colonel were waiting. There was a tray of coffee and cups along with some finger food. The three shook hands and sat down. Mike poured everyone a cup of coffee and ensured the milk and sugar were within reach.

"It is good to see you, CAPT," Colonel Nelson said, "we have been quite eager to finally meet you."

The CAPT nodded and took a sip of his coffee, "This has been a tedious and tiring mission. A lot of stealth and near misses, I dare say. But we have the information. We have found their new home world along with shipyards and resupply points." He shook his head, "And a lot more. Earth needs this information."

Mike nodded. "Colonel, this is so important that we need to load it into one of our hyperspace communication drones and get it back to Earth."

The Colonel replied, "Mike, we only have three of those; why can't they use one of theirs?"

The CAPT answered, "We don't have one. We left Earth before that tech was developed."

She growled. Those are precious commodities, and she hated giving up even one.

"It is obvious that you are not headed back to Earth so, how do you plan to get any more information to them?"

"We have one other sector to explore. Once we have done that, we are to head back to Earth."

She nodded, "All right then. Transfer all the information you have to us so we can get it into the communication device. We have been advised by a potential ally that we are on the edge of Kammorrigan space and could be discovered at any moment. We need to get out of here."

CAPT Ortega nodded, and the three left the conference room. Within a few hours the communication device would be loaded with all the information the *Sabachi* had gathered and launched back to Earth through hyperspace.

Mike informed them, he needed enough of the information for the upcoming meeting between their potential coalition partners. After all, they would desire to know the new home world and how they could work together to destroy the Kammorrigans once and for all.

* * *

"Sorry General, but we can't get the hyperdrive working. It is gone. Whatever they hit this poor ship with has fried the entire system."

Paul sat back in his chair. He was in his office with the *Cyane's* Chief Engineer on his viewer.

"Fried? The computer also? What about the self-destruct?"

"Yes Sir. If you are asking, can someone pull data from it? Maybe, I don't know. The self-destruct system is completely gone."

Paul nodded.

"Have you been able to get anything working on the ship?"

"Well, life support really wasn't affected though a lot of the systems are down. We have been able to get the ion drive somewhat functional. She can move but she can't maneuver."

"Ok," Paul sat thoughtfully. He was thinking to himself. The Engineer waited. He had seen commanders do this before and knew to wait for his instructions.

"All right, I want you to maintain that drive. Get the helm operational along with the autopilot."

"Yes Sir."

Paul switched off his viewer and keyed his Communication Officer.

"Have Colonel Smith come to my office."

After a few moments, the Colonel was sitting across from the General who was scanning through something on his screen. Then General Connington smiled and turned to her.

"As you know, Jeanine, your ship is lost. We can't repair her to make the trip home."

"Yes Sir. I've seen the reports. The crew and I don't like it obviously."

Paul was somber. Of course, it would be hard for any commander and crew to hear their ship was lost.

"All right, well we do need to destroy her. I could simply place a hydrogen missile with a detonator and do it that way. But several of us have wondered about using a sun to destroy a ship. So, I want to use the *Cyane* as an experiment."

Colonel Smith looked at the General in bewilderment for a few moments, then sighed. She sat there for a few minutes, then slowly nodded.

"I see, try to use her death in a useful manner."

"Yes, exactly. So, I want you to take a very small team of engineers and pilots onboard and set a course straight for the sun. We will follow and before you cross the corona zone, set the autopilot and get everyone back to the *Hood*. We will place some smaller explosive devices onboard ensuring her destruction."

Five days later, the three ships had reached the outer zone of the sun's corona.

The *Hood* and *Chesapeake* were in position at a thousand kilometers from the corona sphere. Paul watched as the two transports were making their way back to the *Hood*. Five minutes later, the *Cyane's* ion drive came online, and the ship began moving toward its final leg to the sun. Everyone onboard the two ships and the transports were watching as it moved slowly toward its fate. Thirty minutes later as it entered the corona it began heating up and buckling. She was rocking side to side but maintained a heading toward the chromosphere. Soon the *Cyane* passed through the corona and five minutes later she exploded. All scanners on the ship were recording and transmitting everything to the *Hood*. The *Hood's* own scanners were picking up what debris of the doomed ship there was and how they were being drawn into the sun by its gravitational pull. Nothing of it was left.

When the two transports were onboard the *Hood*, Paul gave the order for the two ships to make best speed to Zeta Prime. The hyperspace well opened and both ships entered.

* * *

The *Sabachi* had been traveling for twenty days in hyperspace and was approaching its last sector to explore. Captain Ortega was asleep in his cabin. A half-eaten sandwich lay on his secretariat. His coveralls were over his boots so he could easily slip into them if required.

The bridge crew on duty was the night shift under the newly promoted First Lieutenant Michaels. He was excited about his new rank and position as a watch commander. He was being quite meticulous with the checklist as his crew were preparing to come out of hyperspace.

Technical Sergeant Anderson was the Helmsman for this crew. She had made three transitions from hyperspace to normal space before this event. She was very alert to all the issues while preparing along with the Hyperspace Engineer on the bridge for a smooth transition.

"Ten seconds to normal space," Tech Sergeant Anderson announced.

"Five seconds."

"Cutting Hyperspace drive now," the Engineer announced.

The *Sabachi* made a smooth transition from hyperspace to normal space.

Then the proximity klaxons softly sounded across the bridge. First Lt Michaels quickly looked at both the main viewer and tactical display, finding they had jumped into the middle of five Kammorrigan ships.

"OPEN FIRE WITH EVERYTHING WE HAVE." He shouted. "Sound Battle Stations," he barked.

The *Sabachi* lasers reached out to all five Kammorrigan ships with a salvo of torpedoes. Every ship was hit. The Kammorrigan crews on all five ships were taken by surprise. They were not aware of the *Sabachi*. The Kammorrigan warriors were experienced on the five warships and quickly raised their shields, executed damage control, and returned fire on the enemy ship they found in their midst.

The klaxons sounded extremely loud, waking Captain Ortega abruptly. He quickly swung his legs up and into the coveralls and his boots. He quickly pulled them up and while buckling his belt headed for his door. As he exited his cabin, he turned to his right and entered the bridge, there was chaos among his bridge crew. They were all shouting incoherently at each other. He was dismayed that one of his bridge crews were acting as if they were recruits. He moved swiftly to his chair and shouted for all hands to be quiet. They all stopped shouting and looked at him. The CAPT quickly scanned all the screens and saw they had jumped into the middle of a group of Kammorrigan ships. His damage control board started showing red. His shields were on the verge of collapse as they were taking fire from all five Kammorrigan ships.

CAPT Ortega reached down, picked up a phone, and punched a button, "Engineering, how fast can you bring the hyperdrive online? We need to make a jump right now."

"Bridge, the hyperdrive is offline. It has taken damage. I can't even give you the ion drive; it is barely operational."

"Can you get the hyperdrive online at all?"

"No Sir. It is now gone. We have a main space fire down here. I'm about to lose the ion drive right now if we can't stop the fire."

"Do what you can." CAPT Ortega slowly sat down in his chair as he hung up his receiver. He looked around his bridge. The controls were starting to burn out and fires were starting in half a dozen places. The crew was trying to put them out.

Damn, he thought, *how the hell did this happen?*

"Weapons and Engineering, it is time. We need to blow the ship," he announced.

He then keyed into his board several codes and the self-destruct system came online.

"Weapons and Engineering, I am now entering my self-destruct codes; you two do the same."

They both stared at him and then at each other. They both hesitated till they looked at the monitors and saw the shield was seconds away from collapsing, then they hurried and entered their codes.

The *Sabachi*'s shields glowed a bright rainbow of colors and as it fell, she ignited into a ball of white and yellow fire. All five Kammorrigan ships were hit by her debris as she exploded. In her dying moments, she delivered massive damage to her enemies.

The Grand High Viscount Nayxaphex of the Kammorrigan Superior Royal Regime Fleet sat on his three-legged stool reading a very disturbing report on his monitor concerning a patrol's strange encounter with an alien ship in sector twenty-three.

This encounter surely was with a Human ship, the Grand One was sure. As he continued to read the report, his tentacles began to twitch and he bared his sharp teeth in a clenched grimace. The more he read the faster his tentacles twitched, knocking items off his desk.

The guard outside the Grand High Viscount Nayxaphex 's cabin began to get agitated hearing the noise from within. His own tentacles began to twitch in this agitated state, and he began shifting his weapon from one hand to another. Then he remembered his meditation techniques and immediately began taking control of his breathing to enter into a meditative state for the purpose of calming down. He wrapped his tentacles about his body and with their tips began to stroke his ears.

Meanwhile, the Grand One was still in an extremely agitated state.

How could they disobey their orders? He fumed. His purple skin was growing darker with each thought.

Every Kammorrigan Commander had the same strict regulation, capture any and all Human ships, no matter the cost. And here, five ships destroyed a Human ship. "DAMN THEM!" he screamed. Then he caught something out of his right eye and immediately focused on the monitor going quite still. He then began to shake in rage, his own guard was asleep. He keyed his communication system for Security.

"Yes, your Magnificent Exalted Grand One," the Chief Security Officer answered.

"My guard is asleep. Come and arrest him at once and confine him in the torture section."

"At once, Your Magnificent Exalted Grand One." But the Grand One had already closed his communication system and began reading the report again.

He did notice when four Security officers showed up on his monitor. Two of them took immediate custody of the guard and escorted him away while the other two positioned themselves outside his door. He smiled to himself then turned back to the report.

Two of the ships were so damaged they would have to be destroyed and the other three would be spending weeks in the shipyards being repaired. He snapped his teeth together and kept them that way till saliva was dripping down his chin. With a quick flash of a tentacle, he wiped away the drool and keyed his communication system for his personal inquisitors.

"How may I serve your Magnificent Exalted Grand One?" The Chief Inquisitor asked.

"You've seen the report from Sector Twenty-three?" He asked.

"Yes, your Magnificent Exalted Grand One."

"Good. Send a team out there. I want all five of the commanders and their first officers to be publicly executed. Ensure it is transmitted to the Superior Royal Regime Fleet to the lowest and insignificant ship we have. Reiterate to all of my commanders that I want a Human ship captured; NOT DESTROYED! Is that understood?"

"Yes, your Magnificent Exalted Grand One. We will depart within the hour to execute your orders."

"Good." The Grand One closed his communication link and licked his lips with his pointed tongue.

I must reinforce my authority across the Regime, he thought.

Since the Humans had destroyed their home world along with the Chancellor and Ruling Council, he was now the sole authority in the Kammorrigan Space Regime, and he was determined to keep it that way. But to do so, he must locate the Human world and destroy it. Otherwise, others of the Nayxaphex would attempt to assassinate him to take his spot, or worse yet, a new Ruling Council could be formed.

He snapped his teeth yet again at this thought. He stared with malice at the monitor showing his door and the two new guards.

Well, at least I will get the entertainment of watching the slouch of a guard get tortured, he thought, *I will keep that going till I get bored then have him executed.*

He got up and exited his cabin and was immediately followed by one of the guards as he headed for the torture section of his flagship.

CHAPTER 13

Task Force Colony had been traveling in hyperspace for six months. Fleet Captain Lindsey kept them in hyperspace to avoid wasting time. After her arrival at Plymouth Station, it took another month before the colony ships with three other warships to arrive. They stayed for one week ensuring a shipment of crystals were loaded onto each ship and cross-decked key personnel onto her own ship, the *Rapture*.

When the rest of the task force had jumped into the space around 237 Prime, everyone was astonished at the immense size of the four behemoth colony ships. They dwarfed every ship around them. They were elongated cylinders measuring one thousand feet long and eight hundred feet wide. Each ship carried five hundred colonists. Two of the ships each carried ten US Army Striker vehicles for one hundred Soldiers, totaling two hundred for the colony's ground defense force. The light cruiser and two destroyers would be the colony's orbital defense. The other eighteen hundred colonists consisted of engineers, miners, scientists, various technicians, farmers/hydroponics, and various other skilled workers for the colony's multiple operations.

Jo sat in her office with the Director of the Kyrmménos Colony, Dr. Anthony Phillips. He was a tall, lanky man with olive skin and dark hair. He had brown eyes that, at times, seemed to look right through you. Both he and Jo had become good friends over the last six months traveling together. Now, he seemed to have withdrawn into himself. She took a sip of her coffee.

"You seem to be somewhere else, Anthony."

"Mmm." He stirred and focused in on her.

"Oh yes," he said with a grin, "it's just…well it is, we are almost to our destination, and it seems strange. Finally, we are here and yet it is…well, it is difficult to describe." He then took a drink of his coffee.

"I know something about what you mean but it is different. With EXPLORER, we knew we would go back to Earth. But you and your folks are staying here for the rest of your lives," she responded.

Anthony nodded. "Indeed. Yes, we all were carefully selected to ensure we would be able to colonize a planet with the expectation of never returning to Earth. Still, it is a strange sensation thinking we will most likely never see Earth again. Our colony ships are designed to land on the planet and be taken apart to build the colony. No way home."

Jo took another sip of her coffee.

"At least there will be transport ships coming for crystal shipments and will bring supplies and news. That ought to be helpful."

"I hope so. Especially if we do run into some behavioral issues and need to send someone back. We have been prepared quite extensively for this mission and thankfully, we have some great mental health professionals with us."

"That is good," Jo responded, "that is helpful. Besides you will be quite busy, I'm sure with the construction and then mining operations. You have the plans to ensure the colony can grow and eventually become a shipyard."

"Yes, but I suspect that will be at least ten years from now. We have to get the colony established near a major crystal vein so we can start pulling them out fast and refine them for use. That is planned for six months to a year. It will take that long."

She nodded. "But as we have discussed, we have to ensure the system is still uninhabited before we land you. Your ships will park in orbit to scan the planet while my cruisers check out the system. That should take at least a week."

Anthony nodded in turn. "Yes, that is what we are anticipating. Also, the whole climate and weather patterns need to be established before we land. We need to understand these factors, so we don't willy nilly land and then disaster hits us because we didn't do our homework properly." He smiled.

She smiled back, "Tomorrow we should enter normal space near the system. I'll take the *Rapture* and *Tiber* into the system and slowly approach the planet while the other ships remain outside waiting for our report. I hope that we can establish the system is safe, quickly. This location is a backup for me in case the information I need comes early; however, I need to move off to a rendezvous location soon. Your colony is to remain hidden, even from the vast majority of Earth. Only a few will know about you and your location. It is to be kept a secret for quite a long time. Not even the majority of our world leaders or even in the US know about this colony, let alone where it is."

Anthony took another drink, "I know. Outside of those transports, we are truly on our own." He rubbed his lower jaw with his left hand. "That is something else. That makes me the sole ruler out here. The laws that were written for me to enact and the military as my secondary police force." He shook his head while frowning. "That is a tall order for a scientist who is also an administrator. I only have a few personnel that are true law enforcement. A very heavy responsibility." He took another drink of coffee.

Jo sat there with a reassuring look on her face knowing how he must be feeling. After all, she was the judge and jury of all the ships under her command and, like Anthony, all alone out here to ensure discipline, morale, and mission success all at the same time.

Late the following day, Task Force Colony came out of hyperspace. They were two hundred thousand kilometers from the system. Jo sat in her command chair and waited. It was her standing order that all ships of the task force would perform system checks unless they were in combat. An hour later all the ships had reported in. As expected, every ship stated all systems were green, but their hyperdrives required maintenance. Jo reviewed the ships' status; they also noted that the hyperdrives were operational but would need minor work before making any long-distance jumps. She gave the order for the two heavy cruisers to make their way into the system while the other ships remained on station.

Both the *Rapture* and *Tiber* moved off at an angle toward the system at flank speed. Jo wanted to perform a quick survey of the system but was being cautious; she didn't want any surprises. As they approached the system, the sensors showed a yellow star with six planets in orbit. The target planet for the colony would be the fourth planet from the sun. It was in the habitable zone of the system. The scanners reported that the sixth planet was a giant gas planet with four moons. The fifth planet was a medium sized ice planet. The fourth was a desert world with areas showing vegetation; it had a singular moon. The third planet was an iron rock in space. The second planet was of medium size with no atmosphere and the first planet was of molten lead. But so far, no sign of any form of civilization. It still appeared to be a system that no other race had visited.

It took the two ships five days to run their survey around each planet. There were no signs of intelligent life. Fleet Captain Lindsey sent a message to the remaining task force they could now head for the fourth planet to begin their survey. Three days later, the colony ships reached the planet. They immediately maneuvered themselves into four equal distances along the equator of the planet and immediately began scanning for the largest crystal deposits along with the climate, weather and ecosystems. It took eight days for them to map the surface along with the deposits.

Jo shuttled over to the colony's primary ship to meet with the colony leaders. A young woman escorted her from the shuttle bay to the elevator, which was the only entrance to the control room. As Jo stepped out of the elevator, she found herself in a large room, shaped roughly like a ball. The elevator opened onto the top floor of the room. She glanced to her right seeing several offices lining the curved wall. In front of her was a square table and to her left on the level were two command chairs and a rail. As she turned to her left, she saw stairs leading down. She walked over to the railing. The far wall had several large monitors on the top of a rather large window made of transparent duraplastic, which descended into the command room's conical shaped well. The window was reinforced with a lattice work of vertical and horizontal beams. It had a protective shield, made of composite materials, which was closed during the trip and could be closed during storms. She noticed a descending terracing of two levels below her ending in a third level. Along the walls of the two immediate levels were several stations for monitoring the colony and mining operations. The bottom level, had the window ending on one side, with a square table in the middle of the floor and along the wall were the space control stations.

When the fleet came out of hyperspace, Dr. Phillips had shuttled over to the primary colony ship. He along with the Deputy Director, the Chief Engineer, the Chief Mining Officer and Col Davenport (the military commander) enthusiastically met Fleet Captain Lindsey after she had surveyed the control room. They gathered around the table on the top level, which had holographic capabilities. Above the table was a holographic image of the planet. The technician operating the table had the image rotate on its axis at a greater rotation to allow all the members to view the various surfaces. There were three continents, two of which crossed the equator, and one continent was contained solely in the northern hemisphere. Oceans separated all of them. Both poles were ice caps. The northern hemisphere had signs of vegetation and at this point in time the land masses in the south didn't seem to have any. There were signs of water across all hemispheres, but they were not sure how much of them were underground lakes and rivers.

At a signal from Dr. Phillips, several silverish images showed just under the surface of the planet with two extremely large ones. One located in the northern hemisphere and one in the southern hemisphere but on different continents.

"Well, there it is." Dr. Phillips said with a sigh.

CAPT Lindsey turned to him, "What does that mean?"

He shook his head in response and said, "Sadly, this is all we have been able to map out in eight days. We have a lot of unknowns as to what to do."

Jo looked around the table and back at the hologram.

"Ok, so I'll ask the question: What does that mean?"

Colonel Davenport responded, "CAPT, it means we have to pick one of the two large locations. The colony ships are not duplicate ships. They are very similar but with enough differences that we can only establish one colony. There was enough duplication to allow the loss of one ship but no more. If we had lost two, we would have had to turn back."

"Aaah," she responded. "Ok, so if you sent one ship to a location, it couldn't sustain itself."

"That is correct, CAPT," The Col answered.

"Ok, well, I need to move my three heavy cruisers to a different location to find out where our coalition system will be, but I have time," CAPT Lindsey said. "So, Anthony, why don't you do some on-the-ground site surveys. Find out which is best suited and try to establish risks and dangers. Take your time since this colony is so important to Earth."

The others stared at her with curious looks.

"You know you are a secret colony. You are also our backup Earth in case we lose the war against the Kammorrigans. Then, your colony becomes Earth. Your databanks are full of our history, technology, multiple cultures, religions, etc. In fact, only three of you know the codes to access Earth's location. You have to ensure you pass those codes to your future successors. Only a few on Earth will know your location. Not even the transport captains will know where this system is. Their ships will have your special location locked into their astrogation computers and won't be changeable. When they jump, the people onboard will be blind as to where they are going. So, it is best you take the time to do this right, especially since all four ships are the single colony on the planet." CAPT Lindsey stated. "My ships will remain here. We will run defense drills with your three defense ships and perform some surveys of the system while you figure out where you will set up. Be sure to try and identify any creatures that could harm you while you develop the planet."

Everyone nodded. As CAPT Lindsey departed the control room for her shuttle, Dr. Phillips had various personnel and shuttles displayed on the holographic table so they could pick their survey teams.

Fleet Captain Lindsey checked her viewers. The five warship commanders were on the main screen. The other viewers showed each of the six ships and their various statuses'.

"All right Gentlemen," she began, "let's get started with the workups. My three ships will be the antagonists. The *Guardian*, *Castle* and

Fortress, you are the assigned defense ships for the colony. You are on defense. We will run through the tactics, techniques and procedures you will need to defend this colony. Be ready for one-on-one contact to full three-on-three contact. Keep weapons at the minimum power to register hits only. No torpedoes; those will be simulated. Shields up when in contact. Questions?"

"Yes, Captain," replied LtCol Arthur, commander of the *Guardian*, "how long will we be conducting these drills?"

"Until I am satisfied that you are ready to assume your duties, Colonel," she responded. She held her gaze steady on the viewers waiting. No one had any further questions.

"Ok," she began, "Colonel Jackson, start scanning the system, starting with the interior planets. Colonel Nelson, you are with me. We will move off to the outer section of the system and start an approach toward the colony planet. Let's see how the Colony ships respond." All the commanders confirmed her orders and the three heavy cruisers moved off while LtCol Arthur coordinated with his two destroyer commanders, Major Paul of the *Castle* and Major Thomas of the *Fortress*.

The Deputy Director of the Colony, Dr. Kristen Reynolds, and the Military Commander, Colonel Davenport approached the Directors' door, the Col pressed the buzzer and the door slid open. They entered, and Dr. Phillips indicated seats for them to take. As they sat down the Colonel opened his binder.

"Good evening, Sir," the Colonel began, "we would like to send two transports to the two sites. We can do this at the same time without any delays. We have already selected the shuttles and the crews pending your approval." He handed the Director a flexi sheet with the information and continued.

"As you can see, each survey will have a military shuttle for their protection and one shuttle for the actual survey. Each survey team will have a mining expert, climate, agronomist, geologists, and a construction engineer." He stopped as the Director raised his hand, and he continued to scan the flexi sheet. Finally, he put it down and looked up at Dr. Reynolds.

"Do you agree with the Colonel?" He asked. He had been briefed that the military can be overbearing. During their training, Dr. Reynolds demonstrated level-headedness and good judgment, but this was their first actual decision that had long-lasting effects. He watched her intently. She smiled.

"Yes, I do. Everyone had their input into these teams and they are sound. I like to send them down in the morning."

"All right, assemble your teams tonight and prep them. Ensure they are well rested. We don't want any issues due to a lack of preparation or rest," he said and the two left his office.

Dr. Reynolds and Colonel Davenport agreed that the team leaders would be the senior military member on each survey. Their survival and safety were the highest concern. The colony was provided ten Striker teams under two companies for their ground defense force. The Colonel assigned the lead Striker team of each company to the survey mission. Captain Smith from Company A would lead the southern survey team and Captain Baker from Company B would the northern survey team. Both Captains were given very specific instructions. Let the survey teams do their job. Only interfere with them if hostile species appear, bad weather, or an unforeseen threat. Then they were to get them onboard and lift off immediately. The military force would set a perimeter about the camp with an alarm system. Never let a survey member out of their site. Otherwise, stay out of their way.

Both Captains were standing a few feet away from their shuttles as their Soldiers were loading them. The military shuttles were large enough to house a Striker vehicle, communications center, and weapons rack (both projectile and power rifles, various side arms, and launchers). They had a limited berthing area. The Soldiers were placing a small habitant system on each shuttle along with various camp sensors. The habitant would house the majority of the Soldiers while they were on the ground. They had already loaded enough food and other supplies for ten days. The mission was to last no more than seven days.

The two non-military shuttles were larger. Each shuttle could easily hold fifty passengers, or a large amount of cargo or a mix of both. In this case, they would be the habitat for the survey teams. The shuttles had organic berthing, kitchen, facilities, and even a med center. Each survey team consisted of seven members, one of which was the lead, who was a research expert and a medic. The crew consisted of two pilots who could double as astrogators, since the shuttles were designed to operate in both space and an atmosphere plus one loadmaster. Currently, the loadmasters were supervising the various research and supplies being loaded onto their respective shuttles.

The Captains both turned to see the other team members by their shuttles as Dr. Reynolds was talking to them. They could see where she must have been telling them the two Captains were in charge by the way the members were looking displeased and a couple looking angry. But she handled them well, and they started to calm down. She must have been informing them of the military's purpose and how they would be allowed to do their job. Now and then the Captains would look at their respective Soldiers to see how the loading was going. They noticed the Colonel approaching along with their commanding officer. They saluted them as they approached.

"Captains," the Colonel said after returning their salute. "Everything ready?"

"Nearly Sir," they each responded.

"Good. I see you have been watching the little drama over there." Neither Captain responded. The Colonel nodded his head.

"Yes, nothing more to say really. Just keep constant comms with us, understood?"

They both acknowledged him. He then shook their hands and the Captains moved to their respective shuttles. After inspecting the load out, they ordered the Soldiers into their respective shuttles and settle down. Both Captains approached the civilian shuttles to check on their status.

The two shuttle pilots came over to meet with them.

"Well, your shuttles ready?" Asked Captain Smith.

"Almost. They are still settling their equipment, but we should be able to launch in thirty minutes," answered Pilot Marcia Simmons.

Captain Smith nodded, "Seen the weather reports?"

"Yeah," said the pilot assigned to Captain Smith's area. "Going to be rough on us going to the South. You, Joe?"

"Pretty calm for us. We shouldn't have any problems with entering the atmosphere and heading for our sector."

The first pilot pursed her lips while shaking her head. Captain Smith inquired, "What is wrong?"

"Well, you know we want to circle as much of the identified fields as possible before setting down but with this storm, I'm not sure we can do it."

"How long before we can launch if we wait for more favorable weather?" The Captain asked.

The Pilot waived someone over and they conversed for a few minutes. Then she turned back to Captain Smith.

"Looks like another hour or hour and a half."

The Captain nodded, "Ok, let's wait for the storm to calm down. I'll alert control to advise them." He then turned to the other two,

"Why don't you guys take off now and get a start on your area." They both nodded and headed for their shuttles.

Three hours later, all four shuttles left the hangar. They had been instructed to depart at the same time. Meteorology had declared that both sites were now clear, and the forecast was favorable over the next eight days. The last-minute checks were occurring onboard each shuttle. The atmosphere on the planet was not favorable without a breathing mask, though the pressure was normal for humans. It was decided since this would be the first landing everyone would be in a full suit vice just masks. Risk was not to be tolerated. Each suit came with a utility belt to include a grappling line in case anyone fell into a trench and needed to either get themselves out or be rescued. The loadmasters double-checked the security of all equipment and returned to their seats. The four pilots had signaled everyone stay strapped in their seats. The heat shields were being activated as the shuttles approached their entry points into the atmosphere.

The four shuttles entered the atmosphere. It was a rocky ride down the well but they came out of it with no injuries or cargo straps breaking loose which secured the equipment and supplies. Two shuttles were going to the northern field and the other two to the southern field, their approach paths placed them nearly identical to the arrival time to their respective fields. As they approached and began their aerial survey, the pilots indicated the teams could unbuckle and begin taking readings. Each team circled the areas for two hours. After which they located their respective landing sites and began their descents. All four shuttles touched down without event. Only the military shuttles opened, and the Soldiers dispersed into a perimeter and scouted their respective areas to ensure there were no hostiles.

In the South, Captain Smith stood by his comm center watching via his screen as his Soldiers spread out. The terrain was a rocky desert one. Some of the rocks stood over thirteen feet in height. His Soldiers went fifty feet in a circle out from the two shuttles. They maintained an open comm system on each suit and ensured they would make visual contact with each other every few feet. No issues they reported to the Captain. Captain Smith acknowledged and had them place the sensors and ran the tests ensuring he had a sound perimeter. Then he ordered them to return and begin setting up camp along with the survey team.

The area for the northern survey, was a dune sea. Captain Baker's shuttles touched down thirty feet from a dune. Fifty feet in front of the dune and leading away from it, in a two-hundred-fifty-degree arc, was relatively flat, but the dune itself, was over sixty feet in height. This bothered him but the scanners reported this area was the largest portion of the crystal field and the construction engineer really wanted to inspect the area for the shuttles and colony development.

Captain Baker stood staring up at the dune. His sensors were in place except on top of the dune. He did not like this area. He couldn't see what was on the other side. The fly-by didn't show anything but other dunes beyond it. He couldn't place any perimeter sensors on the other side of it. He ensured there were sensors right up and even on the dune that was safe enough for his men to place. Now he watched as the camp was being set up.

Fleet Captain Lindsey stepped onto the control room of the primary colony ship. Drs Phillips, Reynolds, and Gupta along with Colonel Davenport and Mr. Pernell were standing around the holographic table with the planet displayed on it. She joined them.

"How is the survey going?" She asked.

It was the evening of the fifth day of the surveys on the planet surface.

Dr. Phillips sighed.

Mr. Pernell had a big grin on his face while he examined the reports. Dr. Reynolds was smiling but her eyes didn't reflect her smile, indicating there was indecision. Colonel Davenport just frowned as he shifted from one foot to the other. Dr. Gupta stood there stoically.

With a heavy sigh, Dr. Phillips looked at her.

"Hi, Captain. It is a good report. Both fields are large. The North is just over two thousand acres in diameter and the South is three thousand five hundred acres in diameter. The issue boils down to which can support the weight of the ships along with the tunneling we will need for the colony. The South is rocky with pinnacle-like rocks, while the North has several dunes with flat areas. The North would be easier to get to the crystals, but we are not sure about the foundation of the entire area. Anyway, the teams have two to three more days left for collecting data and their preliminary analysis. Meanwhile, our labs are attempting to determine the best location for us."

She nodded. "Ok. Well, I have run through all the drills we can do with your orbital defense. They are ready and I am prepared to turn them over to you. I will want to do this in a ceremony so the three skippers understand they fall under Colonel Davenport's command."

Everyone nodded their agreement.

"What about your survey of the system?" Dr. Reynolds inquired.

"Very good," Captain Lindsey said, "You are totally alone in this system. Which means you are on your own once you land these ships. You better be positive about your landing choice. The data from the other planets will be downloaded to you before you begin your landing procedures so you will have it. That way your shuttles can pinpoint any other exploration you may desire to do while you set up mining and manufacturing operations here."

"On our own," Dr. Phillips muttered. "Everything now depends on this choice and what we do from here on out. No help from Earth." He turned to Dr. Reynolds. "Kristen, better keep excellent tracking of our population here. With only two thousand of us, we need to ensure we operate with the maximum risk mitigation procedures in place. Plus, we better ensure the married couples start having babies while we figure out who the single population will marry. We need to start our colony growth while setting up all the habitation and begin the mining operations." As she acknowledged what he said, Dr. Phillips addressed all of them. "We all need to be mindful of all of our people and how we are managing them. Before Captain Lindsey departs, I want to go over my legal authorities and responsibilities and where all of you fit into the chain of command." Everyone nodded.

Captain Lindsey glanced at both Dr. Phillips and Colonel Davenport. "I would like to transfer the command of your orbital defense force tomorrow if that is ok with you?"

The Colonel replied, "Yes that will work. We will bring the three commanders onto the hangar deck for the changeover."

Captain Lindsey smiled at them and departed the control room for her shuttle.

Sergeant Thomas stopped. He looked across the flats toward the horizon as the morning's first light streamed across it. The red streak along the horizon with dunes accented in the distance, he found beautiful. He stood there staring through the Plexiglass of his helmet. He had polished it the night before just in case he saw something as amazing as this sunrise.

He could hear Isaac's heavy breathing.

"Hey, Doc, slow it down." He said through the open microphone in his helmet. He stood there in his armored suit resting his projectile rifle in crossed arms as he gazed at the morning light. But the Geologist was still hurrying along. He wanted an early start to collect some samples. They were already two hundred fifty yards beyond the camp's perimeter. Dr. Isaac Corrothers was twenty yards ahead of him.

Sgt Thomas sighed and began to move forward at a rapid pace when Isaac screamed. The scream happened so fast, the dampeners in his helmet didn't reduce the volume quick enough. Sgt Thomas bent over in a moment of pain.

"Doc, what happened?" As he scanned ahead of him, but Sgt Thomas couldn't see him. He started running forward while scanning the ground ahead of him for any sign of the Geologist.

Captain Baker was walking from the kitchen area with a cup of coffee. He was thinking how things were going well despite his earlier fears. This morning of the sixth day should see them wrapping things up. He looked up to see a warning light on the communications panel and noticed Sgt Thomas' view camera showing the ground jostling as the Sgt was running. He moved quickly to the panel and depressed the audio button.

"Doc, where are you? What is happening?" He heard the Sergeant calling. He quickly scanned the panel and noticed a viewscreen with Dr. Corrothers' camera on. But it was dark. He checked the vitals monitor and saw the Geologist's pulse rate was at an accelerated level and his breathing was erratic.

"All hands, alert!" He yelled.

In response, three Soldiers approached.

"Get the vehicle ready. I need you to roll out when we figure out where these two are at."

Two of the Soldiers acknowledged the order, ran to the vehicle, and began the prep cycle.

Sergeant Thomas reached a hole in the ground and slid to a stop just before he fell in.

"Hey Doc, you down there?"

He could hear the Geologist's breathing in his ear. It was erratic. He sounded as if he was sucking in his breath at times as if he was in pain.

"Isaac, can you hear me?" He said, trying to make his voice calm.

"Sgt Thomas, this is Captain Baker. Do you read me?"

"Yes Sir. We are two hundred seventy, seventy-five yards to the west of the perimeter. I'm standing at the opening of a hole. My helmet light can't penetrate too far into the darkness. I think this is where Dr. Corrothers fell. I can hear his breathing. It sounds as if he is hurt."

"Solid copy. We will send the Striker vehicle to you with the Medic onboard. I gather you don't have a sense of the depth."

"Correct Sir. I don't have a visual on the Doc nor the bottom of the hole."

"Damn," Captain Baker breathed out softly. He called over to the other shuttle.

"Dr. Corrothers is injured and has fallen into a hole. Get the Medic over here ASAP. We are mounting a rescue now." He clicked off when they acknowledged what he had said.

"How is the vehicle prep going? Also, rig for scaling a wall for rescue. We will need a basket!" He yelled to the Soldiers.

Sergeant Thomas reached into his utility belt and pulled out a chem light.

"Doc, if you can hear me. I'm dropping a chem light down. I need you to retrieve it. I need you to speak to me when you see it."

He then snapped it quickly, breaking the element inside it. He shook the light vigorously till it lit and then dropped it into the hole. He watched it fall, getting smaller and fainter.

Dr. Isaac Corrothers graduated from the University of Oklahoma as a PhD in Geology. He was doing research into various geological formations, in particular, crystallization at the Grand Canyon University when EXPLORER returned with a new crystal technology. He had written several papers on crystallization and was chosen as a researcher of these new crystals. It led him to revisit the petrified forest, where he performed tests on different petrified items. When he finished, he placed them back where he found them. His next visit was to the Grand Canyon. He was seeking certain formations in a cave. That is where the government men found him. They asked him to join a secret colony to a world full of crystals. They told him his research caught the attention of those who were putting together the colonists, and they wanted him because of his work on the crystals. Isaac was excited; he had never understood people and had found his voice through his geological research. The ability to settle on a planet with these crystals would give him a greater range of voice, he believed. He said yes.

He now woke up in darkness. His left leg hurt. The lights in his suit were off. He whimpered as he shifted his weight and felt more pain throughout his body. He could faintly hear Sergeant Thomas in his earpiece. The ear piece that was supposed to be in his left ear was gone. The one in his right ear was still in place, but something had to be wrong with the suit. He moved his head to the right and left. It was all dark here. He tried to look up, again wincing in pain as he had to shift himself to see upwards. As he peered upwards, he noticed a faint light way above him.

That must be the opening I fell through, he thought.

Then he noticed a light falling toward him. It grew in its intensity as it approached. It was green. The chem light fell three feet to his right. He stretched toward it and yelled in pain, but he got his right hand on the light. He lay there breathing heavily while trying to calm down. At least the Sergeant was still with him. He scanned around himself and found the cavern's wall. He crawled over to it so he could lean his back against it. The pain in his left leg was agonizing as he moved to the wall and sat up.

"Doc, can you hear me?" the voice came over his earpiece though it was faint.

"Yes, Sergeant, I can, but something must be wrong with the suit. My left leg is broken, I think. I'm really hurt."

Sergeant Thomas barely heard his charge, but he was able to read that he was really hurt and had a broken leg. He relayed this information to Captain Baker.

"Doc, we are coming to get you," he yelled into his microphone. "We are bringing the vehicle. We will get you out of that hole. Just hang on."

The Sgt could barely make out the chem light, or so he thought. Those damn things could be tricky to see at any real distance.

At least he could sit up against the wall. It helped him to look around the area. *That was fortunate* he thought. He held the chem light in his right hand and moved it from the top of his chest to his lap. The suit wasn't punctured. The chest control was banged up pretty badly, though. He then eased forward and moved the light over his two legs. There were no punctures on his right, and he could bend the knee. But, the left leg. He began to get sick when he saw blood oozing through the suit and a bit of bone. He had to turn away before he threw up in his helmet. He drew in several sharp breaths due to the pain.

"Sergeant, I'm hurt badly. Please hurry."

Sgt Thomas was checking his belt and backpack for rope. He had about twenty feet of rope. He was looking around for some way to secure it so he could rappel down to the Geologist. He was having difficulty finding anything to help him.

"Captain, how long before you guys get here?"

"We are ten minutes out."

"Dammit, can't you get here now?" He asked sharply. He stopped, "Sorry Sir."

"No problem. We finally have everything loaded and are now scanning for your tracker. Once we are locked onto you then we will be there."

"Yes Sir."

Something was moving around in the darkness. Isaac sat straight up.

"Sergeant, something is down here with me," he whispered. "Please hurry."

"Repeat. Did you say something, Doc?"

"Please hurry."

Isaac sat there daring not to move. There definitely was something down here moving around. The way it was shuffling around made Isaac think it was big. Big or small didn't matter. He couldn't move to get away if he had to.

What to do, he thought. He looked at the chem light. He then aimed it straight in front of him and threw it.

The light thumped against something black and fell to the ground. He saw the thing moving over the light toward him. It had a head with teeth and glowing eyes. It was on him before he knew it. It bit into his helmet. The glass stopped it. He screamed in terror and grabbed the thing that had a hold of his helmet. It bit black teeth onto his helmet and began to shake back and forth. Finally, the teeth penetrated the top of the helmet.

"HELP ME! HELP ME!" He screamed. "No. No. NO. NOOoooooooo!" He cried out in sheer terror as the creature tore through the top of his helmet and ripped into his skull.

Sergeant Thomas stood petrified at the sound of Isaac's last scream.

What just happened? he thought.

He then aimed his rifle down the hole and stopped himself from squeezing off any rounds. *What if I hit him?* He then fired a three-round burst. Nothing happened.

Captain Baker stood at the edge of the hole as two of his Soldiers rappelled down.

"Nothing Sir, but blood. A lot of blood and pieces of what appears to be the suit's helmet," they reported.

"Captain, this is a small cavern, approximately twenty by thirty. The floor is a mixture of sand, dirt, and small rocks. There are rock projections from the floor scattered about. There are several openings around the cavern. We see a blood trail heading down one opening. We are preparing to enter the opening to look for the Doc."

Captain Baker thought for a moment.

"No. Get up here double quick."

"But Sir. We need to find the Doc."

"You heard me. Get back up here now."

The two Soldiers looked at each other then back at the opening. One took the safety off his rifle and started moving toward the opening. He knelt down to peer into the tunnel and shined a light down it. It went back ten feet then angled off toward his right. He could only see a faint blood trail and nothing else. He thought about the order. He could crawl in there and maybe find the Doc's body. He could drag it back.

"Hey, let's get back up there," the Private said. His mic channel was set so the Corporal was the only one to hear him.

After a heavy sigh, they picked up what was left of the Geologist's helmet and attached themselves to the cable. They signaled for the vehicle to pull them up.

Dr. Gupta stared hotly at Colonel Davenport with his eyes narrowed and lips drawn tight. He started to say something when Dr. Reynolds stopped him.

The Colonel started, "The report is clear. They left before dawn so Dr. Corrothers could collect some samples. He was quite excited. They had not explored that portion of the field. It appears the ground gave way, and he fell twenty-five feet. He broke his leg or legs and couldn't move. The Sergeant couldn't tie his rope off in order to rappel down to him. From what the Sergeant reported and the Corporal that was in the hole. There was some creature that tore the top of his helmet off," Col Davenport finished and looked at the hologram of the planet.

Dr. Phillips breathed heavily. "So, there are hostile life forms down there." He glanced at the Colonel then back at the hologram.

"What about Sgt Thomas?"

"Aah. Oh yes. He isn't injured but he is quite shaken over the whole thing. He is feeling guilty and is blaming himself for not getting to Dr. Corrothers. That is why the Captain sent down two other Soldiers. The last thing he wanted was Sgt Thomas going after something that could have killed him."

Dr. Phillips nodded. "Makes sense. Why have two casualties? One is enough."

Captain Lindsey entered the control room. She was frowning and her steps were brisk as she approached them.

"Colonel Davenport, I've been waiting for you to transfer command of the orbital defense force."

He looked up at her and realized she hadn't heard.

"My apologies, Captain. We just lost a geologist to some creature on the planet."

Her gaze changed from one of anger to astonishment and then looked at each of the persons around the table.

"Where was the attack?"

"Northern group. A geologist fell into a hole and before the team could get to him something killed him."

She nodded slowly. Her lips were pursed tightly.

"Dr. Phillips, in light of this, do you still desire to colonize the planet?"

He looked quickly at her in astonishment.

"What?"

She stared at them. "In light of a hostile lifeform, do you still desire to colonize the planet? You were sent here to do just that but with hostile lifeforms, it is now your decision to either continue with colonization or return to Earth. And remember, once you land it might be possible for you to take off again, but only once. And if you deploy the colony, you won't be able to take off at all."

He looked at each of his directors in turn. They returned his gaze. Each one had a puzzled look on their faces.

"I didn't realize that was an option." He looked down at the table.

"If we can vote." Dr. Reynolds started and then stopped and gazed at the hologram of the planet.

Dr. Phillips looked over at Mike Pernell, the Chief of Mining Operations.

Mr. Pernell said, "We came here to mine crystals. We understood there would be dangers and risks. I say we land. The northern site would have been better for mining, I think, but that is your decision.

Dr. Phillips looked at Dr. Gupta, the Chief Engineer.

While shaking his head, Dr. Gupta slowly said, "I hate losing people, but we did come here to mine and manufacture. Land."

Dr. Phillips then shifted his gaze to Colonel Davenport.

"We have two hundred military with us plus three ships in orbit. That is over ten percent of the colony that is military. We will protect the colony. Provided everyone follows protocols that we will update after this last incident. I vote we continue and land."

Dr. Phillips nodded his appreciation and looked right at Dr. Reynolds.

She sighed, "We came here to colonize. Let's do what we came here to do."

"Ok, thank you all and I agree with the assessment. We will land in the South since there have not been any reports of any creatures. I'm sure there are but that is the target area. How long before we land?"

Mr. Pernell responded slowly, "Well, probably another six or seven days." He picked up his palm pilot while shifting the holographic image to the southern field, "We have those pesky rocks to clear and I would want more flyovers to ensure we pick a very stable area to land the ships. Oh yes, we most likely will have to have some pre-drilling done to ensure we can land the ships."

Captain Lindsey frowned and furrowed her eyebrows.

Dr. Phillips saw the frown, "What is wrong, Captain?"

She sighed heavily, "Another seven days to hang around just to see you land and begin to colonize." She shook her head.

Everyone around the table gazed at her with confused looks. The Captain returned their gaze in turn.

"I have to get out of here and reach a rendezvous location for communications from our delegation to the alien species we have discovered. In that location, I am to learn where a coalition system will be set up and get there fast. I'm to work with the other species on combat tactics so we can win our fight. However, I can't depart until you have successfully landed and deployed the first of your colony. My orders are clear. I have to witness the hidden colony of Earth. In case we lose against the Kammorrigans, then you will be the source of all Earth's history, cultures, peoples, technology, etc. You become the new location of all human existence. I'm to ensure you get a good start."

Colonel Davenport nodded.

"I get it, Captain. But if we choose the safest location, which also is the larger field, then we must prepare the ground accordingly. Otherwise, we could have disaster with our landing."

"Oh, I agree, Colonel. For me, it is the time lag for my follow-on mission."

Everyone around the table nodded.

"Anyway, you have made your decision. I recommend you get on with the site location and preparation. Meanwhile, Colonel, please accompany me to the hangar for the change of command ceremony of your three ships. Then I'll head back to my ship to monitor the situation."

Both military officers left the control room together as the others began planning for the landing.

Ten days later, Fleet Captain Josephine Lindsey sat in her command chair onboard her ship, the *Rapture*. She glanced around her bridge at the various monitors and rested her gaze upon the main view screen. The planet almost filled the viewer. She could see the horizon as the sun was about to break over the eastern horizon. The four large colony ships were maneuvering into position to begin their landing. She glanced at her tactical monitor. The three orbital defense ships were in position, one to the right, one to the left, and one near the bottom of the four colony ships. One of her ships, the *Tiber*, was at the northern pole of the planet, while the other, *Andromeda* was on the outskirts of the system. Her own ship was far enough away to monitor the landing. Telemetry was being sent to the four colony ships by the various warships. Meteorology had reported a clear day with no winds. A perfect day to execute this landing.

Captain Lindsey waited for the day to progress. Her appearance was stern; she was pleased the day finally arrived for the landing but was growing impatient with the delays. Three days more than was projected. But the terrain proved difficult. After a day of scouting, the colonists had decided on a landing site. It was south of the crystal field. The ground was solid. It took several days for their transports and teams to try and clear the area of rock projections. Finally, the Director called for one of the defense ships to come in and use their ship's weapons to clear the area. Jo was impressed by the accuracy of the *Fortress* fire team and weapon skills. She had asked her Executive Officer, Colonel Ron Davis, if their own Weapons Officer could handle their weapons with such precision. He smiled at her and shrugged.

It took the remaining days to finish prepping the site for the four large ships. Now, she waited for the hour to arrive where one ship, then another, would begin their landing. She glanced over at the monitor that displayed the orbiting structure that one of the colony ships had launched two days previously. This structure, when fully deployed, would be a transfer station orbiting the planet. Ships from Earth would dock with it, along with transports from the colony. There, they would exchange crystals, personnel, equipment and supplies.

Dr. Phillips, the colony's Director sat in his command chair in the control room. Behind him was the holographic table, and in a semi-circle around it were offices, including his own. He could see the three tiers of stations in front and below him. The massive window was now sealed with its protective plating. The main monitor showed the sunlight radiating onto the planet's surface. The geosynchronous orbit they were in was above their landing site. He was nervous. The tension from the control room crew was almost deafening to his senses. Now more than ever, he wished he had that command presence that Captain Lindsey possessed. He wished he knew what to say to his people to have them calm down. His mouth was dry and he reached for his water as he watched helplessly the monitors before him.

"Dr. Phillips, we are ready to begin the landing. Alpha ship reports ready."

He would have jumped clean out of his chair if the straps didn't hold him in place. He fervently searched for the person who spoke. Then he remembered the audio system and keyed his mic.

"Yes, good. Ok, begin the landing," he said and quickly clicked off the mic.

The crew members began sending the signal for Alpha ship to begin its landing while the warships monitored the situation and sent their telemetry to the main ship, which was designated Delta, the last ship to land.

Alpha Colony ship altered her orbit, pointing her aft engine exhaust ports toward the planet, and fired her maneuvering rockets to begin the descent. She clicked on her electronic heat shields to displace the extreme temperatures across the shields to protect the ship as it entered the planet's atmosphere. Reports came in that she was in her approach pattern. The descent to the atmosphere took ten minutes. Everyone across the task force could see the giant ball of fire as the ship entered the atmosphere.

Klaxons across all the ships started going off. Alpha Colony was descending too fast. The crew onboard the colony ship fired the retro rockets attempting to slow her down. Telemetry readings indicated the ship slowed but was still descending too fast. The crew poured on more power to the retros. After two minutes, the ship slowed to the point where she started to gain altitude. Quickly, the crew adjusted the power levels to stop the ascent. The klaxons sounded again; Alpha Colony was just out of its descent path. The crew again adjusted the maneuvering jets to bring them back onto the descent path. Three minutes later and at thirty thousand feet, the ship was back on the proper descent path with the correct descent rate.

The crew made new adjustments, and the ship began to drop its nose and level off. They were now outside of the descent path and made hurried adjustments to correct the angle and pitch of the ship. They had to get this correct. The misalignment of the ship, if too much off the correct position, would require extensive adjustments to deploy the colony modules and connect the four ships on the ground. They were on the upper end of the required speed for the landing. They extended the landing gears along the underside of their ship. They were still too high when they did this maneuver and the ship shifted again. Quickly more adjustments were made.

The ship landed hard, kicking dirt, rock, and dust high into the air, jarring the ship's hull, which the entire crew felt.

Captain Lindsey was standing over the shoulder of her crewman who was taking readings of the Alpha Colony ship's landing position. They heard the report from Alpha Colony to Delta Colony. They reported they were point zero three degrees off position.

Captain Lindsey growled deep in her throat. The crewman checked his readings.

"Captain, they are close enough to their designated landing. If the other ships can do better then everything ought to be ok."

She acknowledged him and had her Communications Officer send the data to Delta Colony ship.

The crew in the control room of Delta Colony was running their figures. After ten minutes, they informed the Director that the Alpha Colony ship's position was close enough. However, each ship must match the degree angle or be off their mark for the ships to deploy the colony modules correctly. He acknowledged the order and informed them to advise Bravo Colony ship to begin its descent but to double-check their systems and learn from Alpha Colony ship's mistakes.

The day proved to be extremely rough for the colony. They had several near misses. The entire colony was exhausted. Bravo Colony ship had performed its descent at near textbook perfection. The ship's landing site was at a ninety-degree angle to the Alpha Colony ship's aft end. Bravo Colony ship landed hard since the crew didn't brake soon enough, jarring both the ship and crew. Also, she was ten meters too close to the Alpha ship.

Charlie Colony Ship made more mistakes than Alpha Colony ship on its descent nearly crashing into Alpha. Her landing spot was designated to be at a forty-five-degree angle to the bow pointing to Alpha's port side. Only at the last second did the crew make an adjustment which avoided the ship crashing into Alpha. Her landing was especially hard. Despite their exhaustion, the crew was inspecting the ship to determine the extent of the damage that the sensors alerted them to. They were fifteen meters too close to Alpha. The crew was determining if they would have to attempt to move the ship in order to deploy the colony modules.

Delta Colony began its descent favorably. Her landing zone was at a forty-five-degree angle off Bravo's port nose. Soon after entering the atmosphere and passing through the ion zone, a massive gust of wind hit the ship, knocking it off course. The crew was frantic while trying to bring the ship back on course. The descent became precarious. The crew kept over-compensating as she continued down. At one point, everyone thought she would miss the mark completely. Another adjustment meant the ship would crash into both the Alpha and Bravo Colony ships. Finally, after several adjustments, they landed. It was another hard landing, breaking two of the landing gears. They were also eighteen meters too far from Bravo Colony ship and would not be able to adjust her position. Her colonists were inspecting the ship for additional damages and determined they could connect to Bravo Colony ship. They landed at the upper connection range.

All the ships were at the correct angle from one another. However, the damage assessment parties, and the level of exhaustion made the deployment of the colony impractical for that day. Several colonists reported to medical but with light injuries. With rest, they would be able to continue. Captain Lindsey sighed heavily. Another day, most likely two or three, before she could depart the system.

Captain Lindsey sat in her office onboard the *Rapture*. It took the colonists three days to begin deploying their modules, but now all four ships were connected, and they could begin. She continued to read the reports from all the ships.

Well, she thought, *at least they did it, and now I can be off to the rendezvous point tomorrow.*

She nodded to herself as she continued to pour over the reports when the buzzer to her hatch rang. She pressed the button, allowing entry to her office. Colonel Ron Davis, her XO, entered.

"Captain," he said as she gestured for him to take a seat.

"Well, they did it, Jo."

"Yes, indeed they did. Though it was a close one. Tomorrow, we should be able to depart from here, yes?"

"Yes, we can."

"How long before we reach our designated coordinates, Ron?"

"Now that we can travel at our rated speed, Astrogation says four full weeks."

She grimaced and turned to her computer screen. Right now, the display showed her family.

"Damn, that long. We are still that far away."

"Yes. And I know, we are behind schedule. But the delays are justified."

"I agree. We should have considered these obstacles back on Earth. Ron, I want to launch one of our own hyperspace communication drones with all the details of this mission since we left Plymouth Station. Also, I have checked our number of drones. Give three of them over to the colony. They really don't have enough of them. Three more may make a difference on their success. We can spare them."

Colonel Davis nodded, "Will do. I will have the reports collated by tonight and ready to launch the drone tomorrow before we depart. Anything you desire from the colony?"

"No. Just the reports. I'll speak with the Director myself tomorrow morning before we depart."

He nodded as he stood up to leave.

"I'll see you at breakfast then."

She smiled as he departed and turned back to the display. She had no idea how long she would be out here and away from her family. She missed her kids. They would probably be grown before this was over, and she would have missed it all. She began putting together a message for them. Part of the communication drone would contain messages from the colonists and her own ships' crewmembers to their various families, not only the reports to command.

"I want to thank you for the three communication drones. I do hope they are extras only and not needed. But I do appreciate them." Dr. Phillips said.

"I hope so too, Anthony. Well, you are set. We are launching the drone now. Remember, it is going to take a month for any of these drones to reach Earth. So, remember to be very clear. Only a few people know you are out here. These drones are encrypted. That means after a month of travel; it still will take weeks for the parties to understand what is in them. The right people have to be alerted after retrieval. They need to decrypt them and then attempt to understand what is being said."

Anthony frowned. "Really?"

"Oh yes. Written and spoken communications can be so misinterpreted. You will have to be very clear as to the situation and what it is you desire. Remember, it will take two and most likely three to four months before anyone shows up after you send a drone. You will have to continue your drills to ensure you can fight off anything till help arrives. I hope Colonel Davenport has rewritten your procedures to protect you from those creatures."

"Yes, yes, he has," Anthony said, nodding vigorously. "Ok, I didn't realize how difficult communicating with them might be."

"It can be. Just really think it through. One method you can use is have someone who knows nothing about what you are trying to say listen and read your communiqué. If they can relay it back to you as you mean it, then you are probably safe to send. If they say something completely different, then you missed it."

"Thanks. I didn't think of that."

"Well, I think that is it, Anthony. We will be departing in approximately two hours. I'll send a final farewell to you just before we hit hyperspace."

"Good. Safe travels and a successful mission." He smiled.

They both clicked off and Jo sat back in her office chair. Two hours before her Space Action Group would make a jump. Her Chief Engineer had assured her he would push the engines along with the two other ships to the upper end of their rated speed to stay with the four weeks or shave off as much time as possible. She yawned as she stretched her arms over her arched back and laid her head onto her hands on her desk.

A nap would be worthwhile right now, she thought.

CHAPTER 14

Mike O'Shea was sitting in the office portion of his cabin. His desk had three monitors on it. One monitor displayed the Earth fleet that was being built. The second one had the talking points from Earth's leaders concerning a coalition, and the last one was Mike's work as he continued adjusting the words for the upcoming meeting. On the bulkhead was another monitor displaying the scene from the main viewer on the bridge. Occasionally he would glance at it but was deep into the speech and the possible questions he may receive from the other delegates at the meeting.

Colonel Nelson sat in her command chair onboard the bridge of the *Diplomat,* she was sipping her coffee and watching the various monitors. She was getting tired of the waiting. They had been at this rendezvous spot for three weeks now. She allowed the ship to drift occasionally only to bring it back to its original position. Her scanners were passive only. They were at the edge of Kammorrigan space.

"Colonel, a hyperspace well is opening," the Scanner Technician called out.

"Thank you," she responded, "prepare to go to General Quarters and maintain passive scanning."

The crew responded efficiently. They had learned early on not to question but do. Colonel Nelson had proven herself to be extremely competent. She keyed her comm channel on her chair and asked Mike to come to the bridge. A ship was inbound.

A ship entered normal space from the well. It was five thousand kilometers away and moving toward their position. Colonel Nelson sipped some more of her coffee as she watched the monitors. It was big, three times the size of the *Diplomat*. It had a flat nose and curved away from the front along all sides, similar to a cylinder, then sharply sloped down to an elongated hull toward its aft engine ports. Scanners reported it had various weapons and shields, that were off at this time. They waited for the approach.

At one thousand kilometers, they were hailed by the ship.

"Open a channel," the Colonel said.

The view screen switched from the ship to a figure. Like the other Wooxunas, this one had four legs, black in color with black pointed ears over a black head. His muzzle was all black with dark fur below his eyes and along his head. The brown eyes fixed onto Colonel Nelson.

"*Diplomat,* I am Kuro, the captain of the battle wagon *Roofunas.* We have arrived as directed by our government."

"I am Colonel Nelson, commander of the *Diplomat.* We are glad to see you, Captain Kuro."

He gave her a very cold stare.

By this time, Mike had arrived on the bridge.

"Jennifer, I see our escort has arrived," he said to Colonel Nelson.

"NO!" Captain Kuro responded with a sharp tone in his voice and turned his cold stare at Mike.

"Soon, we will launch a transport to come alongside your ship. It carries a very special passenger. He will provide you with the coordinates to the meeting location and remain with you." He paused as he stared at both of them. "To assist you in preparation for the upcoming meeting." Next, he showed his teeth and leaned forward.

"I assure you Humans, if anything happens to him, I will hunt you down and destroy you. If he is taken by the Kammorrigans, then I will ensure you endure great pain before I finally slay you. You understand, Humans?" Captain Kuro growled the last.

Mike was a bit taken back but stood steady with a blank gaze.

Colonel Nelson stood up while placing her cup down. Spread her legs shoulder width and put her hands behind her.

"Rest assured, Captain. We will take care of our guest. No harm will come to him. Be aware, if Kammorrigans show up we will jump out of the space they are in. Understand, all Earth ships have the same orders. Self-destruct before capture by any species, especially the Kammorrigans. If we are going to be captured or killed, our guest will die alongside us." She returned his cold stare.

Captain Kuro continued to stare coldly at her for a few moments. He then turned his head to one of his boards. After studying for a moment, he depressed a couple of buttons and turned back to Colonel Nelson.

"Good. We are sending one of our top government officials to you. He will be our delegate at the conference. His shuttle is departing now." He then clicked off the viewer.

Mike and Jennifer looked at each other.

"Damn," he breathed.

"Yes. I never expected something like that from the Wooxuna, but we had only known two of them. Guess we better get to the airlock."

The Colonel turned and opened up her mic.

"Security and Protocol, meet us at the." She checked her monitors, "port airlock. Prepare to render honors to an ambassador." She clicked off her mic. "Ready for your true first diplomatic meeting?" She asked Mike, smiling as she moved toward the bridge hatch. Mike shook his head and followed her.

Mike sat at the conference room table, sipping his coffee. Colonel Nelson sat to his right with a cup of coffee in front of her, but she didn't seem interested in it. Chief Seymour sat to his left with a glass of water. The Wooxuna sat across the table. He was drinking from a bowl he was holding to his mouth between his two paws or hands. Unlike a dog on Earth, the Wooxuna thumb was closer to the position of a human thumb plus they could open their paws and use each digit like a human finger.

He sat the bowl down and started smacking his lips. He was fawn all over his back, but his chest and stomach were white with black fur as a border. His muzzle was black which ran along both eyes and the nose bridge. He had a white patch of fur on both sides of his muzzle.

Mike put down his cup. "Should we address you as Ambassador or Delegate?"

The Wooxuna looked at him for a moment while he finished smacking his lips.

"Good drink. I assume Magos or Thunder told you how to make it. Thank you, it was refreshing."

The three Humans looked at each other with puzzlement.

The Wooxuna chuckled.

"I do have a translator on me. However, we now have examples of your language and I among others have been attempting to learn it. Please, call me Kuma. We will save the formal language for the conference. I appreciate the honor you provided me and my team with."

"I trust you will find the quarters satisfactory," Col Nelson said.

"I think we will. There are only three of us and the space is sufficient," Kuma responded, looking them over.

"We are curious about this species on Earth called dog."

"Why?" Inquired the Chief.

"From what Magos reported, they sound similar to us. My people are interested in seeing one. It may answer a lot of questions for us about our ancient past." He sighed, "But that is for another time. Your Astrogator has the coordinates to the meeting?"

Colonel Nelson depressed a couple of buttons, "Commander to Astrogation."

"Astrogation, here," a voice came over the comm system.

"You have a plot for the coordinates provided by the Wooxunas?"

"Yes, Colonel. We have plotted. Duration in hyperspace will be three weeks."

Mike slouched back in his chair with a despondent look on his face.

Chief Seymour sighed and shook his head.

"Why that location?" He asked Kuma.

Kuma turned his head to the Chief, "Simple. It is hidden. The Kammorrigans do not know about the place or the meeting. Three weeks, not too long. We will need the time Mr. O'Shea to prepare you for the meeting. Who will attend for your planet?"

Mike nodded and responded to Colonel Nelson, "Go ahead, Jennifer, and make the jump."

She spoke into the comm system, "Helm, take the plot and make the jump to hyperspace. See if Engineering can give us more speed." She closed the mic after the orders were acknowledged. Mike turned back to Kuma.

"Colonel Nelson, the Chief and I will be the Earth delegation."

"Well, then," Kuma said, "we best get started. There will be eleven total planets represented. That is all either we or the Alians could get to agree to come."

Mike nodded, "I hope it will be enough."

Kuma then stood up and made his excuses. He needed to check on the room and ensure the materials were ready to be presented. They agreed to meet again after dinner.

Three weeks later, the *Diplomat* came out of hyperspace. Colonel Nelson leaned forward in her command chair. There was nothing but space on the viewer. She scanned all the monitors. In the distance was a faint star, but they would have to make a short jump to get near it. Her crew began scanning the area.

"Colonel, no contacts at all. Normal space radiation, etc. The only thing we are picking up is an asteroid field. Parts of it is dense," the Technician reported.

She furrowed her brows, frowned, and sat back in her chair.

"Astrogation, double-check our position," she ordered.

After a moment, Astrogation said, "Colonel, we are where we are supposed to be according to the coordinates the Wooxuna gave us."

"Thank you."

She started to open up her comm system when Chief Seymour and Kuma strolled onto the bridge. She turned her chair to look at them. Kuma glanced at the viewer and then at her.

"I felt us come out of hyperspace," he said, "I asked the Chief to bring me here. Have you found the asteroid belt?"

She gave him a cold stare. "Are we going into an asteroid field?"

He smiled, or what could be called a smile. "Yes, Colonel, we are. This location has been a secret meeting place for the civilizations that the Kammorrigans have either destroyed, raided and/or enslaved. They don't know where it is. Yes, it can be dangerous to maneuver through them. My assistant can take over at the helm, if you prefer. He knows the way in and the docking procedures at the base. Your decision. Naturally, we will provide all the technical information as required."

She continued to hold his gaze.

Great, give my ship over to an alien, she thought. She began to weigh the risks of entering an asteroid field.

"Helm, are you able to maneuver through the field to the destination?"

The Helmsman began checking his board and the information coming to his station from the other stations. Everyone waited on the Helmsman. Jennifer didn't want to turn the helm over to an alien but no one had maneuvered through an asteroid field before.

"I know I can make it, but it will be rough going. I don't know the route through the field."

She stood up and walked over to the scanning stations. She had the techs bring up the field. As she leaned over the Technician, she studied the output from the monitors. Finally, with a heavy sigh, she stood straight up and turned to Kuma.

"Sir, please bring your assistant to the bridge. I am requesting he maneuver us through the asteroid field to our destination."

Kuma nodded and asked Chief Seymour to have his assistant come to the bridge.

A few moments later, Kuma's assistant came onto the bridge. He had the same bulk as Kuma but a bit shorter. His coat was white with a couple of brown spots, and he sported a white mask. He walked calmly toward Kuma who pointed him to the Helm station. The Helmsman pressed a few buttons and then stood up, offering his chair to the new Wooxuna. The Wooxuna stepped lightly onto the chair and seated himself. He thanked the Helmsman and began looking over the board. They discussed the controls of the board and how the ship would react. After a few minutes, the Wooxuna started working the controls with the Helmsman guiding him. He looked up at the Colonel signaling he was ready. As the Helmsman was stepping away, the Wooxuna asked him to stay, saying he might need his assistance. Also, he could show the Helmsman how to maneuver around the asteroids. After a few minutes more, the Colonel told him to proceed.

The Wooxuna depressed the maneuver buttons and made speed adjustments, bringing the ion drive online. The *USS Diplomat* thrusters started the ship along a forty-five-degree angle to its port, and the sub-light engines kicked in, increasing her speed. The ship was angling along the X-axis of the asteroid belt and closing. The Wooxuna was monitoring the main viewer, and another monitor showing relative position to the asteroid belt along with the velocity gauge and the helm monitors on the helm board. He was maintaining both speed and approach vector to the belt.

After ten minutes on this course, the Wooxuna saw what he was looking for. He powered thrusters bringing the ship on a Z positive of one thousand kilometers and changed the direction along the X-axis to a forty-five-degree angle to the starboard of the ship. The Colonel was impressed by the way he handled the controls and how smoothly the ship responded to the course change. Now comes the fun he indicated to the Helmsman. He continued to angle the ship into a gap between two large asteroids and slowed the speed of the ship. As the *Diplomat* slipped between the two asteroids, the Wooxuna slowed the ship, then turned toward the port and maneuvered the ship around the first large asteroid and paralleled it to its halfway point. Then he turned the ship hard to its starboard and accelerated to slip past two asteroids. As the ship began to clear the two asteroids, the Wooxuna dropped the ship to Z minus two thousand kilometers and angled to the starboard thirty degrees. Once the ship reached this new spot, he angled it out to run alongside an asteroid to the starboard side. After passing this asteroid, he then turned hard to port and slipped past another asteroid. Then he brought the ship to a Z positive fifteen hundred kilometers and slowed as he made a hard turn to the starboard and after a few seconds, dropped the ship two thousand kilometers on the Z-axis and turned hard to port. He accelerated past four asteroids, then dropped speed and turned hard to starboard ninety degrees. He then leveled out and flew past several asteroids.

Kuma then stood up and strolled over to the Communications station.

He began keying in some frequencies while saying to the Officer, "Keep these frequencies stored, but be ready to destroy them. These are the frequencies and codes for the station." He then keyed the system.

"Station Renauldot, this is Senator Kuma of Wooxuna. I'm escorting the Human ship, *Diplomat,* which is carrying the Human delegation. Please transmit beam for approach."

After a couple of moments, a voice said, "Human ship *Diplomat,* we are transmitting." Helm acknowledged the beam.

"Welcome to Station Renauldot both Wooxuna and Human delegates." The Communication Officer indicated they were receiving both audio and visual. The Colonel told her to place the video feed on the main viewer. The main viewer display went from the asteroids to displaying a control room with a blue-skinned creature. The creature had large green eyes outlined in red. It scanned the bridge and then smiled when it saw the Wooxuna at the helm controls.

"Hi ho, hi ho, Neefrus. I see you are at controls. Good. Smart Humans. It is good to see you again."

"Hello, my friend. What landing pad do you have for us?"

"Can the ship land or not?"

Neefrus, the Wooxuna, looked at the Helmsman, "Do you have landing gears?"

"Yes, we do," he said while gesturing to another set of controls.

"Good." He then turned back to the viewer, "They have landing gears. Scan the ship, please, and advise if we can proceed inside the station."

A few moments more passed while Neefrus continued to maneuver the ship around several more asteroids.

"We have you now. Yes, the ship can land inside the hangar. You will take pad number two. That way we can fully bring you inside the station. Do the Humans require additional environmental adjustments?"

Kuma spoke up, "We have been with them for three weeks. No, the station's atmosphere and pressure are sufficient to support everyone."

The creature nodded and affirmed the information.

"Good, should we prepare quarters for them?"

The Colonel answered, "No, thank you. We will remain on the ship in between any discussions."

The creature again nodded and affirmed the information.

Kuma asked, "How many delegates have arrived?"

The creature checked a board. "To include you, six out of the expected eleven have arrived. The other five are due here tomorrow." It paused and checked another system. "There will be a gathering in a few hours after your arrival should you be inclined to refreshments."

Kuma thanked him and said they would discuss it; meanwhile, he asked that it ensure they arrived safely. The creature smiled again.

Neefrus brought the *Diplomat* through the last asteroids. The ship's sensors picked up a bubble in the belt with an enormous asteroid in the middle of it. Neefrus informed them there was a repulse system set up to maintain an asteroid shield wall around the station. He had already slowed the ship down considerably as they approached the behemoth of an asteroid. There were several points of light coming from the side of the asteroid they could see. It had an extremely rugged terrain, but the ship's sensors picked up various systems along the surface including shields, weapons, communication arrays, and sensors. As the ship approached, two extremely large hangar doors began to open horizontally, and light began to stream out of the hangar.

As the ship entered the hangar, the crew could see an enormous circular room. On their starboard side, approximately halfway between the floor and ceiling, was the control booth for the hangar. All around the wall were various items for ship servicing. On the floor were two large landing pads. These pads could easily receive a ship the size of *Diplomat* and even bigger. The light came from several different sources around the hangar.

Neefrus deftly maneuvered the ship along the middle of the hangar and started employing the landing gears. As the ship entered the hangar six landing gears deployed. When the ship was inside the hangar completely, Neefrus maneuvered it to the midpoint and then brought it to its port, leveled it, and proceeded to place the ship on landing pad two. After cutting the engines, the hangar doors were closed, and the pad began to recede to a lower level. As the pad came to a stop, they could see they were in a chamber with eight pads laid out in a circle; the whole system cycled bringing another pad to the elevator slot, and it rose, closing the upper level. Neefrus informed them the same hangar configuration existed under landing pad one. The sensors showed that a breathable atmosphere was available.

A few hours later, in the conference room, Kuma and Mike O'Shea were having a polite argument about going to the gathering. Colonel Nelson with Chief Seymour sat listening.

"Mike, we should stay here in the ship and not go" Kuma said.

"I don't understand. As a diplomat, I have found negotiating with other entities to be done during social gatherings. A lot gets done in those times versus a formal meeting. I tell you; we can get agreements before the conference."

Kuma shook his head. "Maybe on Earth that works, but not here. Please, understand that all of these species are paranoid. We all have suffered at the hands of the Kammorrigans. They don't trust you yet."

Mike smiled. "They will when I can meet with them one on one."

Kuma shook his head again. "Maybe on Earth. But this group would start thinking you are making private deals with each other group to take them down. This would destroy any opportunity to form a coalition. Trust me, I know them all too well."

Mike started to say something when the Colonel broke in, "Mike, perhaps we should trust the Senator's wisdom and knowledge on this. After all, he has been working with these species while we are just meeting them. Maybe their trust is earned in an open meeting instead of private meetings."

Mike turned his gaze on her while considering what she said. After a brief moment, he nodded his head slowly.

"You're right, Jennifer. My apologies, Kuma, we are new here and we want a strong coalition. We will stay inboard until the conference."

Kuma thanked him and advised Colonel Nelson that a member of her staff ought to augment the station's control room. They would welcome the person as it would show trust and cooperation. Besides, she would have her own person to alert them of any situation outside of the station.

Throughout the next day, five ships arrived and were placed under landing pad one since six ships occupied the slots under landing pad two. The *Diplomat* was informed the conference would take place in two days now that the delegates had all arrived. The station's crew was ensuring all protocols would be met. The agenda would start at the end of the next day with an evening gathering of all diplomats; then, the conference would begin the following morning. Kuma informed them there shouldn't be much discussion during the evening gathering. Each of the delegates desired to get a look at the Humans.

CHAPTER 15

Ambassador Mike O'Shea and party arrived at the conference room first, as he desired. His party included Colonel Nelson and Chief Petty Officer Seymour. He was advised that each delegate was allowed one security guard. He had decided against taking one. Mike desired to demonstrate that he trusted the other delegates with his own security. Colonel Nelson was to attend since she had destroyed a Kammorrigan warship and Chief Seymour since he was on Kammorriga during the EXPLORER mission.

Senator Kuma, along with his Aide, Neefrus who carried important documents, was with them. Kuma had shown them the way to the conference room. Kuma did bring his own security. This Wooxuna was rather large and extremely muscular. Mike estimated the Wooxuna weighed two hundred or two hundred fifty pounds. He had a coat of body armor over his chest and back and carried a rifle across his back with a sidearm at his waist. His eyes kept shifting along the hallways while it constantly sniffed the air. He was the last in the group.

Kuma had been informed that the chamber was ready for the delegates. The group rounded a corner and could see the metal, pocket doors were open. When they were closed, the room would be sealed, offering maximum security, similar to a top-secret room on Earth.

The conference room was a large circular chamber formed out of rock. The fifteen-foot ceiling and floors were smooth and flat. It had two doors leading off it, one to the station's control room, and the other door led to a support room for the chamber. The center of the room was dominated by a horseshoe table, with the ends nearly touching, that could seat fifteen easily.

The walls were lined with diamond-shaped lights. Over the table itself was the chamber's main light source. These lights could be dimmed as required. The table had lights for each delegate, which they could adjust them to their respective light spectrum. Additionally, translators were at each delegate seat.

When they sat, Mike was informed there would only be eleven nations represented at this conference. Except for the Humans, each delegate would be the representative and have one Aide. Each delegate would have a security guard stationed behind them along the wall.

As they moved around the table to take their seats, the Humans noticed the other delegate seats varied in size and shape for their comfort. Some were very similar to themselves and some very different.

Mike and his team sat at the far end of the table, opposite from the main door. Mike in the middle with Colonel Neslon to his right and the Chief to his left. Senator Kuma sat next to the Chief with Neefrus next to him.

Kuma had informed Mike that the station was a neutral site between a consortium of nations. Its top-secret location was known only to a few of the political leadership and commanders authorized to approach it. Any nation could utilize the station. But to hold a conference required a nation to be the host. Most of the expenses would be paid for by the host, in this case, the Alia. Therefore, they were the last to arrive. Kuma indicated; the Alia wanted to host the conference since they believed they had the most to gain from a coalition.

Mike pulled out his chair and placed his briefcase on the table, and unbuttoned the blazer of his black suit. He adjusted his black tie, ensuring it remained clipped to his white shirt as he sat down. Mike noticed the chair conformed to his body and had temperature controls on it. Chief Seymour was unbuttoning his dress blue jacket as he pulled out his chair and noticed Colonel Nelson doing the same for her Space Force blue uniform. He was glad to see her frown at her own discomfort with the uniform. Neither of them had worn these uniforms since they left Earth and both were a bit uncomfortable in them. Chief had to wear his blues with ribbons only since the Space Force didn't have an equivalent uniform with medals. Both his and the Colonel's uniforms had their ribbons, warfare devices, and rank, Mike being the only civilian.

When Kuma, who wore a red sash with gold borders and a gold waistband, reached his chair, the security officer pulled it out for him and moved to his position by the wall. Kuma sat. Neefrus, wearing a brown sash and a gold waistband, settled into his chair next to him.

Mike opened his briefcase and organized his papers on the table. He handed the Chief a pad of paper for notes and started to hand the Colonel some when he noticed she had her palm device. The Colonel was bringing up the information she would require. She then checked her communications with her Executive Officer, Major Alexander, who was in the control room. The station's personnel insisted on checking her communication device ensuring it would only be able to reach the control room. They had double-checked the signal so no one could listen in on the conference.

The ShiLoeeza entered next. They appeared to be human, though their features were slightly elongated. Their guard wore full body armor with a rifle over its back, and a sidearm at the waist. The

Delegate, Bopt, wore a black uniform with two red sashes, one over each shoulder. His Aide had one red sash over his left shoulder. They took their seats next to Neefrus. Once seated, Bopt nodded at those already in the room while his Aide took documents out of a bag and laid them in front of him before taking his seat.

Next, Mockaseus of the Nmaeurvena Order entered. They were pale skin with red eyes. Mockaseus wore a blue robe; his Aide's robe was blue and silver. Their guard was in full, black body armor with a rifle and sidearm. They took their seats next to the ShiLoeeza.

Graplees of the Gopp Block followed. These people were large and bulky. They had broad shoulders, thick necks, and barrel-like chests. Graplees wore green body armor over his chest with leg armor and grieves along his four legs. His upper arms were bare, and he wore bracers on his forearms. He took his seat next to the Nmaeurvena Order while his Aide, who wore similar green armor, took out documents for him and sat down. Their guard, who was fully encapsulated in green armor, took up position by the wall. She also had a rifle and a sidearm.

Entered Loraineas of the Saemeennaee system. He, along with his Aide, were shorter than the Humans. They had blue skin with large green eyes rimmed in red. Loraineas wore a blue shirt and pants flecked with gold. His shirt sported a red V that ran from his shoulders to the middle of his shirt ending in a blue jewel. His Aide wore a black shirt flecked with red with a blue V ending in a blue jewel. They took their seats next to the Gopp while their guard, dressed in brown and carrying a rifle and sidearm, took his place behind them.

Everyone who had entered the chamber thus far was seated to the left of the Humans. The next group to arrive took the seats to the right of the of the Humans. The first to enter was the delegation from Zzssizzkpent, who were bipedal lizards. They had elongated heads with razor-sharp teeth. Their eyes were slits along the top of their heads. They had lean torsos and tails. At the end of the tail was a metal device. Their hands were talons with three very sharp nails and an additional sharp nail similar to an opposable thumb. Their feet had similar nails but were webbed. They wore green sashes. They took the seats that were five away from the Humans. Their Delegate, SssLu-rapee sat closest to the Humans. The Aide placed documents in front of the Delegate. The guard, who wore a form of body armor, took its position along the wall and sported both a rifle and a sidearm.

After they were seated, three boulders rolled into the chamber and headed next to the Zzssizzkpent. The largest boulder rolled over to the wall and came to a stop. The next boulders rolled to the table, presumably with the Delegate, Garrble, closest to the Humans. The Kluba remained in their boulder form.

Next came the Ccaayuba. They were tall bipeds with short hair that resembled fur. They had four eyes in a square formation. The Delegate, Sheeosai, wore a brown jerkin with multiple gems on it and brown leggings. His Aide had similar clothes but with three gems. The guard took up its position. While he had jerkins and leggings, these were of a heavier material. He also was armed with a rifle and sidearm.

No sooner did the Ccaayuba reach their chairs that, the Ghuzanee delegation entered the chamber. Their skin was of different hues of grey, tending to a dark coloring. They didn't have any hair, and they had pointed ears. The Delegate, Runares, wore grey slacks with a dark red shirt and a purple sash. His Aide wore similar clothes and no sash. Mike noticed the Aide's skin was a lighter grey. The guard was almost all grey and a bit stockier than the other two. He wore all brown clothes and was armed with a rifle and sidearm. He took up his position against the wall.

All the Delegates were present save one. Once all the parties had settled into place, a chime sounded. Everyone stood up as the host of the conference, Prince Alianeese of the Alia, entered, followed by his Aide and their guard. They moved rapidly along the right side of the table toward the Humans and their seats on their two arms and two legs. They were short, had short brown fur, and moved like chimpanzees. Prince Alianeese wore blue pants with a gold shirt and a blue sash with red borders and a bright red jewel on his chest. His Aide had the same style of clothing but a brown sash with no jewel. His guard had brown body armor and carried a rifle and a sidearm. The guard took his place, and the Delegate and his Aide stood next to their chairs. The chime sounded again, and the two main doors slid to a close. Everyone took their seats.

Prince Alianeese scanned the room fixing his gaze upon each member around the table. After a few moments, he nodded and then stood up. He fixed the earpiece of the translator into his left ear and adjusted the microphone near his mouth. As he was doing this, all the other Delegates did the same.

"My friends, thank you all for coming to this conference on such short notice," he began. He stopped for a moment and glanced about the room. "The reason for this conference is to discuss the formation of a coalition for the eradication of the Kammorrigan Space Regime." He paused and glanced around to see the reactions around the room. He nodded. "We all have suffered at their hands. They have taken our worlds. They have destroyed some of them and have enslaved all of our people. Now, a new species has appeared. They destroyed the Kammorrigan home world. They have come, seeking to join with us, for the total defeat and hopefully the obliteration of the Kammor-rigans." He turned to the Humans. "I, Prince Alianeese of the Alia people, welcome you Humans here. I am hopeful that we can come to an arrangement for a coalition to wipe out this pestilence upon all of us." He then sat down.

Senator Kuma, then motioned for their attention, and began laying out the agenda. The rest of the day was spent introducing each Del-egate and the people they represented. After several hours, Senator Kuma dismissed them. He stated they would begin laying out their positions and desires concerning the coalition in the morning.

Three days later, Colonel Nelson was in her quarters on the *Diplomat*. She had entered the room, tossed her blazer onto a chair, and opened her small fridge. She was kneeling down, scanning the contents of the unit when she saw it, a bottle of vodka. She grabbed it and stood up, looking at the glasses on top of the unit. Nope, she decided against the smaller one and reached for the taller glass. She filled it halfway with vodka, placed the bottle back in the fridge, and picking up the glass, turned to the water and ice dispenser. She filled the glass up with ice.

She took a sip of the vodka and placed the cold glass against her fore-head with her eyes closed. She then raised the glass and toasted the health of Admiral Brannigan and thanked him for allowing alcohol aboard his ships. She needed a stiff drink after these past three days. She took a full drink and went back to the fridge to refill the glass. Afterward, she went to a recliner and sat down, kicking off her shoes and reclining. She took another sip from her glass and was thankful she was a Space Force officer and not a diplomat.

The last three days had been painful for her. She could tell it was the same for the Chief. Only Mike was in his element. It proved difficult to understand the other species in the chamber, even with the translators. Their dialects and strange pronunciations made her head ache. The Gopp had angered her during the second day. She was asked to recount the destruction of the Kammorrigan warship. Graplees accused her of cowardice for attacking the ship from behind. The Gopp attack only from the front. He was a brute about the whole affair. She attempted to explain the sensitivities of the mission and how they had to win fast before the Kammorrigan called for reinforcements. The whole discussion soon spiraled out of control with both her and the Gopp standing up, leaning on the table and nearly shouting at each other over tactics. Mike attempted to get her to calm down when Prince Alianeese banged on the table and demanded silence. He explained how grateful he was to the Colonel and told Graplees that it was his own ship that was under attack. If the Humans had not destroyed the Kammorrigan ship, he would have been captured, and think how devastating that would have been. Graplees acknowledged the fact and sat down with a huff.

Prince Alianeese informed the group, that he is the crowned prince of the Alia Kingdom. When his father dies, he will be king. He again expressed his sincere thanks to the Colonel. Then he explained that the Kammorrigans did not honor the way they fought and that they needed to learn the methods that the Humans would employ and also teach.

Nope, she thought, *Mike was the only one in his element.*

He studied each attendee, trying to discover their non-verbal language and cues. He tried to figure out what each member was thinking by their reactions to what was being said. After each session, he would sit down to compare notes with her and the Chief. The Chief was finding it difficult to keep up at first, but by this third day, he was getting it. He fell back on his special operations training and found he could do the job. When he relayed what had happened on Kammorriga with his team, he found all members were intent on what he had to tell them. They all appeared to be impressed by how Admiral Brannigan had stopped the Kammorrigans with a stare and later, when he commanded the annihilation of the planet.

The only group that didn't react was the Kluba. They remained in their boulder configuration. Mike asked both the Colonel and Chief repeatedly if they had noticed any change. He was bothered by their lack of reaction. Senator Kuma told them that the Kluba have the ability to change their form. He further stated that he was surprised at their lack of reaction. He had no idea what that meant.

The third day was the hardest on the Humans, thus the stiff drink. The Ccaayuba and the Saemeennaee accused the Humans and the Alians, of having created an alliance already. After all, the Chief had attempted to rescue one on Kammorriga and the Colonel had saved the crown prince. Surely, they were already working together with full trade and diplomatic efforts. Crown Prince Alianeese was able to dissuade the accusation with a series of arguments that Mike admitted he had not thought of.

By the end of this third day, the coalition was supported by four of the attendees: the Alia, Wooxuna, ShiLoeeza and the Ghuzanee. The others remained uncommitted, but no one had departed the confer-ence. Colonel Nelson took another drink from her glass and shook her head. A lot of the discussions centered around trade negotiations and who would lead the coalition. Several of the species didn't have war-making abilities. The Zzssizzkpent, for instance, were not a war-rior caste. They had great technology but were isolationist. They were attending due to the suffering of their people at the hands of the Kammorrigans. Mike had met with them alone to attempt to figure out a compromise. They didn't have warriors or ships to contribute, but maybe Mike could convince them to aid with their technological advantages. This effort was proving difficult, as was the whole affair.

Colonel Nelson finished her glass of vodka and was thinking about pouring another.

No, she thought, *better not. Tomorrow will be another tough day. Better to eat dinner and get ready for bed.*

Thankfully, her officers were taking care of the ship and crew so she could help Mike.

The start of the fourth day found all Delegates seated around the table. Everyone was quietly studying their documents, except for the Kluba; they remained in their boulder configuration. Senator Kuma called for everyone's attention.

"Well, here we are," he began. "Let me refresh why we are here. We are seeking a coalition to destroy the Kammorrigan Space Regime once and for all. They have conquered our planets and terrorized our people for far too long. We are not seeking individual or group alliances, though that could come in the future. No, we are seeking a coalition, which means we all fight together for one or some limited goals, in this case, the destruction of the Kammorrigans. There are four of us willing to join the Humans in this endeavor. But we all need to be a part of this coalition. Each of us has the strengths to accomplish the goal together but not separately. Do we not desire to be free of these most vile of creatures? Do we not desire the freedom of travel and trade? The Humans have demonstrated they have weapons and the willingness to make war on the Kammorrigans."

"How many ships do they have?" Inquired Delegate Loraineas of the Saemeennaee.

"Admiral Brannigan is building one hundred ships centered around nine battle carriers," Mike stated. The Colonel started to object then remembered he was authorized to discuss certain material matters.

"The battle carriers are more than a match for two or three of the largest Kammorrigan warships. We did get a lot of information on their ships and their disposition from another battle, which you are not aware of. We lost a ship with the destruction of a Kammorrigan warship. And yes, it was a frontal battle. I was there. I saw it. Our battle carriers will be devastating to the Kammorrigans. Also, we will have ships designed to launch ground troops on certain planets to capture them and wreak havoc on the Kammorrigans. This won't be a single battle. No, Admiral Brannigan is confident that it will take several space and planetary battles to destroy them. We can't be everywhere at once. We need your assistance for major battles and for separate actions. Already, we have Fleet Captain Lindsey waiting for the results of this conference to begin the training and development of coordination between all of our fleets. She also was with us at Kammorriga." He finished.

There was silence around the room as the Delegates turned to look at each other and back to their notes.

"You are committing this much effort to their destruction?" Asked Sheeosai of the Ccaayuba.

"Yes, it is important to eliminate this threat to all of us," Mike answered.

"In fact, we already have another ship deep in Kammorriga space seeking additional intelligence on them," Mike stated. This time Colonel Nelson started to object, but Mike silenced her with a wave of his hand. In this matter, he was in charge. That simply meant he had total discretion as to what to tell this group.

All the Delegates, except the Kluba, stared at him.

Ok, that got their attention, Mike thought.

The door to Mike's right, the one leading to the station's control room, opened, and an Alian and two Saemeennaees came in rather quickly. They went over to Prince Alianeese and spoke quickly to him. As they spoke to him, the other door opened, and several of the station's crew came in and took several translators, including Mike's and the Colonel's, and departed the room. Mike and the other two looked at one another quizzically. Then, the Colonel keyed her communication device.

"Major Alexander, what is going on? She asked.

"I don't know, Colonel. Everyone in the control room is extremely excited," the Major responded.

"Are we in danger?"

"No Colonel. I don't think so. They are excited but not alarmed. And I mean a lot of excitement. Aah, a moment, please," the Major said.

"Colonel, got it. Another ship is coming out of the asteroid boundary and heading for the hangar. It is already depressurized and opening to receive it." He paused for a moment. "The ship, well, it appears to be a beetle: conical shape with two distinct parts. The main body appears to have three parts to it. It is approaching the hangar bay and decelerating. It should arrive in a few minutes."

"Ok, thank you. Advise me if there is a threat. Colonel out," she said as she closed her link. The three Humans turned their gaze onto Kuma. He just finished speaking in a hurried manner with the station's crew and watched them while five crewmembers brought in three new seats configured and different from the rest.

"To use a Human expression," Kuma started, "WOW! Something that no one expected is happening. A ship from Minurva is arriving.

We have not had contact with them as long as we can remember. No one here has ever seen a Minurvan. Every time one of their ships is spotted, they jump into hyperspace before anyone can contact them. This is a momentous event. We will be joined shortly by a delegation from Minurva."

Mike asked, "Who are they?"

Kuma shook his head. "We don't really know. It is rumored they are descendants of the Daemoulaoumari, whose republic was one of the great civilizations of the past. They controlled roughly twenty-seven percent of the known galaxy. The Kammorriga home world was on the outer edge of their republic. We did not invite the Minurva to the conference since they have avoided contact with anyone for centuries. But now, they are here."

Mike turned to look at each of the Delegates as they were adjusting their seats and documents. He could tell they were all nervous. Even the Kluba had changed their configuration. The two at the table now had a head and torso with two arms. However, their guard remained as a boulder. The technicians returned with their translators, indicating they had configured them with the Minurva language, though their data was old. Then, the main doors to the chamber opened.

Everyone watched the doorway. Soon, they could hear the sound of claws scratching on the stone floor. The noise grew louder by the moment, indicating multiple beings were approaching the room. Then, two figures appeared in the doorway and took up positions on either side of it. Mike could only think of praying mantis as he gazed upon them. They were dark green in color with black wings folded over the top of their bodies; their multi-faceted eyes were black, and they were approximately five feet tall. They had six legs, the top two holding what appeared to be power rifles. He couldn't tell whether they wore armor or not. Next came two other similar figures, standing at about six feet or so. They had the same body configuration; except they had brown wings folded over very dark green bodies with multi-faceted black eyes. After they entered the room, they took positions closer to the table and within the width of the two guards. The scrapings outside of the room grew louder as more of the creatures were approaching the room. At last, three more emerged around the corner and entered the room. They resembled the other four. The first stood at seven feet with a light green body. Its chest was yellow and had red wings folded over its body with yellow streaks running down the middle of each one. Its eyes were red. The last two followed the first and stopped slightly behind it. They had the same body configuration, except they had red wings folded over their dark green bodies, and their multi-faceted eyes were red. They came closer to the table and stood on either side of the two chairs. The doors closed behind the party. The chairs were made so that the Minurvan could lay its body along it. Instead, they stood to their full height and turned their gaze upon each of the Delegates.

Mike sensed an intensity to the Minurvan gaze. He naturally felt a discomfort with insects, as most humans did. But he was doing his best to overcome any dislikes or anxiety regarding them. He needed this coalition and didn't need his feelings to interfere with the goal.

After several clicks between the three main Minurvans, which the translators couldn't decipher, the lead one spoke, "This is the group considering a coalition against the Kammorrigan Space Regime?"

"Yes," stated Kuma.

The Minurvan lifted its left claw and pointed at Mike. "And are these the Humans?"

"We are," answered Mike.

"And you are?" It clicked.

"I am Ambassador Mike O'Shea of Earth."

"Interesting," *it responded with surprise,* Mike thought. "One of the heroes of the Battle of Kammorriga. And is this the hero Admiral Brannigan?" It asked, pointing at Colonel Nelson.

"No, this is Colonel Nelson, the commander of our ship, the *Diplomat,*" Mike answered, wondering how the Minurvan knew who was at Kammorriga.

"Interesting," it responded. "How many ships will you provide to the coalition?"

Mike found the Minurvan to be blunt. "As I informed everyone here, we will provide one hundred ships. Ships capable of destroying planets, win space battles, and provide ground assault capabilities to take planets."

"Interesting," the Minurvan said, sounding impressed.

"And Admiral Brannigan will lead your effort"

"No," Mike answered. "General Connington is slated to lead the fleet."

"Interesting," the Minurvan said, sounding disappointed, "why not the hero of the Battle of Kammorriga?"

Mike shrugged. "He is preparing the fleet, but we will most likely have him defend our home world."

Several clicks occurred between the three Minurvans.

"How many ships will each race be contributing to the coalition?" The Minurvan asked.

"Not everyone has yet agreed to join the coalition," Kuma responded.

"Interesting," the Minurvan responded, but this time, the tone showed both disappointment and disapproval.

"Why? All of you have suffered at their hands. They have destroyed you, and now you have an opportunity to destroy them, utterly," the Minurvan said, turning its gaze upon each Delegate in turn.

Graplees of Gopp responded with indignation. "Where have you been? You could destroy them."

The Minurvan turned its gaze upon him. It made several clicking noises that sounded like disappointment. Then, it gazed upon each of them.

"There was a time when each of you could have defeated the Kammorrigans in the distant past. The Daemoulaoumari Theologic Republic was one of the three great civilizations that fell to the Galactic Plague. All of the galaxy was in chaos and turmoil. Then, Kammorriga was a minor planet on the outer edge of the Republic. Any of us could have destroyed them, but who could see the future? In turn, we had to recover from the loss of all. Only the Kammorrigans were able to take advantage of the chaos. They grew and conquered, taking from each of you but giving nothing to the Universe," the Minurvan responded. "Now you need each other, the Humans, and us."

"Have the Kammorrigans found your world?" Mike asked.

"No. Every time one of their ships have approached our sphere of influence, we have destroyed it. They don't know where we are," it responded.

"Well, we would like to know where the Humans come from," Sheeosai of Ccaayuba said.

"Why?" Clicked the Minurvan. "All of you hide the location of your home world or new home world. And with good reason. The Kammorrigans find and destroy them. You don't need to know the Humans' home world just like you don't need to know ours," it clicked several times at them.

There was a heavy silence in the chamber.

The Minurvan clicked some more. "Minurva has decided to join this coalition and we expect all of you to do so also." It turned its gaze at each of them in turn. "Further, we demand that Humans lead the coalition. Each of you will participate to the utmost of your abilities. We will provide ships. You will provide ships, warriors, people, tactics, technology. Whatever can be."

The silence that followed felt extremely heavy as the Minurvan gazed at them. Finally, each Delegate took turns pledging support to the coalition.

Mike sat at the conference room table aboard the *Diplomat,* sipping on his drink. Colonel Nelson was with him; the Chief had gone to his quarters. Mike sighed.

"What is it, Mike?" Jennifer asked. "You got the coalition we were sent here to get."

Mike nodded slowly and took another sip, "Yes, but I don't think I like how we got it. Who are the Minurvans, and how could they just command the others and they give in? What are they? What influence can they exert, especially when no one has interacted with them for centuries? I don't trust it."

Jennifer thought for a few moments and took a drink of her vodka. "Ok. So, like any coalition, we have to watch them. Trust them to a point and be ready for anything."

Mike snorted a short laugh. "Really?"

Jennifer smiled at him. "I think that has been the history of any coalition and maybe even alliances across our history. Why should this be any different?"

"Indeed," Mike said, finishing his drink. He then reached for the bourbon and refilled his glass.

"So, what is left?" Jennifer asked as she refilled her glass.

"Now, we have to figure out just what each member will contribute. Thankfully, the Wooxunas know a system where we can concentrate our forces." He paused as he took another drink. "We need to warn Josephine about the Minurvans. She will have her hands full. We also need to tell Kevin what we know about them. He may need to send a ship under deep cover to discover what we don't know about them."

"Ok. Let's put it all onto a coded disk for her."

"What?" Mike turned and gave her a confused look. "Why not send a drone?"

She shook her head. "We only have two left. I want to save them for the time we can't use an intermediary. Kuma said they could relay messages for us and provide any items to Captain Lindsey that we require. I trust him."

Mike was in deep thought as he took another drink.

CHAPTER 16

Josephine sat in her command chair, sipping her coffee. For three weeks her three ships had sat here in deep space. They were waiting, scanning the space for any sign of a hyperspace communication drone from the *Diplomat*. When would they get it? She didn't like just sitting in one part of space. Odds were against them being discovered in this location, but damn it, Mike, where is the information?

The Technician in charge of sensors called out, "Captain, a hyperspace well is opening."

"Main viewer," she responded.

The well opened, and a ship came through, and the well closed. Sensors reported the configuration of the ship didn't match anything in the databases. All three of her ships clicked on their shields and charged all their batteries. Sensors reported the ship had not engaged either shields or weapons. Communication reported that a signal was coming through. "Main viewer," she told them.

As the main viewer switched on, she saw the face of a dog. It had a black muzzle with fawn and white fur around it and pointed ears standing straight up.

"Are you Captain Lindsey, one of the heroes from the Battle of Kammorriga?" It asked.

Her crew turned to her with amusement.

"I am Fleet Captain Lindsey, yes," she responded.

The dog opened its mouth like it was smiling.

"Good, I am honored to meet one of the heroes. I am Thunder of Wooxuna. Ambassador O'Shea has sent me to escort you to the coalition system. He has been successful. I'm sending you the coordinates to the system. Plus, we have some coded items for you. Colonel Nelson requests you send them to the hero of the Battle of Kammorriga, Admiral Brannigan." He continued to smile at her.

Ok, she thought, *what is all this hero crap?* She acknowledged Thunder's comments. *Just what is Colonel Nelson up to sending a messenger vice a drone?*

She turned her gaze to the Communications Officer. "Receive the transmissions and prepare a drone to be sent to HQ. Let's get the coded items from Thunder and review them. We may need to send them along also."

She turned to Thunder. "We will probably need a few days before we can move to the system."

He nodded, "Of course. No hurry, Captain. This area of space is well outside of Kammorriga influence. We have time."

Three days later, they launched a hyperspace communication drone to Plymouth Station. Two hours later, they opened the hyperspace well, and all four ships made the jump. They estimated a week in hyperspace before reaching the system, where they would begin receiving ships from the coalition and begin training with them.

CHAPTER 17

Kevin handed Paul a cup of coffee as he rounded his desk, heading to his chair. LtGen Connington had recently returned from his mission. Kevin sat down as both men took a sip of the hot coffee.

"It is good to have you back, Paul. Very good indeed." Kevin sighed. "Soon, you will pick up your fourth star and, after some much deserved leave, take up your new assignment."

"Thank you, Admiral," Paul said.

Kevin shook his head. "Enough of that, Paul. We have been through enough for first names."

Kevin set his cup down and adjusted his monitor as he picked up a report. He smiled.

"We have had success across the board. You have succeeded in your mission. Zeta Prime has been secured, pirates destroyed, Josephine delivered colonists to a secret location, and Mike has created a coalition." He frowned a bit after he said the last item.

Paul, watching him, said, "Then why the frown?"

"Mmmm," Kevin murmured and looked up. "I think Mike has hit on something. The report shows a pretty straightforward series of events. The conference was going as any coalition conference could be expected; that is, until this delegation from Minurva showed up. Mike is concerned, and I agree with him, about how the Minurvans commanded all delegates to join the coalition, and they did. What influence do the Minurvans have over these races? What power do they have?" Kevin put the report down and leaned back in his seat. "Maybe he can find something out. After the conference, he is traveling to several of their planets. The Prince of Alia invited them to their home world to decorate Colonel Nelson and her crew for saving their butts. As he travels about, perhaps they can learn more about Minurva and who they are."

He picked up his cup and took a sip.

"Plymouth Station seems quite happy these days," Paul said.

Kevin smiled. "Yes, we have had great success there also. The pirate threat at this time is nullified. Colonel Clark did a great job, and Josephine's ships destroyed a pirate fleet that attacked the planet. We should be good there for a while."

"What are the plans for John?"

"BGen John Roberts of the Galactic Marines will be promoted very soon to MGen and be made a Deputy Commandant of the Galactic Marines. After his leave, he will be transferred to Mars to take over all Marine development. His primary job is to make them ready to take down planetary and satellite installations," Kevin said.

Paul nodded. "You said Josephine has dropped the colonists off on the planet we found. Where is she now?"

"She should be at a system where the coalition will form up. She will be training them in different tactics, working out the communication systems, and figuring out combat positions. She has her hands full. We have sent a supply ship to the system. The Wooxuna whom Mike found, were the only race who knew about this system. They are working with her on intelligence gathering. Apparently, that is one of their strengths." Kevin took another sip of coffee and frowned. "That reminds me. The *Sabachi* has not contacted us since they met up with the *Diplomat*. I am hoping that nothing has happened to them. But they should have returned by now. They had one area left to explore before heading home. Maybe the Wooxuna can find out what became of them."

Paul frowned at this and finished his coffee.

"Kevin, I'm concerned about Zeta Station. All was well when we departed there. But when we were on the enemy's planet, they said they had created an alliance with the Kammorrigans. It is only a matter of time before they show up at Zeta."

Kevin keyed his system, bringing Zeta Station onto his wall screen with a tactical of the surrounding space.

"Yes, you're right, Paul. That was important news you gathered. Colonel Williams has done quite well since we returned from EXPLORER. We will promote him to Brigadier General." Kevin shook his head. "Damn, another delay, but we need to send a fleet of ships to Zeta Station. We will have Williams take command of the fleet and get him out there." Kevin stood up, motioning Paul to remain seated as he walked over to his screen.

"His fleet will number fifteen ships," Kevin said, more to himself. "The only question is the complement of his fleet. Well, best get this figured out now and get him out there." He had looked down and shook his head again as he returned to his chair. "Ralph isn't going to like hearing I am sending a fleet out and need more ships for the battle fleet. But we can't afford Zeta falling to the Kammorrigans and them finding Earth."

Paul nodded.

"Need another cup, Paul?"

"Yes. I'll get it." Paul stood up and retrieved the thermos and poured coffee for both of them. He sat down while placing the thermos on the desk.

"What is my next assignment?" Paul asked.

Kevin turned toward him and smiled.

"You will be the Fleet Commander of our battle fleet."

"Oh," Paul said. Kevin noticed he didn't seem happy with this.

"What is it, Paul?"

Paul sat there drinking his coffee. His eyes seemed to be looking at something very far off. Kevin noticed the stare in his eyes.

"Well, Paul. What is wrong with the assignment? You have more than earned it. You found an enemy with limited information and soundly defeated him. I told you to eliminate this threat by any means at your disposal and you did it." Kevin had a sharp edge to his tone.

Paul shuddered.

"Yes. You did, and I did just that. I killed all of them. You gave me the means and told me to do it, and I did. I didn't hesitate. I destroyed their planet and their outposts. I slaughtered them."

Kevin took a deep, slow breath. He took another drink, stood up, and turned to look out his port window. He shook his head.

"I see."

"No Sir. You don't." Paul said. There was an edge in his voice. "You weren't there. I killed all of them. I committed genocide."

Kevin nodded.

"But Paul, that is what I told you to do. I knew what I meant when I told you to hunt them down and eliminate them. What did you think I was asking?"

Paul stared at the Admiral's back, slightly shocked.

"You gave me an order to eliminate, not genocide."

Kevin sighed and turned to face him.

"No, Paul. I told you to commit genocide. Just like I did at Kammorriga."

"That was different," Paul retorted.

"No, Paul. It isn't different. What makes you think destroying a planet isn't committing genocide?"

Paul stared at him in shock.

"You need to realize that this is a war of genocide, Paul. The difference between Kammorriga and this planet was time. We didn't have time to ponder anything at Kammorriga. I watched the bombs drop and destroy the planet. You and the others didn't. All of you were in the fight of our lives against their ships. Then we ran. No one had time to realize what I had ordered and everyone executed. You, on the other hand, had finished your space battle and won. They refused to surrender and so you destroyed them. But you watched it. You and your crew had the time to watch the planet get obliterated. You did the same at the outposts. All of you had the time to realize you were committing genocide. Now, I am sending you out there to wipe out an entire race of beings. To knowingly and with a clear head to commit genocide on a galactic scale. That is what this is about."

Kevin watched Paul as he assimilated what he said.

"You mean with intent; we are to commit genocide on all of them?"

"Yes, Paul. I want you to track down every Kammorrigan and exterminate them, completely wipe out every single one of them. We can't afford to have even one left alive to possibly regenerate their race."

Paul looked Kevin square in the eyes and saw no humor in those blue eyes, only hardness.

"I didn't realize that. What if they surrender?"

Kevin smirked.

"They won't. And even if they did, well, that would be a ruse to buy time to regroup and grow in strength to come after us. What we saw on their planet was their intent to find our world and commit genocide on us. And if there were any survivors, they would enslave, torture, and experiment on us. Meanwhile, they would strip every planet in our system of its resources. Then, they would terrorize any and all creatures out here. No, Paul, not a single Kammorrigan is to be allowed to live. We will do to them that which they will do to us minus the enslavement and torture."

"I see," Paul said.

Kevin studied him for a few minutes. He quickly looked up as it dawned on him about Paul's entire crew. He turned to his board and pressed a call button.

"Yes, Admiral," his secretary responded.

"I want the Head of Mental Health and the Chief of Chaplains to meet General Connington at his shuttle. Tell them to pack for several days. They are to head over to his Strike Group and perform a survey on the entire crew to determine what mental trauma they may be going through. No one is authorized leave from the Group till I have their assessment and how they plan to deal with the crew. I don't want to hear any grumblings from them."

"Yes Sir. I will make it happen."

"Thank you." He closed the mic.

Paul was watching him.

"I didn't think about this, Paul when I sent you out there. Your entire crew must have been watching. We will evaluate them and get them any assistance they need."

Paul nodded. "Thank you. I didn't think about them. I have been torturing myself. Dammit," he said and started to get up.

"Paul. No. If you haven't prepared yourself for such things then it does come as a surprise. Don't worry about it, and forgive yourself for not thinking about them. Just make sure you get them any help they may need. And take care of yourself. I mean it. You are taking out the fleet to hunt down and destroy those bastards. They must be eliminated."

Paul nodded and Kevin noticed his strength was returning.

"Ok, no problem. I'll get that done."

Paul stood up. "Anything else?"

"Plenty, but it can wait. Go ahead and meet those two. Give me an update as they are doing their evaluation."

Paul nodded and saluted. Kevin returned the salute, and Paul left the office. Kevin silently watched him go. He turned around and walked over to his window. He placed his hands on either side of the window and leaned forward. His forehead was furrowed and his lips were squeezed tightly together as he watched his Mother Earth rotate into view. A tear fell from his left eye. He had that horrible, sickening feeling of fear in the pit of his stomach. He wondered if he could keep her safe in the upcoming war with the Kammorrigans.

Find out in the conclusion:

EARTH FORCE ONE